Fimí sílẹ̀ Forever

Published April 2017 by Team Angelica Publishing,
an imprint of Angelica Entertainments Ltd

Team Angelica Publishing
51 Coningham Road
London W12 8BS

TEAM
ANGELICA

www.teamangelica.com

A CIP catalogue record for this book is available from the
British Library

ISBN 978-0-9955162-0-5

Printed and bound by Lightning Source

Fimí sílẹ̀ Forever

Heaven gave it to me

Nnanna Ikpo

TEAM
ANGELICA

"*Fimí sílè Forever* is a brave work that seeks to counter the narrative of victim homosexuals in Nigeria's state-sanctioned homophobia. Twins, young, lawyers, would-be Afropolitans, Wale and Wole Damian are LGBT defenders and litigators determined to challenge Nigeria's anti-homosexuality law and change social mores around multiple sexualities and gender identities. In *Fimí sílè Forever* the twins and Nigeria's LGBTI community are determined to live their lives to the fullest, in the closet and out, get married, go underground, and have lovers. It's a survival that engages and is presented with richness and complexities. Wale explains his need for women as central to his life, but he is also aware of the difference between love and desire. In this case one may love women, but it is men that are desired.

The tensions and fear aroused by the passing of the anti-homosexuality bill, and the multiple challenges that survival and life require, are woven throughout the text. We are never quite sure if the twins will survive the risk it takes to live an LGBTIQ reality in Nigeria.

I congratulate the author and look forward to hearing more from him about this work, and what it means for them personally, and their community in Nigeria."

Sokari Ekine, *Queer Africa Reader*

"Nnanna Ikpo is that rare thing, a Nigerian in Nigeria writing about LGBT life there. For that, he is to be treasured."

Rev. Jide Macaulay, founder, House of Rainbow

"Honestly well written. A great ability to capture a scene in a few telling words and a character through dialogue. Nnanna succeeds in vernacularising and humanising LGBT, mixing personal and political deftly."

Frans Viljoen, Director: Centre for Human Rights, Professor of International Human Rights Law, University of Pretoria

"Nnanna has created a loving, exasperated, optimistic, and troubling depiction of contemporary Nigeria, rich with insights that enrich our understanding of the struggles for human rights and sexual health throughout the continent. Beautiful and idealistic, thoughtful and horny, his young characters navigate the shoals of sexuality, family, social media, and careers in the context of shifting traditional values, Nigeria's fraught political scene, and today's easy global connections."

Marc Epprecht, *Sexuality and Social Justice in Africa; Hungochani*

"The creativity in *Fìmí sílè Forever* is mind blowing. In a legalistic world Nnanna [has] found an exciting means to communicate the need for respect and tolerance among humans of all races, colour and orientation. *Fìmí sílè Forever* is indeed a timely call to let every man be and follow his chosen path."

Dr. Azubike Onuora Oguno, International human rights lawyer and advocate, lecturer, University of Ilorin, Nigeria

"A fascinating first novel. Nnanna's story of twin Nigerian lawyer brothers grappling with sexual identity, against the backdrop of legal, cultural and religious opposition to anything other than the heteronorm, is exciting, troubling, passionate and earnest. Nnanna makes a compelling case for Africans to celebrate sexual and gender diversity, without necessarily rejecting the traditions and ways which root citizens in their homelands."

Pierre Brouard, Deputy Director, Centre for Sexualities, AIDS & Gender, University of Pretoria

"Outside Africa – and even within – the situation of sexual minorities is usually seen in black-and-white terms: as a heroic struggle against unrelenting hate or as a perverse, 'unAfrican' conspiracy. *Fimí sílẹ̀ Forever* is a fascinating corrective to these simplistic myths. A sprawling, complex saga of courage and compromise, hope and betrayal, harmony and hate that unfolds against the colourful background of Africa's most dynamic society, Nnanna Ikpo's debut novel challenges us to see African modernity in all its rich and contradictory exuberance."

Prof. John McAllister, Dept. of English (rtd), University of Botswana

To
God Almighty,
for the perfect gifts of Love, Nigeria and Martins O. Ibeh

Even before I formed you in the womb I knew you; even before you were born I set you apart...

Jeremiah 1:5, the Holy Bible

Ile Erupe/Sand House

A storm has blown and left the dust to rest
And all our conquests are now lies.
A storm has taken away my best,
Yet the rest of the world passes by.
Our lives of warmth and dust
And the ones unlived and dry
The ones that once loved the most
This still land now denies

This home is that of sand
Unworthy to be kept alive
Please come in just to rest
And at sunrise, pass on by.
For the winds that come
Don't sleep too long
They return at noon and night
To steal the best and silence songs

My home is that of sand
This is my lot in life
My home is that of sand
Be my friend, share my life

Prologue

The media blew it about like confetti and blew it up like fireworks. But I knew exactly what happened.

At four a.m. on August 15th the police crashed into the Atlantic Night Club on Omore Street, to raid an 'illegal gathering of societal misfits' who, they said, had 'terrorised Omore Street and the rest of Amara State for too long'.

They lobbed in tear-gas grenades and set about the club's emerging patrons with whips and truncheons. In the chaos of stinging smoke and blows, no-one could escape. The few who got out and tried to run were gunned down in the street.

The news had it that the residents of Omore Street poured out in large numbers with torches, leafed branches and canes to flog the suspected, cheer on the police, and boo the arrested as they filed into the waiting police vans. The latter were about thirty in number, and included the internationally-bestselling author and veteran actor Amobi Dike; Ken Fubara, the African blogging sensation; Fola X, one of Nigeria's top models and the founder of Fola Foundation; and some very recent graduates of Kola University.

Immediately after the arrests were made a press conference was held at the scene, to allow the media to capture the faces of the suspects on camera. Interviews with the demonstrating neighbours were also conducted.

'Look, there is nothing hidden under the sun o! One day dem go catch all of them wey dey our country,' one resident said. Another said, 'It is sin. Homosexuality is an abomination. How man go dey gbenj him fellow man?' 'Ko gbadu, I no follow, guy.'

The police had come to Omore's rescue. They had made an example; razed a landmark to immoral deviation.

The policemen, who had worked themselves up into a fury during the raid, then began to flog and curse the residents for being slow in getting out of the way as they returned to their vehicles, forcing people to jump aside or be mown down as they sped away in convoy, and leaving them to choke on thick clouds of dust and fume.

The mob then broke into the premises of the Atlantic Night Club, evicted the caretaker and his family, defaced the building, slopped in petrol and threw in matches.

The whole street broke into gyrations. The mob grew wilder and wilder with excitement as they jeered, danced, drummed and watched the Atlantic go up in flames.

This was a sweet horror of a sort that had already occurred twice within Nigeria that year, and now for the first time in Omore; an event that once more put Nigeria on the map of international human rights violations. It was followed by talk, talk and more talk, bouncing back and forth and colliding on the airwaves – talk by union leaders, church ministers, bloggers in favour of and against the raid, Facebook-posters and Twitter activists; Nigerians at home and in the diaspora, and the judiciary. The suspects were charged and taken to court. There the stale power of precedent and *stare decisis* would not only be regularly invoked but submitted to as to some slave-driver. Prejudice is not stale, and it seems to grow more complex. Would it be there in court as well?

What these men were accused of would win them a special place in our civilised society as unnatural offenders, even monsters. And unlike other criminals, who after all, if to excess, followed natural urges – greed for money, for status, for the fulfilment of normal sexual desires – the accused were more than deserving of the great retribution demanded of them: they had, it was generally agreed, brought this upon themselves.

Even at a point in history such as this, they had brought it upon themselves.

Omore had to wake up, everyone said. This had been going on for too long a time.

It has always been this same story: the law for the people – and, more often than not, the law against them.

Now it concerned me, and they will have to listen. I swear it, they will have to.

An eka aro (a good morning) like that

From: ahmed@sugarbooks.com
To: waledamian@afrospark.com

Dear Wale,

My name is Ahmed Azeez, male, 37, Nigerian. I was recently appointed CEO of Sugar Books Inc. and I work at our head office here in Europe. I am resident in the Netherlands but I visit home from time to time.

While we value our international audience, I must say that I was both excited and impressed to learn that it was your youthful and daring first novel, Hot Sundays, *that turned it around for us in Nigeria. As you know, sales were not huge, but it won a lot of attention with its controversial themes coming from so young an author.*

Your photograph has been in front of me for almost an hour now. I know it is not polite to stare but I am led so fiercely to reach out for you with the truth as it burdens me. I hope I am as honest as I should be. I also hope that you are as open as you should be.

I am writing to ask that we meet soon, perhaps on my next visit, if your schedule permits. This, Wale, is on personal grounds. I believe that we share a lot and that there is some other great stuff we could accomplish together. No pressure. I shall send you emails from time to time in this regard.

I am thrilled by as much as I know right now about you. But I want to go deeper.

Regards,

Ahmed

I t was March 2013, and I was on a midnight flight to Addis Ababa from Maputo. I had gone to Maputo to present a paper on 'The Art of Writing Black: The Voice of Our Laws' at the seventh gathering of the Pan-African Literary Arts (PALA) Convention. My talk had comprised some fairly informal thoughts about the late Professor Chinua Achebe, arranged around excerpts from his Biafran memoir, *There Was a Country*. I had uploaded most of it onto my blog prior to submission, but whilst in Maputo made a few last-minute alterations to give it a more academic tone.

The PALA convention had taken up a whole week. I spoke on the fourth day, and was also on a panel with two other professors and Kwame Osei, an undergraduate from Accra, and spent much of the rest of my time attending various other lectures and discussions, some interesting, some less so, as is usual with such things. Some of the lectures were in English, others in Portuguese or French, with provision for simultaneous translation, though most of the printed materials were only available in Portuguese. French and English versions were sent to the panellists, and uploaded onto the organiser's website – most of which was also in Portuguese, and as such quite difficult for non-lusophones such as myself to use. Speak of disability!

A highlight of the week was the opening ceremony, because as well as stage performances it included the premiere of a Hollywood-Nollywood collaboration feature-film, *The Broken Wind* – in English and unsubtitled in Portuguese – sorry lusophones! – or French. The movie was about the power of our African traditions, and the need to question them ourselves, or at least not get in the way when others try to do so. But it was also about love, dance and finding oneself – universal themes which could flow without language.

At the screening I found myself seated next to the teenage lead actress. It was a night of glitz following, I was told by the enthusiastic organisers, a week-long build-up of buzz about the movie, and actors, actresses and paparazzi were everywhere: there were so many camera-flashes that my retinas burned.

The young lead actress seemed quite a charm – something to be caught by – though there was not the opportunity to have an actual conversation with her. Perhaps this was just as well as, embarrassingly, though it was blazoned in huge letters on the opening and closing credits of the film, I had failed to take in her name. I was nonetheless thrilled that I could see her up on the screen, and then, at the turn of my head, seated beside me. It was, we were told by the director before the film began, her first major role. She is, I think, gifted, but has a long way to go to snatch the crown from actresses like Genevieve Nnaji – whom I adored as a child, and dreamt of growing up to find and run away with.

The final day was wonderful too – another cultural festival – but by then I had had enough of being in a foreign land, confined in my free time to my room by the Portuguese I did not understand. Yes, Maputo is still within Africa, but the feel is different: not the particular Nigerian craziness that charms me so sweetly I know that I am home.

Whenever I am leaving Nigeria, I feel a surge of ecstasy. The chores of having to fill out the many obligatory forms, queue at the embassy for my visa (except when the visas are to be issued on entry), and shop for necessities, are sweetened by my anticipation of the adventure ahead. The joy of knowing that I am leaving for some hopefully-inspiring academic endeavour, or that I have been recognized somewhere beyond the nation's borders for my work, is such a good feeling – the secret or not-so-secret pride I take in having been heard or seen amongst so many more gifted individuals. The feeling that I might, in my rambling and shambling, have done something right.

Having my passport stamped and endorsed to leave Nigeria used to feel like winning a trophy. But now, though I still enjoy my journeys, my euphoria dampens more rapidly with each trip.

Simultaneously, or seemingly so, the joy of returning home has increased in folds. Nothing compares to the feeling I have each time I arrive back in Nigeria. Still time becomes a rush, a smooth flow struck by lightning that is raised into a song both distant and fleeting. A song that cries 'everything is possible', and never stops enchanting me.

For all that, Nigeria has not exactly been friendly to me these past few years. Litigation, property disputes, real estate deals and the servicing of corporate concerns were not exactly what I envisioned when I signed up for a career in the law. And then when the practice was spiced up by some controversy or other, the excitement and wahala that followed could be alarming. For instance, the Tani Cross case – Cross was a schoolboy almost lynched by fellow pupils for allegedly attempting to sodomise a sleeping classmate – and its media blow-out made our firm for a few months the target of FOLABON and other homophobic bloggers in Nigeria, as well as an object of discussion by those who were annoyingly 'neutral' and 'balanced' on the matter. As a result of this publicity we attracted more cases of assault on suspected LGBT persons and, consequently, threats to our lives. These died down after a while, but, as the months advanced, a storm approached: I could feel it.

Shades of blue, silver and grey twirled up in puffs of cloud outside my window. So dark a world it seemed, so still and quiet.

It was cold on board the plane, and everyone around me seemed to be hibernating, knocked out by the plummeting temperature. Some of them had been watching one thing or another on their mini-screens; now the screens returned the favour, watching them drool in their sleep.

I couldn't sleep. Fortunately for me I was seated next to another wakeful traveller, Kwame, the student who had spoken on my panel, and his 'new girlfriend' – the lead actress from *The Broken Wind* – who had gone to sit and chat with other members of her film crew for a while. 'My luck,' I thought. 'My boy,' I said, gently grabbing Kwame's knee when he took his seat on returning from a trip to the lavatory, 'I did not have the opportunity to commend you for your performance at the session.'

'I thought I was mumbling most of the time,' he said.

'You might have done better if you had lost most of the references and citations.'

'But they demonstrated how much research I'd done.'

'I would have loved to see more of you.'

'How?'

'Well, like the part at the end when you finally ran out of academic journal articles to quote from and spoke as yourself.'

'Oh, that.'

'That was what caught me the most. The convention was about art, you know, not statistics and precedent.'

'Hmm... coming from one of the Tani Cross lawyers, I was expecting a more legalistic critique.'

'Well, citations aside, you did well and I loved it.'

'Thank you. You were also quite phenomenal,' he added, his face warming into a smile then into a charm.

'So you are headed back to school?' I asked.

'I want to spend a few days in Lagos before I head home – I'm meeting up with some friends there.'

'Classmates?' To think how small the world had gotten: that social calls were no longer made from neighbourhood to neighbourhood but from country to country, perhaps even across continents.

'Well...'

'Hmm?' I was now curious.

He started talking about the affiliations he had built over the internet with Nigerian students with whom he shared common interests. 'But my going to Lagos is particularly to see Tayo Davis.'

'Tayo Davis?' I had heard the name before in connection with something that must have caught my interest, but couldn't immediately place it. 'The blogger – and he's one of Nigeria's A-list models.'

That was him, of course – and in fact I knew Tayo slightly: we had met once, a few years back, at a mutual friend's son's graduation party, but had never been properly introduced. Tayo was, as you would expect, quite a lot to look at – a tall dark glass of chocolate sensation. At the time his hair had been cut very low, and was linked to his goatee by thin lines of side-beard rising up from his jaw-line. He had thick but well-shaped eyebrows, somewhat sunken brown eyes, and dark lips that more often than not were stretched into his winning 'Tayo smile'. As well as modelling he had co-authored two self-improvement books with two South African authors, and gist had it that he was considering going into film-making.

Aside from running into Tayo on the pages of Nigerian celebrity magazines I had not seen or heard of him for a while. '...and he is very intellectual too,' Kwame went on. 'I respect how he combines glamour, business and brains. For me, he is everything the African man should be.'

'How did you meet?' Tayo was hardly ever in Nigeria these days, or so the magazines said, but so far as I knew he was not in Ghana much either.

'On Facebook,' Kwame said, and he winked at me.

'You know, you should be careful with social networks,' I warned, knowing how fearless and naïve the youthful mind can be. I was myself quite familiar with the excitement that comes with disclosing one's deepest, wildest, most uncensored thoughts to that 'new best friend' with whom one seems to share such strong feelings of attraction, enthusiasm and other small tinini tanana. In such a situation, intense feelings of romance and jealousy were not uncommon. I also knew there was no guarantee of fidelity or long term companionship: on social networks we live in the moment, all the while cultivating other possibilities with other new 'best friends'.

Occasionally the most – or perhaps least – fortunate of these online relationships would see daylight as the longing to see each other face to face became overwhelming. Once the plan to meet was made, however, anxiety would bubble up and stretch already tense emotions to rupturing point. In Nigeria we call it Facebook love – and yes, I understood what drew Kwame to Nigeria, to Tayo: the several deep status updates too fiercely direct to be general, yet too open to interpretation and ambiguous to be specific; the urgent instant messages demanding as instant a response, the night-long chats, video-calls, unfounded promises and apparent common ground that jumped up out of nowhere and evaporated in the morning, and may indeed never have existed in the first place. That was the beauty of it: Facebook.

But hey! This chap, hopping international flights just to meet up with an internet fling? Did he know of the possible danger that he was being set up by an impersonator? Did he know that social media has been used to lure unsuspecting victims into situations of blackmail, humiliation, violation and, in the worst cases, death? Did he know that he could be making the most stupid mistake ever?

The fling had better, at the least, be smeared with gold. But sha, an internationally-successful male model who was also a businessman and intellectually accomplished, sounded like a worthwhile attraction – if he was truly the one at the other end of Facebook.

The actress returned to her seat. 'Sorry. Did I take so long?' – buckling her belt and tucking her hair behind her ears.

'Naa... the Prof here is actually good company,' Kwame replied.

'Please, it's Wale. Wale Damian,' I said as I shook hands with her.

'Kelechi Adiele, Kay for short,' she said, clearly not remembering I had been sitting beside her at the screening. Perhaps she had expected me to know her name more generally, because she added, 'You don't see home videos?'

'Only once in a while, when life permits,' I said.

'Or when his case-load permits,' Kwame said.

'A professor at his age, a lot must be on his plate at every given second,' Kay said.

'He is not just a professor,' Kwame enthused. 'He is Nigeria's own Wale Damian: author, blogger, lawyer, and troublemaker – '

Laughing and a little flattered I asked, 'Where did you get all that from?'

'This *is* the age of the internet,' Kay said.

Kwame nodded. 'Everything at the finger's touch.'

The air hostesses came round to attend to us. One wore thickly-applied purple lipstick, and her uneasiness in her role tickled me. I had earlier, on boarding the plane, pointed out to Kwame that one of the buttons on her blouse had come undone where the material strained across her substantial bust.

I could not pronounce her name as I saw it on her tag, so I just thought to myself, 'Here comes Lisa.'

'Coffee, sir?' she asked, avoiding my eyes while waving the metal jug towards me dangerously. I shuddered. From the corner of my eye I saw Kay pushing down an impulse to laugh.

'Oh, no, please. But water will be perfect,' I said. She poured me a glass of water, and had to look at me to hand it over. 'Thanks, darling.'

'Coffee, sir, madam?' she asked Kwame and Kay. They shook their heads and she rolled away, pushing the trolley jerkily along the aisle, waving the jug at other passengers. Neither she nor her better-poised colleague came around much after that.

About an hour later Kay and Kwame fell asleep tucked beneath blue blankets. I gazed at their intertwined fingers. How much is said in silence, and done in sleep? We almost do not have control over it.

Everywhere was now completely still for me.

I had shut out so much since the Maputo trip came into the picture. I could either let it all back in, or just try to enjoy the simple things around me: the warmth Kay and Kwame shared holding hands.

Holding hands.

So simple a thing, yet I knew there was a huge chance that Kwame was gay, given how he had talked about Tayo – the glint in his eyes and the excited restlessness of his legs. His playing out his new-found fondness for this Kay chick, even while he must have been thinking and dreaming Tayo all the way, just made things more interesting to whoever had the eyes for such intricacies; to whoever had activated his 'gaydar'. And yet watching this young man and woman together also reminded me quite sincerely of my first picture of love.

So many years ago, before Wale became Nigeria's wahala, he was a little boy who believed only in Baba, Maami and the remote rural life that was all he knew; who believed that the world was black and white and orderly. There were seven days in a week, and at each one's conclusion I would look forward to the nights in Ilaro, when Baba's house would be still and dark. A pink bungalow, with a roof that had always been reddish-brown with rust, it had five bedrooms, a large living-room and an outstretched half-moon foyer. The kitchen was six bamboo stems holding up a dry raffia roof;

the bathroom and lavatory were in separate roofless rooms built of zinc, situated behind the main house. The earth in our compound was powdery, sparsely bejewelled with stones of red and brown, and stretched forth until the walls separated her from the rest of Ilaro.

At sunrise, and again at sunset, gold streaks of light would pierce the living-room through its facing windows, coming to rest on the woven cane furniture and the earthenware and wooden figurines, lined up by height from one end of the room to the other, that Baba collected on his visits to neighbouring towns.

Framed black and white pictures, large and small, hung in line, tracing the perimeter of the room, beginning after and stopping before the narrow wooden grandfather clock whose finials brushed the ceiling. The sun only got to them shortly before it set.

The other rooms were modestly furnished, hung with light blue curtains, and had a six-spring bed, a chair and reading table in each; save for Baba and Maami's room, which had a tall, free-standing wood-framed mirror and a larger, more pillow-dominated bed.

Our home was always warm, and not so comfortable in the late afternoon. But when it got dark it would be enchanted by multitudinous cricket symphonies, and lit up by fleeting fireflies and the light thrown from the kerosene lamp on the balcony where Baba, Maami and I would sit to unwind; and I would listen to them take turns in telling tales of distant animal kingdoms – their quirky elaborations making me believe, now that I think of it, that the tortoise was actually James Bond.

Baba was my first example of masculine beauty. Tall, dark and solid, everything about him caught my eyes. His kind brown eyes, dark nails; the measured way he chewed; how neatly his silver goatee and moustache framed his pink lips. He was bald and always wore a hat whenever he went beyond the gate. Though his polished ebony face had always been punctuated by six deeply-engraved tribal marks – three long parallel vertical lines on each cheek – it lit up whenever he smiled – especially when we visited Eden Kekere, his cocoa farm – a lush, mini cocoa forest.

Brother Gbenro was his second in command, and the farm's manager in his absence.

Light-skinned and lanky, with a clean-shaven chin and thriving moustache, and hair cut fairly short, he was always tidily-dressed in spite of his working on the farm. Baba always addressed him in Yoruba while it was strictly English for the rest of the staff, and seemed to spend more time talking to him than he did to the others. Brother Gbenro was part of the family, I understood, though at the time there were no grounds for this closeness that I could see beyond Baba's obvious fondness for him.

Maami was not so tall, though like Baba she was dark and had parallel scars on her cheeks, and was beautiful inside and out. She was gifted with her hands, and industrious. She would rise each morning with Yoruba gospel songs. I would hear her voice stream softly from the kitchen as she prepared breakfast – her first solo waking Baba and me. I would also always hear her say 'Ifemi eka-aro' to him, which means, 'Good morning, my love.' I would rise to say my eka–aros as well, prostrating on the floor before both of them. We always began our day by praying together in the living-room, kneeling around a flickering candle-flame while it was yet dark outside, Baba, Maami and I taking turns to pray in Yoruba.

Maami would serve Baba and me breakfast then go back to the kitchen to put the finishing touches to the moi-moi and akara she sold to those who went early to their farms from her small stand just outside our gate.

Maami was the Queen of Ilaro, our town – or at least I thought so. The women there frequently paid her visits for one thing or another, and she would attend to everyone as though she were their mother. 'Iya-titi' they would call her whenever they came around, whether individually or as a group – 'Titi's mother' – and I would wonder who this Titi was, as I had no brothers or sisters. She had a gift for weaving cornrows on women's heads so tiny, so neat, that the 'shuku' (cornrows woven into a bun at the crown of the head) would turn out like a healthy, evenly studded corn-cob – provided, that was, the woman's hair was healthy and long; otherwise, for all Maami's skill, the shuku would be like the several splash pillars of a stricken red sea, swearing never to submerge or form a healthy bun in its lifetime. Regardless, the braids were always tight and symmetrical, and the women would return for a reweave week after week, either because they were bored of the style they had in, or they simply wanted to hang with Iya Titi.

'Your water, sir,' Lisa said as she handed me a cup.

'Oh, thanks, dear,' I said, and she smiled at me, revealing bits of lipstick on her teeth.

The cabin-lights had dimmed, save for a few which were being used to read by. We had spent a long time sitting, and the low temperature had left me feeling torpid but unable to sleep.

Further along our row of seats, Kay was now awake. Tucked completely beneath her blanket, she was watching her mini-screen intently, with both ears plugged in. Perhaps she was in the film she was watching. Kwame slept heavily. I took a glance at the view outside my window – black nothing – and settled once more into myself.

The best of my days at Ilaro were Saturdays. I loved them because I would either be at Eden Kekere with my family, working with the staff, or we would all stay home to work on adireh with Maami. Brother Gbenro always came by to participate in adireh days.

Prior to dipping the white cloth in the dye, all three 'men' – Baba, Brother Gbenro and I – would engage ourselves in tying it with raffia palm-strands and stones to make patterns, and Brother Gbenro would tell me silver secrets – wise spirit sayings that he said would remain in the fabric long after they had been spoken. Once, while knotting a piece of fabric, he said, 'Olawale?'

'Brother mi,' I answered.

Fixing his eyes on mine as he pulled the knot tight, he said, 'You know, men's lives are like tall, strong trees that make the wind bearable, and useful for plants, animals and humans, which is why it is our job to bind the material in the raffia. On the other hand, women's lives are the beautiful wind that needs to be cared for and directed where to go and where not to. This is why it is their part to mix the dye and colour the material.'

'What about when the wind is too strong and the tree breaks? ' Baba asked as he dropped his bound fabric.

'Disaster!' Brother Gbenro whispered, with a serious look in his eyes, sweat trickling down between his eyebrows.

Disaster? I thought, frightened to my bones.

'Yes.' Baba responded. 'So you need to make those knots as tight and strong as possible.'

I nodded and we carried on with our work, my palms and fingers sore from tying the raffia.

We were a great family, Baba, Maami and I, and I would give anything to go back to those years when I watched the romance play out between Baba and Maami. On Sundays they would sit in the back row at church, and they would create such a spectacle as they danced out together afterwards, like newlyweds, in their matching ashoke attire. Of course such strongly-demonstrated love didn't mean there were no disagreements. Though these were never addressed or acted on outside their bedroom, when they had squabbles the tension was felt by the rest of us. The eka-aro was usually sour then, and I'd have to prostrate twice because they would avoid being in the same room before our morning prayers together, and the adireh process was quieter.

It was at times like these that Brother Gbenro would try to distract me with his silver secrets. He was a perfect big brother, and I would soon learn that he meant more to my family than just being a loyal employee.

The tension never lasted: I do not remember two eka aros playing out consecutively like that, or not more than once in a very long while. My parents were my pride, the joyful picture of my childhood, and each time I look at a couple with a future I see Baba's arms gently yoking Maami from behind as he whispers in her ear, 'Eka-aro, my love.'

'Please move your seats into the upright position and fasten your seatbelts...'

Touchdown Addis Ababa!

Ethiopia love, the horn of Africa. Interesting factoids about this great land: it is one of the earliest spots where humanity originated. It is proud to be the first and only African country to defend and retain its independence and sovereignty in the heat of colonialism and, on independence, the designs of most of the national flags of African states flowed from that of Ethiopia. It was also the first independent African country in the League of Nations. It is multilingual and has about eighty ethnic groups; and the Ethiopian people have, in my and their own opinion, beautiful skin-colour, beautiful hair.

After a lengthy descent that made my ears pop, the plane finally touched down. The five-hour flight had taken its toll on us all, and everyone was crumpled and exhausted but Kwame, who looked irritatingly rested.

'Are we there yet?' he asked, stretching and yawning as the plane taxied.

I grunted. I hadn't blinked once throughout the entire flight, and I felt stoned.

The plane came to a gentle halt. It was still dark outside. Kay whispered into Kwame's ear. Transit romance. The excitement of the moment for them and the fatigue for me.

'Sir? I will be staying with my crew, but hopefully we will be put in the same hotel,' she said to me as Kwame got her hand-luggage down for her from the compartment overhead. She shook my hand and went and re-joined them. Kwame looked after her wistfully.

After waiting in the several queues – to leave the plane; get a transit visa; and, finally, for the shuttle to get to the hotels allocated – my feet had grown sore and I needed to sit down.

Some thirty minutes later Kwame and I, seated next to each other on the shuttle bus, were on our way to the Hotel Ararat. Kay and her crew were nowhere in sight. However, she was at the end of Kwame's BlackBerry Messenger: 'They are at their hotel already!' he said, clearly disappointed that it was not the same as ours.

'You can see her later in the day,' I said. 'We don't take off again until 3:30 p.m.'

'I hope their hotel is close to ours.'

I said it probably was, and he remained engrossed in messaging for most of the ride.

My own hopes were for a warm meal and a warm bed – I was still chilled from the flight, and the vigorously air-conditioned airport bus was not helping matters.

Through the window I saw the streets of Addis passing in the paling dawn. It looked just like Port Harcourt: the same flyovers, the same large billboards blazoned with bold statements. I could not make much of the Amharic script, but an expensive car or apartment is the same in any language.

We finally got to the hotel. The warmth bathed me so suddenly on stepping down from the bus that half my shirt-buttons were undone before we got to the reception-desk. We were led in by a tall Ethiopian man wearing a deep blue suit.

First stop after checking in? Breakfast!

We were shown to the dinner hall. There was a buffet, and I helped myself to scrambled eggs, white bread and orange juice.

'Beautiful,' Kwame said as he took a seat opposite me.

'What is beautiful?' I asked, forking in eggs.

'Don't talk with your mouth full,' Kwame scolded. 'You must be very hungry, sir.'

'I am. And Kwame –' I reached for my glass '– the name is Wale, okay?'

I appreciated how he expressed his respect, but I believe that in the twenty-first century regard can be expressed in more innovative and mature ways. I agree that this stance is not entirely African, but I find it impossible to relax around anyone who calls me 'sir'. There always seems this tacit expectation or call to live up to a rather superhuman standard.

Kwame smiled warmly. 'I'm sorry. Wale.'

'It's okay.' I smiled back.

'The hotel is beautiful,' he said, looking round at the rather grand whitewashed hall with its grey marble floors, dark blue drapes and thick gold pillars, its flotilla of round tables, each of which was surrounded by three chairs neatly draped in a dark blue cotton that contrasted pleasingly with the light-blue table napkins.

'One of the pleasures of avoiding the direct flights.'

'I'm hoping Kay can make it down here afterwards.'

'Could it be the beginnings of love?' I asked.

'I don't know about love,' he said, sipping his orange juice. 'But I think she is great to be with.'

'How so?'

'She knows how to keep up a conversation, she is in the arts and she is good at what she does.'

'As good as Tayo?'

Kwame almost choked on his omelette. 'What?'

'Easy, man,' I said as he cleared his throat. 'Have some water.' He took the glass I handed to him and his eyes, now red from coughing, fixed on me as he took a gulp.

'I'm sorry,' I said.

'No, it's okay,' he said. 'But I think I've had my fill of the eggs.'

'I think I've had enough of consciousness,' I said.

'How do you intend to solve that?' he asked. 'Do you...?' He gesticulated with his hands, smoking an imaginary joint.

'Naa,' I said. 'I need something stronger...'

His eyes widened. 'Stronger like...?' He gesticulated with two hooked fingers towards the crook of his arm, injecting himself with imaginary drugs.

'Naa,' I said, my eye drawn to the bulge of his bicep. 'Much stronger.'

'Sex!' he said, with the broadest smile I've ever seen.

'Oh Lord,' I said, with my head bowed and my palms together, 'please cleanse sweet Kwame's mind of all filth.'

He laughed. 'Amen!' It was laughter that made my heart race. Laughter that lit up his face and the room; that made me realise that though the hall was full of guests I felt in that moment it was just the two of us. I had only meant a glass of whisky, but... would he – ? I dismissed the thought. The possibility remained in the air between us for a moment longer, then passed. Still, the eggs tasted better; the juice tasted fresher. I felt lighter, more alive. We chatted some more, I forget what about; though after initiating a flirtation and then pulling back from it, tired as I was I felt an obligation to be at least pleasant and entertaining.

Shortly after, we assembled in the lobby with the other transit passengers. There we were given our room keys, and Kwame and I found that we were neighbours.

The manager instructed his staff to show us to our rooms

and make sure we were comfortable. The flight had been full, and I guess because they were so outnumbered by us he condescended to take ten of us to our floor himself. Kwame and I stepped into the elevator still talking and laughing. The others were too tired for words. The manager, perhaps relieved to have at least two guests who were not zombies, joined in with us cheerfully. Despite my tiredness we flitted from subject to subject, Kwame always having something witty to say.

'Here it is. Room 508,' I said on getting to my door.

'And... Room 509,' Kwame said as we opened our doors together.

After a courteous 'Goodnight' I locked the door behind me, then scrambled my way to the restroom to offload my water. Boy, was that a relief: my bladder had been pressing me since the airport bus, though sitting with Kwame for a meal had temporarily distracted it.

I undressed and lay on the bed nude, with the now very welcome air-conditioner softly chilling away. I took a deep breath and sighed, relishing the cool air on my body. As the room got cooler I crawled beneath the duvet and took a quick glance at my phone: 9:30 a.m. Enough time to get in a quick one. 'I had better ask Kwame to wake me when he is set,' I thought. 'I'll call his room in a minute or two.' My limbs felt leaden.

Gradually my determination to reach Kwame waned. I ordered myself up: 'Oya! Wale! Get up now. You will miss your flight o... Wale? Wale! Wale... Wa.... Wa... Wrrrrrrrrrrrr.' In vain. Wale was already flying first class to Neverland, snoring all the way.

'Wale? Wale? Wale, wake up!' I felt a warm hand touching my shoulder. I looked up. Kwame and the hotel manager were standing over me, looking concerned.

'Mm, what?'

'Are you alright?' Kwame asked, sitting beside me on the bed and feeling my neck with his palm. His touch was pleasant.

'I'm fine. I'm so sorry, I must have slept so deep,' I said, searching around for my phone to check the time.

'Mr Kwame thought you might be having some crisis so we used the master key-card to open the door,' the manager explained.

'It's okay,' I said. 'Oh my, it's 3:30. We've missed our flight!' I started to struggle to my feet but, on recalling that I was naked, I stayed still, safely beneath the duvet.

'Relax. The flight's been delayed by four hours,' Kwame said, taking off his shoes.

'I'll be leaving you now,' the manager said, shutting the door behind him as he withdrew.

I fell back onto my pillow. 'Thanks man,' I said to Kwame as I reached up for a handshake. 'I don't know when I would have woken up.'

'It's okay,' he said, taking my hand and smiling at me.

I was now wide awake and hoping he would leave soon so that I could throw on some clothing.

Perhaps sensing this, he went over to the window and looked out on Addis. I wrapped the duvet around myself, gathered up my boxers and vest from my open suitcase, and shuffled into the bathroom to ease myself and put them on. When I returned he was sitting in the reading chair, which he had turned to face the bed.

'The flight did a huge number on me,' I said as I put on my wristwatch.

'Yeah.' – sounding distracted as he fiddled with his phone. Enthused and chatty Kwame had vanished.

'Kwame?'

'Yep?' – waking up to me.

Is everything alright?'

'Well...' He tossed his phone onto the bed. 'Most of it.'

'Most of what?'

'Can we talk?'

'Of course. What about?'

'*Hot Sundays.*'

This surprised me. *Hot Sundays* is a short novel I wrote while an undergraduate. I wrote it because I needed to resolve so much about my roles as a Christian, son, brother and, even at so young an age, author in my society. Though it was fiction, my real-life experiences were embedded in every page. And though it was published, as the years passed I forgot that I could be read in it by anyone who chose to open its pages; that I could be found there, quite easily, beneath the ink.

'Okay,' I said, sitting back on the bed and drawing the duvet to myself.

'Is it true what they say, that a writer's first story is mostly his own?'

'Perhaps,' I said. 'What do you think?'

'I think it's true.'

'Perhaps you are right. Perhaps this writer couldn't resist the temptation to mix his actual memories with some of the fantasies that insist on being eternally desirable,' I said. 'Or perhaps it was entirely other people's stories and none of his own.'

Kwame wrinkled his brow. 'You mined the themes of hard work, romance, spirituality and family life,' he said, seeming not to have caught what I said. 'But when it came to the issues of rights, morality and sexuality, you left an incomplete flow of thought...'

His back was to the window. The bright light silhouetted him. My eyes were beginning to hurt so I asked him to bring me my spectacles from the table.

'Here' he said, handing them to me.

I put them on, then took his hand and drew him to me. 'Sit close. I'd like to see you better.'

'Okay.' He came and joined me on the bed. 'Wale, I need to ask... was that a deliberate omission or was it – cowardice?'

I looked at him for a while, searching for the most appropriate words with which to respond, wishing he did not avoid my eyes so much.

'Kwame,' I said gently. 'Do not forget I was still quite young – only twenty – and had just gotten into the university, and though for my age I had seen and learned a lot about my society, I still had a long way to go. I wrote it under the supervision of one of my lecturers and someone else, a friend, so the plot and the themes were all discussed and decided upon before and during writing – and after, during editing under their guidance. So it wasn't out of cowardice. Of course I had my views, which have developed over the years.'

'What are those views now?'

'On what specifically?'

'Sexuality! Your views on sexuality. In an article you wrote you quoted Brené Brown when she talks about the power of vulnerability, and how "imperfections are not inadequacies but are reminders that we're all in this together" just before referring to how different being gay must feel but how human it is – '

Hearing my thoughts stream from someone else's lips reminded me of how hard it had been to try and find my feet in the dust-storm of confusion that engulfed me as an adolescent.

'So what are your thoughts now?'

'I hope you are not a student journalist,' I said, feigning a stern look. Despite my playful tone, however, I was beginning to get a little worried: journalists had their way of going undercover to get the juicy stories at all cost. Had my flirtation in the dining hall put me at risk of a scourging in that sun?

He laughed. 'I'm sorry. Am I being too inquisitive?'

'No, it's just that *Hot Sundays* is an old, long-finished project, and I'm focused on a whole lot of other things now. How interested would you be in going into the complexities of what you thought fifteen years ago – especially when there are things you are trying so hard to forget?'

'Oh, okay,' Kwame said, abruptly giving up on the interrogation.

There was a long moment of silence, during which he sat there glowering. 'Kwame,' I said, 'tell me: are you part of the pro-LGBT movement, or are you asking these things because you don't believe there is any space for homosexuals in our society?'

'What is it to you?' he replied, getting to his feet.

'Well, I have been on the hot seat for some minutes now. Don't you think it is only fair that you tell me a little about yourself? Besides, you will never know why I am asking until you tell.'

He hesitated. 'I need you to promise me that whatever I say to you will remain between us,' he said.

'Lips sealed. I cross my heart.'

'And under no circumstance will you spill it to anyone?'

'Kwame, I assure you that you are safe.'

He shut his eyes and took a deep breath. Then he began.

This is the story of so many African youths. Strong enough to commence an argument, yet too cautious to risk more: to really communicate. He did not tell me instantly. He struggled. But I knew. It is really not hard to tell: from the first conversation, in words or eyes or handshakes, there is always something instantly sweet, warm, betraying and revolutionary. This one? Definitely!

A few hours later I was standing before the large mirror by the door of my hotel room, contemplating my reflection and considering how time had taken its toll on me. Suddenly resenting this, I took off my glasses and untied my locks, letting them fall freely about my shoulders. My mirror-image flashed before me in soft-focus, at that instant somehow stellar, a man but androgynous and, dare I say, a perfect gentleman. Nothing like me, yet all of me and much more. I left my locks untied.

'Are you set?' Kwame called from the hallway as he closed his door.

'Yeah.'

He looked in through my open doorway and smiled. 'They look better like that.'

'Thanks.'

On our way down we had the elevator to ourselves. I smiled at Kwame's reflection in the elevator door, tall, handsome, seemingly so confident in his masculinity, in himself. I put my arm around his shoulder. I wanted to tell him that he was everything he could be and more; that he had his whole life ahead of him to figure out all the simple questions that now seemed so fiercely difficult. I wanted to embrace him and tell him that he was beautiful and perfect. Yet I stayed silent: the words choked themselves in my throat.

'I'll always be an email away if you need anything,' I managed to say as we reached the lobby. I slipped my card into his breast-pocket as the elevator chimed and its door slid open to reveal, standing there waiting, Kay.

'Are you serious?!' she exclaimed, and she turned and stormed away, an alarmed Kwame running and calling after her.

In addition to our fellow-passengers, the lobby was packed with Ethiopian photographers, bloggers and journalists who had come to catch up with and interview the cast and crew of *The Broken Wind*. As I pushed through them, through the thick glass doors I could see Kay and Kwame arguing in front of the hotel. It was getting intense and people had started to watch. I observed that Kwame was mostly on the listening side while Kay seemed to be raving more and more. I pushed one of the doors open and leant out.

'What is going on?' I asked.

'W. Damian, the gay lawyer,' Kay said sneeringly. Her voice was loud and her eyes were hard and bright. 'I see the hotel rooms were not enough space for you both.' She waved her arm theatrically, threatening to draw the attention of passers-by. 'Oh no, you have to mark the elevator too. You mark here as well. Like dogs. You disgust me. You are all sick, mad, queer, stupid, disgraceful and shameless – '

'Zip it!' I snarled. 'Kay, this is very inappropriate.'

'The jig is up,' she said, snapping her fingers in my face. 'In fact it has always been up. When I – '

'Shut up, Kay,' Kwame interjected angrily.

'What?'

'Shut up,' he repeated. 'Look around you.'

Everyone was now watching: passers-by, visitors to the hotel, and our fellow airline passengers, amongst whom were the journalists who had come with *The Broken Wind* cast and crew to cover the Maputo premiere. Phones were held up, pictures were taken, videos were uploaded. Inside my head I cursed.

'Kay?' one of the actors in *The Broken Wind* called from the lobby. 'Amadi wants you inside.'

It was a quiet ride back to the airport and a long flight back to Nigeria. Kwame, Kay and I sat in different parts of the bus and then the plane.

*

I was reading emails on my iPad before we boarded when I came across Ahmed Azeez's mail from Sugar Books. My first thought was, 'Too much from *Hot Sundays* for one day.' However, since the subject-line referenced proofing a contribution I had made to an anthology which was being prepared for imminent publication, I grudgingly opened it and felt moved to reply:

Dear Ahmed,

I do appreciate your letter: thanks. Sugar Books will always have a special place in my heart. I consider anyone from there a very salient part of my success story, such as it is.

Still, I don't advise that you be looking at my photo-graphs so long that you develop a headache. Lol. Regardless, I do like the tone of your letter and it leaves me hoping that you know only the good things about me – the internet reveals quite a lot these days – and wondering what it could be that we share.

I do look forward to meeting. Hopefully, that would be whenever you visit Nigeria in the future.

I also look forward to a great relationship with you.

Best of the day,

Wale

We had been airbound for some time when, glancing up from the book I was reading, I caught sight of Kay's shuku sticking up above the seat in the front row. She was sitting with Amadi, the director of the movie. He had approached me just before take off to apologise on behalf of Kay and the production team. Kay was then made to apologise herself, which she did in a flat voice and with a stone face. No doubt she felt this was beneath her as a rising movie star, but because footage of the argument had escaped onto the internet, Amadi promised he would ensure that she also made a public apology on Twitter and Facebook. Kwame, who was not considered significant enough to receive an apology, sat a few rows behind me, watching all this. I turned to look at him after Amadi had retreated. He gave me a warm smile: I still had my friend.

I read on for a while – mostly downloaded conference invitations and solicitations of papers, legal and academic, for – usually – enthusiastic online journals offering little to no payment – before dozing off.

'Wale? Wale!' Kwame was shaking me gently by the shoulder. 'We are in Nigeria, and you are the last person on board.'

I said a short silent prayer of thanksgiving, unclasped the seatbelt, tied my hair up and got my luggage down from the overhead compartment. Kwame and I joined the tail-end of the line of people shuffling off the plane.

As soon as I turned on my phone a text came in: *Welcome home sweets. I missed you.* It was Tega, my fiancée.

My mood was suddenly so light that I did not feel the Nigerian heat smack me across the face as I entered the terminal building, and I forgot to take off my jacket. My heart raced and my pace hastened as sweat blotted my underarms.

We Nigerians finished our immigration formalities quickly, and I had to force myself to wait for Kwame as, being a non-national, his were taking longer. Eventually he was done, and we got our suitcases from baggage reclaim and headed for the arrival hall together. People trooped out ahead of us, all of them walking briskly, as if eager to escape the impersonality of the airport. We neared the Arrivals exit. Beyond the glass doors was a crowd, some of them holding up placards with names displayed on them, others just watching and waiting.

'Kwame, stay close.'

'I'm right behind you.'

'Has Tayo called you?'

'He sent a text. He is here. Who is coming to get you?'

'My brother Wole. But he hasn't texted me.'

We passed through the doors and the heat outside was instantly unbearable. It was three in the afternoon but it felt like the hottest noon ever. Beneath my clothing I felt as if a thousand tiny ants were digging into my skin. Kwame had already unbuttoned his shirt half-way in the heat.

'Oga, cab service?' A man who must have been around forty touched my arm, hoping to win my custom before I reached the cab-rank.

'No thanks.'

'Oga, Island?' another, who was lounging on the bonnet of a Peugeot 406, called out. I shook my head.

'Oga welcome! Cab service!' They all lined up, eager for our business.

Craning my neck over the heads of the crowd around me, I looked around for Wole. As I did so a convoy of three tinted-windowed cars came to a halt in front of the main entrance. As if by prearrangement, like dancers executing a routine, the cab drivers slid into their cabs and locked the doors. An armed policeman stepped out of the frontmost car and headed straight for me and Kwame. We stood still, tense.

'What's going on?' Kwame asked out of the corner of his mouth.

'I don't know,' I said, fearing the worst.

Then, to my partial relief, Wole, and, to both my and Kwame's surprise, Tayo emerged from the back of the third car, along with two more officers, also armed. The officers fell into step in front and behind them as they made their way through the spaces between the cabs. From their bearing they didn't seem to be under arrest.

'Brother mi,' Wole said as we hugged. Tayo shook Kwame's hand and they exchanged uncertain smiles.

'What's happening?' I asked.

'Ma beru,' he said. 'All is well.'

'Welcome home, bro,' Tayo said to me, taking Kwame's backpack and slinging it onto his own back, throwing his arm around Kwame's shoulders and shaking my hand. 'It's been too long.'

Looking from me to Wole and back, Kwame must have

thought he was seeing double – the only difference being that I preferred to stick to my glasses while Wole had his contacts in – finally and unexpectedly beholding the notorious Damian twins, both of us tall, dark-complexioned, clean-shaven, with long locks, deep-voiced and, if I may say so, stellarly charming.

I made the introductions: 'Kwame, this is my more spontaneous half. He is also W. Damian.'

'Abegi don't mind him, dear,' Wole laughed, shaking the still-disconcerted Kwame's hand. 'I'm Wole, the elder one.'

'Carry the elder go market na,' I said, to water down the statement.

'Unfortunately for some people.' Wole winked at me and then turned to Kwame. 'Tayo has been expecting you – '

One of the blank-faced policemen standing nearby sneezed and slapped the palm of his hand on the machine-gun slung across his belly.

'We have been receiving some death-threats at the office,' Wole said, dropping his voice, 'so our friend in the State Security Service insisted that Fred moves with me to wherever.' He managed to sound casual.

'Threats again?' I said. 'I thought it was over and done with.'

'Post-judgement beef. We are their wahala, but thanks to our "oga at the top" they still spare us some protection. He insisted that the other two came today because of some YouTube video we saw of you and some Nollywood chick. What's up with that?'

'It's no big deal. She has apologised.'

'He isn't taking it lightly, sha. I'm sure you'll get your escort too, once you get home. He is Yoruba,' Wole added in a half-mocking, half-consoling tone. The queuing cabs had cleared out, and the road now seemed unusually free of traffic. He hugged me once more and whispered, 'Welcome home, man,' patting me on the back. I pulled back and frowned at him. He smiled. Wole had gotten used to this terrain: living in the face of the cold fact that some people somewhere do not think you deserve to stay alive. It had become part of him. This was what he lived for, and he was certain that 'Nobody is going to intimidate me out of my fatherland. Nigeria's mine – she had better get used to it.' I hated to imagine a scene where the powers-that-be decided that his stubbornness had got out of hand, and sent the same police who were now acting as our bodyguards to handle us as I had feared they had come to do today.

As the four of us drove away from Murtala Mohammed airport, escorted by armed police, and in a convoy of three Chevrolet cars, our windows tinted and wound up for security, volts ran through my feet and my heart raced.

'So I'm home,' I thought.

Eka aro *my love*

The morning is beautiful my love
With the brilliant sun greeting us afresh
God pleases that we see another day
Eka aro my love

Please wake up to the daunting freshness of this peaceful
day
When all but the darkness is awake
That I may share life and light with you at least once
more
Eka aro my love

I am open to new adventures
Embracing both you and your imperfections
I am once more beside you and in love with you
Eka aro my love

You are not responding my love
And the sun's sweetness no longer tickles your skin
Please wake up my love, my heart waits
Eka aro my love

I am closer now my love
With my palms greeting your face
Is all well my love? I yearn for your love's embrace
Eka aro my love

You are no longer breathing – I am scared my love
My heart has now one new emotion
Please do not tease me, you are my solution
Eka aro my love

I am still beside you
Just like that morning you passed away
I still love and, like this morning, here to stay

I greet you, Eka aro my love

It is raining my love
And like the sun, our love is still brilliant and silent
So I am standing here for all you mean
Because you are still sweet and true
Eka aro my love, it is I who greets you.

The Tani Cross Case

My love,

You know it hurts me to see you this way. What we share is beautiful and promising. And yes, it has inflamed our hearts and lives beyond anything that we had earlier planned for. This is why I am trying my best to see that we protect what we have for as long as we can.

I am married and a father. I never kept this away from you; you have always had an understanding of what I can share. What has changed that?

That we have each other matters to me. Secrecy makes it safe and all the more desirable. Let's not be like those who don't understand that we, as African men, have our place of honour which must be respected and protected in spite of what (or who) we are doing.

I love you very very much. And no matter how hot it gets I won't leave. Please be the man you are. This is Nigeria.

Madly Yours,

Iska

The Kaka Foundation, South Africa, established in 1999, is dedicated to promoting equality and diversity in Africa in line with the vision of its deceased founder, Kaka Kasala, and the pursuit of the global Millennium Development Goals. It launched its three-year 'Write Me a Forever' project on St. Valentine's Day, 2011. The aim of the project was to celebrate, and to promote to the world, accurate African versions of human realities through storytelling – in books, music and movies – by awarding the Kaka Grant (worth two million U.S. dollars) annually to a variety of worthy recipients.

Surprisingly, it seemed that Nigeria was oblivious to the opportunities the grant afforded. A select few whose ears were always to the ground pursued it fiercely but stealthily, mostly Nigerian film-makers in the Diaspora.

It was our mother, who was by then living in the United States, who alerted Wole and me to the possibilities it offered. 'You know you can hardly change Africa's take on this gay issue only by going to court all the time,' she said when she phoned us the day the call for submissions was officially announced.

'We're lawyers, Ma,' Wole said, putting her on speaker-phone. 'Litigation is one of the most formidable superpowers we have to fight this thing right now.'

'And besides,' I added, 'neither of us knows jack about film-making. Or music production. And for me to come up with another book, I'd have to drop all I am doing now.'

'Yes, but this grant could go a long way to boost your careers as activists for this cause,' Mum said. 'And you do not have to be Mel Gibson to shoot a great movie these days.'

'I'm sure Kaka won't settle for regular Nollywood,' I said.

'True,' Wole chirped.

'All I am saying is that you must want to change the world very badly to do what you did for Tani Cross. That case blew minds even here in the U.S. The fact that you both risked ending your very young careers on that case? Crazy. Stupid. But brave.'

'And we don't regret it, Ma,' I said.

'But going into film-making now will make us seem like we're desperate and frustrated,' Wole said. 'It has not been done before. Practising lawyers do not make movies. Besides the Nollywood ministry is overstaffed, and we have enough movies already to last us a lifetime.'

'But not on this subject, and not made thoughtfully. What we have now are movies that fan the flames of prejudice, where gay people are either confused or demonic or the products of abuse, or troubled and mentally ill. The people who should be thinking and researching are too lazy to get out of their blind enclaves to see new horizons. To consider that perhaps history is history and we have to make a new present. Nobody wants to rise against the tempest. But you have done this. And I am proud of you. It may not seem so now, but Africa is headed where it should be. Seize this chance to lead this change in Nigeria. Now we have the world's attention, let's say all that we can. I'd hate that tomorrow comes and we regret not exploring all the chances we had. Craig is quite keen, and professional. He's dying to speak or even meet up with you guys.'

Neither of us said anything. I could tell something was churning deep within Wole. A chord equally thrummed in my chest.

'This Craig chap you talked about, how did you meet him?' I asked eventually.

'He is a Nigerian student of film-making here in New York, interning with a Nigerian production company,' Mum said. 'He was born in Harlem but his parents are Fulani. You don't have to do this if you don't want to, but why not meet him at least?'

'When did you become a film producer, Ma?' Wole asked.

'Who says I am?'

'Well, you are mingling with them so much,' I said.

'The black community here is somewhat closely-knit among those who are doing things,' she said. 'Almost everyone knows almost everyone.'

'Almost everyone knows almost everyone' translated to months of planning and discussion. Craig got the Kaka grant in November 2012, naming us as his collaborators on the continent, and we scheduled his first visit to Nigeria for later that month. The foundation thought it novel that a pair of self-employed human rights lawyers might want to participate in the making of a feature film, and that had helped with the application, particularly because of our role in the Tani Cross case – they had heard about that too.

I had been spared the numerous initial phone calls and wrestling with scheduling logistics because of my Maputo engagement, but on my return to Nigeria they subsumed me completely and strapped us all in Lagos for a while.

On the day of our scheduled return to Port Harcourt, which was where Wole and I were based, and also the Afrospark Foundation, our art and human rights organisation, we spent most of the day with Brother Gbenro on Lagos Island, pleading with him to withdraw the police escort. He eventually caved in, but insisted that they would return to escort us to the airport, as there was no telling where the next homophobic outrage might break out. We had to be careful, he reminded us: we had been labelled as so many things since Tani Cross. We had not come out, and had not been openly confronted, and we should keep it that way. People would try to stir things, he said, and this possibility was to be guarded against. It was not a wise decision to be openly gay in Lagos. Everyone knew what could follow: hate, rejection, oppression, bullying, marginalisation, assault, death.

But even so, some dared the kpims out of Lagos and stood firm in spite of her, proving time and time again that freedom is impracticable without some level of independence, influence and audacity – leg and liver, if you like.

Lagos has always been a magnet for homosexuals. At first glance it was unimaginable that there were gay men, lesbian women, transgender and intersex people, bold and discreet who lived, worked, loved and cohabited with each other here. But here they were – clandestine lovers walking the streets, driving on the roads, meeting up for dates, throwing underground parties, thriving in amongst everyone else. Individuals who blended in like chameleons, save for the theatrical wave of a hand, the too-beautiful-to-be-ordinary handsomeness, the piercing look at another of the same gender that lingered a moment too long. The handshake that felt like a hug that sent a thousand volts across the chest and down to the groin. The familiarity that sprouted and blossomed in seconds.

With our escort in tow we set out to beat the traffic to the airport. We failed. We spent the latter part of the day on the third mainland bridge, making calls on our mobiles to reschedule the meetings we would now be missing back in

Port Harcourt. Subsequently Wole called one of his contacts at the airline to have our tickets cancelled and rebooked for another day.

Wole suggested that we bunk for the night at one of Tayo's properties in Surulere, it being closer to the airport than the Island. 'Kwame is staying there: he can let us in.'

A detached cream-yellow two-bedroom flat surrounded by a jagged-tipped walled compound, it was one of five similar-looking two-bedroom flats arranged in an L. It could pass for a human-size doll-house arrangement, and was peaceful – save for the hurricane sound-lashes of blaring generator sets from behind three of the flats – and tidy, with flowerbeds and rectangles of lawn in front of each flat, and the cars neatly parked in a prefabricated shed. This was in sharp contrast to the adjoining street and the major road that led to it: it seemed like all of Lagos had broken out there.

The sun's last streaks were leaving the sky by the time we reached Surulere, and yet it seemed the working day was just beginning there: shop-owners were entertaining more and more customers; roadside sellers set up their tarpaulin floor-carpet ground-level supermarts of 'okrika'; and the many grill operators were stealing the show – and the untainted air – with the smoky aroma of roasted masara, boleh, yam and akara. The narrowing roads got more and more difficult to navigate as increasing numbers of maruwa, buses and bumblebee-ing okada riders seem to surface from nowhere, with kpekereh, sausage roll and 'la casera' hawkers – young and daring children bearing large trays or cartons on their heads – darting in the opposite direction on missions of their own, the light-beams from the approaching vehicles falling on their fearless faces and bouncing off their dreams, the glinting la casera bottles and the night ahead.

Craig, I was informed, had been having a hectic week getting used to the Nigerian city that never goes to sleep, with Tega, who had left for Port Harcourt earlier that day, playing host on behalf of the Afrospark Foundation. I had not met him yet, and since our return to Port Harcourt had been delayed, a meeting was scheduled for the next afternoon at Shoprite, Surulere, for me to do so.

The power was out when we arrived. Kwame came down

to the gate and let us in; Tayo was already in bed. I decided I would catch a few hasty hours' sleep in the apartment, and without more talk fumbled my way in darkness to the bedroom I was sharing with Wole.

The spicy aroma of jollof rice woke me with a start at 11:30 a.m. To think all the usual rattle and rumble of traffic, and the early-morning Muslim calls to prayer that streamed through almost all the neighbourhoods of the Lagos Mainland had not woken me: unimaginable! But there it was. Wole, who was no longer in bed, must have been responsible for the aroma. I could picture Kwame, who had passed the night in Tayo's room, sweaty and with a runny nose as he shovelled in spoonfuls of Wole's hot rice, accompanied by several gulps of water. The Nigerian taste for chilli pepper knows no rival.

I had not seen the room properly the night before because Tayo's generator set was out of petrol. Now I saw that it had nothing in it save for the king-size mattress on the floor, a sadly-immobile ceiling fan, and a large picture of Jesus's mother, Mary, looking beatific on one wall. After washing and dressing I said my prayers and read some psalms. Then I went about the house to greet the guys.

Tayo wasn't there. I was told he had rushed out for a photo shoot on Lagos Island around four a.m. in order to beat the traffic, and would be returning with Craig at three p.m. or thereabout, depending on the same traffic. Wole and Kwame were chatting away cheerily in the other bedroom – and in a spasm of I suppose jealousy I made sure I left the door wide open after going in to greet them. I had breakfast by myself and went over our contract documents with Craig. It was uncomfortably warm, but I stayed put with the hope that the power would be restored as unexpectedly as it usually seized up – which had happened briefly twice in the course of the night.

My mobile beeped. *Walemi*, Wole texted. *What's up?*
I'm okay, I replied.
Oga Dee dey Lag o.
Danjuma?
Yeah.

So?
I just thought that you might want to see him.
I don't.
'Oga! You harsh jor!' he screamed from the other room.
I love you too, I texted.

I was having my third bath of the day when I heard Tayo's vehicle pull up beside the house. I checked my phone: it was 6:30 p.m. I dried myself off and dressed.

Craig was an American Fulani who, unlike other Fulanis I know, was stocky and dark-skinned. His dark, wavy, widow's-peaked hair was pulled back in a full, kinky bun. He had unmistakable youth in his eyes, a spring in his step, and a sway to his hips. His pearl-studded ears, his large bespectacled eyes, soft-looking pink lower lip and scanty beard, meant he could easily pass for the black African version of Tinker-bell the fairy. Like all the Fulanis I know, he had perfect, dazzling white teeth, and a beautiful smile that rarely left his face – and those dimples. I had been informed that he was a kid the last time he visited Naija.

Tayo took two sachets of cold 'pure water' from the fridge, served one on a china saucer to Craig, and said, 'Kwame, let's leave the gentlemen to discuss business, shall we?'

'Aaa. True. Pardon me,' Kwame said, getting to his feet and heading for their bedroom.

'Make una tidy una business make I tidy my own,' Tayo said, winking.

'Take am easy o,' Wole replied.

'Na you I suppose dey tell that one,' Tayo said to Wole. 'Craig, my man, you're welcome, alright.'

'Thanks man,' Craig responded.

Kwame and Tayo vanished into the bedroom. The door closed and I heard the lock click.

'Craig, we haven't met before,' I said, extending a hand.

'We haven't,' he said, taking it.

'You've spoken with my brother and associate, Wole?'

'Yes.'

'I see you've already done some impressive work on setting out the terms of our arrangement.'

'Thank you, sir.'

'No "sir"s.'

'Okay.'

'Do you work with a lawyer?'

'No.'

'Have you ever worked with one?'

'No.'

'You must be very good with legal documentations, then.'

'I'm good with words. And words are all documents are.'

'Profound!'

'Well, I am a writer, sir – Wale. I Googled you and I know you are too.'

The discussion went on in that way, Wole and I keeping it as formal as we could. Of course what mattered most to us was that not only was Craig a competent director and film-maker, with an understanding of all the production and pre- and post-production requirements we ourselves were unfamiliar with, along with distribution and other practical matters, but that his attitude towards the subject-matter was in line with what we stood for.

About an hour into it, Craig was talking about his family back in the U.S., and how it was very difficult for him to be around them whenever the issues of sexuality or career choices came up. Being the first son, his deeply conservative dad had decided that he would be the next Ben Carson or nothing: it was not up for negotiation, however many Lara Croft and Terminator cut-outs Craig stuck to his door or the walls of his room. He was studying film on sufferance, with the assumption that, having learned how to use the power of the media, he would afterwards go into politics. As far as the issue of sexuality – one would think that Nigerians abroad should be more liberal, given their exposure to different types of people and ways of living. But quite often we see that a person being travelled does not guarantee such a person's maturity or wisdom. Craig said that whenever the Nigerian news came up, and it was mentioned that the homophobic bill was making progress through the Senate, his mum would rush out to the living room, her wooden spatula coated with the residue of the hot eba she was stirring, excited. And his dad would break out in Hausa with his friends, and they would loudly insist that the government was not trying hard enough; that the bill should be enacted as soon as possible instead of being delayed by rigorous official processes.

Just as we were getting around to discussing the actual film script (up to this point we had read only brief synopses and plot-outlines) the bedroom door was unlocked and Tayo and Kwame came out into the living-room all glammed up. Both were wearing tight-fitting short-sleeve plaid shirts – Kwame's neatly tucked in and buttoned, Tayo's with the top two buttons undone – white leather belts, skinny blue jeans and black suede shoes. Tayo's eyes glittered from the contacts he had put in, and their lips shone with lip-balm. Tayo announced that he was going to show Kwame the best of Lagos's nightlife. Kwame's eyes sparkled. This was his night.

As I listened to Tayo's car heading out of the compound I wanted to run after them, to accompany them on their adventure; I wanted all of us to accompany them. Then again, I wanted everyone else to leave so that Kwame and I could be together, just the two of us. I hated myself for thinking so confusedly. Part of me chimed that we had some unfinished business that his outing with Tayo could eclipse. I did not know Tayo too well, but I would break his neck if Kwame came to any harm. Yet what was I thinking? Kwame had come all the way to Nigeria to see Tayo, not me. We were only in the same apartment through coincidence, a traffic jam.

From that moment on, most of what Craig said sounded French to me, and I do not speak French. His fresh Fulani face was not as charming to me as it had been a few minutes before. Our conversation lost its flow. I scolded myself: this was important. 'We will deal with all the location permits,' I said. 'I can see the budget is already stretched, and you would be charged American prices.'

Not too long after that Craig got a call: he had to dash back to the Island to meet up with some agents of the Kaka Foundation who were visiting Lagos on unrelated issues, and with whom it would be prudent to build a good relationship. Wole called one of his taxi-driver friends to come pick Craig up. While we were waiting I caught Craig saying, 'Right now I feel like I'm where I should be, doing exactly what I should be doing,' and made myself nod earnestly.

He left two spiral-bound copies of the story outline, scene breakdowns and first draft of the script, with his business card stapled to the front cover of each. He encouraged us to look through the draft and pen down as many suggestions as we liked, for us all to discuss later. He would adjust the script as pre-production progressed. 'Just being here for a week has given me so many new ideas,' he enthused, the sweat running down his smiling face. 'I'm open to whatever you want to throw in: I want you guys to have ownership in the process.'

Wole got a text, and we escorted Craig to the cab, a yellow sports car parked outside the gate. He embraced each of us separately, briefly and gently slipping his fingers into the left front pocket of my trousers as he did so, before he got in. As we waved him off I felt my pocket: he had slipped me a note. It was 7:10 p.m. I fleetingly considered asking Wole if he too had received a note – after all, why should Craig flirt with one twin and not the other? – but didn't.

Wole and I went to buy hot suya and fresh apples from some roadside stalls a few blocks away and returned to the apartment.

Just as I finished washing the apples, the power went out again. Tayo had brought petrol when he came back earlier, but Wole refused to go and battle with his generator, insisting that it was too technical for him. I did not try to put it on either. We ate our suya and apples in a darkness broken only by Tayo's rechargeable but failing fluorescent lamp, which just about lit the suya and its path to our mouths. The power did not return, the heat grew stifling, and I became restless.

It was our last night in Lagos and I was relieved that I hadn't unpacked anything. *How I for do for that kind darkness?* The house had become an oven turned to maximum. Tayo and Kwame were out, and I had no idea how late they would be back. I was irritable. I had been looking forward to tonight not just so I could spend more time with Kwame, but because of another meeting, here in Surulere, that I had hoped to take him to, and that our missed flight meant I had the opportunity to attend.

9:30 p.m. Wole and I were climbing into the back seat of an air-conditioned SUV that was steaming as it waited for us outside the gate. David Archuleta's 'A Litte Too Not Over You' blared from the car-stereo.

'Is this the other half?' a light but undoubtedly male voice pitched in delight from the front passenger seat as the driver pulled away.

'Abeg jor. He is my brother and he is also engaged,' Wole teased.

'Ah-ah, Wole,' the driver said in a voice that vibrated the car, 'abi na you be him mouth?'

'Ee abeg, ma binu,' Wole retorted, 'Olawale abeg carry your cross.'

'You no go like introduce me before you begin to dey talk plenty plenty,' I said, teasing Wole.

'No mind me jaree.'

'Leave am make him talk the one wey nobody ask am,' the front passenger said.

'Wale, the guy behind the wheel is Ibinabo. I.B. for short.'

'I.B., it's my pleasure to meet you.'

'Likewise, my brother,' I.B. responded. 'But we already met.'

'When?'

'I was here earlier to pick your friend up.'

'You were the cab guy?'

'Yes, sir.'

'How is business in Lagos?'

'Save for traffic, pot-holes and fuel, everything else is okay.'

'I.B. also runs a car hire company and a fleet of taxi-cabs covering Lagos.'

'He is also married with three kids,' the man with the light voice chirped.

'Oya Roy, we don hear you oo,' I.B. said, clapping his hands briefly before resuming manning the wheel. 'Abeg Wole, try introduce am before him die of amebaitis.'

'Wetin come be amebaitis?'

'Na amebo cancer,' I.B. said. 'Strictly reserved for shelleh dem wey dey chook mouth anyhow, anyhow.'

'Gerrout jor,' the man with the light voice said, sounding as though he had picked offence.

'Abeg Roy, no vex na,' Wole said, trying to placate him. 'Wale, the guy wey dey front na Roy,' He reached out and fondled the head of the one with the light voice.

'Roy, it's nice to meet you,'

'The pleasure is mine, dearie,' he said.

'But just for clarity, him name na Kosisochukwu.' Wole said.

'Nna! the name be like paragraph,' I.B. said, chuckling.

'Dem ask you? Amebaitis!' Roy fired back. Everyone burst out laughing.

We were all members of the Rainbow Talk, an LGBTI group – though unfortunately, due to the way it came into existence, one with very few L, T or I. It had been established about a decade earlier by a group of gay Nigerian men spread across the country, who, thanks to the MTN free midnight call facility, would connect by conference call every Friday night. They would share the challenges they faced as gay men in their schools, churches and homes. Members local to each state in Nigeria would also meet twice every year.

Rainbow Talk was started by two gay men who used to date each other until, to placate his family, one of them decided to relocate and get married to a woman. This ended their intimacy, but they continued to have long telephone conversations every Friday night. On some Friday nights the single gay man would have another man in his bed, and instead of stealing away to whisper secretly like the married one did, he would put the call on loudspeaker, and the three men would talk. The next Friday a different man was in his bed, but the married one requested that the man from the previous week be rung up and put on conference too, and the phone be put on speaker – and so four men talked that night. Soon there were seven men on the conference call. Soon enough too the married man started having flings during business trips, and the Friday night talk got all the more interesting.

Flings of flings joined the conversation as time went on – then friends of flings of flings of flings in an endless chain. Soon it was a mobile phone community of gay and bisexual men from all over Nigeria. Professionals, students, politicians, public office holders, lawyers, doctors, engineers and experts from various other fields were joining in. Having had their fill of staging multiple phone-sex sessions, other subjects crept to the table: everything theoretically sexual and queer, everything serious and funny, formal and informal; soccer, politics, fashion, law, government policies, religion, culture, gay health, HIV, human rights, current affairs. Of course it was a standing rule that we use ti bii code-names for security purposes. And we had only ten numbers to which everyone else could connect – which I assume were those of the initial flings. Through our network men were getting great job offers off the floor; and pretty much everyone who wanted to was getting laid at least every other weekend. Initially I too used it to have me some, and a little more often than just at weekends.

Rainbow Talk was also how Wole and I got involved with the Tani Cross case, given that Nigerian lawyers are not ethically permitted to solicit for cases or clients in any form, but must wait to be approached.

Tonight was one of the twice-yearly meetings, and would be my first in Lagos. We arrived at the venue to find cars already lining both sides of the street, which looked peaceful, and was also lined on both sides with duplexes. I.B. had told us that no attendees exchanged pleasantries until they got inside the premises where the meeting was being held. After we had found a space to park we flanked I.B. like X-Men as he led us up to one of the houses, about seven SUVs away from where we had pulled up.

After the security check and confiscation of our phones and electronic gadgets at the gate by two dark-skinned, hefty-looking guards – with both of whom Roy flirted, and whose chest and bicep muscles threatened to break free from their shirts at any second – we were permitted entrance. One of the guards flashed me a flirtatious look and for a second he seemed avian.

The white-walled and glass-balconied duplex and its grounds were pleasantly proportioned, though the house and the three Mercedes parked by the outer wall took up most of the land. Concrete tiles of grey and brick red interlocked smoothly on the wide footpaths and in the parking-spaces. Yellow Ixora shrubs laced the foundations, and patches of lawn glittered green in the rays the night-lights cast on them.

On walking through the door I was caressed by the sweet fragrance of frosty citrus essence, the soothing rush of air-conditioning, the subtle stream of Waje and M.I.'s 'One Naira' on the home theatre, and the mild chatter that was going on all over the house. In the first room we entered we met a tall, slender man in corn-rows and skinny jeans, who had a name-tag that read 'Titan', and into whose arms Roy ran instantly.

'Break it up. Break it up,' I.B. said, getting in between them.

'Oh sorry, Oga is here. My bad,' Titan said, winking at I.B.

Titan stuck tags on our shirts, onto which he wrote our ti bii code-names as we told him them. I.B. was Silver. Roy was Roy. Wole was Nicole. I was Storm – after the X-Men character played by Halle Berry.

'You are Storm?' Titan asked, looking at me quizzically.

'Yes, why?'

'Iska? You know him?'

'What about him?'

'He has been out here like only a gazillion times to check had I endorsed any Storm. He crazy.'

I had forgotten that Danjuma – who also liked to go by the name Iska – lived in Lagos. Of course he would be here tonight. I groaned inwardly as we were ushered into a large lounge where the more structured part of the Rainbow Talk meeting was taking place, hoping I could somehow avoid being cornered by him. It was really a party. So many men of all different shades and sizes were there, and all of them were beautiful. All had their ti bii code-names stuck on their shirts. Most of the formal stuff, such as opening prayers and the discussing of urgent issues, was over: we were late. Even so, it felt more organised than the ones I had attended in other cities: this was Lagos, and the big boys were paying. I was part-hoping that Tayo would have brought Kwame here, but we were told by a mutual friend, who Wole knew by his real name, that Tayo had not shown up all evening.

Every man who was not already paired up was hunting for eyes to lock onto his. My own eyes were safely and seriously fixed on the meat kebab and can of Maltina I had just been served. The only people I knew in the Lagos gay circle were my brother and Tayo, and though the atmosphere was friendly, I kept feeling like something was going to go wrong.

Wole sensed my uneasiness. He was taking me around to introduce me to a few more people when Psquare's 'No One Like You' burst out of the speakers and someone tapped me on the back. It was, inevitably, Iska.

'Hi,' he shouted over the music.

'Good evening,' I responded flatly.

He leaned forward to whisper in my ear and the alcohol on his breath stung me. He asked me to dance. I shifted away in an attempt to turn him down. I hoped that Wole would help me out but instead he offered to hold my drink and kebab, and instantly turned and danced away. Danjuma, who used to look so charming and boyish, now had dark circles around his eyes and looked really tired. His hair had thinned, receded and was almost all greyed out. I pitied him: law practice in Lagos is tedious and unrelenting. I wondered how he could make the time to be here. Back in Port Harcourt we had worked closely on the Tani Cross case, and before his relocation we had shared an intense moment that I regretted. He had an exceptionally sharp mind: once he had the power to make me love reading large volumes of verbose judicial precedent simply because I wanted to out-reference him.

Iska and I danced, with him occasionally getting too close and me guiding his hands away from my hair, my waist and my chest, and we talked afterwards about his law practice in Lagos, the corruption in Nigeria and other generic topics. All the while I was planning my walk-away line. He was disgusting me, but not enough to justify my being impolite in front of people he knew. Later he asked me for my card. I told him that I did not have one on me. I lied. He gave me his, slipping it into my back pocket, feeling my butt gently as he did so, his alcoholic breath assaulting my nostrils some more. I had to excuse myself. As Titan would say, he crazy!

I tossed his card on the road just before I zoomed off with Kwame and Tayo, who had by then dropped by briefly to register their presence – done and dusted. We left Wole, who insisted on staying longer, behind, engrossed in lively talk with Titan.

Kwame was silent all through the ride home, and I wondered if something had happened between him and Tayo, who was driving rather hastily. He explained he had an overnight engagement he had to rush to on the Island, dropped us off at his apartment and sped away.

The power was yet to be restored. Kwame and I groped our way to our separate rooms.

About an hour later I was awoken by banging from the house next door. This was followed by the splintering of wood: someone was breaking in. Kwame knocked gently at my door and came in. He said he wanted to go check what was happening. I advised him against it. He went on about how it could be a criminal. I told him that it could be a gang, and there was no telling how many they were. I was about to call Brother Gbenro so he could send me the number of the nearest police station when we heard a woman's voice out in the open courtyard:

'Stupid man! Foolish man! That is how you will be drinking up and down like a fish. Like a fish. Looking at your mates out there making millions.'

Then we heard a man's voice, presumably her husband, 'Me?! You are talking to me like that?'

'Yes! You. It is you oo foolish man!'

We heard a slap, then the sound of someone throwing up.

'Chei... Oya sorry na. It's okay.' The woman's voice.

A few minutes later the voices died down. We heard no other voice interfere with them. 'Those are the criminals,' I said to Kwame.

'We should still go and check on them,' he said.

I said that domestic affairs were best left domestic. Especially when it concerned husband and wife – except of course in extreme circumstances, when the woman – or the man – calls for help. And even then one would get little thanks for interfering.

I left the room to get some water. Kwame came along. We stood in front of the fridge and gulped it down in silence, staring into each others' silhouettes. We were alone in the house. Kwame said that Nigeria scared him. I said that, for me, without fear Nigeria would not be half as exciting as it is. I suggested he sleep in my room, so that I could shield him from Nigeria 'when they jump into our premises again.' He laughed, and stretched to his full height, his arms in the air, in front of me. 'Okay,' he said.

Later, watching him sleep, memories of Tani Cross came into my mind.

Tani Cross was, as I have mentioned before, a fourteen-year-old student at Night Flower Memorial Secondary School in Port Harcourt, who was almost lynched by fellow students after allegedly attempting to sodomise a sleeping classmate of his in the hostel they shared. Tani was badly injured in the attack and was hospitalised in a private clinic near the school. This was reported to us by his uncle Danjuma (Iska) during a Rainbow Talk in 2012, and many of us had read accounts of it in the press and on social media that of course focused on fear-mongering ideas of 'predatory homosexual deviants' penetrating boys' hostels to recruit students. We quickly agreed that a team of three lawyers – Danjuma, Wole and I – would visit Tani in the clinic. At the time Danjuma was working at Ataba & Co, a firm specialising in oil and gas law, while Wole and I worked with Ipali & Co, one of the most flourishing law firms in Port Harcourt.

At the clinic Danjuma introduced us to Tani's mother, Mrs Fola Cross, and we were permitted to see him. His father, she said, would have nothing to do with an allegedly gay son.

A slightly-built fourteen-year-old, Tani looked like he had been knocked down by a truck. Cuts across his face and on both forearms had been stitched but still looked raw. His body was discoloured and swollen with bruises. His upper lip was split. He was asleep, but he was breathing hard and was not at peace. There was the worry of a blood-clot on his brain.

His term exams had already started, and, from what his mother was saying, the school had not sent anyone to visit him in the clinic. Whenever she went there to request permission to see the principal, Mrs Ajatala, the receptionist would tell her that she was in one meeting or another, and unavailable. Mrs Cross had resorted to focusing on Tani's health for the time being.

'Where there is life there is hope,' she said tonelessly.

We visited the school to commence the negotiation process between Tani's family and the administration, which had done nothing to punish the pupils involved in the

lynching attempt, but were told that the principal had no
wish to see us. The second time we went there the security
guard told us to our faces that the school was 'not Sodom and
Gomorrah'.

And so we opened fire. We petitioned the Citizens' Rights
Department of the Federal Ministry of Justice in Abuja. We
sent out pictures of Tani Cross before and after the lynching
attempt; he and his mum in the clinic; and Danjuma, Wole
and I at the school gate being refused entrance, to national
daily newspapers, which published them; and we requested
that other students in the school be withdrawn in protest.

Our campaign worked: that weekend half the school's
student population were withdrawn by their parents and
guardians.

The Attorney General wrote to us and instructed us to
come to Abuja to commence the mediation process. The day
the A.G.'s letter reached us Mrs Ajatala called Tani's mum
and asked to meet with her privately at the school. Suspecting
some sort of ambush, we turned her down, insisting that the
principal came to the hospital if she was interested in
speaking to Mrs Cross.

The school authorities were silent for a few days. Suddenly the principal appeared at the hospital unannounced.
We weren't there, but were told afterwards that she had
begged Mrs Cross to send Tani back to the school once he had
recovered, and to forgive the administration and look past
their error. Mrs Cross avoided saying anything definite in
reply, and came to see us. I wondered aloud how can an error
be ignored when we see it has knocked a child into a pulp,
and seen to it that he is strung up in a hospital bed while
those of his classmates who were responsible for the attack
are sitting their exams and getting ahead in their lives and
careers. This error, we agreed, had to be looked at, thoroughly.

After further pressure had been brought to bear, Mrs
Ajatala staged a televised conversation in the hospital foyer
with Mrs Cross and her three lawyers. The principal opened
by claiming that she had been away receiving medical
attention when the incident occurred. She apologised on
behalf of the school authorities for their silence on the

matter. She then gave Tani Cross's mum a wad of five hundred naira notes and a carton of beverages and corn-flakes. Mrs. Cross made eye contact with us before she accepted it.

Wole then pushed further:

'You have apologised for your silence. And we have accepted your apology. Now we want you to speak.'

'I just did,' Mrs Ajatala said, sweating in the heat and in the blood-red skirt-suit she was wearing.

'Well, yes. But we want you to address the cause,' Dan-juma said.

I then spoke up: 'We don't want Tani Cross to happen again. We need you to tell us how you intend to ensure it does not. More clearly we want you to speak and act!'

We had prepared a document that would serve as the terms of our settlement, and I handed a copy to her. It included, amongst other things that she should publish the names of all the students who brutalised Tani, and those of the staff who were on duty that day; and that they should be suspended from school and be properly chastised, to serve as a deterrent to other students. We also demanded the sum of four million naira by way of compensation for Tani Cross and his family, and that the school should foot all Tani's hospital bills. We added that all Tani's academic activities should be graded by external examiners approved by the government; that the principal was to re-introduce Tani during the school assembly as a student who was under her personal care; and that in the event of further discomfort coming to Tani or other boys or girls in similar cases, she undertake to compen-sate such a student with the sum of ten million naira, regard-less of the degree of discomfort.

The document was accompanied by a copy of the writ of summons as evidence of the civil case already instituted against Night Flower Memorial School for the sum of fifteen million naira, and a coloured photocopy of a petition signed by two hundred parents of students withdrawn from the school, calling for it to be shut down. We gave her a two week deadline to revert to us.

Our terms of settlement were sent out to the national dailies and were published the next day.

Nigeria roared.

Soon enough, however, some individuals fought back, saying that the terms were unreasonable and oppressive. Others said that the school should be left to decide how best to discipline its students. Some people were of the opinion that the terms were trying to justify the practice of homosexuality in schools. A number of parents who had access to the press wrote elaborate statements demonising us for representing the Cross family. Ipali & C° received letters from a number of high-profile Nigerians, some of them fellow lawyers, describing our methods and our participation in the matter as unethical. Most threatened to report us and our law offices to the Legal Practitioners' Disciplinary Committee for sanction. It was claimed that we were forcing ourselves on the Cross family, and had succeeded in blowing up a trivial matter into an internationally-known incident of human rights violation, shaming Nigeria. As if this was not enough, we started receiving private messages and threat calls. We started a file where we stored copies of this bullshit.

Embarrassed by the direction things were now taking, our principal partners at Ipali & C°, who had previously commended us for conducting the case *pro bono* while keeping up with our regular caseload, withdrew their support for the Tani Cross case and threatened to dismiss us if we did not do the same. Though he at least had the defence of being obliged to support a relative in difficulties, Danjuma too was under great pressure, from both his wife and his principal.

It was on the fourth day of that difficult week, and I was just exiting the Federal High Court car park, having attended to my own matters for the day, when a little wooden cylinder with small black feathers bound to it by a fraying strip of red cloth rolled out from beneath the front passenger seat. That night Danjuma reported that he had almost been run down by a car just outside his law office. Wole's phone was constantly buzzing with threat messages.

Some people were more desperate than we had bargained for.

We brought all this up during the Rainbow Talk meeting of the Port Harcourt Chapter, which coincidentally fell on the Friday before the Monday deadline, at which time the school would have to agree to, or refuse, the terms of our settlement. The pastors amongst us led a hot prayer session and declared a compulsory two-day dry fast for all members.

In the meantime we received letters from American, South African and British human rights non-governmental organisations, commending our efforts and assuring us that we had their support all the way in the fight for the promotion and protection of human rights in Nigeria.

On Sunday, the eve of the deadline, Danjuma came over to the apartment Wole and I shared for a brief meeting. We discussed the possibility of success and the threats that would multiply as a consequence. Even the ones that we had had already had terrified us: Wole confessed to having nightmares, and none of us was sleeping well.

We held hands and prayed together. Afterwards Wole went off to meet up with one of his flings.

'I wonder where you both get the energy from,' Danjuma said after he had gone.

'How do you mean?'

'Two single, sexy, and ravishingly desirable men with all the possibilities in the world, stuck on a case that could kill them.'

'Are you saying I'm energetic?'

'I said other things too.' His eyes dipped below my belt.

'Stop that,' I said.

'Stop what?'

'Dee. Let us both put our energies to this case that could kill us.'

We had our laugh and worked a little on our laptops, responding to the emails that had been pouring in, both related and unrelated to the case.

An hour later we had read and talked back and forth until our throats, heads and eyes ached, so we decided to take a break and watch a film. After going through the stack of dvds by the TV, most of which were Wole's, we eventually agreed on the candyfloss escapism of *The Princess Diaries*, and slumped on the sofa together to watch it. Only half an hour in, we were already making out. Two exhausted men tiredly looking into each other's eyes, holding hands, gently touching each other. At some point he went through to the kitchen to get water for both of us, his boner jutting out before him. Speaking gently, cuddling me in that way of his that was both avuncular and passionate – the possibility of this moment had been lingering since we met. And I had always hoped to be rational enough to refuse him when the time came. I understand all too well the forces that drive a man who fundamentally prefers men to take a wife and father children, and I pitied him. But still, he was married; he was a father.

And yet, when it came to it, I did not say no.

Every time I tried to bring us to climax he would gently move my hand away. 'I'm not ready yet,' he would say.

And so there we were, shirtless, with our belt-buckles undone, sitting on the floor next to each other, our boners rigid in our trousers, our pelvises inflamed with craving, and our heads, ideas. Princess Mia was having her coronation makeover. Then there was a power failure. I felt him reach for my hips, then my lips, nipples. He was tonguing my navel when the power was restored.

When he looked up, his eyes had that look in them – the one that every man has when he has become his sensuality. The look that consumes the moment but does not last beyond the orgasm.

I didn't ask him to stop.

Afterwards, saying nothing, we showered. Just before he drove off that night, he told me sheepishly that he was being made to choose between a transfer from the Port Harcourt to the Lagos branch of Ataba & C⁰ and being permanently dismissed from the firm. Unsurprisingly, he had decided to opt for the transfer.

He also said that his family was falling apart. His wife had threatened to leave with the children so that he could, in her words, 'concentrate on your pursuit of realising Sodom and Gomorrah in Nigeria.' He mentioned pressure from his church, and said something about how he had been content with his peaceful career before all of this.

I was too tired to respond the way I wanted to, but I had to confirm that he would be at the clinic the next day. He said no: he was leaving on the first flight to Lagos that morning.

Wole hadn't returned by the time I went to bed.

*

Wole and I arrived at 10.45 a.m. to find the hospital foyer packed with journalists and reporters. Mrs Ajatala arrived at eleven, in the company of two smartly-dressed men I recognised from Nigerian Bar Association Conference meetings as top lawyers. We inspected the documents, okayed them, and they were signed without reservation. A few cameras flashed. There were no handshakes. The three of them left without saying a word.

When we handed the documents to Mrs Cross she embraced Wole and then me. She was crying. A press conference followed at which Wole spoke briefly. A journalist asked whether we thought it was safe for Tani to return to his school. We said we hoped so. Another asked whether we would take up more cases like Tani's in the future. We reminded them that lawyers are not permitted to solicit for cases. We were asked whether we would fight for gay marriage to be legalised in Nigeria. We replied that we were lawyers, not activists. Someone asked if we were gay. We declined to comment. The signed copy of the terms of settlement was filed in court, and afterwards the terms themselves were published in national newspapers.

When we returned to the office that afternoon, drained but proud, Wole and I were given notice of our dismissal.

A few months after that, Night Flower Memorial commenced a new session, and we and Tani's mother were invited by the principal to witness the playing out of one of the terms of the settlement at the school's morning assembly. She announced the suspension of several male students who were known to have been involved in the bullying of Tani Cross. Furthermore, she instructed those assembled that if there was a repeat of such an incident of students taking laws into their own hands, such students would be expelled from her 'prestigious school'.

Courtesy of some film-makers who were also members of the Rainbow Talk, a long interview with me and Wole, intercut with bits of TV news footage, and chronicling the Tani Cross case from its inception to what was still ongoing, was shot and made available on YouTube, and was posted and reposted numerous times.

With each reposting the death threats seemed to increase in arithmetical progression.

Danjuma, now in Lagos, called and kept calling. Wole didn't hold a grudge against him for long. At some points I even thought that Wole was taking sides with him, defending his making sacrifices for his family, at which point I had an urge to tell Wole about what had happened that final night between us. Since I hated myself for giving in to him, I didn't. And even in the face of the death-threats I wished Danjuma had been brave enough to see it through to the end. He continued to insist that he was besotted with me.

Eventually I said that if he wanted me to listen to him he should return to Port Harcourt for a weekend so we could speak in person. He declined my invitation, but kept calling. I stopped taking his calls. One day, however, he used an unfamiliar number to call me from. Although unknown numbers often meant death-threats, by chance I picked up. He babbled on about wanting me to understand that he really missed me and needed me in his life.

After his having chickened out on Tani (who was, after all, his nephew) Wole and me, as well as on the broader fight for human rights, I said I didn't want *him* in *my* life. I wanted to be around people who inspired me to be braver, not more timid. I threatened to report his activities to his wife if he ever contacted me outside of the Rainbow Talk. He then sent me some email about African standards and some love bullshit. I did not respond, but found myself getting more and more angry about it.

Eventually I called his home one Sunday morning. His wife answered, and after exchanging some rather stilted pleasantries with her I asked that she hand him the phone. He sounded cold when she said it was me.

'Baby boo,' I told him, 'If you ever contact me again I'll be on the next flight to Lagos and I'll kiss you before your wife and the rest of Lagos. The world already thinks me gay. You are the "respectable" married one. I'm not bluffing.'

And so he had been stacked away with the history books – until a few hours ago, at the Rainbow Talk meeting, where, annoyingly, he had acted as if we had parted on excellent terms.

I had never wanted to set my eyes on Danjuma again, or on any married bisexual man who hinted that I could be the 'moi-moi' on the side.

But then here I was, a man engaged to be married to a lovely girl in Port Harcourt, gazing longingly at the silhouette of the beautiful man who now lay asleep beside me, shamelessly yearning to slip my arm around him, and sure he would welcome me doing so.

When I finally fell asleep I dreamt of sex, confusion and Tega, my woman. I awoke restless, seeing flashes of her face, just before rolling into Kwame – rolling into him one time too many. I slipped my fingers into his and squeezed. 'You are one hot man,' I whispered.

It was 4:30 a.m.

He didn't respond.

I was both relieved and disappointed.

I got out of bed before the Muslims to freshen up for the flight to Port Harcourt. It was still dark when I returned from the bathroom. I slipped on my blue jeans and went back to bed to say a short prayer.

Just after I said amen Kwame drew so close that vibes ran through me. 'I love you,' he said.

'What a crazy night,' I whispered as I turned to him and placed my hand on his waist.

'I couldn't sleep all night.'

'Why?'

'I was hoping you would hold me.'

'I didn't want to offend you or Tayo.'

'How do you mean, "offend"?' he asked, pressing his chest against mine, his fingers tracing my spine. 'It's not like we're seeing each other.'

'So why did you come all the way to Nigeria?'

'I wanted to meet him and attend the Rainbow Talk meeting.'

'Really?'

'I was fascinated by the idea that such a thing existed and I needed to know how it worked.'

'Are you satisfied with what you know?'

'I'll be in Lagos for two months. I could be satisfied then.'

Leaning forward, he kissed my neck and fondled my locks.

'I'm sorry,' I said, though doing nothing to resist him, 'I can't do this.'

'Do what?' he asked, his cold tongue-tip shivering on my chin, his grip tightening in my locks.

'I'm married.'

'Married?' He pulled back, taking his hands off me.

'Well, not married yet, but very much engaged.'

'Oh.' His hands resumed moving slowly on my sides. 'So when are you leaving Nigeria?'

'For what?'

'To get married,' he said, ducking down to suck on one of my nipples as he squeezed my butt fiercely, breathing hard on my chest. Desire flushed through me, and I grabbed his hands and slid on top of him, spreading his arms apart and pinning him. He panted heavily. I could feel sweat trickle down my back, and it dripped from my chest onto his, and I could not make out the details of his face in the dark.

'It's to a woman,' I said. 'I can't do this anymore. I'm sorry.' And with great reluctance I got off him, my swollen penis pressing painfully against the zipper of my jeans, threatening to break free and wreck my life. I turned away from him to unzip and tuck myself in more comfortably.

He watched me as I buttoned my shirt in the same way I must have watched Danjuma get dressed to go back to his wife.

I avoided his gaze. My heart pounded heavily but slowly. I knew I had lost Kwame's friendship. He did not say much to me. What was there to say?

Morning came. The convoy arrived to convey me and Wole to the airport. I walked to the car without looking back. The last thing Kwame said, in a voice thick with emotion, was, 'It'll kill me not to see you again.'

On the way to the airport I thanked God that I had been strong enough to resist cheating on my woman. I had proved to myself that my sexuality was mine to control and define – this time. I had not been so successful in the past, especially when distance and opportunity were in sync. Often I would blame it on the excitement of suddenly having so many men available to me and willing, and too little time to do other than plunge into that hot, sweaty, sensual world of male desire. I would blame it on the little man, 'ifentinye', down south, who wants what he wants. Crazy, I would think afterwards – but not at the time.

At the airport I saw – was suddenly aware of – women, for the first time in days: dark-skinned and light, calm and high-spirited, colourful and demure. Women with curves and protrusions. One flirted with her eyes as I passed her wheeling my luggage. Another locked my stare, the colours on her eyelids and full lips vivid and provocative. A third was touchingly absorbed in cuddling her baby. A fourth was immersed in Adiche's *Purple Hibiscus*, while, next to her, another was frowning at her iPad. Being around so many women made me feel like I was breathing another oxygen; as if I had traded the intrigue of twilight for the bright clarity of the morning. Like a part of me was waking while another was falling asleep.

Just before we took off, I tried to imagine a world in which no woman would be central to me. I could not. Perhaps it is because, on several levels, nothing is really complete without their naughtiness, sassiness, interference, wisdom, friendship and leadership; they are our sisters, daughters and mothers, and their love is different, and important.

Yet love is not desire.

I had a woman. And I wanted to share myself with her. I even wanted to share those moments where confusion is god and ghost. I wanted to love her as I had loved lovers before her. I wanted to risk exploring new and secret places with her. I wanted to take chances because when I was with her nothing felt the same. I did not know what this interesting new feeling was. Love, perhaps. But no woman, absolutely no woman, had made me feel 'in love' before.

'Oremi Alhaji'/'My Friend the Stranger'

You see me because there is an eye in your soul
An eye for my kind
Because I have been hidden from all save a few
Of the few and you

You hear me even when I've said nothing
Because what you listen to isn't my voice
But instructions from the universe
Music inspiring you

You walk with me because you have become a friend
Even while still the most exciting of strangers
And I walk with you because I understand
I see you too

You tell me that I'm different
When in fact it's you
And your falling heart
With the seasons that now vent

I'm saying Oremi and letting you sing
Because I see your eyes longing too
I'm still listening
Because I hear you

With you I see myself again
Feel the first
And the next
And the next

With you I see I have fallen in love a lot
And that this is your first
I should listen
Because you are my next

So I won't hold on

Nnanna Ikpo

Because I know you won't let go
Either way we'll be together
Saying innasunka for a while
And perhaps, forever

Eden Kekere/Little Eden

From: ahmed@sugarbooks.com
To: waledamian@damianbros.com

Dear Wale,

I do appreciate your reply. And yes, I also look forward to a great relationship with you. Thanks for accepting my Facebook request. I'm certain that your Maputo outing was rewarding. Your photo and status updates on your timeline say it all.

At least one of us is having a good time.

Today I am writing from my 'secret place' and there seems to be a lot on my mind.

Sometimes life hits me so hard that I fall to the ground, and the lonely winding road stretches out before me. The intensity of the moment chokes off my lucidity. So I retire to the nearest peace I can find.

It's usually some place that is calm but alive in its theme and mood. There will usually be soft music – I love Westlife – silence occasionally, fresh air and the perfect temperature – a place where the moment and its intensity beautifully fade away. In there it would be just me, God, and my heartbeat as I shut out the countless voices in my head.

Well, all this goes on in my study once every week, when I take time out to reflect on certain issues that surround my life – which these days includes you. It is my secret place.

Now considering you, who is thirty-five and such a

celebrated jurist, I would love to know your thoughts on secret places, if you have any, and the things that go on in there.

I would also want to know your next step in the light of academics, it being the case that you don't seem as fond of litigation as your brother, Wole.

I reread the opening paragraphs of Hot Sundays *today after reflecting and I fell in love with you afresh. Pardon my saying this, it's just that sometimes caution seems a burden to me when honesty is most called for. You were a great writer in your teens and I am wondering what happened to your literary side? Academic research is valuable but it says little or nothing about the soul of the writer. Your soul is beautiful, Wale, so beautiful.*

Wale my man – if I can call you that now – I would appreciate that you update your status more often on Facebook along with photos, and also that you tweet more. I may not be always available to chat, but I always want to know how your day is going and be sure that you are fine.

Please do send my love to your family. And for you, inshallah, I remain

Yours truly,

Ahmed.

On an otherwise-beautiful Christmas evening at our house in Port Harcourt we sat down to supper under the crystal chandelier exchanging heavy glances. I felt the weight of what had been happening, and the fear of what would follow on from it, pressing down on all of us: Wole; his fiancée Lola; Brother Gbenro, our 'father'; Tega, my fiancée; and me.

In front of us were spread out dishes of spicy ewedu soup, fresh fish and dark amala. I ate quietly, reflecting on how we had come to this; on the unspoken bond that none of us could explain. But we all knew it was built around Wole. Yet as we ate I found myself wishing that my life was as simple as it had been before him, back in Ilaro.

Not that it had ever been wholly simple, of course. My first few days at Ilaro Community Secondary School everyone stared at me. Dreadlocks were not a taboo in our community, but they were very rare, and no matter how many times I reintroduced myself to establish my name as Olawale, my classmates and teachers insisted that I was either 'Bob Marley' or, less obviously, 'Dada'.

Myth has it that the ancient god of vegetables, Dada – who reigned as Alaafin of Oyo in the time before his brother Sango, god of thunder and lightning, came to power – had thick and dense hair. And so some called dreadlocks Irun Dada, while others called them Dada Awure, and so I was 'Dada'. They were also worn by Orisha, the priest of the god of the deep oceans, Olokun.

I was born with my locks. Except for one brief period in my life, I have always had them.

Maami and Baba took turns to groom them on Saturdays, telling me that I was lucky to have hair like my great grandfather, and Samson in the Bible, who was very strong, and whose strength resided in his hair. Like Samson's, mine was never cut.

Initially, although I was proud of it, I did not give much thought to the meanings that might reside in my hair – though my reservations about being called Dada never did wane. I made friends in school, studied hard, and even made a best friend, Seun, with whom I shared many 'boyish escapades', as well as doing our homework together and watching the school soccer team – god forbid they ever pick either of us to play! My life seemed straightforward. But things soon took a different and more dramatic turn.

I was eleven. Baba's diabetes had intensified, and he became too weak to leave the house. Brother Gbenro moved in with us and took over the day to day management of the farm, reporting to Baba at the end of each day. He also assisted Maami by attending to Baba in the evenings while she prepared dinner, and he was always the last to go to bed. He shared my room, but despite Maami instructing me to lay the bed out for him, he always insisted on passing the night on the raffia mat on the floor. If I attempted to take the mat he would tap me gently till I got up, insisting that I take the bed. Though I did not understand this, it would have been disrespectful to question it.

This had been going on for about two weeks when one day I returned from school to find a white Peugeot saloon car parked in our compound. From inside the house came the sound of a woman crying and apologising in Yoruba. My heart skipped a beat and goose-pimples shot from my skin.

Reluctantly I went in and found the woman kneeling before Baba and Maami. I had seen her face before, some-where, somehow, but she was a stranger to me.

'Olawale, you are back?' Maami asked as the woman turned her tear-stained face to look at me. She was as light-skinned as Brother Gbenro. Her hair was dark, straight, flowing and unbound. She wore a fitted yellow dress, short-sleeved and stylishly cinched at the waist with a metallic-looking belt, and red high-heeled shoes. She was alarmingly 'un-Ilaro' to my young eyes.

'This is Titilayo Ajayi,' Maami said. 'She is your mother, and – '

Titi's Maami.

Before Maami could finish the introduction Mum had caught me in her arms and lifted me high in the air, hugging me, crying, kissing me. She was different from the women I had known until then. Her embrace was soft, unlike the coarse suffocation of ashoke usually worn by women in Ilaro. She smelled of a new kind of sweetness that perhaps even then I knew was expensive. Her chest throbbed against mine in a rhythm that was new yet suddenly familiar, as if I had always known it.

'Olawale, we will always be your parents, and we will always be here, okay?' Baba assured me a few days later as he reached in to shake my hand through the Peugeot's window. My few possessions were in a bag in the car's boot.

'But you must learn to love and respect her o. Remember she gave birth to you. You must behave. Don't forget you are a man,' Maami continued.

I nodded and didn't say anything. There had been two days of discussions which I had not been a part of, and this was the outcome. Mum and I sat in the rear seats with the driver in front. Our journey began. She held my hand and looked the other way. I didn't really understand what was happening until the parts of Ilaro I knew were left behind, and a road strange to me stretched ahead. At once I was broken, yet still. From the corner of my eye I watched her. She saw me watching and her eyes flashed.

And then I realised where I had seen this face before.

It was the day rain almost destroyed one of our adireh-backed photo-albums, which Baba kept stacked on his reading table. He asked me to spread them out on the living room floor to dry. The album usually on top, which he looked at the most often, was the most badly damaged. I opened it randomly at a picture of an unfamiliar but beautiful woman – Titilayo Ajayi – in bridal dress, accompanied by Maami holding two babies, one cradled in each arm. When Baba caught me looking at it he snapped at me and I dropped the album on the floor. But the bride had burned into my brain. Now she had broken free from the photo to snatch me from all I knew.

Frightened, alone, shivering with cold: the air-conditioner did not make it any easier for me. Tears rolled down my cheeks, and my heart kept skipping beats until I felt Mum's hand caress my nape.

'Come,' she said.

I slid close to her and she hugged me, and she was warm. This wind was too strong and the tree snapped. Suddenly all my emotions broke loose in a rush. I screamed. I cried. I saw Maami waving goodbye as she receded into the distance. I saw Baba and Brother Gbenro vanish from sight as the road curved away from Eden Kekere. I saw Ilaro and all the classmates I would perhaps never see again. I saw my best friend Seun, to whom I had had no chance to say goodbye. The life I knew was gone, the life ahead I had no idea about. Yet what was this safety I now felt?

'You look and feel just like him,' she said as she kissed my locks and cuddled me. I didn't understand, but remained in her arms sobbing off and on until eventually I drifted into sleep.

When I awoke it seemed hours had passed: it was nightfall, and I lay there with my head on Mum's thighs, her hand caressing my arm. The vehicle now felt pleasantly cool rather than cold, and soft music was playing on the stereo. My feelings of loss returned, but I was more at peace now, and even feeling a little anticipation.

The car slowed and turned off the road. As we drove onto a fenced premises I sat up and saw a brightly-lit space spread with well-tended lawns, the borders busy with flowers. In the middle was a white duplex, the place I was now to call home. Though the house was big, to my surprise Mum said she occupied it by herself. I thought she was brave to do that. Here I would have my own room, she said, as she led me in. She took me through to it, snapping on the light as she opened the door, but letting me enter first. Strangely my pictures were already on the walls, and brand-new clothes of my exact size were laid out on the bed, as if waiting for me. She showed me the bathroom and how to use the taps and turn the water heater on and off; and how to use the intercom for the kitchen.

'Do you want something to eat?' she asked.

I shook my head.

'Now, now, this is your home,' she said smiling at me, fondling my locks. 'I'll make us some noodles and fish for dinner.' She pressed the intercom and asked someone named Biola to defrost the fish. I sat on the bed, still holding onto my bag. *My home*, I thought. My eye was caught by a framed photograph on a shelf. It was a picture of me aged perhaps eight or nine, holding a big round cake with candles on it. A tightness passed through my chest: I had never dressed like that or had such a cake in my life.

Mum was watching me. I forced a smile. She smiled back.

To begin with I did not leave the house much, save on Saturdays, when she took me to the salon to have my locks washed – she retwisted the roots at home herself, and these were perhaps our most intimate times. On weekdays she left early in the mornings, after preparing my breakfast and lunch: she worked as a nurse at a private hospital in town. She usually left me in the care of Biola, her female help, who attended to all the domestic work except making my meals. A slim, dark-skinned girl in her teens who was slightly taller than me, Biola was banished to the kitchen or the studio flat behind the house except when she emerged with a broom or mop.

When Mum's shifts meant she returned late, if I was still awake she would come into my room and tell me tales of her patients, of suffering and healing, of pain averted or endured, of her fellow-nurses, the doctors and administrators, and their humour and wisdom and stupidity. Often there were times when nurse, mother and son drifted off to sleep side by side. If I was asleep when she came in, or pretending to be asleep, she would gently tuck me in, run her hands across my forehead into my hair, then stare at me for a while with the strangest expression on her face – before turning off the light and going out, always carefully leaving the door open just enough to cast a gash of light across the floor that ended at the foot of my bed. Other times we would sit up and watch *The Lion King* over and over again – on my demand. She often made fun of Rafiki's butt and how tomato-red it would look in reality. Sometimes she made me laugh so much I had to run to the restroom to relieve myself.

I quickly got used to calling her Mum. For all the strangeness of the situation, I had fallen in love with her, and became extremely attentive to her moods. There were times when she would have this look in her eyes and they would get all teary. She would notice me watching her and smile and turn her head away, and I would pretend I hadn't seen. Other times she would seem to be carried away with grooming my hair and perhaps pretend not to notice I was staring at her, fighting the questions and doubts that haunted me. Yet her presence filled me with a growing sense of peace and familiarity.

I thought of Baba and Maami often, but I couldn't help melting in Mum's arms whenever she hugged and kissed me goodnight. I hoped that Baba and Brother Gbenro would not pick offence if he learned that I waved and swayed willingly in this wind that had become my mum – yielding almost instantly and without putting up a fight. I also wondered what Maami had meant by, 'Don't forget you are a man.' That was the first time she ever said that to me.

After I had been living with Mum for what felt like a long time, but was in reality only a few weeks, she told me that I had been transferred to Junior Secondary Two at Nigerian Navy Secondary School, Borikiri, Port Harcourt. The plan, she informed me, was that I would be living at school most of the time. Having barely settled into my new home I tried to protest but she kept saying, 'Trust me, love, you'll have a lot of fun with him.'

'Who is "him"?' I asked.

'What flavour of ice-cream will you have this evening?' she responded, heading off that line of conversation; and the resolution of that chapter was for the umpteenth time adjourned. I could do nothing but keep on looking forward to meeting this 'him' with whom I would apparently have so much fun.

On the day of my resumption of my education at Nigerian Navy – a Monday – we both woke early to pack the last of my luggage: bedspreads; a pillow; stainless steel plates; spoons; beverages; cereals; disinfectants; soap – if I had not known better, I would have thought that we were going to stock a shop. We also printed my initials on each item – even the bars of soap had their wraps initialled with permanent-ink felt-tipped pens.

'Mum, why do we have to go through all this?' I complained.

'So you can recognise that which is yours amidst every other person's,' she replied. 'It's a boarding school, love. All the students are made to buy similar-looking wares.'

She advised that I be careful, prayerful and studious – and kept advising in a similar vein till, after an hour's drive, we pulled up before the school's smart white gate.

Two men in black berets, blue short-sleeved shirts, black combat trousers and boots flanked the gate. I fancied their uniforms and imagined how I would look in one. I was excited, thinking they were students, though they looked tougher and older than the students at Ilaro.

'Yes, good day,' one of them said as he bent to look into our vehicle.

'Good day,' we replied.

The driver explained that I was resuming my education as a transfer student, and we were permitted to drive onto the premises.

Beyond the gates the smell of freshly-cut grass greeted us. Bent-over palm branches brushed the windshield. There was a lush green field to the left and a basketball court a little further in on the right. We passed a number of two-storeyed buildings and bungalows, and I wondered which of them would be my classroom. Everywhere appeared tranquil. I looked out for other students, but at that hour there were none to be seen.

Our car came to a halt on a large square of land that was smeared smooth and black, and shimmered. From there a sand path stretched away to a cluster of buildings separate from the rest and all blue in colour – the main school; another path led to a building signposted 'Admin Block'. Mum and I headed over to that. We went in and out of various offices for the requisite registration and endorsements. One of the registrars, an older woman with half-rimmed spectacles, looked at my documentation and then up at me from behind her desk and said, 'They look so much alike.'

My attention was drawn to a student who was the same size and perhaps age as me, as he jogged up to one of the water taps to wash his hands. 'This must be a junior student,' I thought to myself. He had a white caped shirt on, along with a navy blue tie and trousers, white stockings and brown sandals. As I had with the blue and black uniforms of the security guards, I also fell in love with this fashion. To my eleven-year-old eyes he looked like Superman, with his cape bouncing up and down as he jogged off back the way he had come.

No sooner had we rounded off registration than a bell sounded. The students – all boys at first – poured out of the buildings on every side. Girls trickled out subsequently, sashaying, a good number of them walking in pairs holding hands. They seemed to me at the time to be in their thousands, heading in a crowd for what I later discovered was the school's tuck-shop, and all the boys wore white-caped shirts.

Mum and I went back to the car to collect my luggage. 'Now, you wait here,' she said. 'I'll be right back.' And she smiled at me – that secretive smile I had become so used to, so intrigued and frustrated by – and headed off towards one of the blue buildings.

Some of the passing students gave me odd looks that seemed to me to go beyond curiosity. One waved at me in an uncertain way, frowning when I didn't respond. Feeling awkward, I got back in the car. While I was seated there in the silent vehicle with Mum's uncommunicative driver my excitement began to wane. I felt as though I stood once more at our gate at Ilaro, as if something was about to be ripped from me. My locks were suddenly too tightly bound, so I loosened them to let the blood flow and tension pass, and shut my eyes.

A moment later I heard the car door swing open and someone get in. My eyes snapped open, I turned my head and I beheld him. An exact replica of me. Long, thin, well-kept locks bound behind his head by rubber bands; shrewd brown eyes, pink lips, dark skin, pointed nose... Immaculate in his uniform, he was beautiful. He was me.

He pulled the door closed. As if by prearrangement the driver got out and stood outside, leaving us sitting side by side in silence. After a few minutes Mum came and sat in the front passenger seat. Looking at us in the rear-view mirror she said, 'I know how shocked you both must be. But there will be no better time in the world than now. You are my sons, my only children. Oluwole, this is Olawale, your twin brother.'

'Yes, Mum,' he replied. He sounded like me save that I had a Yoruba accent at the time and he did not.

'Olawale, this is Oluwole, your twin brother.'

'Yes, Mum,' I said, watching her watching me in the rear-view mirror.

'Do you have any questions?'

Petrified in that moment, neither of us could utter a word. She twisted round and kissed and hugged us both, Wole first, then me, then we all awkwardly got out of the car. She escorted us to the housemaster's office, and after I had been assigned to the same room as Wole, she bade us farewell and left.

That was how I met Wole, twenty-five years ago. And ever since then he has been an inalienable part of my life.

After eating our fill, Wole, Brother Gbenro and I went and sat in the lounge to unwind over the last of the wine while Tega and Lola did the dishes. They were such noble women – and that's not because they insisted on doing the dishes: Wole and I were simply blessed to have them in our lives. Brother Gbenro equally shared our sentiments.

Lola is a tall, slim and light-skinned girl of twenty-eight who hails from Ile-Ife. She bagged a law degree from Obafemi Awolowo University and worked in the Federal Ministry of Justice before joining the Afrospark Foundation as our legal representative. She's very driven, academic, analytical and meticulous. Nothing gets past her – and so she's exactly Wole's match.

Tega is darker, as tall, but has a larger frame, a more embellished silhouette and an amazing derrière. She is twenty-seven, hails from Delta State, and studied at the London Film Academy. She worked with MNET Africa for a while before joining the Afrospark Foundation as the head of our documentary filming unit. Added to this she wielded my magic – my 'mumu button'. She was, in a good way, my tsunami.

'Wole, your mother will be so proud of you,' Brother Gbenro said.

'Why?'

From the kitchen came the clink of the washing-up, and Lola laughing at something Tega had said.

'Her. Lola. Taking the bull by the horn and proving everybody wrong.'

Wole raised an eyebrow.

'You have such great chemistry. You could almost pass for best friends or siblings.'

'That's what it should be, shouldn't it?' I asked.

'Well, not everyone gets that lucky,' Brother Gbenro replied, reaching for his wine-glass and sipping from it. 'As men, we all set out to find the next great woman in our lives who is neither our mother nor sister, but should be capable of playing both those roles in addition to being a lover.'

'You mean that every man wants a version of his mother or sister for a spouse? Mm, that would make it all such a bore,' I said, shrugging.

'When a man is born, his first sensation is touch,' Brother Gbenro said. 'Therefore he always wants to be touched. Physically first, then spiritually, emotionally, in all spheres of his life a part of him would always crave to be touched. However, as he advances in age he learns to attach this feeling of pleasure to the people who are closest in his life: mother, father, brother, sister, if they are available. Then again, in Africa the women more often than not are the ones in charge of the nurture and loving and caring and hugging and spending time. So a man attaches feelings of happiness to the particular class, taste, texture, mode and means of nurture which the women in his life afford him. That's why if a woman is light-skinned, more often than not her son or little brother would fancy a light-skinned woman above a dark-skinned one. If a woman always bought her son or little brother blue shirts on his birthday, more often than not her son or little brother would fall in love with any woman who buys him blue shirts on his birthday.'

'Choi! Brother Gbenro Sigmund Freud,' Wole teased, and we all laughed so loudly that the girls came out. 'Brother Gbenro was giving us psychology lessons,' Wole said by way of explanation, chuckling.

'We heard the end of it,' Lola said as she sat beside Wole and Tega sat beside me.

'And what did you think?' I asked.

'What if,' Lola said, 'the boy grows up in millennial Africa, where a good number of the mothers and big sisters are storming the offices and ministries and calling the shots?'

'Yeah,' Tega continued. 'When the women are darting from one international summit to the other so fast they hardly have time for the boys or the blue shirts.'

'A mother will always have time for the boys and the blue shirts,' Wole said. 'That's what makes her mum.'

'What about in Africa, where many of the mums are too taunted by sexism and angry, or too poor, to be mums to the boys or even the girls?' I asked.

'A mum can never be too poor to be mum,' Lola said.

'Aah,' I exclaimed. 'A mum can be too poor to be a mum sometimes. And I'm not talking about cash.'

'If you put it like that,' Brother Gbenro said, 'times are changing really. Back in my day, once you give a child life, you must mother or father him or her o. Wo! It is by force o!'

We all laughed.

'But now we have crèche and nurseries and nannies,' Lola said.

'Nanny ke?!' I said jokingly. 'See this babe o!'

'Wetin?' Wole exclaimed back. 'I dey complain?'

'Thank God say I don clear Tee,' I said, stroking Tega's thigh. 'Shebi you sabi tie pikin for your back.'

'Ehhhh?' Tega screamed. 'Back ke?! When we have carriers?'

What?! Our women did not intend to carry our babies on their backs? 'Carriers ke?' I cried, holding my head comically in my hands.

'Correct, babe!' Lola gave Tega a thumbs-up.

'And then you will be shocked when the baby calls the carrier "mama"?' Brother Gbenro teased.

'A baby has several sources of affection besides his mama,' Wole said.

'Like his dad,' Lola agreed, 'his uncles, aunties and future spouses.'

'For a baby?' Tega quizzed. 'Aaaa, Omolola. Babies can't source affection from their future spouses. Abeg.'

'Don't you believe in love at first sight?' I teased, catching her by the waist.

'Well, not when some crèches and schools teach kids to sit boys to one end of the class and girls to the other,' Lola said, rolling her eyes.

'That stops nothing,' Wole said, 'given that boys can love boys – '

'– and girls can love girls,' I finished.

'Babies can't love like that that early,' Lola said, making a face.

'That's not true,' I said. 'There really are gay babies.'

'Bisexual babies too,' Tega said.

'I don't agree with that,' Brother Gbenro said. 'Sexuality is a choice thing. And to be able to choose, your mind needs to be mature enough to articulate, or at least recognise distinctions.'

'Are you saying a baby can't make distinctions between "akamu" and breast milk?' I asked.

'Especially when everything from pencil to python are the baby's favourite chew thing.'

'I quite agree,' Lola said.

'I hope God does not decide that you know for sure,' I said, reaching for my drink.

'How so?'

'I don't know,' I said, looking into my drink. 'By giving you a gay child.'

'God forbid!' Lola and Tega shouted, snapping their fingers. Wole choked on his drink, slightly mouth-spraying it in front of him, causing everyone to jerk and sit up.

Lola held him, rubbing his back. 'Take it easy, babe.'

'Are you okay?' Brother Gbenro asked.

'I'm fine,' Wole said, darting a sharp glance at me before sitting up once more. 'Just fine.'

'Besides,' Tega cut in, 'you'll need to have a gay parent to be gay.'

'Sisi, that's the biggest lie ever told,' Brother Gbenro said. 'If that was true, how would there be gay people? Two men, or two women?'

'It all depends on how you look at it, sir,' I said, in an attempt to brush two birds with a pebble: placate Wole and defend Tega. 'A gay parent might let a gay child be more honest about themselves, rather than lying and covering up.'

'True, but their nature would still be the same...'

The night was young and we chatted away, arguing boisterously, laughing, moving on to topics less controversial. Finally we got to the crux of why we were all together that night: my leaving for Amara to take up my new job at Kola University.

'Tega,' Brother Gbenro began, 'what do you have to stay about this?'

'Brother Gbenro,' Tega replied, 'Wale is passionate about academics. He and I have both discussed this and he really wants this exposure. It's going to look great on his resumé and will also be good for the Foundation. He is a wonderful teacher and will be a blessing to the students there.'

'You do know that he and his brother are alumni of that university – '

Tega nodded.

'– and that they did not have too many fans in the school's administration when they were there,' Brother Gbenro continued. 'They got into a lot of trouble for their, let us say nonconformity.'

'But they offered him the job,' she pointed out. 'And they invited him to apply.'

'We still do not understand the rationale behind Kola offering a job to Wale now. And with the death threats that have been coming in recently you know we have to be careful, so – '

'Brother Gbenro,' Wole cut in, 'Wale is an adult and he knows what he wants. It is our place to support him regardless of death threats, alumni wahala, whatever it is. These threats are empty and I'm sure that – '

'Sure that what, Wole?' Lola interrupted. 'You shouldn't take these things lightly. You both greatly support the LGBT community here in Nigeria. You run the Afrospark Foundation. Since next year's theme was announced, Nigeria has believed that you both are gay – which I think is most ridiculous given...' She gestured to herself and Tega.

Wole and I avoided exchanging glances but I couldn't help smiling. Brother Gbenro sipped his wine once more, and didn't comment.

'The "Save the Colours" theme isn't – ' Wole began.

'The job offer at Amara could be a trap,' Lola continued, 'to get either or both of you away from where you have support and a set-up where you have security. Let's be rational: this is Nigeria; activism gets tagged as a lot of things. It is better we stick together and you forget this job,' she finished abruptly. Her eyes were bright and she was breathing hard.

'Wale.' Brother Gbenro spoke up again. 'Inasmuch as I don't want you to do anything risky, I believe that you have to do what you have to do. You are grown up.'

Picking up his phones, iPad and walking-stick, he stood to leave. At the door he turned back to us. 'When is your flight?'

'New Year's Eve, sir,' I replied.

'Well, that's enough time for you to sleep on it. We are solidly behind you no matter what you finally decide. I'll be here then, just in case.'

And that was Brother Gbenro: a worrier and an overprotective dictator to those dear to him, when it came to things like this he was a different man: firm, unruffled. Perhaps that was part of his job description: quite extraordinarily he had risen from farm manager for Baba at Eden Kekere to be a senior officer in the State Security Service, one of the most highly-regarded law enforcement agencies in the country, known mostly for its stealth, underground and unconventional modes of operation. Even more extraordinarily, he was invested in supporting the pro-LGBT human rights work Wole and I were doing. Without his backing we would soon have found it impossible to function in the hostile political environment in which we were increasingly finding ourselves.

Shortly after Mum came to get me, and after recruiting an impressive replacement to manage Eden Kekere for Baba, Brother Gbenro left Ilaro to study, of all the unlikely things, criminology in England. He kept in frequent touch with Baba by letter, and when he returned he mechanized Eden Kekere and attracted several foreign investors to it. It blossomed so much that a good percentage of the Foundation's funding still comes from there. Baba, who had been satisfied with the scale of things as they were, was initially sceptical of the new approach, especially as news was spreading that factories were springing up all over the area and farms were going down, and that the government was taking over people's land. But the investors who came were a still-thriving English family company, and they made a favourable impression on him. Brother Gbenro had good lawyers and the deal he made was good. It is still really good. Safe and private.

Eventually Baba passed on, and Eden Kekere was bequeathed to Wole and me.

The girls spent a little more time with us after Brother Gbenro had gone and then left, each of them clearly wishing that I would call off my acceptance of the teaching post at K.U. and stick primarily, like Wole, to the Afrospark Foundation. Tega in particular struggled. When she kissed me goodnight at the front door it felt different.

'I'll be fine,' I said. I even begged her to spend the night and help me pack when we hugged outside.

'I don't doubt that you'll be fine,' she said. 'I just can't imagine not seeing you for such a long time.'

'You can visit.'

'So that I'll be the lecturer's flown-in lover?'

'That's not a bad idea,' I said, trying to snuggle, our hips meeting.

'Leave me jor,' she said. 'We're outside.' Trying to pound softly on my chest. She smelled of milk, gentleness.

'I love you,' I said. 'You know that, right?'

'That's all I need to know.'

As I packed I thought about our project. Afrospark was an offshoot of one of Wole's visions in his final year at school, during his tenure as leader of the stage production service unit in our campus Pentecostal fellowship. He saw it as a means through which he could, as he modestly put it, 'change the world'; repair lives that were being blighted by prejudice, and change certain psychological orientations that he felt were baseless in our society. He was very passionate about anything that concerned it. Everyone except me thought that he was only being a dreamer, but besides being the logical thing to do after our involvement in the Tani Cross case left us stripped of our jobs, it was also his way of immortalizing our father – and yes, perhaps himself too – while learning every day to love and heal himself.

Dad. Our dad, Aderopo Toluwani Damian. 'Tolu'. A man whose role in our lives has never been simple to comprehend. Growing ever more complex with the years.

There was no representation of him in my childhood environment beyond a single faded black-and-white childhood photograph of him and Brother Gbenro – who was his younger brother and so our uncle, I learned once I had left Ilaro. Wole and I were eventually and grudgingly told by Mum that he was serving a jail term at the Kirikiri Maximum Security Prison in Lagos. Why, we asked excitedly. She refused to tell us, but promised to take us to see him during our first long August vacation together. The plan clearly did not thrill her; presumably it was his idea. But I knew she would fulfil her promise: she was trying hard to repair tears we were barely aware of, and make everything right.

Often Wole and I would talk into the night, imagining what Daddy was like. We wondered whether or not he was friendly – the idea of his being a convict was scary. We assumed that Mum would only be taking us if she thought he wanted to see us. We assumed that he and Mum had shared a great love story, so great it had birthed twins. Wole repeated this idea often. I wondered to myself though, if the story was so great why were Wole and I separated at birth? Why had Mum only just come into my life? And my biggest worry of all: why was Dad in prison? – a maximum security prison for that matter!

Mum had to pay several preparatory visits to the prison to make it possible for us to go. She had to take a lawyer to notify our father that she would be bringing us to see him; seek the permission of the Nigerian prison officials for us to come as independent visitors; and verify the visiting days and hours. It felt strange and intimidating – as if we were attending some important personage. She explained to us that she had to go through all these hoops because she wasn't a direct relative of his – they had never married – and we were not going under the umbrella of any charity or non-governmental organisation. Above all, in the four years he had been in prison she had never once gone there, and she wanted to check it out prior to our visit.

That first time she did not speak beyond introducing us to him. It was the same as when she had introduced me to Wole: no information, no explanation. That was her way with the things she felt most deeply.

The memory of that first meeting often haunts me. Pressure breathes from the walls.

When my eyes met our father's, my heart split and something bright jammed in. He smiled a festival of suns. He had magic in his brown eyes – like Wole – and even though to my twelve-year-old self he looked wild and was unshaven, he was beautiful.

He was a darker, taller version of Brother Gbenro. He had long, thick, leonine locks, dark with light-brown tips. When he spoke his voice was deep and had a Yoruba spice to it that was slightly more intense than mine. When he held our hands his touch felt like harmattan-hushing rain, taming, peaceful, sweet. We had so much to ask, and it was difficult to begin. The time allotted to us was short. It seemed to shrink with every subsequent visit, and it became provoking to leave in what always felt like the middle of a conversation. And, like our mother, our father was evasive about details. But so it was that, in a strange and unexpected way, Kikiri – or rather the jewel that we sought within her grim walls – become our Wonderland, our treat.

Wole and I enjoyed this new fountain of fondness. We keenly looked forward to our father's release, though the actual date somehow remained forever in the middle distance.

Mum was not as excited by that prospect as we were, and we didn't understand why. She didn't discuss him much after she had made the initial introduction. She took us in to visit him faithfully, but it was soon clear to us that she could not stand his presence.

'I'm here because the boys insisted,' she said to him once, early on, before we had even sat down.

'That's a good reason,' he replied.

'I'm also here to tell you you are the most irresponsible scum of an excuse for a man,' she went on. Wole and I gasped, and our eyes swivelled from her face to his.

'Mind your language in the presence of my kids,' he said without anger.

'Your kids? You might have fatherered them but they will never be yours!'

'Please don't say that to me.'

'You will pay for every single evil you did to me,' she said breathlessly. 'For every single time you crushed my life.'

'Damn it!' he snapped, banging his clenched fists on the table. It was the first time Wole and I had seen anger in him. 'Isn't it enough for you I'm in here?' He looked around with hard eyes. 'I want this woman out!' he said loudly. 'I want her out now!'

'You are a beast, Tolu! A beast! I curse the day I met you!' she screamed as a warder took her arm and pulled her out of the visitors' room. We stood there awkwardly, not sure if we should go too. Our father gestured that we sit. Reluctantly, and exchanging looks, we did so, and he asked about our doings as though the argument had never happened. He transformed instantly from beast to berry. I had goose bumps.

Subsequently, Mum waited in the car when we visited. But she always asked us to extend her greetings to our father.

'Mum is mad that Dad is in prison,' Wole would say as the prison warden took us through, pressing for no deeper explanation.

Dad, on the other hand, was breezy about the issue whenever we brought it up, as if it was no more than a marital tiff, easily put right. 'You know your mother,' he would say, once again foreclosing questions about the past with a shrug and a wry smile.

For a man in his predicament he was a very cheerful person, never complaining about the smell, the food, the overcrowding, the lack of sanitation. Calm, and at times witty in disposition, he was both worldly and widely-read. He was very spirited about us – we were not only his sons, we connected him to the world outside, to the future. I saw this in his clear brown eyes as he looked deeply into ours before and after the prayers we shared each time we were leaving. Every fortnight he wrote each of us beautiful letters, instructing that we read them separately and keep them secret from each other. I never peeked at Wole's; I don't think he ever peeked at mine. But they had the same effect on both on us, leaving us thinking, laughing, praying, feeling, and loving him all the more for treating us as separate individuals, not 'the twins'.

We went on like this, visiting in the school holidays, and sometimes at weekends in term-time, up until after we completed our West African Senior Secondary Certificate exams.

Then he was released.

The first we knew of this was when a parcel arrived at the school for us. It had no sender's name or address written on it and a Lagos postmark. Intrigued, we opened it. It contained two Motorola GSM phones, SIM packs, and a card on which his phone-number was written. We were seventeen.

A welcome-home party was thrown for him at Ilaro, in his family home. Wole, Mum and I travelled there to grace the occasion, collecting Baba and Maami on the way. This was my first time in Ilaro since Mum took me away five years earlier. I was excited because Brother Gbenro had returned to Nigeria for a holiday, and so would be there too. I knew the house, but had never been inside it.

The party was already in full swing by the time we arrived. It was a typical Yoruba indoor owambe that had overflowed outside, and the house and yard were packed with guests: uncles, aunts, cousins, distant relatives. The women were all rad, clad in their native ashoke, buba and iro, with large damask headgears of varied colours and sizes on their heads. The men were sumptuously adorned in their agbada gowns, and festooned with coral beads. The boys were all clad in white agbada and red ashoke abiti-aja hats, and the dun-dun drumming streamed out loudly from the Damian family compound as singers and dancers mounted the stage set up in front of the house, entertaining everyone.

Despite all this festivity, there was an air of awkwardness on our arrival. Before we – Baba, Maami, Mum, Wole and I – got past the gate, one of the guests saw us and dashed inside the house. Dad emerged almost immediately and fell – head and agbada – to the ground to greet us. Brother Gbenro came out behind him and followed suit. They got to their feet and Dad hugged Baba fully and tightly while Maami rubbed Brother Gbenro's back – a pseudo hug perhaps. Somehow it seemed odd. Mum and Dad looked at each other. Mum stretched out her hand to shake Dad's hand, but Dad went in for a hug. Time stopped. Mum did not hug back. I fought an urge to blurt, 'What did he do? What was so terrible? If it was so terrible, why are we having a party?' Other guests watched. Darkness flashed in Brother Gbenro's eyes as Mum's eyes met his during the awkward embrace. Brother Gbenro hugged Wole and me together, and whispered, 'Welcome,' without looking at us. He felt cold, different.

We were taken around for introductions in the company of the adults. Wole and I had to keep prostrating each time Maami or Baba introduced us to a relative. The younger ones, those in Mum and Dad's age-bracket, were fine with our just bowing, and would pat us lightly on our backs. An awkward moment came when a large man with his back to us turned and Baba jerked and said, 'Jesu!' and looked shocked. His expression impassive, the man bowed and touched his toes but Baba shook his head slowly in displeasure, refusing to acknowledge him. Maami, however, rubbed his shoulder and broke the moment. When the man straightened up I saw he was a dark giant with a full red lower lip and a full beard. After he and Baba had exchanged a few chilly pleasantries Baba leaned over, whispered something into Dad's ear, then turned away, asking him to carry on the introductions as he did so.

'Boys, this is Uncle Ola,' Dad said. 'My best friend.' With his arm around Uncle Ola's big shoulders he flashed a glance at the back of Baba's head. 'He is responsible for organising this wonderful party.'

We bent to touch our toes, but the giant reached out for a handshake. We took a hand each, clasping them tightly between our two palms. 'Ola, these are my boys.'

'I need not be told.'

'Of course you know Titi,' Dad said.

'Good afternoon, sir,' Mum said, smiling that plastic smile of hers.

'It's Ola, please,' Uncle Ola said. 'And you look fabulous.'

'Thank you.'

'I haven't seen Gbenro, though,' Uncle Ola said, looking past her into the crowded room.

Brother Gbenro had vanished amongst the guests the moment we entered the living room. He kept his distance from both Dad and Uncle Ola for the duration of the party.

The formal introductions over, we were free to mix with the younger people. The girls were so beautiful. I imagined how good it would feel to flaunt a photograph on hi5 of me with my arms around one of them. Though they also wore the buba and iro, their wrappers were knee-length, exposing their smooth, straight legs, and I couldn't help flirting with them whenever they served us refreshment. They preferred to speak Yoruba, and I loved them for it. It reminded me that I had never really considered dating, and also that I missed my school at Ilaro, and Seun, who had been my best friend, and who I had not seen since leaving. Wole, whose Yoruba was still a work in progress, owing to his limited exposure to the language, kept quiet and to himself most of the time; and Uncle Ola smiled a festival of suns.

At first glance it seemed very much a village affair, with most guests, male and female, dressing customarily. However, after a while I began to notice there were some men present who did not blend in. They seemed, in fact, to hate the idea of doing so, wearing form-fitting brocade jumpers instead of the agbada that every other male was wearing. I first noticed one of them when he fluttered his fingers at me. I blushed and looked away: they talked and acted so feminine it sent icy shudders racing down my back. They clapped their hands at the slightest statement. When their hands were not clapping or mounted on their waists, they were thrust out like the legs of a cattle egret. Unfortunately Dad insisted on introducing us to all of them. When one of them touched my head during our introduction it felt like a hundred soldier ants were pillaging my locks. I slapped his hand off a thousand times in my head.

Then Dad, filled with joy and alcohol, dragged Wole and me off to the dancefloor outside, and it seemed everyone else joined in. He out-danced them all – including the ones who danced for the village. While dancing I thought how beautiful it would be to see Mum dance with her man. I searched for her with my eyes, not finding her, and while doing so I saw Brother Gbenro, who I only then realised had been absent from the centre of things. He was observing from the elevated balcony. When he noticed me looking at him, he forced a smile and gave me a thumbs-up. I quizzed him with my eyes and hands: 'Are you okay?' He nodded and smoothed his chest with his right palm. Only then did he smile genuinely. Wole caught my hand and yanked me back into the throng.

A few minutes later, after I had danced myself into a sweaty mop, I returned to the living room to cool off and catch my breath. I sank into a seat beside Uncle Ola. Dad joined us, oozing alcohol, drenched in sweat, laughing, alive, his locks all over the place.

'You sure do know how to get your groove on,' Uncle Ola said.

'To commot for sanko na beans?' Dad said, wiping the sweat from his face, panting, sprawling in the chair.

'Flex my guy,' Uncle Ola ordered him, and stroked dad's thigh close to the hip. Dad put his palm over Uncle Ola's hand and squeezed it, and rested his head on Uncle Ola's shoulder and closed his eyes. An elderly female guest who passed by us at that moment hissed so loud that Dad opened his eyes. He looked at her and she glared at him, and he took his head off Uncle Ola's shoulder and settled back into the chair instead. But he kept his hand where it was.

'Wole, are you having a good time?' he asked, turning to look at me.

'Yes, Dad,' I said.

'Okay,' he said.

'Daddy?'

'Yes, darling?'

'I'm Wale.'

'Oh my. Are you sure?'

'Yep.'

'You both are too physically similar. How does your mum cope?'

'When she gets it wrong we don't tell her, so she thinks she always knows... Speaking of Mum, she didn't come out to dance, and I haven't set eyes on her.'

'She will be fine,' Uncle Ola said.

'She is okay,' Dad said, shaking Uncle Ola's hand off his and frowning at him. Then he smiled at me and said, 'She must be close by.'

'Wale, dear,' Uncle Ola said.

'Yes, Uncle.'

'Please go ask one of the girls to bring us some food.'

I got up and went over to one of the girls serving and delivered the message. She asked me what exactly they wanted to eat. So I went back to get their proper orders but they were no longer in their chairs. I looked around but did not see them. But I did run into the men with the cattle egret hands. They were quieter now. They were eating, and somehow seemed to be staring a lot. The one with the soldier ant palm called out to me:

'Omo Tolu!'

I pretended not to hear him above the music.

'Omo Tolu!' he screeched again.

Someone tapped me from behind. 'Boy! He is calling you!' – another one of them. This one left his hand too long on my shoulder. He ushered me over to their nest, all the while with his hand on my shoulder. I hated it. I hated him.

'Hello, Omo Tolu. How are you?' the one who had called me said, making space and motioning me to sit beside him.

'Please sir, my name is Olawale and I'm on an errand for my dad.'

'It's nice to meet you, Olawale.' His voice sounded like a strained accordion.

'We have met before, sir.'

'Yes, but you can't recall my name, so it's necessary we meet again.'

As if this second encounter with this man was not disturbing enough, the other men in jumpers were looking at me, into me, smiling.

'My name is Biodun,' he said, 'and I don't like being called sir. Sit.'

'Okay.' Reluctantly I did so.

'I used to work for Baba, and was very, very close to Tolu, your dad,' he said.

The man beside me nudged him sharply and said, 'Haba Biodun!'

'What?' he said to him. 'Am I lying?' Then he turned back to me. 'Even closer than Ola,' he added, with emphasis.

'It's nice to meet you, sir.'

'The pleasure is mine, darling,' he said, smiling and crossing his legs. 'You are a lot like your dad.' – now squinting as he looked me over.

'Thank you.'

'I only hope you don't end up like him.' He said this with a straight face.

'Kai Biodun! E don do for you abeg!'; 'It's okay now, Biodun.'; 'Omo you too talk!' the men beside him said, speaking over each other.

I wanted to leave. In my head I had stamped on his feet and plucked out his eyes a hundred times already. But this close I saw that he was more manly than I had earlier thought. His body was skinny but his arms were toned, and thick with soft-looking hair, some of which spread across his chest. His hair was cut low, and he had a neatly trimmed and sharply-outlined moustache. His lips were dark with a dab of pink in the middle and his eyes were feline. And he looked at me like he knew that I understood the crap he was saying. Like he had stripped me naked a thousand times before our first introduction. Like he knew me in a way I was ashamed of being known. I didn't know how he managed all that, or how I knew that we were more similar to each other than was convenient, though I did know that I hated this similarity to the core of my being. Yet I stayed, because a more decisive part of me wanted to be seen by Biodun, the part that was curious, that wanted to be led, to be surprised.

'Abeg abeg! Wo! Let me talk o,' he said, snapping his fingers and waving his palms in the air. When the chatter died down, he faced me again. 'I'd love us to be good friends.'

'Okay.'

'We have a lot to talk about, when my friends will not interrupt.'

'Okay sir.'

'Biodun, please.'

'Okay, Biodun.' I said, getting to my feet.

On turning around and walking away I felt stabbed by the eyes of everyone in the room, especially those of Baba and Maami, who were staring at me, at us, at whatever had just happened. For some reason, though I was guiltless, guilt trapped my feet. Baba motioned me to come to him. With difficulty I did so. He asked me whether I was being disturbed. I said no. He then instructed me to keep away from Biodun because he was a bad influence, and that if he ever approached me again, I should report it to him personally. Baba then motioned to Biodun to approach him. When Biodun came Baba ordered him never to approach any member of his family henceforth, 'Even after I am dead.' Biodun apologised, excused himself, went out through the door and did not return. His friends drifted away, talking quietly among themselves and casting glances at Baba. I went back to where I had been sitting, dried out, and wishing I could go home. But no: we would be here till the bitter end.

Shortly after, a masquerade dance drew all the guests outside.

I was about to follow them when, pushing his way through the crowd, Wole rushed in with another young man breathlessly in tow. For a moment I didn't recognise him. Then I did: Seun. How had Wole known? I didn't care. It seemed all of a piece with everything that was happening that evening. I hurried into his arms. I held him tight. He squeezed back. The rush. I felt his hips pressed against mine, a growing hardness between us, his and mine. We lingered like this. My eyes were closed. The whole world could watch for all I cared.

'Walemi... This is you,' he whispered.

'This is me,' I agreed, not understanding him.

Wole, perhaps bored with looking at the ceiling and waiting for us to be done hugging, coughed.

'Oh, my manners,' I said, breaking off the hug as Wole's cough became convulsive, and pulling Seun to my side, my fingers in his. 'Wole, this is Seun, my best friend.'

'He almost strangled me with that same hug outside,' Wole said.

'I'm sorry, it was because I thought – ' Seun tried to explain.

'It's okay,' Wole smirked, 'we get that a lot.'

'I didn't know Wale is a twin,' Seun continued.

'Well, he is,' Wole said, his hand around my neck. 'And this carbon copy loves him so.' He pecked me on the cheek.

'I love you too, darling,' I said, smiling, shocked for a

moment, but looking in Wole's eyes still.

'Me jealous now,' Seun said.

'Oh don't be, dear. This is a battle you won't win,' Wole said. 'Meanwhile, your attire is fabulous! What is that, damask?' – feeling the hem of Seun's flowing, royal blue kaftan.

'Yeah. I'm sorry I didn't know the colour code,' Seun said.

'Mmm, see how Wale is glowing like egusi soup,' Wole teased, winking at me.

'Egusi ke?' I said.

'Abeg, I'm hitting the dancefloor again,' Wole said, 'Man, those guys are killing me! See ya!'

Seun and I found a corner and sat. We talked and the years seemed to thin away between us. His hair was, as it had been even when he was eleven, snow-studded, but there were now soft strokes of sideburns on his cheeks and a moustache above his upper lip. He still had the delicate look he had the first time we met five years ago as junior pupils of the Ilaro Grammar School. But now he exuded a more adult, more alluring air. The kind that made me want to resume holding him; that made the walls around us fly apart, and my world rave and storm within, even while appearing intact and still outside. Thoughts that would ordinarily shock me and make me fight myself spiralled and splayed out inside me. And in that moment I wanted them to. Fighting was not an option.

Suddenly and annoyingly one of Biodun's friends, who should have quietly passed us, stopped for a second in the doorway. He took a look at us, hissed, 'Shelleh!' and cat-walked away. I instantly made to go to Baba, but Seun caught my hand.

'Where are you going?'

'To tell Baba.'

'Tell Baba what?'

'That the man is bothering me, of course.'

'Why will you do that? Are you a kid?'

'What do you mean?'

'It's no big deal, is it?'

I shook my hands away from Seun's. 'You were not here earlier when they called me over and were quizzing me.'

'They?' he asked. 'Which they?'

I pointed to where the rest of them were now seated.

'Who?' Some guests stood in the way: at first he could not see them. 'Christ!' he exclaimed when they moved off. 'Who invited them?'

'They're friends with my dad.'

'Hmm. Well. Okay,' he said, reclining in his chair.

'Okay what?'

'It's nothing,' he said, taking my hand again. 'Besides he was referring to me.'

'Oh, okay. Your name is Shelleh then?' I asked.

'Nope. It's a slang.'

'A slang?'

'Yeah. You know, like "babe",' he said, laughing.

'You are the babe?' I asked, tickled as well.

'Okay, let me lay it out for you. When someone, probably a guy, calls you names like shelleh or ti bii it means he thinks you are camp.'

'Camp?'

'Yeah, you know, girly, colourful, stuff like that.'

'I'm not.'

'I know, but it also could mean either he finds you sexually attractive or believes that you might find guys sexually attractive.'

'Ti bii is a Yoruba word and does not have anything to do with sexual attraction,' I said. 'So please tell me another lie.'

'Now you tell me,' he said, 'what does ti bii literally mean?'

'It means, "of that kind".'

'Yeah, yeah... you see,' he said, sitting up. 'It means "of that kind"; "like that". The guys who like guys like that. Like those guys with Biodun, and Biodun too.'

'Like that,' I echoed.

Darkness drew on. All the older guests seemed to have sneaked away, and the party got wilder. The aroma of freshly-cooked ewedu soup, jollof rice, moi-moi, the stench of alcohol and the sound of the drums of the seventh set of entertainers filled the air. By this time Baba and Maami had left, and Seun too – after slipping me a piece of paper that had his phone number written on it. All at once I noticed Wole leaning in the door of the living room, sweating profusely and coughing. His coughing grew worse. This was not the mock version – this was the real deal. He crouched down, then sat heavily on the floor. His chest began to heave alarmingly and he gaped and gasped like a fish on the riverbank: he was having an asthmatic crisis. He fumbled in his pockets for his inhaler but couldn't seem to find it, and he looked at me with wide eyes and gestured helplessly.

I panicked. I dashed further into the house, pushing through the girls, who were still serving food and drinks, hurrying from room to room, looking for Mum. She knew how to handle this. She would have a spare inhaler. The hall was poorly lit. I yanked a door open to reveal a study with a desk and over-full bookcase. Then an unoccupied bedroom. Opening the next door along, which was a second bedroom, I was smacked in the face with the staleness and density of the air. Dad, naked except for a towel round his waist, lay face-down on a single bed. His locks, now tied back neatly in a single braid, rested along the groove of his spine amongst a thousand sweat-beads. Next to him was a copy of Ola Rotimi's *The Gods Are Not to Blame*. Its cover was smeared with traces and sweeps of white powder, and on it lay a playing card with a frosted edge. The floor was littered with paper serviettes and several used condoms.

'Dad?' I said. He was snoring heavily and didn't respond.

Pulling the door closed I went and tried others, now knocking briefly before opening them. The loudness of the drumming must have drowned out my knocking, however, because my mother and Brother Gbenro didn't look round to see me in the doorway. They were sitting side-by-side on the bed, kissing passionately. At least they were fully dressed. I stepped back into the hallway, knocking a picture-frame off the wall behind me. It fell with a clatter to the floor. At the sound my mother broke off the kiss and looked round. Her eyes met mine, and widened. I reached in, snatched her bag from the side-table, and dashed off.

By the time I got back to Wole the music had stopped: people stood or sat quietly, looking on. I feared that the worst had happened. Wole was surrounded by the ti bii men, lying on his back stretched out on the long sofa, his head on Biodun's thighs. His eyes were closed, and tears had rolled to his ears. He had fought hard this time but he was breathing, alive. My eyes met Biodun's and he smiled and mouthed, 'He's okay,' and showed me the inhaler he had used on Wole, which was, it turned out, his own.

Similar... one of us...

The party was over. My family was a wreck. And unfortunately we were part of it.

Later, when the women were clearing things away and Wole and I were sitting quietly by ourselves, I told him about Mum and Brother Gbenro. He nodded. I didn't tell him about Dad. It dawned on Wole and me then that our never having felt allowed to ask about the relationship between Mum and Dad, or why Dad went to prison, was a sort of conspiracy between them, and others. No-one had mentioned it at the party either; not the ti bii men, not even the sharp-eyed and sharp-tongued older people. And Brother Gbenro and Mum? Suddenly we were part of much more than that which was obvious to the eye.

We would remain at Ilaro far longer than we had planned.

Neither Mum, Dad nor Brother Gbenro would face us the following morning. Leaving Dad and Gbenro behind, Mum drove me and Wole back to Baba and Maami's house, where we had arranged to stay, in silence. Baba and Maami were silent about the dramas of the night before too, acting as though all was well, which confirmed to us that they were in on the conspiracy too, and would give us no answers.

Faced with this wholesale denial and stonewalling by our elders, Wole and I turned to practical matters, shifting our attention to Eden Kekere and administrative work with Baba. We went out to the farm early every morning and returned late at night.

Two months had passed in this way when Mum informed us abruptly, over breakfast, that we would be leaving for Port Harcourt the following morning, and that there would be a family meeting that evening.

Wole and I spent most of the day at Eden Kekere, as usual. All the work for the day was done, but we didn't want to go back for what threatened to be an awkward encounter: we just sat there in the dark office, our faces illumined by the dull beams from the two table-lamps. After a long while we heard the sound of a car pulling up outside and Baba came in.

'Let's take a walk around,' he said.

Nodding, we got up and followed him. The moon was bright overhead. A few minutes later we were all seated on a wooden bench in a cleared spot in the middle of the farm. Eden Kekere had expanded in size and orderliness over the years. It was fenced all round now, and there were flood-lights at strategic positions. There were also night-watchmen on patrol.

'You have both grown into wonderful young men,' Baba began. My brother and I bowed our heads. 'I am proud of who you have become. Great men, with so much potential. Titi says you both made a mark in school with your academic performance. I am happy about that.'

We waited, but he said nothing else, just nodded thoughtfully to himself.

'Baba, I just don't understand this,' I burst out, my fury at how lightly he and the others had been taking the situation with our parents rising up in a rush, and feeling this was our last chance to learn the truth. 'Who is Brother Gbenro to Mum? Is Dad our real father? Why should Mum – ?'

'Olawale, calm down. You are a man.' Baba turned towards Wole, who was now blinking back tears. 'Oluwole, you too. Come closer so that I can feel you both... In fact, let mother earth feel us all,' he said, standing up. Awkwardly he squatted down, then lay on his back on the sand, and we looked down on his silvered face as he looked up at the moon. After a little hesitation we joined him, me on his left and Wole on his right, all of us gazing up into the night sky. Then he started again, this time speaking in Yoruba:

'A long time ago there was a certain young man who came into our lives. He was orphaned, but so handsome and brilliant. Everyone in Ilaro respects him for his speed in learning, his oratory, and the passion with which he works.

He once worked here on this farm. He was so attached to me and I loved him as a son.

'Time soon came when everyone expected that he would be getting married. But he did nothing to encourage the countless women who flocked around him. We hoped that he would bring a woman home before his younger brother, who was himself soon to be married.

'One day he opened up to me as regards how God had made him "special"; told me that though he respected women, and handsome and well-spoken as he was, he preferred to be with another man, who also worked here. They were secretly courting – doing things that only men and women should be doing together – though I did not understand this then, thinking he meant only friendship. But I knew that each time his family would bring up the issue of marriage he would come here to the farm to work himself to exhaustion, and would sometimes cry, and would be bitter all day.

'I tried to encourage him, and prayed with him whenever he was in this state. However, nothing would pacify him other than his friend's cooking. At first we all saw it as a healthy brotherhood of the sort that could develop between any two people, regardless of whether they were of the same gender or not.

'But things got out of hand when his brother and I barged in on them kissing in the warehouse one evening, half-naked and in each other's arms. I was overwhelmed with confusion. "This must have been what he was trying to explain to me," I thought.

'In a fit of rage his brother charged at both of them, hitting and terribly bruising them. They were men, and strong, but they were ashamed and did not defend them-selves, and I eventually broke up the fight.

'I told no-one about what had happened, and assumed his brother would also keep silent. However one day he and his family paid a visit to his brother's fiancée's family, for a formal introduction prior to betrothal, as custom demands. He was most uncomfortable because everything was telling him that he was long overdue for marriage. Some members of his own family then began to make reference to his being disturbed and unreasonable around men – they all knew now, he realised: his brother must have told them. His family did not pass up any opportunity to tongue-lash him and belittle him before his brother's bride and her family.

'The following day this humiliated young man, having deliberately intoxicated himself the night before, forced himself on his brother's fiancée, got her pregnant, left Ilaro and was never heard of for a long time. The next we heard he had been arrested in the company of some international drug traffickers while trying to leave the country, and was jailed.'

'Baba, what happened to the pregnant fiancée?' I asked, a sinking feeling in the pit of my stomach.

'Did she still get married to the man to whom she was betrothed?' Wole asked.

'Well, the pregnant fiancée is Titi, and she gave birth to two wonderful men and – '

Before Baba could finish, Wole jumped to his feet and darted away into the night. Baba and I called out after him, but to no avail. A short time later we heard the sound of a car starting up and driving off.

When Baba and I got home some hours later, we learned that there had been a face-off between Wole and Dad. The family meeting was not held that night. Wole wouldn't tell me what had been said.

The following morning we learned that Dad had left Ilaro with Uncle Ola. We learned that they had been so close they bore similar scars from their work on Baba's farm when they were young.

Dad left us our last letters. Wole ripped his up without reading it, but mine read:

My sweet one,

All through my prison experience I had hoped that I could return to my life at Ilaro as it was. Those were dark times for me, but I returned to a brighter world through getting to know you and your brother.

When we danced at the party, it was the most enchanting time of my life yet. I didn't feel just free-

dom. I felt alive. Everything seemed possible.

However, it seems that Ilaro can never again be home to me. So today I start my life afresh, as a man conscious and free to live for all the right reasons.

I am leaving because I don't have a future here. I am leaving because grudging sympathy and silence can never replace forgiveness and acceptance. I am leaving because you and Wole deserve a better father than I am and can ever be. I leave because I want Titi to fall in love with Gbenro afresh without my shadow cast over her. I also want her to forgive me. I want you all to forgive me. Perhaps that can be done more easily from a distance.

I hope you will understand some day when you are grown that some of our questions are really so big and difficult. I have my big questions too: What is my life about? Why am I homosexual in Nigeria? Why am I homosexual at all? Why did I do what I did to Titi? Why am I still alive? What future is there for me now? Wale I could go on, but life is too short to rehearse and what has been lived can't be unlived.

Ola is my partner, friend, brother, lover, inspiration. He was light to me all through those years in prison despite how badly I treated him. He gives me hope in a different today, with opportunities to make things right, to live afresh. This is something Ilaro and Africa will never understand or give. Perhaps you will understand, someday. This is not for me but because Wole is equally homosexual, and you have to be there for him.

You are both spirited like me, but Wole has the most restless heart. His soul is pure, kind, trusting and driven. You must defend him Wale.

Teach him and teach yourself that love is a journey not because it takes you to places, but because it's always evolving, giving, demanding, inspiring and accepting new things. Love is a language, secret and safe. Love is secretly fast-growing – but it never happens overnight.

You must learn to forgive yourselves and to-gether move on to the next happiness.

Once more I ask for your forgiveness – in spite of how undeserving I am – and that you both accept Titi and Gbenro as your parents. I will always be on my knees praying for you, believing that God de-fines us all in the perfect and beautiful times of our lives. Even times such as this. I hope that some day I will find the strength and sanity to face you both again.

I love you very, very much. And I need you to take your walk with God seriously. I also need you to pray for me. Pray for all of us Wale. Pray.

Please never forget this.

Your father,
T. Damian

I had lost my dad to something I did not then understand. But I understood that I had lost him. I wished that he had written about Biodun; that he knew we were already aware of our big questions. That Wole's homosexuality – subtle to others but very clear to me – was the least of our problems. That I might have an an equally large one of my own to contend with. I wished he knew that I needed him to be here. That I was confused by my body, heart and most candid desires – and that no language was clear enough to explain my dilemma, my battle, my whirl.

Our leaving was postponed not because of Dad's depar-ture, but because Wole insisted on taking off his locks, and if Wole's locks had to go, I wanted mine off as well. Baba sent for the barbers to meet us at Eden Kekere.

Back-to-back we sat on Baba's office balcony and the scissors snipped and snipped, and the locks fell, followed by the clippers on our scalps. Maami and Mum sang and chanted Yoruba worship songs and clapped. My eyes were closed through it all.

'We don finish,' the barbers announced, and my heart sank. I had kept my eyes shut to avoid the hair getting in them. I could hear Mum gasp but I did not hear Baba or

Maami. Wole, whose eyes were apparently also shut, demanded that the first person he wanted to see was me. So the barber brushed me down, helped me to my feet and turned me around. When I opened my eyes I saw a shaven-headed Wole looking as I knew I must now look. My feet grew unsteady, my sight blurred, and I felt myself fall to the ground as if lifeless. Afterwards I was told that Wole and I had both passed out at the same instant. All these years later I still cannot explain this.

On the eve of my departure for my new job at Kola University I lay beside my brother, not knowing what to think. It was dark, and after fighting back his tears and pretending to be at peace with my leaving, he was asleep. I drew closer to him, kissed his cheek, then turned onto my side and went to sleep too.

Ten hours later I was airbound for Amara State. It was a forty-five minute flight from Port Harcourt, followed by an hour's taxi-ride, to get to my alma mater, Kola U. Tega and I were on BlackBerry Messenger exchanging instant messages all through this part of the journey, so it was as though she was there with me. I was grateful, as even the simple act of naming my anxieties to her helped me to control them.

When I arrived at the campus gates the vice-chancellor's orderly was waiting to receive me. He told me that the vice-chancellor, Professor Brown, had had to travel the day before, and that he, Mike, had been instructed to drive me to my lodge and make sure that I was comfortable until the professor returned tomorrow. We transferred my luggage to the vice-chancellor's official car, a white Chevrolet jeep, and got in.

As we drove through the campus goosebumps rose on my skin. Wole and I had raised so much dust when we were students here, dust that in no little way went on to define our future lives.

I had, I realised, expected big changes – after all, my life was wholly different now; why would things here not have changed too? – but Kola University remained Kola University, a sweep of lush green lawns and freshly-painted, sky-blue buildings. From the gate house to the faculty buildings, the hostels, event halls, the Catholic and Pentecostal chapels and the mosque, everything was blue and silent.

We drove past the Faculty of Law. It being the Christmas holidays, it was deserted. I imagined it alive with students clad in white shirts and black skirts and trousers, emerging from the lecture halls and hurrying up and down the spiral staircases that flanked them.

Then I saw her, Themis, the ten-foot statue of the law goddess at whose feet I had had my picture taken one time too many as a student. Just before she passed from view I imagined she blew me a kiss. She used to flirt with me a lot when I studied here – or rather, I used to flirt with her. I had always been in love with her symbolism: her scales for evaluation, her blindfold for impartiality; her sword for sanction. And I was all the more thrilled that she was a woman, for reasons that were complex and hard to express.

Next we drove past the Pentecostal Fellowship and the campus mosque, which sat side by side and shared a common fence. My Muslim interests at the time, and Wole's intense Christianity, had made those neighbouring premises the site of profound spiritual experiences for both of us, and many passionate debates. For stretches of time I alternated between attending the fellowship and the mosque; at other times I avoided both of them altogether. Wole would attempt to drag me to the fellowship and I would pull myself away at the entrance on seeing my friends going into the mosque, embarrassed, even though I had promised to go to church with him and did not call myself a Muslim. I would partici-pate in the Muslim fast and eat really early before the hours started counting, and then avoid the Christian fast because I didn't want to go thirsty like Wole. I would come up for altar-call to give my life to Christ every Sunday I attended the fellowship, and then I would argue the Bible with the church worker who was appointed to help me grow spiritually, just because I wanted to make a point. And if that worker was Wole I would never stop arguing that, although God was real, both religions were pointless given the drama that came with them. I attended the social events of both sides shamelessly, parties and eat-outs, but was fully committed to neither. Wole always urged me to be serious in church, and he would condemn Islam as the religion of angry people.

It's funny how time takes its toll on people's viewpoints. Wole went on to become quite liberal and inclusive, and I became less and less interested in Islam.

The academic facilities behind us, we drove onto the staff residential estate. I was not too optimistic about my accommodation: as an undergraduate our lecturers had often complained of the mosquitoes that terrorised them at night. My spirits lifted considerably, however, when Mike told me that nowadays the entire estate had an effective standby generator; that every room had an air-conditioner in it; and, best of all, that there was a strong and reliable Wi-Fi signal within the residential estate available to all staff.

We pulled up outside my building and Mike helped me take my luggage to my room. I found I had a bed, a reading-table and chair, a large wall-mirror, and a bathroom to myself. From my bathroom window I also had a great view of the surrounding countryside. After giving me some practical information about schedules and campus facilities Mike left and I had the room to myself.

My main reason for returning to Kola University just now was to explore what being an individual would feel like. I had spent most of my life – and all my adult life – with Wole. We went to the same secondary school, university and law school; we had worked in the same law firm; and we now ran Afrospark together. My fiancée also worked at Afrospark. I needed to learn how it felt to be alone as a man. So when the invitation came, a few months after my return from Maputo, to lecture on International Human Rights at Kola University, I jumped at it.

K.U. was government-owned until four years ago, when it was bought by a group of Harvard-trained Nigerian professors. I did not know any of them, though Google had confirmed their *bona fides*, but I was impressed with the showpiece they were turning my alma mater into. And I was hopeful that this high-profile and surely highly ambitious team would offer the students a more dynamic education than I had received in my years as a student there, fondly though I remembered it.

I unpacked, took a shower and washed my locks. Afterwards I stood before the mirror nude and dripped to dry under the air-conditioner, watching my scrotum shrivel in the chill draft as I pushed the blow-drier through my steaming locks, trying not to burn my scalp. I stared at my reflection for a while then moved closer, fogged the mirror with my breath, and drew myself a winking smiley. I winked back. *So I'm here*, I thought.

The sunset sky lit the room pink. It was only a few hours before New Year. I slipped into bed to draw up my usual mental itinerary of unrealistic New Year resolutions – a ritual that Wole and I began the year we were called to the Nigerian Bar and started growing our locks again. *Swear off chocolates; change the world; try rocking my locks blue...* my list went on. When I got to the tenth item, *Get married!* I stopped.

Tega.

My baby.

We still had not had sex: she was one of those girls who celebrated the intactness of her hymen. But she could cuddle and kiss like kai! I hated how high and dry she always left me, but I enjoyed every moment that led to the point where she pushed me away. And truly, I wasn't in a hurry: I was going to marry her, so in time I was going to know everything and feel everything. I had at that point never had sex with a woman, and was curious how it would feel; how far it would be a different category of experience from sex with, say, Kwame. Or Seun. Would it turn out to be so natural that it would forever eclipse my desire for other men? Or would it, as I suspected was more likely to be the case, be one of two circles that, like ripples in an akamu dish, overlapped in me on equal terms?

By eleven p.m. I was done with my list, and had not decided on how to count down to 2014 all by myself. It was my first New Year's Eve away from home, and all efforts to focus on the blessing of the peaceful moment were proving abortive. I missed Wole terribly. I did not even have a bottle of beer to open. Why had I imagined being alone would be so productive?

Wole called at 11:45 p.m. We talked for a while, then video-called on our phones. He was with Lola and Tega, and they were counting down to 2014 in church. The connection was not at its best – blurry, with voices and faces out of sync – but it was good enough for me to see that the church was packed and that they were all ecstatic. I joined in their prayers and determined to see in the new year with them. It was odd having to shout to be heard in the empty silence of my room, but I persevered, while wondering if any neighbours I might have would think I was insane, or deaf.

At 11:55 p.m. our conversation was cut short by a sudden downpour in Amara. Thunder and lightning followed, and abruptly the power went off. I waited for the 'efficient estate generator' to kick in. It didn't.

'Yup. Back to K.U.,' I sighed, sitting alone in the dark. 'So much for 2013.'

At midnight I was in my bathroom, standing at the window looking out on Amara as the rain and lightning electrified her in flashes and rumbles.

It grew unpleasantly chilly and humid so I retired to bed. Sleep was, however, far from me, and I lay awake staring into the pitch dark: I had not travelled with flashlights because I had not foreseen power failure – or, rather, I foresaw it and failed to pack one anyway. It was the Harmattan, and I had hoped that it would not rain.

After a while I activated my Facebook app, to see whether I had received any goodwill messages for the New Year, and thinking I should send a few myself. Amongst others, I saw a rather lengthy instant message from Ahmed.

Of the several things that bothered me about my public life as an academic and activist – discounting the receiving of death-threats – internet relationships topped the list. I could not, however, resist the extra-curricular excitement they afforded me. Some of them fizzled out after a few exchanges; others went on for days, weeks, months; some of them even stretched into years. Arranging a physical meeting was more often than not the theoretical rationale for beginning these conversations, though in actuality we almost never got to that point. My bad. Usually.

Thrilled by the length of his first letter and the somewhat strange feeling it had given me, I went ahead and read Ahmed's message. It gave me a lot to think about; so much in fact that I did not reply immediately.

The storm passed away into the distance. My thoughts rocked me to sleep.

Tega's call woke me at eleven the next morning. She sounded bright. 'Good morning, love!'

'Mm. Your voice is like fresh honey on my skin,' I replied sleepily.

'W. Damian Esquire, there you go again with the words. How are you this morning?'

'Well, I am on my back, in my room, beneath the sheets, and I'm hungry.'

'Still in bed! What are you having for breakfast?'

'Breakfast ke? I should be thinking of lunch now. Before I drag myself out of bed, take a shower and get some clothes on, it should be at least one.'

'You are now a bachelor o!' she teased.

'I have hardly ever been anything else.'

'Yeah, but unlike Wole you are no witch in the kitchen,' she taunted cheerily.

'I miss his cooking. I could have tricked him into a nice warm omelette and pasta. Mmm, I can taste it already.'

'Wake up jor!' she said with a chuckle. Then: 'He really misses you.'

'I miss him too,' I said.

'He was moody until the prayers started yesterday.'

'It was worse here for me. And I missed you.'

Our conversation lasted for over an hour. She finally said, 'It's still August, right?'

'Yes, love. Why wouldn't it be?'

'Nothing, it's just that you are far and I miss you so much. And I still don't know why you left.'

'It's a good job, an opportunity,' I said. 'It won't be for long.'

'I trust that you will come home to us. To me.' A long silence followed.

'Tega?'

'Yes?'

'I am still madly in love with you.'

Mike called round at about 1:30. He drove us to a

restaurant in town and I had breakfast with him. Afterwards he insisted on taking me to the cinema to see a movie. As the credits rolled I realised it was *The Broken Wind*.

'I will be outside,' I said, excusing myself as up on the screen Kelechi Adiele emerged from a limousine, looking chic and bright-eyed with ambition.

As I sat in the car I read Ahmed's message again and got my reply sorted out:

Dear Ahmed,

How have you been? How is work and life generally? Your letter gave me a lot to think about. And honestly, I'm not done thinking. Then again, I need to give you a reply.

Yes, I do have my 'secret places' and they range from a heated church service to the solitary silence of my room. They vary with the circumstances that I am in at any given time. All through my life I have learned to give more than one thought to the interpretation of events around me. This is why I could never be caged to one particular place as my secret place.

Having a secret place comes naturally to humans whether the gift of writing is there or not. This is because, like our nervous systems, there is only so much our minds can bear at a time. We have to deal with fear, confusion, excitement, love, depression and a string of other emotions on a daily basis. That's the way God has made it, perhaps to make our lives all the more exciting and spontaneous.

In the Bible, I see Jesus always retiring to pray by instinct (led by the spirit) and for this He always goes to His secret places. Throughout His ministry they vary from wilderness to mountains to islands to gardens. And for Him so many things happened in His secret places. We could see that He had to stretch His humanity into the realm of supernaturalism and back to the human again, all for His purpose on earth. It is also recorded that each time He emerged from these places remarkable events accompanied Him.

For me as a Christian, and as a human being, secret places are a wonderful transition point into spiritual lucidity, a deeper understanding of who I am, where I am and where I am headed.

As for my literary side... I just recently got employed by Kola University to lecture on International Human Rights Law. I shall be blogging about my experiences here a lot. I do not see myself writing much outside this because activism and Afrospark take up most of my non-teaching time.

This year I see a rather interesting and I hope beautiful experience coming my way because I am far from Wole and my regular life as I know it. I am part excited and part scared. Regardless, I am hopeful.

I have a few days to myself so I shall be seeing the town, to get accustomed once more to Amara and what it has to offer. I shall also be setting up my room and schedule for the school's resumption, which is only a few days away. I hope we can Skype in the course of this time as well – if it is convenient for you.

2014 is wonderful already. I wish you a sensational New Year. I hope to read more from you.

Hugs,

Wale.

P.S. Amongst other things, I cry a lot in my prayers

in secret places and I don't have to be alone to do this. It just happens. and no matter how much I struggle I can't control or restrain what goes on in there. I guess prayer is one of the very few places where I am permitted to never grow up.

A little while after I had proofread and sent my lengthy instant message Mike emerged from the cinema, and we drove back to K.U. He made several efforts to chat with me, starting off by apologising for choosing a film without consulting me, but I was preoccupied with thoughts of what lay ahead.

As we descended the hill on the bumpy road I once again caught sight of the university's green-and-blue grounds looming up ahead. My heart skipped a beat and I felt sweat on my palms. Something remarkable was approaching. Something that would alter my life.

The Kilode (What?) Place

Shola exploded politely
And sweet was her every word
Her thoughts like dance laced
One magic spell into another
A different girl she became
Now bold enough to scribble words untamed
Away to the sun she went
And she returned volcanic
'Kilode?' I ask

Audu now sounds better
His violin-strains purer
His message deep and fiery
I hear him
And now I see him clearly
Calm and fearless glint his eyes
Now the world must listen
A better man he has become
Away with the night and back at dawn
Magic!
'Kilode?' we ask

Like wahala,
We saw, we knew
We didn't mind them
But returning from the Kilode Place
We were suddenly enchanted by them
Kilode?!
Even when we can't but wonder
How they bloom and blast like thunder
And the sun shines down so sweet?
Kilode?!

Most seriously, what is it?
Look I must learn, I'm no fool
But Kilode?
How is it that they do?

Iwo atiemi (You and Me)

Oh my sweet Wale,

I'm excited about your new job. Yeah!!

I wonder how being under your tutelage would feel – especially when it's human rights you are addressing...

However, I do hope that you will be as 'interesting' in this field, as provocative as you were in your book. In the world today, from what I see, every age has its own clichés, its own conventions and limits, and every person has to play slave to some extent to gain acceptance.

The world agreed that regard for the thirty articles of the Universal Declaration of Human Rights shall be the international ideal. Simple and clear as they are, the world's eras and regions, darting from one end of semantics to another, have given us countless corrupt versions of them, so much so that very few of us regard the UDHR as being more than mere aspiration.

Then again, it seems to me exciting to learn when every tutor and text has a different version of a single story. Nothing is what it seems any more. Everything is distorted, I tell you. Beautiful but distorted.

I do know that human rights rest on two pillars: respect for, and protection of, human integrity, which for me is more on the part of 'hey, let's be human in our humanity.' Funny how various versions of these two pillars wash up repeatedly on the shores of our selves.

Well, that aside, I'm eager to know what your visions are for this phase of your life. And also to hear about your first few months on campus.

I'm certain that you are a remarkable man with a gift for making an impact. You are sure to be a great teacher of International Human Rights.

I shall be enthused reading your blog posts even as I spend every day studying and learning you.

Please be yourself. Study, but in the end be yourself, not afraid to face the world as you, Olawale Damian.

I dey believe you die.

Hugs,

Ahmed

idnight in Amara. The sky thundered and the rain was coming down heavily. The power was out.

The crackling noise of the wind hastily flipping the leaves of books filled the campus general library. Words and sentences seemed to read themselves in deep whispering voices, echoing loud. Unsecured papers twirled in the air and lightning flashed repeatedly in the hall and on my face. I shivered in my chair, uncertain of how and when I had come to be in the library. It was a *wili-wili* moment, my worst and most terrifying yet. A pillar of white light dashed in a split-second from the end of one bookshelf to another, torn covers and pages erupting on its tail. My eyes stretched wide and my mouth turned dry as this wild light, with every bedazzled shelf, drew quickly nearer.

Suddenly the power came back on and Nelson Mandela leaned over and winked at me. For a second a thought crossed my mind that I... No, I was certain: I was dead.

The power went off again. The hall was dark and silent

and I was by myself. Too scared to blink, I stood up and began to walk like an automaton stiffly towards the exit. Yet my night had not had its fill of horror, because then I heard the sound of stilettos walking briskly behind me. For some reason this filled me with dread. I darted to the door and, fumbling with the handle, tried to shove it open, unfortunately crashing into hard, unyielding wood: it was locked. I tried to force it. It would not give. The steps behind me were drawing nearer.

Shivering and drenched in sweat I turned and saw before me a young man wearing a well-fitted navy-blue tuxedo who I did not know. As the lightning flashed on his face and remained there I fell to my knees to plead for my life – he looked like the shadow of the sun. He had ghostly white skin and a cold light fluttered about him. His hair was long and locked like mine, only it was of a golden hue. His eyes, which were light grey, were unsteady and did not focus. His lips were pink and smiling. He looked as though he was still in his teens.

Coming closer, he knelt opposite me. I was unable to move. With his palm he felt my face and my locks. His hand was cold. And then he fizzled away like smoke in the wind. Once more I was all by myself.

A car screeched past outside my window, jolting me awake. I was in my room, in bed.

Naked, drenched with sweat and trembling, I lay there, not caring that my duvet had taken to its heels. I felt about for my phone to check the time. It was 3:30 a.m., 4th January 2014, the morning of the official resumption date for the students of Kola U.

To help me gather the temerity to leave my bed I recited Psalm Twenty-Three in a hoarse whisper: 'The Lord is my shepherd, I shall not want, He maketh me to lie down in still pastures...' A few minutes later I was calmer. I quietly pondered the rest of the darkness away, reflecting on what seeing Madiba meant, on the symbolism of the library.

I have always placed value on my dreams and nightmares. Maami used to say that dreams are the spirit's sojourn in delicate and symbolic realms, and that no detail of them should be taken for granted. I had also learned that it is bad for one's brain-functioning to sleep without dreaming. But then when the dreams are 'Frightville' it becomes another tale: 'Bad omen!' – a call to be alert, either for yourself or for those who are a part of you.

At six a.m., and just after I had finished my morning prayer and said 'Amen', I received a phone call.

'Morning, man,' a voice said.

'Good morning,' I replied. 'Please may I know who is speaking?'

'It's the Vice Chancellor, sir.'

'Oh. Good morning, sir.'

'I'll send a driver to get you. Will eight a.m. be okay?'

'Perfect, sir.'

'Swell. See you then.'

'Thank you, sir.'

Two hours later I was walking a stone path through the lush lawn that surrounded the university's administrative block, a predominantly blue, three-storey building that arched slightly at its apex. The building seemed deserted, save for the cleaners, who were rounding off their work for the day. The professor's office was on the top floor. I was in my smartest suit. Taking the staircase I felt like a student again, climbing up to see the school's monarch. I had ascended these stairs several times before, most memorably when I, alongside a few other students, came to seek the then vice-chancellor's permission to represent the school at an international student debate.

I was nineteen. Wole and I were in our second year. I was enjoying the challenges of academic work, and we had both given up most of our social activities to take the various optional professional courses that came with the session. One day, in the course of a constitutional law lecture, the dean announced that there would be a selection exercise to pick the best speakers in the faculty, to represent the student body and the school at an international debate night. It would be held in Kenya, and the theme was to be 'the propriety of African culture'. To be invited to participate was a big break for the faculty: everyone went on and on about it.

Wole caught the fever. He was very enthused with the

idea of speaking, especially as it would give him the chance to talk about Ilaro, and in particular the customary way of expressing respect for one's elders there. He had always been fascinated by the way men fell to the ground to pay their respects, regardless of how expensive or brightly-coloured their clothes were. And he kept on quizzing me about other practices, especially around courtship and marriage, as I had grown up there and he had not. I suspected him of romanticising what he had not experienced, and wilfully ignoring what was smothering and limiting about it. He took copious notes of my haphazard remembrances. I was less enthusiastic about the whole event, and the commitment it required.

'Oh, c'mon, Wale. Look, flying the flag for Kola internationally is not a chance you get every day,' he insisted.

'It's not about flying, oga. This competition adds nothing to your cumulative grade point average. It simply takes from your time and academic performance.'

'Abegi... you know we can comfortably squeeze out a mere thirty minutes every day for extracurricular research. We can take out ten minutes from siesta time and skip movies for three months.'

'Even at that, our time is already fully booked,' I said. 'Administrative law requires more than its allotment. You said so yourself.'

It was typical of Wole: no matter how much reason there was not to, he wanted to take the leap. And I always had to take it with him – the story of my life. We kept late nights, practiced our tongue-twisters, and rehearsed in front of our less-than-thrilled classmates – who, unlike Wole, saw how much this debate was taking from our – and their – study time.

A few weeks later he was waving to me from the other end of the row as we stood in line with twenty of the most accomplished student oralists in the final year, waiting to give our presentations. Only four of us would be chosen.

We were appearing before the entire student body and a judging panel made up of the university's deans and the vice-chancellor, Professor Daniels, and were to make our presentations in order of seniority. The competition was stiff, with high-sounding vocabulary flying out of one speaker's mouth

after another, as each hoped to elicit thunderous applause
from the watching students and smash the earlier speaker's
ego. It soon grew too warm in the crowded hall, and I
loosened my tie a little, though not so much as to appear
rattled or undisciplined. I was getting nervous. Wole was
called before me.

He got to his feet and went straight to the lectern.

'Due regard to the panel. I am Wole Damian and Africa is
my home...' Ah, Wole. Everyone who heard the sound of his
voice fell under his spell. He told stories that were clear and
true, that any listener could identify with. He was, in the best
way, simple.

'Yoruba culture is not a history book from distant lands.
It's like that garden patch we never planted but somehow
grew up and found its way over our walls and spilled into our
backyards, no matter how civilised we may pretend we have
become, and however close we keep our front lawns clipped.

'A child is the community's treasure, and as such everyone answers to her tears. That's why it feels like our parents
are immortal, because their love never goes away. And it
seems, in some silly light, that nobody ever fully grows up.
Nobody ever gets so old that they cannot be subjected to a
slap across the face by the elders – even if you are the
commander of the federal republic. What came before can
still slap what happens now.' Wole laughed, infecting others.
Then he resumed his speech, gliding away from humour,
slipping into his core argument. Wole did not believe in
sugar-coating anything: although he told stories, he did not
believe, like me, that the tortoise was James Bond. The
stories he told picked at the roots of substantial questions
about the pointless persistence of baseless values and empty
gestures of honour, and questioned the rationale for postrat-
ing to our elders when the heart is bitter and the respect is
gone. He made it clear that disrespect was not his version of
where the Yoruba civilisation should go, but that mindless
obeisance to tradition was not admirable either. For a
minute I thought that Fela Kuti's ghost had appeared to him
the night before and possessed him.

He finished. Everyone was still, and his voice seemed to
reverberate in my chest. I could see myself speaking as he

spoke, and as always I saw myself going the distance. He drove me. He still does.

'Thank you.' – and only then, after a long moment, did the applause and cheering follow.

Now it was my turn.

Knowing I lacked Wole's charm, instead I discussed African culture in the light of its becoming lost beneath the ever-growing tidal wave of modernisation, in which a child is nurtured more by gadgets than by the community. I recall saying that the parental love that would ordinarily be expressed through physical intimacy, sharing food and chores, supervision and conversation and story-telling, is now expressed in more remote styles, where the child is literally raised by his or her computer – and, of course, books, which were the beginning of the end of oral cultures. African culture, I concluded, was not really in existence any more, except unfortunately in the case of age-old prejudices that encouraged nepotism and inter-tribal tension.

Although I did not speak as well as Wole, and my argument did not extol traditional African virtues in a crowd-pleasing way, we both made the selection, along with two final-year students of law, Oluchi and Kate. We were going to make history – or at least we thought so. The news reached home. Everyone was excited.

It was a standing rule that the selection was subject to the vice-chancellor's final approval. Normally this was merely a formality: we didn't know of anyone who had been denied approval. However, to our shock, on getting to the vice-chancellor's office he insisted that neither Wole nor I were good enough to represent the university. I didn't understand why he was dropping us. Neither did our dean, until the vice-chancellor eventually said to him angrily, 'Please get me real Christians fit enough for this task.'

'They are Christians, sir,' our dean said.

'I said real Christians! Am I blind?'

'I don't understand, sir. Please, what do you mean?' our dean asked, while Wole, Oluchi, Kate and I stood there with our hearts racing.

'I have my eyes all over the campus. I always see these boys sitting outside the mosque and parading themselves around with that crazy boy, Ali.' Ali was a voluble classmate we often studied with after class, and sometimes socialised with. 'You know what these Muslims are capable of, don't you? This is Kola University, and here it is totally unacceptable,' the vice-chancellor finished, breathing hard.

What? I thought. *But we have a mosque on campus!* But he wouldn't be swayed. We were replaced by two other students, 'real Christians' who got to go to Kenya in our place.

Well, here I was outside that office again. I knocked and entered.

'The pictures do you no justice,' the vice-chancellor said as he stood, reaching out to shake my hand across his desk. He was a bald man of average height, with dark skin and grey eyes – coloured contact lenses – and was younger than I had expected, around my own age, I guessed. He wore a well-cut black suit, black shirt and a sky-blue tie, and gave me a smile that seemed too good to be true.

'Good morning, sir,' I said, shaking his hand, trying to maintain the formality expected of me in such a situation despite his youth.

'Relax, senior. Please call me Brown. I'm also an alumnus.' He motioned me to a seat while retaking his.

'Okay,' I said, trying to place his still-smiling face.

'I came in when you and your brother were in the fourth year. You used to tutor my friends in the law library. I still have the notes on public international law you handed over to me on your graduation.'

'I gave my notes to one Dele Fatade,' I said.

'I now use my middle name more, Brown. Brown Fatade,' he said.

Now I remembered. We had not had much of a relationship outside academics, but he was one of those boys I always had to be ready for in my final year, as whenever I saw him he had some knotty academic question to pose. Sometimes I hid under the library table or pretended to be Wole to escape his challenges. Then again, I had to be extremely lucky not to get caught out, so persistent was he.

I wasn't surprised that he had gone on to become a professor, but I was most unsettled that he had also become the administrative monarch of Kola University.

'My guy... wetin happen now?' I asked after a laugh of shared recognition, pushing down my unease.

'Well, I went all around the world and decided that I wanted to turn things around at home.'

'How do you mean?'

His smile brightened. 'Wale, this is my alma mater. I came here with dreams not of just getting a law degree, I came here with dreams of good mentorship, of being free to question, and to challenge. And I was disappointed. So much was staid and stale. The lectures, the student life. All those words that seemed so bland and cold that had to be committed to memory. It was cram or die! But I was not at all disappointed by the quality of the students: to see the likes of you, Wole, Ikechukwu, Raymond, Ali, Obinna... I could go on: there were so many phenomenal students here at K.U. who were ready to seize opportunities and make the boldest statements. I remember how the authorities here mistreated you over the matter of the debating team. I am Muslim, but I came to the understanding that God's love and blessing breaks through the barriers of religion and race. I have also learned that if the academic space is not kept open, safe and liberal, and if this openness is not protected, the development of Africa will remain only a vision. We are all in this together. For God's sake, Nigeria's Civil War and past pogroms are no justification for choking the lives of students today with religious bigotry and discrimination. This is the world we live in: we will always have those who have decided against civilisation, the crazy ones consumed by inflamed versions of their faiths. It doesn't mean that everyone is crazy. We all deserve a fair chance.' His eyes were shining now, and he spoke quickly.

'The gist of what the authorities did to you because they thought you were Muslim lingered amongst us, and several other similar instances occurred after you left. If my faith was that much of a curse within the academic world I feared for what would become of my life outside it, but you and your brother went out there and did well, and that gave me hope. And now you run a foundation that brings love and care to humanity regardless of who or what they are. You both inspired me so much.

'After my studies here, I had the opportunity to go to Harvard for further studies. I went, and I did well. A few of my friends there and I got wind of the government's move to sell off Kola University, and we jumped at it. And so I am here to make things right.'

'Hm, this is music to my ears,' I said. 'So how long have you been here?'

'Long enough to know that it won't be an easy task, but that more and better heads are more formidable than fewer and worse.'

I didn't at once understand what Brown wanted from me. It became clearer when he said that, though there was a predetermined course outline for international human rights law, he desired that I improve its content; that I make it as challenging as I could. He also put me in charge of the University's newly-formed student debate team.

'Come,' he said, and led me to my office. It was only a few doors away from his, and everything was brand new, from the chairs to the desk to the curtains.

'I had it refurnished for you,' he said as I spun round in my chair. 'I hope you like it.'

'It's great. Thanks.'

We admired the office in silence. Then he said, 'I believe in you. So much Wale, I believe in you.' He went and looked out of the window and continued, 'There are other, older staff here who do not approve of my methods. They think I'm too idealistic to survive. But I will prove them wrong. I need you to stand by me. Break the right conventions. Take the students out of their comfort zone. Teach them to live up to their individuality on the one hand, and their community on the other.'

After going through the lecture notes my predecessor had left me, which were penned on moth-eaten paper that had gone beige with age, I could see why Brown had had so much to say that morning. Most of us had given up on the educational system in Nigeria. There was so much that had become mechanical: the students were all being narrowly schooled for nothing beyond white collar jobs. They did not have much exposure to international standards and competition, or access to good-quality mentorship, and going to school had become a mere rite of passage which had no relevance outside the formal process of label-gathering. Nationally, we had just pulled through a six-month strike – in effect a compulsory unpaid holiday – by the Academic Staff Union of Universities which, though it had no direct impact on privately-run K.U., would have a big impact on our country's future. A half-trained life-saver will struggle to save a life effectively, and worse, will make others take risks thinking an effective life-saver is standing by.

Once Brown left me I got down to work, researching and browsing our e-library from my office computer. I became so engrossed in what I was doing that I did not realise it was six p.m. until a tap came at my door – the vice-chancellor checking in on me before he left the building. I bade him goodnight and worked on, leaving an hour later after setting up sticky notes and reminders to myself for the following day. My driver was waiting outside.

'Tobi? I'm so sorry you had to stay this late.'

'It's okay, oga. It's my job,' he said as he took my file and put it in the car. 'Where to?'

'Into town. Please stop at an eatery when you see one.'

We drove smoothly through the campus. The streets were sepia and gold-toned under the streetlights. Looking out at students walking along, paired up or in groups, probably catching up on the holiday gist, I was almost tearing up with nostalgia when I remembered I had had my glasses on all day.

I had been given a week to settle in and organise my commitments before beginning lecturing. It was wonderful that my new boss believed this much in me. My head was still buzzing with thoughts and ideas for the debate society. I would have to work closely with the youths; I would have to get to know each of them on an almost personal level. I would... My phone rang.

'Hi love,' Tega whispered.

'Hi babe,' I said cheerily. 'Good evening. How are you?'

'I miss you.' She sighed, then went on wearily: 'These emails don't stop coming and the files have refused to attend to themselves. The – '

'What are you doing with the files?' I cut in. 'Where are you?' Tega never went near the files, save when she was in Lola's office and had to create space on Lola's usually overloaded desk for her laptop.

'You know how Wole has been all about "Save the Colours" since last year? Well, it just got worse this morning. He had a face-off with Lola about some problem with the spreadsheets she'd done, she stormed out of his office and off the premises, and I haven't heard from her since. Wole is still in his office, sweating over the figures. He asked that I speed up the production of *Eyimofe*. But I can't magic the necessary location permits out of thin air or stop the editing suite crashing whenever there's a power cut. And then Craig is always insisting that perfection takes time and he can't be rushed. What can I say to that? And then Wole directed that I – '

'I miss you too, my sweet,' I interrupted.

Realising that the work gist was a turn-off, she apologised. 'I'm sorry,' she sighed. 'That's what you get when two individuals share career and romance.'

'I know it's frustrating, and I'm sorry I'm not there to help sort things out. But I would love to know how you've been missing me whilst buried under all those files and spreadsheets.'

She giggled. 'Well... it's kinda boring having to work late alone so often. Wole's great, of course, but you two are just too dissimilar for substitution.'

Intrigued, I tried to enquire more. But she didn't say anything definite, just that, 'The energy from you feels different. When he is around, I feel my big brother and boss is watching. With you, I feel like a naughty little girl – and sometimes a big sister.'

'Hm.'

Tega's coming into my life was my first serious diversion from Wole. She was brilliant, creative, polite, warm, fun, girly, spontaneous and practical. She loved white and bright colours, and wouldn't be caught dead without her smartphone and high heels. She and Wole had an instant connection. She had a knack for achieving quality to deadline which he particularly appreciated: at Afrospark we were forever trying to get too much done with too few resources in too little time. It was Wole who hired her, and after a few weeks, during which he had noticed how much I liked her, he talked me into letting her come round to our apartment one evening, to run a few ideas past us informally over a home-made dinner. She came earlier than expected – or perhaps I should say, earlier than I expected.

'Fine boy,' Wole called out to me – as he usually did when he was up to no good – from the living room. I emerged from the hot kitchen to answer his call in only my boxer briefs and an apron, to find to my embarrassment that Tega was already there and already seated. She looked immaculate in white. I was sweating and smelt of frying.

'Fine boy,' Wole continued, 'I won go pick up more drinks from that shop wey dey down the street. I won't be long.' He winked mischievously at me and did his funny cartoon dance behind Tega, then hurried out of the house before I had the chance to protest. This was his seventh attempt to match-mate me since we were called to the Nigerian Bar, and the second since we set up Afrospark. Six failed romances had followed hard on the heels of his efforts, so I didn't have a great deal of trust in his judgement by this point.

So there I stood, shiny, under-dressed and awkward, before some girl who was on my payroll, stumbling to make conversation. 'I didn't know you would make it this early,' I said.

'I'm so sorry,' she said. 'Wole said 6.30.'

'Not seven?'

'I hope it's no trouble.'

'No, no, no, it's okay. It's good.' I forced a smile even though I wished I could cut and paste her back into her house till I was showered and dressed.

We had a short conversation which led to her taking over most of the cooking while I quickly went and put some clothes on, and us getting on quite well. I liked the way she briskly shredded the onions, and that her palms were seemingly too numb to feel the scourging heat of the pots and pans she lifted every now and then. She was very tidy too

– it was difficult for me to cook and tidy at the same time, but somehow she managed it quite effortlessly, and in an unfamiliar kitchen.

We talked, and I discovered that Tega was the last of three children in her family – two girls and one boy. She grew up in Delta State but managed to escape the unique Warri subculture and its accent. Her parents are retired civil servants who jointly run a beverage store in Asaba. The family are quite closely knit and in regular touch with each other by phone, but they all seem to lead very busy and rather separate lives.

She asked me about myself, and I told her a little while we waited for Wole's return. But to further complicate – or, as he thought, 'speed up' – issues Wole sent the drinks home ahead of himself. Then, after two hours had passed awkwardly between Tega and I as we groped for topics of conversation, he called her to say that he had to attend to some other 'official matters' in town. He called me some minutes later: 'Fine boy... Fine... boy.'

'Bros, wetin?' I said, trying not to lose my composure before Tega.

'No vex abeg,' he apologised. 'Oya, the deal is I really want you to hook up with that babe. She is clean. I checked her out myself.'

I stole a glance at her, then excused myself so that I could lash out at Wole properly.

'Bros, there is this thing called "agreement",' I whispered as I paced the balcony of our duplex. 'You never tire for all these match-mating.'

He sighed and said, 'Olawale' – now sounding very serious – 'you need to settle down. Look, I know that you will make a great husband and father. What is holding you back?'

'I always tell you,' I said. 'We will walk down that aisle together. I still stand my ground.'

'Ehn, no wahala. Whatever you say,' he said abruptly, trying to end the conversation.

'I no dey joke o,' I insisted. 'In fact, let's make this deal. If I take this one, I will get one for you as well.'

He laughed. 'You ke? Oya no wahala. I'm game. But yan me now... shey you gbadun Tega?'

I smiled. 'I'll tell you when you come home.'

'I'm at the neighbours',' he said. 'I'll step in once she leaves. Take your time.'

A few months after this shaky start Tega and I began officially dating.

Talk between us soon became easier, and quickly grew in intimacy. She told me about the time she crushed on a classmate for a whole session during her university days, but was too shy to speak to him. She bought a new SIM card and took up the name Sandra, so she could call him under the pretence that they used to attend secondary school together, even feigning anger when he said he could not remember any Sandra.

'And this was easier than just speaking to him as yourself?' I said.

'I know.' She laughed lightly. 'But I was younger, and it was quite exciting and dramatic.'

Difficulties arose when he began to hint at wanting more than phone sex, and she was very close to confessing her deception. The spell was broken, however, when he started to complain to 'Sandra' about some 'annoyingly disgusting chick named Tega from the Niger-Delta', who did not have any dress sense and just did not know how to mind her business in class, 'always putting her hands up and making everyone look so dumb.' She broke the SIM card in two, and made sure she stepped on him once a week for the following two months.

She also told me about the time she dreamt that a girl kissed her and she told her pastor. She fasted for three days on his instruction, after he told her that she was under a satanic attack by marine spirits. She said that it terrified her at the time because the girl had looked like an actress she idolised. She stopped seeing her movies afterwards. Tega confessed that it excited her, though; and that she had had to take the fast seriously in order to purge herself of all attachment to the actress or her movies.

She had interesting views on a wide range of subjects. There was so much for me to learn – and unlearn. 'An African woman,' she would say, 'is a like a book of green leaves. You can look at her, feel her, and celebrate that you have her. But you may never know the particular roots she grew from. More often than not it is better to trust her and grow slowly with her than to study or rationalize her.' She would always tell me this when surprising me with some unexpected viewpoint, or when she wanted to defend her female crew members at Afrospark from some unwelcome patriarchal critique. And if she discovered that she had done so unjustly, she would always 'apologize' by saying something like, 'You know there is a feminist in every woman. I'll sort things out, okay.'

We vowed to keep our relationship platonic, but I was fiercely drawn to her. The chemistry between us strung me like a puppet. She was, I thought, a female version of Seun: they were to my eyes strikingly similar. She was incredible on the dance-floor – like Seun. She did this thing with her eyes that Seun did too, and I knew that she knew it caught me every time – as Seun had known; so much so that it turned my masculinity to popcorn. As I heard her voice over the phone now, images of Seun flashed through my mind, and I felt weak, then warm, then firm.

We pulled up at a restaurant close to the campus entrance. In my student days it had been an almost 24-hour mini open market, with large tables, shelves and tarpaulin shelters, that we nicknamed 'Gbo-gbo-eh' because everything was sold there from flip-flops to fried akara, 'akamu-oku' hot enough to cause real damage to the tongue, buckets of pirated textbooks and photocopied class notes of alumni who had been rumoured to have had high grades – although the rumours were unverified. Now it was a much more exotic place, though was still popular with the students for their payday outings on account of its proximity to the campus, and had become a regular unwinding point for K.U. staff – I even learned later that they made the best pepper soup in Amara.

I sat in the vehicle chatting with Tega for a few more minutes more before ending the call, but I wasn't really listening: I was thinking how crazy it would have been with Seun. Though it was Tega there at the other end of the line, she was all the more and at the same time Seun. 'Tega, Tega... you no go kill me o,' I groaned in half-response to some remark of hers. She laughed.

After dinner all I could think of was my bed, and how much Lola and Wole needed to be patient with each other. *For God's sake, we are all getting married in August.* Healthy and spirited dialogues every now and then to clear the air are a good thing, but no matter how spirited the dialogue is, it should be kept between the two parties involved, not yelled across an office to become gist among co-workers.

I had planned on maintaining my silence on this issue, but that night Wole called. Tobi had dropped me off at my accommodation, and I was already half-asleep.

'Fine boy,' he said, hailing me.

'Oga, how you dey?'

'Your bros no dey well o. Lola is not making matters any less complicated for us,' he complained.

When I went on to enquire how, he said that Lola was irritated by the increasing number of effeminate men who sashayed in and out of the office, and would not be attended to by anyone except him – mostly men from the Rainbow Talk, and the ones who did not care that a man had only five days a week to build a business. The ones Wole enjoyed meeting up with too much. The ones who had cat fights and always called Wole in to settle them, or had some trivial legal issue that could easily be dispensed with over the phone but were hell-bent on seeing their friend face-to-face, strutting their stuff all the way in, then all the way out when they were done – talking loudly of his charm and handsomeness even when his wife-to-be was in the same set of offices and could overhear them. The ones who would not dare come any-where near me.

'This morning she, being on the legal team and all, tried to sit in for me when I was off with Tega at the *Eyimofe* set to sort out the latest crisis. And naturally one of the more effeminate men came in and refused to be attended to until "dear Wole" returned. She left him to wait and went to handle her matter in court. And then, on her return in the afternoon she walked in on me holding hands with him across my desk – '

'Wole...'

'– purely in friendliness. But at that point, she lost it.'

'Wole... wetin?' I groaned.

'Fine boy, I, I...' There was a tremor in his voice.

'I, I wetin? Your wedding is in August o,' I said, hushing him. There was silence before I went on: 'I'm here at K.U. because you promised me that you can handle things there.'

'I know. I can.'

'You don't have to do this,' I said. Despite my earlier insistence that I would only date Tega if he dated Lola, Wole didn't really have to get married to her: it wasn't a promise I would hold him to. In fact, it was now one I very much regretted making him make. But whenever I said this he insisted that she was the love of his life. Though we both knew better, he was unrepentantly adamant on this point – even if Lola herself surely knew somewhere within the drawers and files of her mind that he might have a queer splint glowing. I thought of our father's parting letter to me and sighed.

They had met at a client's house-warming party – Mazi Amanze. Lola was a friend of Mazi's. Quick-witted, striking, shapely and sophisticated, Lola caught the fancy of both single and married men at the event. Her manner was aloof, but Wole soon got her chatting and laughing, and the next thing I knew she was volunteering with the foundation, enchanted, she said, by our saying out loud the things that people were mostly too scared to talk about above a whisper. She said that this was the law she had always dreamt of practising. She was one of the most outstanding young female – or, for that matter, male – lawyers in the state, but she initially struck me as an egoistic diva who was so full of her expertise that she would never give in to Wole's charms. In fact she turned out to be the reverse of all that, unaffected and idealistic – and I lost three brand-new long-sleeved white T. M. Lewin shirts to Wole in a bet when I dared him to kiss her at our office reception desk on the Monday of her second week with the Afrospark team. The smartass had asked her into a relationship with him the night before.

'Wale, it really was nothing. I only reached out to hold his hand when he got a bit emotional Please believe me.'

'I do. But she is getting the picture that this year's edition is not just a project for you.'

Wole had always tried to disguise his being gay, and his natural inclination to advance LGBTI rights, by using the general pursuit of human rights protection as his mask. I understood that. But I also let him know that if he insisted on getting married to Lola, out of fairness he had to draw a line.

Now Lola was pushing for him to let her take the interviews with any gay-seeming clients. Evidently the persistent rumours that both Wole and I were gay, which at first she had laughed off, had begun to take their toll on her.

'She says it's because she's concerned for the reputation of Afrospark, but...'

'Make it right, man,' I said. 'Look, I know this isn't easy for you. But don't step into what you can't finish.'

'I won't.'

'Are you still up to this?'

'Fine boy, relax jor. Na me be this,' he said, and he laughed.

We talked about other things for a while – he was, of course, interested to hear of the changes that had come to our alma mater – and I dozed off with my phone cradled to my ear.

Wole was such a sweet talker: Don Juan had nothing on him. The next day, at about two p.m., Lola uploaded a photo on Instagram of herself and Wole cuddling, with the tag *#lovingmybootobits*. I looked at it, and sighed.

It was nine p.m. and I was about rounding off my work for the day when my mobile rang: a call from Abuja: 'Olawale, where are you?' It was Brother Gbenro, sounding tense.

'I'm in the office, sir,' I said.

'Have you seen the news?'

'No. What is it?'

'The Same Sex Marriage Prohibition Bill was passed into law,' he whispered. 'Today.'

'What?!' I exclaimed. Although we had all been following the law's progress through the Assembly and then the Senate with sinking hearts, I was still shocked that such a draconian piece of legislation could actually be approved in what purports to be a democracy with some regard for human rights.

'I know. Just be calm. I'll send an official vehicle to get you. You and Wole leave for the United Kingdom on Friday. Your mum is in England briefly for a course, and she will be at Heathrow to receive you. And afterwards, with the help of some contacts we have there, you can commence the asylum process. Everything – '

'Woah, woah, woah. Wait,' I interrupted. 'Slow down, sir. I just got this job and there is no way I'm leaving so soon. I – '

'What nonsense job?' he burst out. 'Do you think I can bear to lose any of you? I will never forgive myself. In fact, I'm coming to get you. I'm leaving Abuja for Port Harcourt first thing in the morning. Put your things together. Job ko. Job ni.' And the line went dead.

I called Wole. 'Everybody is affected. Absolutely everybody!' he said. 'This isn't good enough, oga, at all.'

Connecting from Port Harcourt and Amara, Wole and I spent the better part of the night discussing the situation on Skype with Mum in England and Brother Gbenro in Abuja.

'Look, nothing is going to happen here,' I said. 'Or at least not right away. The campus is quite secure and has the United Nations' endorsement, and we have private security. No-one comes in uninvited.'

'What about your brother?' Mum asked. 'You know he has a knack for going all out with his projects. And so many international NGOs here in the U.K. and even the U.N. are endorsing "Save the Colours" simply because it is LGBTI rights-inclined, and that is known.'

'The U.N. is endorsing us? You didn't tell me that,' I said to Wole.

'I'm sorry, I was going to tell you today.'

'Oh, congrats, my man,' I said, and we both laughed in slightly hysterical excitement.

'See these children o – Titi, look, they have to leave,' Brother Gbenro pressed.

'Brother Gbenro, please now. Please,' Wole and I begged. 'We can't just drop everything and run away.'

We finally reached an agreement that Brother Gbenro

would arrange for some policemen to be attached to the Afrospark premises, and that Wole would always be in the company of at least one of them. For my part I agreed that I would not leave Amara without taking a mobile policeman with me.

That tense negotiation out of the way, I was able to turn to getting the remainder of my preparations done before the semester began in the protective bubble of K.U. By Saturday I was free to catch up with my laundry, Skype with a few friends from Port Harcourt, and read the numerous links that had been posted on the Afrospark wall.

The news was uniformly bad. The newly-passed anti-gay law was fast raging through Nigeria: numerous arrests had been made of individuals, and members of groups that were alleged to be homosexual or supporters of homosexual rights. Parents were being threatened to produce their homosexual wards for punishment. None of the ten Rainbow Talk lines were available – and they would not be for the rest of 2014.

I had seen enough for one day and was just about to sign off when another Skype call came in. It was Ahmed Azeez. I took it.

'Ahmed! It's you!' I exclaimed as his face came into slightly blurry view.

'My brother... Finally,' he said. He had a slight Hausa accent. 'Wallah, the pictures don't do you any justice.'

'Oga, calm down,' I said, adding jokily, 'You might be misunderstood.'

'I was worried: I heard that they arrested you,' he said.

'Arrest me ke.'

'With everything you are posting online these days. That's why I had to call.'

'If they arrest me for what I put online, then what will they do when they find out what I put in my bedroom?'

'You mean, what you put and where you put it?'

'And how I put it too.'

'Mmm, this law needs to have plans for you.'

It was now my turn to be serious: 'It does. And it's really closing in.'

'Don't be negative man.'

'It's not about being negative, Azeez. Have you not been reading the news?'

'Of course I have.'

Initially I had found nothing fascinating about his appearance, but now his mirror-smooth head and dark complexion struck me like the face of a Sango in the lightning. He caught me looking and smiled, and I couldn't help muttering, 'Damn! You are beautiful.'

'What did you say?'

'Did I say something?'

'Okay,' he said, chuckling. 'Thanks. I think you're beautiful too.'

My heart squealed out several notes. My loins throbbed. But I did not want to have this conversation now. 'Okay, thanks,' I said, trying to sound casual but probably not succeeding.

Azeez cleared his throat. 'How is Wole?'

'Wole is great.'

'Are you okay?'

'Yes, I'm alright.' He gave me a 'C'mon I can read your mind' look, so I added, 'You know I'm not gay, right?'

'Neither am I. What about it?'

'Nothing. Let's just change the topic.'

'And Wole is,' he said, 'and it's okay.'

'What is this, Azeez?' I said uneasily. 'I'd rather we move to something else.' I hardly ever discussed Wole's sexuality with anyone, never mind my own; and with the passing of a law that placed an obligation on all citizens to report anyone even suspected of being gay to the authorities, this was a particularly inopportune moment to do so.

'I'm sorry, sir,' Azeez said politely. And he moved on to discussing international markets for African literature, and the challenges of marketing to European and North American readers, and I was glad.

The call went on pleasantly enough and I lost track of time. Eventually I noticed that the sun had gone down and my body was asking for sugar.

'Ziz my guy,' I hailed him, as it felt like we were about to conclude our conversation for the evening.

'Wale, if you don't mind my saying this...' he said, then

tailed off, as if hesitating to proceed.

'Go on, my brother.'

'It's okay to be honest and verbal with your thoughts sometimes. It doesn't make you any less of a man. It only makes you more open to other people and to yourself.'

'Restraint is a form of discipline and integrity,' I said.

'But baseless restraint is just fear. What are you afraid of?'

I asked him what he meant. He went on to explain that he had nothing against my saying that he was beautiful.

'My son says that sometimes, and I reciprocate to reassure him that polite and decent comments are an important part of fostering good relationships, regardless of our gender or sexuality.' Azeez leaned forward, coming nearer to the screen. 'Sexuality is so big a topic, yet in all seriousness, isn't it too little to make us so uneasy? You know this.'

I didn't reply.

'As straight men who are in the lives of other individuals, we consciously and unconsciously adapt to their physical, mental and emotional environments even as they adapt to ours.'

'Agreed,' I said, a little reluctantly. I had not, after all, said I was straight, just that I was not gay.

'And this adaptation neither alters the substance of who we are nor our sexuality. It only aids us in building better relationships with others, supporting them, and through interdependence we all help each other grow.'

'A very African viewpoint,' I said.

'Given the state of Nigeria now, you should be proud of all your hard work on "Save the Colours". Sugar Books is endorsing the project. We believe it will be a great break-through for Nigeria. And perhaps for you.'

Azeez had gone all activist on me – I liked it. 'Oga... no vex na,' I said, in a bid to placate him, but he did not stop at that: 'My boy – the one I told you about? He is only eight years old. But he is gay.'

'What makes you so sure at so young an age?' I asked.

'Well, I'm only 60% certain. But hey! A parent knows these things if he looks closely,' he said.

'I suppose every child is special in some way that defies

convention,' I said.

'And that is one way.'

To hear an avowedly heterosexual man talk that way was encouraging. However, I think he misunderstood my reticence. I did not care to spend much time talking about homosexuality because my life already revolved around it, and not in a theoretical way. Nonetheless, he got me pondering about Wole's sexuality and my own. Why should one of us struggle with the problem of a singular proscribed desire, while the other battled with the conflict between two separate desires – one taboo, one approved – each bringing problems of its own? Had Mum known that side of our natures before she heard? I had never asked her. I wondered if she could tell the difference between us in that regard – Wole of course being the transparent one.

The next day I attended the university's Pentecostal church service. It was a full house. The first Sunday of the year is always heated up, the New Year's resolution to take God seriously being fresh from the oven. Both staff and students who are Pentecostals worship on campus. I came in while the sermon was being delivered by a student pastor. A male usher in a neatly-tucked-in pink short-sleeved shirt and black trousers escorted me to a seat near the front. I said a short prayer and started listening.

I had hoped to blend in, but my lateness and my locks would not have it: people began giving me the 'he-is-definitely-new' look. An announcement was made from the lectern that 'P. Wole, the former papa of the publicity department' was in the house. Wild volts spurted through me as whistles, applause and drumbeats raced across the hall. Ushers raced in my direction, eager to drag me to the front as the damn floor refused to fold me in and swallow me up. 'I am not Papa Wole,' I muttered behind clenched teeth. Papa Wole was in Port Harcourt. I shut my eyes to wake from this nightmare of social awkwardness.

Before the excited ushers could reach me I felt a hand on my shoulder. 'Papa Wole, welcome sir.'

I turned round to see sitting behind me a slender student with a small afro who would later introduce himself as

Tunde, the incumbent head of the publicity department. I let him lead me by the hand onto the red carpet that ran the length of the aisle, wondering how it was that almost a decade after our leaving K.U. the Pentecostal fellowship still remembered that Wole had been a campus fellowship leader of note.

I tried to wriggle myself out of the mix. But my hand was being held firmly. Feeling uncharismatic, I made a short, awkward speech explaining who I actually was, then returned to my seat for the rest of the service.

Afterwards I had a drink with Tunde in the cafeteria. His continual bowing and calling me 'sir' made it difficult for us to have an actual conversation. He welcomed me over and over again. He kept saying how glad he was 'to be in the same room with Papa Wole – sorry, Barrister Wale.'

Yeah, this has been the story of my life. I don't mind. Most of the time.

I spent the rest of the evening with my laptop on the lawn outside my lodge, uploading material onto a blog I had created specifically for my academic engagements at K.U. All my notes, reference materials and reference links would be posted there, so my students would need to spend less time taking notes during my lectures, and we would be able to spend more time sharing their – our – thoughts.

The next morning I woke early, feeling strong. The sky was clear, the air fresh. It was a perfect day for my first lecture. 'My first day of "de koko",' as Wole had called it when we spoke briefly the previous night. Not quite sure what to wear, I finally opted for a pair of slim grey trousers, a fitted navy-blue short-sleeved shirt and tie, and suede shoes. Formal but not staid.

Before I left my room I stole one last glance in the mirror and took a moment to tie my hair back in a neat ponytail. On impulse I traded my traditional boring spectacles for a pair of tinted oversize ones, and ran my fingers across my brows. It was my first day: I was going be in my most 'me' state.

I had been in the office reviewing my PowerPoint presentation for some time when I glanced at my watch to discover, to my alarm, that it had been showing 6:55 since I arrived.

My watch had killed my time: how late was I? The time on my laptop was far ahead. I snapped it shut, snatched up my iPad, and dashed across to the faculty building. I was already nervous: I was scheduled to lecture the final year students in two-hour sessions twice a week, and I didn't know whether they would accept my methods. Too late now! I hurried up the staircase clutching my iPad. It felt strange to be arriving as a teacher, not a student.

A teacher who was late.

When I arrived at the hall the door was shut.

I took a few seconds to catch my breath, then quietly let myself in.

The blinds were down and it was dark inside, save for a video projection on one wall. The students were quietly watching a documentary film on the creation of the International Criminal Court, and in the low light few of them noticed my entrance. I made my way to the back of the class and the source of the projection. A student there was monitoring the display from a laptop. He looked up as I reached him.

'Hello,' I whispered as I offered him my hand.

'Good day, sir,' he said, shaking it.

'I am Wale Damian, I shall be taking the class on I.H.R.'

'Oh yes, we were told.' He moved over to offer me a seat beside him. 'Will you be using the board or do you have a presentation?'

'I have a presentation.' I handed him a USB stick. After he uploaded my PowerPoint presentation he stopped the video and apologised to his colleagues, using the public address headphones, explaining that the I.H.R. class was now due to commence, and that the latter had been an alternative to it: anyone who wanted to watch the rest of the video should meet him with a flash disk at the end of the lecture.

My PowerPoint presentation was launched and so was my teaching career as a full-time lecturer. The slide show began with a few formal photos of me and bullet points from my resumé, and then it displayed my first topic, 'What Is Human Rights?' At that point I reached across and stopped it and quietly asked that the projector be turned off. The hall was now completely dark. The students began to murmur. Using my iPad as a torch I groped my way over to one of the blinds and pulled it up. Sunshine fired across the hall and the students shielded their faces.

I had no idea why I was doing what I was doing – bringing the sort of theatricality Wole might have done to my inaugural lecture, perhaps, to ensure I made an impact. It felt crazy – good crazy – and spontaneous. I went from window to window, ensuring that the blinds were pulled up so high they could not be pulled any further. With the flooding in of the light I began to get a rough estimate of what I was up against. *Man, there has to be at least a hundred and fifty students in this hall...* So many bright and beautiful boys and girls seated there watching me intently.

Taking off my tie, I said, 'I want us to form a big circle. Everyone push your desk to the wall.' They stared at me. 'Now!' I ordered. There was puzzled excitement on their faces as they hesitantly got to their feet. I was excited too.

After breaking all the protocols I knew how to – asking them to remove their ties, instructing them not to take any notes – I took my seat in that great circle, a seat that was, as I had intended, no more important than any of the others, between an ebony-skinned young woman and a light-skinned young man. I was in my space and I was alive.

Holding the hands of my new friends on either side of me, I shut my eyes and said a prayer: 'God Almighty, gracious and kind in all things. We come into Your courts unworthy, to ask for the wisdom and blessing to teach and learn. Please inspire our minds to give and receive. Enchant our understandings to grow and connect, even as we look into the matters of today for our tomorrow. Do take pre-eminence, Dear Friend and Father, now and forever, in Jesus' name, amen.'

There were not too many amens. It occurred to me then that we would likely not all be Christians, so I said, 'In God's name we have prayed.' Then the amens gushed in. Now we were all on board.

When I opened my eyes, the hall was silent, the students focused, receptive.

'"We hold this truth to be self-evident",' I began, '"that all men are created equal. That they are endowed by their creator with certain inalienable rights, among these life, liberty and the pursuit of happiness." This is an excerpt from the American Declaration of Human Rights of 1776. At one point in my life that used to be the most beautiful, breath-taking piece of poetry for me. However, I soon came to understand that its aspirations and expectations are often far removed from what is realistic and attainable.' I looked around, and all eyes were on me. 'When I said a prayer, a good number of you said amen. And that was beautiful. Nonetheless, it wasn't complete until we all said amen. Do you agree?' There was murmuring. 'I think it's best we speak one at a time. Yes, you.' I pointed to a girl who had her pen up. 'Please tell us your name first.'

'I'm Amaka,' she said as she stood up.

'Amaka, dear, it's okay to sit down,' I said. One of the other female students coughed loudly. Amaka eyed her.

'Thank you, sir.' She sat. I motioned her to resume speaking. 'I'm Amaka Oriji,' she said. 'Yes. I agree with you.'

'Why is that?'

'Seeing that this is a multi-religious academic environment, full participation by all students in a spiritual activity such as a prayer which is said in class would be more productive than the exclusion of some. This is further inclined towards the respect and recognition of the equality of human beings amongst themselves, and as regards rights and access to dignity and the protection of self-worth.'

Chei! Grammar! I do not think she took one breath in the course of her monologue. And she earned a round of applause.

'Okay,' I said. 'Well put. But I was hoping for something simpler. You.' I pointed at a student who was engrossed in cleaning his spectacles. 'Harry Potter.' Every other student who wore glasses quickly 'de-harrypotterized'. He was tapped by the student seated next to him and looked up.

'Sorry, sir.'

'It's okay,' I said. 'Just tell us whether or not a complete prayer demands us all saying amen to it and why.'

'Okay, I don't necessarily – '

'Your name, please,' I interrupted.

'Oh, okay, my names are Rasheed Daudu, sir.'

'My name is,' I corrected.

'Sorry sir. My name is Rasheed Daudu, sir.'

'Very well. You may proceed.'

'Thank you, sir. The validity or completeness of a prayer is not necessarily contingent on whether it is accepted by everyone who hears it.' He put on his glasses and looked at me. Another round of applause ensued.

'So what then does the completeness or validity of a prayer depend on?' I asked. He went on to say that a prayer is a spiritual exercise that serves as a symbol of what a certain category of people hold dear to themselves as right, proper, holy and spiritually relevant.

'I am a Muslim', he said, 'and how I pray is particular to my religion. However, this does not in any way make the Christian prayer less credible. I still respect it, because it is a means through which a people have chosen to connect with the Almighty God. This is the same connection that we all seek and believe in, regardless of our faiths and other slightly dissimilar expectations.'

I nodded. After Rasheed there was a slight pause and no-one made to speak. But after I said I would award marks to those who made comments, many hands were raised high in the air.

One student said that whether or not everyone says amen is irrelevant. According to the Bible, he said, once at least two people had said amen, God would be okay.

'Choi, pastor!' one of the other boys shouted. I called on him to share his own thoughts.

'Sir, what the Bible actually says is that where two or more are gathered, God is there in their midst. Not when at least two say amen.' The class responded with applause. The 'pastor' rolled his eyes.

'Well, at least the Bible mentions two,' I said in the pastor's defence, and he responded with, 'Exactly.'

Some students talked about how prayers should be said with discipline and timing as they are in Islam, rather than at any time, anywhere and anyhow.

Then I said, 'No-one here has talked about the prayers of the traditional religion.'

I had shocked them. 'You mean juju worship sir?' Amaka asked hesitantly.

'That's what it's called now. But I mean the ancient religion of our origins. The one without the books or sermons or excessive kneeling.'

'But sir,' pastor quizzed, 'how can "winches" and wizards be praying when they are the ones committing all the havoc, and they are even the main people we are praying against?'

'Can anyone attempt a response to that?'

Rasheed raised his hand.

'Well, I don't know much about whether they are allowed to say amen when Christians and Muslims pray together or separately,' he said. 'But I know that they pray. And contrary to what my colleague here said, that they have a now not-so-conventional religious preference does not make them witches and wizards.'

Pastor raised his hand.

'To add to that,' I continued, 'some of them are very interesting and busy people. And I don't think they would have the time to be witches and wizards. Take for instance Professor Akinwade Oluwole Soyinka, the first African and black writer to win the Nobel Prize in literature as far back as 1986.'

'But sir,' Pastor spoke up, 'I thought Wole Soyinka was Catholic.' The whole class roared at him. I raised my hands and managed to instil some peace.

When the class was quiet again I said, 'Wole Soyinka is traditionalist not Catholic.'

We took some other viewpoints before I resumed addressing the class:

'You've all spoken beautifully. Some of you argued that prayers draw their validity from public assent. Others said praying and prayers are too subjective a matter to need to be generally accepted in order to be valid. And for some of us, prayer is a mark of good manners and a pious upbringing – something that says that, no matter how educated or exposed to the wideness of the world we are, we still conform to the family traditions we started with, our core ideals. Nonetheless, we have all come to the understanding that a prayer is for most of us a spiritual exercise and a means of connecting with God.

'Now, it's the same thing with International Human Rights Law: the ideals are, more often than not, removed from the realistic and what is obtainable. And this, my dear friends, is as a result of the different definitions, religions, philosophies, viewpoints, perceptions and inclinations that we have as individuals, and in our lives as a community. Do you understand?'

Referring to the two different religions that we had in class, Islam and Christianity – and the third one, traditional religion, which was still a topic that visibly disconcerted my students – I went on, 'We all want the right things happening to us, connecting with God at every point in our lives. Whether we admit it or not, this is a fact. But there are variances in regard to what this connection would amount to, and even as regards who "God" would amount to. While some of us see Him as a king and superior, others see Him as tender and friendly. Others see Him as too busy to attend to us directly, and believe that He needs the assistance of smaller gods – which we see also in Catholicism, where worshippers ask for the intercession of saints. The same thing applies to International Human Rights Law. The classic description of Human Rights today is that it is the rights that we are entitled to simply because we are human, regardless of what we have done. Obviously being human needs no further description – flesh, blood, breath, and, generally speaking, as we can all get carried away by our passions, rationality. But what then would be the complete expression of rights? What is the "rights" story? What is the meaning of rights? When we say a person has a right, what do we mean? What do you really think that rights are – that is, outside what the classic definition says?' My adrenalin pumped. The floor was open. Hands flagged the air.

'Yes – you?' I pointed to a student who had not yet spoken.

'Rights is what lawyers shout about when they are stopped and detained at roadblocks by the police, especially when their driver's or vehicle documents are incomplete!'

I pointed to another.

'Rights are women's authority to come out and do more

important things with their lives and not to be locked in the kitchen all day cooking egusi soup for a man who eventually complains of too much salt or pepper!'

Pastor said, 'Rights are those things that drive teenagers crazy in America and make them talk to their parents anyhow.'

'Kai pastor,' Rasheed said. 'Have you ever been to America?'

'No. But I watch American films. And the children are always slamming the door on their parents. I even heard that they can call police to arrest their parents if their parents flog them.'

'Sir,' Amaka spoke up, 'Pastor has never crossed the Nigerian border before.' The whole class roared with laughter.

'Stop,' I demanded, raising my voice. 'He is always bold enough to air his views and you make fun of it. Henceforth anyone who laughs at what Pastor says in class, except it's a deliberate joke, will have to answer to me.' Then I smiled. 'That's if he does not mind my calling him Pastor.'

'Pastor is fine, sir. Thank you.'

The class fell quiet then and everyone avoided my eyes. 'You know, we are all here to learn. We all have a right to speak and be listened to. But not when another person will get to feel worse because we want to feel better. Pastor is one of us. Okay?'

'Yes, sir,' they all responded.

Then Rasheed summoned up the courage to speak and, though still avoiding my eyes, said quietly that rights were freedoms that each of us enjoyed, limited by accommodating the freedom of others.

Michael, a plump boy who sat beside Rasheed, shook his head and said, stuttering between words, that rights were really only what the powerful and those in authority permitted us to enjoy, 'after making sure that it does not in any way tamper with their own enjoyment and interests.' Rasheed and a few others clapped.

Someone else said that rights were concessions by others made in favour of one person, and that that person would eventually be expected to return the favour, 'like in a romantic relationship between a boy and a girl.' To which another –

male – student said, 'The boy does the spending, while the girl delivers the merchandise.' The boys in the class applauded thunderously, laughing, and he added, 'You scratch my back and I scratch yours.'

I laughed too. 'Now, now,' I said. I wished Tega were here to hear that. I wondered what she would think. She would probably argue that the statement was sexist and chauvinist, that it was disrespectful of women and equality, and that human rights and the habit of over-sexualising women should never be permitted to sneak into the same room.

As though he had read my mind, a dark, skinny boy with a light voice spoke up, saying that human rights have nothing to with mutuality or what two or more parties think is acceptable or feasible. He said that human rights stemmed from an independent individual's standpoint and what benefited that person.

'What about in Africa,' someone else asked, 'where we are never really just independent individuals, but shoots tightly bound to the roots of our families, society and ancestry?'

The boy who spoke first argued back, saying that, 'Even in a place like Africa, our being bound to our families is not enough justification to deny the individualistic nature of human rights.' He then pulled in the instance of child marriage: 'A girl who is bound to her ancestry as an African, should, by your argument, be compelled to submit to it, whatever it says, however it says it. Even if it says that she is mature enough for conjugal duties at the age of ten.'

'I haven't said that.'

'But by implication you have. Our ancestry and family, and our being bound to that, is part of who we are. But it is definitely not all of who we are enough to expel who are independently, and what we should be allowed to do as a result.'

The largest fraction of the student circle was of the opinion that rights are privileges or gifts, rather than innate; and that they are contingent on general societal approval. Others were of the opinion that rights translated to circumstances that formed, transformed, informed and regulated a certain status quo. Amaka, Rasheed and a few others considered rights as a mechanism designed to preserve and protect a particular human being's dignity, identity and expectations of life up to the point where those of another human being began.

I did my share of listening that day, offering gentle challenges as we went along to the views I found most limited. I was reminded that subjective versions of truth never go out stock. This being the introductory lecture, we only scratched the surface of the subject, talking about the preamble and Chapter IV of the Nigerian Constitution of 1999 (as amended), and what it should mean when set beside the Universal Declaration of Human Rights. And I talked about how human rights protection may be a battle that will never be won, especially with the world as it is.

The talk was so lively that I didn't realise our two hours had flown by until we were interrupted by another lecturer, whose period we had run on into. This was wholly accidental, but to him it was a calculated insult, and, aggrieved, he took it out on all of us. Initially he needed to be convinced that I was not a student, given the way I was dressed. Tall and grey-haired, in a grey suit and grey tie, he was rather harsh in the manner in which he bossed the students around, telling them to put the seats and desks back in their 'proper' places, put their ties back on, lower the blinds and turn the lights back off. It was interesting to watch the room relapse into a morgue, and see my lively students become as inert as dead bodies. I wrote down my contact number and university blog address for the class rep, reminding him it contained my notes and other course-materials for the use of the students, and everything fell back into its former place: 'neat and tidy' in my colleague's eyes – rather too much so in mine.

Since I had overrun my allotted time I would have let his discourteous manner slide, had this same lecturer not made a point of confronting me that evening. Having had a similarly exciting session with the debating society I was in the staff cafeteria, reading my emails, putting my thoughts down for the next day's lecture and soothing my throat with a cool drink when he sat at my table and began to tell me off:

'Good day, son. I know we have not been formally introduced. But you should have been properly oriented that here in K.U. we have quality, discipline and balance. It will be in your best interest to conform to the school's standards. They were set up for the good of the students and also for the benefit of the staff...'

He went on about the importance of the students having their ties properly knotted around their necks while in class. He challenged the 'evil' of allowing them to sit in 'indecent' poses for an academic lecture. He was one of those who had mastered the art of trashing others with verbal put-downs too politely phrased to be challenged. I was planning to applaud him at the end of his long Chinese monologue, but found that I had stopped listening when he stopped making sense. 'Your methods are too distracting for these young minds,' he concluded eventually. 'They just won't do. Please do look before you leap next time, alright?' Then, mustering a smile since I was declining to argue back, he said, 'I am Professor Afolabi. What's your name?'

I said, 'I'm Wale, sir,' shaking his hand.

'Okay. Wale. Nice to meet you,' he said. 'Are those real?'

'Are what real?'

'Your dada? Are they real or extensions?' Now he had a mocking grin on his face.

'They are real,' I said, taking a last gulp of water from my bottle. 'I'm sorry, Professor Afolabi, Wale needs to attend to a few other things before the close of work.'

'Oh, it's okay. Try to get some rest, though. You have a whole year ahead of you.' He laughed pleasantly enough as he stood. I nodded and went back to my emails.

I continued to conduct my lectures in that sweet circle, but to avoid further wahala made sure to conclude and have the seats returned to their 'proper' places before this egoistic silver trophy came in. My students willingly colluded in this small 'cover-up'.

Later that month Professor Brown presided over the first staff meeting of the year. We assembled at the Falcon Arena, a place I had last been in on the day of my convocation. Then rather dilapidated, it had been modernised since, and was now a tinted glass domed amphitheatre jealously guarded by a lush carpet of lawn. Inside it was cool and soothing, with hound-tooth leather seats, a black marble tiled floor, powerful sound and cooling systems, a raised stage and a large white projector screen.

I had hoped to sit quietly and keep to myself, but then I saw 'Silver Trophy' and his comrades – the other aristocrats of Kola University's academia. Of course I greeted him well: 'Oh, good morning Prof.' – while bowing down to tap the tip of my toes, as is customary for us Yorubas. 'How is this thing done?'

'Morning, my boy! How are you?' he said, undoubtedly flattered that I had bowed to him in the full glare of the faculty, with everyone watching. 'Won't you join us?' I bowed courteously to the three other men he was with, who sported similar rimless spectacles and grey beards, and took my place beside him in the seat he gestured me to.

The meeting kicked off shortly before noon. A few administrative issues were discussed, anchored by the administrative secretary and the public relations officer. The latter then announced the four new staff members who had been recruited for the coming academic year: twenty-nine-year-old Professor Daisy Yusuf to the Management Science Faculty; thirty-two-year-old Professor Dennis Okolo to the Faculty of Arts; twenty-seven-year-old Doctor Sandra Timi to the Computer Science Department; and thirty-five-year-old Professor Wale Damian to the Faculty of Law. There was polite applause, then the vice-chancellor, Professor Brown Fatade, stepped up to the podium.

'This is a new age,' he said, 'wherein the future is taking over the present. All of us who are here today are witnessing the arrival of this future. We, of course, stand for established excellence: traditional knowledge, scholarship and teaching practices. Yet at the same time as I expect that these revolutionary young minds should be guided and supported in accordance with that established excellence, I also expect that they should be learned from... Yes, we have quality. We have balance. But the future isn't about just these two. The future demands speed of adaptation and spontaneity. That we rock the boat just a bit; that we stir up the waters to return vigour and life to our journey. The future demands more from us than just hoping that respecting custom will create some miraculously revolutionary effect. So, as the poet says, "Let us play with the white man's ways and work with the black man's brains". Let us embrace this new birth, which is not just a fusion of both approaches, but the potentially explosively productive result of their remarkable union.'

He stopped abruptly. Silence threw a large blanket over the dome. I could not let this slide. I clapped. The non-academic staff joined in, then the new staff, and then, eventually and resentfully, the aristocrats, their faces strait-jacketed with contempt.

A strained expression on his face, Professor Brown Fatade nodded and sat down.

The speech was followed by light cocktail refreshments, during which Brown asked after Wole, about Afrospark, and how we were coping in the new legal – or rather illegal – climate. I told him that we were doing okay, but were having to be considerably more stealthy in our operations now. I felt obligated to say I was hopeful our activities would not bring embarrassment to K.U. Waving this aside, he mentioned that a colleague of his had been arrested in Jos a few days back. He said that he had been reliably informed that the police were conducting a series of medical examinations on him to determine whether he indulged in homosexual acts. My heart skipped a beat as I imagined the kind of 'medical examination' that could supposedly objectively uncover a person's sexuality; how near it would come to rape with a surgical instrument.

I knew that arrests were continuing, and that lists of homosexuals and suspected homosexuals were being compiled all around the country. I also knew that, as well as the usual blackmailers and extortionists, the police were going under cover, often through social media, pretending to be gay, then arresting their unsuspecting victims after they had made the mistake of opening up. Any purely LGBTI-focused NGOs had instantly been forced underground.

The heat was really on, but here at K.U., surrounded by sprawling, manicured lawns and under a cloudless sky, the news sounded like stories from distant lands that could never concern us outside of the academic and largely theoretical discussions we had in class, and online, about what rights and freedoms meant.

I had hoped to catch up with big bros Professor Afolabi and ask him, with seeming innocence, what he made of the Vice-Chancellor's words. However, our paths never seemed to cross much after that day, so I do not think he took Brown's speech too well. On the rare occasions our paths did cross he always seemed to be in a hurry, or was too far away to hear me hailing him.

The demands of my job were a welcome distraction from the fear that haunted me every night when I thought of Afrospark, Craig, Wole, the production of the *Eyimofe* movie, and the new law. I had a great rapport with my students, who on the whole made me optimistic for the future. They would drop countless comments on the blog. I couldn't cope with responding to them exhaustively on a daily basis, so they decided to create their own Facebook group, Gani 14 – named after the late human rights activist Gani Fawehimi, and for the year, 2014 – for I.H.R. They added me into their group chats, and would exchange instant messages all evening, with me dipping in and out of the discussions on my lecture-free days, among my other activities. News of the group spread, and after a while there were more members in Gani 14 than there were students in the I.H.R. class. The debate society was equally fired up by the permission its members felt they had been given to discuss provocative topics. Though they comprised students from all the faculties on campus, most were either from the Faculty of Arts or the Faculty of Law, and they joined Gani 14 too. To the delight of the students Wole and Tega sometimes joined in the discussions – real human rights activists who could share with them how things played out on the ground.

Generally on the Gani 14 page we shared universal re-source location links to sites containing information on such international human rights concerns as were relevant to our coursework. I also made general announcements to the class and the debate society. At some point it seemed to me that my I.H.R. class and the debate society were extensions of

each other, and there was hardly ever a dull – or even silent
– moment for my inbox. My students' minds grew in leaps as
their skill in articulating issues increased; and though they
always obeyed the conventions of proper presentation, they
never flinched from dropping it like it was hot.

The Same Sex (Marriage) Prohibition Act and its implications were, of course, hot topics, and the students stood at
various spectrum frets of the conversation. Some of them
wrote that the Nigerian government was finally doing
something that all citizens agreed with, and as such should
be applauded by the people – and people *were* applauding,
after all. Others pointed out that blanket majority rule could
never pass for democracy; that it was no more legitimate
than mob rule. What about the citizens who thought differ-
ently, they argued, and perhaps more progressively? Did
their views count for nothing? Still others wrote that the law
was God-sent, to prevent Nigeria from incurring more of His
curses. Someone internationally-minded pointed out that
countries that tolerated LGBT people were in the main
prosperous and orderly, and didn't seem 'cursed'. Some
students wrote that it was not a human rights topic at all, but
was simply a consolidation of the state's already-established
stance. This argument was 'blog-lashed' by another student,
who argued that not only this, but also the previous law that
criminalised same-sex relations, were in error, and that the
state had no mandate to decide what was allowed to happen
in people's bedrooms or private lives. 'We have the Constitution and rights,' he wrote. 'Privacy is a very strong element of
our lives as citizens and part of the community. Today it's the
homosexuals. Tomorrow, it could be Christians or tradition-
alists.'

This reaction, with which I, of course, agreed, struck me
powerfully. We are not ruled by the church or the mosque –
and if we were, which of the many conflicting sects or
denominations would lead? We are ruled, at least in theory,
by our respect for diversity; by our constitution. Our rights
are not a majority decision: they are – or should be –
sancrosanct, and beyond the reach of popular opinion and
vote-chasing. The Nigerian anti-gay law is clearly in breach
of this concept. It is ignorant bigotry, and of a piece with the

divisive tribalism that haunts our history and blights our lives.

How could those who framed the law not foresee that it would drain Nigeria of a substantial chunk of our most brilliant dreamers and rainmakers, those of our children, siblings and parents who can afford to migrate to safer spaces elsewhere? I suppose they will happily weather the loss. And as for those who cannot afford to go, they will be crushed by a fear fuelled by hate, as the law intends. LGBTI-focused projects, even those run by civil society groups, have been criminalised, their activities stifled. Our children, the little curious ones whose homes stink with homophobic domination, will have no-one to ask those special questions, and so may grow up making the most terrible, life-scarring mistakes, or end their lives in the heat of their depression, their spirits crushed by a nation that should have celebrated them. To think that most of us have been taught to believe that the ownership of condoms is a mark of indecency and promiscuity rather than of being health conscious!

Worse still, we live in a land where our doctors and nurses are not prepared to handle simple incontinence, or treat STIs without thrusting large chunks of hate gospel down the patient's throat. And the ones who are ready to patiently take up this task have been prohibited by the law from doing so. This is in a land where the population keeps swelling like boiling ofe-ogbono, as do the rates of HIV infection, which left untreated lead to AIDS, to death. And our sexual culture, so secretly diverse and exciting, where gay men have multiple sexual partners then come home to devout and faithful wives who bet their lives that their husbands are 'saints', and so have no reason to negotiate safer sex practices, what of that? What of them? The anti-gay law has recruited ignorant criminals to police policies that are of no benefit to our development as a people.

The Nigerian Human Rights Commission, and people of influence in general, encourage this by their silence. And Teriah Ebah, who has spoken up, has been hushed because he is not part of the LGBTI community. They say he has no business participating in the human rights conversation. Does he have to be gay to understand that an anti-gay law speaks against our constitutional pledge to embrace diversity? Does he have to be gay to understand that this coldly-enacted hatred will finish Nigeria even before she begins? That is, when our law eventually permits – even encourages – public interest litigation.

In the heat of the moment we had a session on basic blogging, conducted by Tega over Skype during one of our lecture periods, and soon my students had stormed WordPress, Blogger, Flickr, Tumblr, creating their own amazing worlds of human rights expressions, descriptions, visions and versions. It was amazing seeing so many blog and vlog links on Gani 14, and all this felt like a wonderful adjunct to the work of Afrospark. To my surprise I found I was having the time of my life.

The blog ideas and posts and debates on the Gani 14 page gave me the opportunity to get to know my students on an informal and sometimes highly personal level. Shielded as we were within the campus community, it didn't strike me then how dangerous all this self-exposure might be for them.

There was one student, Ella, who blogged regularly. A quiet, chubby girl, she was a devout fan of Chimamanda Ngozi Adichie, whose image was her profile picture on Facebook more than half the time. She hardly ever updated her blog without alluding to Adichie, no matter how slightly – and her blog posts always made an interesting read.

One day she came up with this post, which resonated with me:

> I am a twin. My parents say that Emmanuel – my twin brother – and I are two bodies wielding one soul. Is that a good thing? They promised to give us both the best of everything. When we were kids we got the best clothes, shoes and toys. Everything identical – or at least as far as it could be in terms of clothes. However, on our tenth birthday we were taken to a store to pick bicycles of our choice. While Emma – as we fondly call him – went for a black and deep-blue bike, I went for a pink tricycle. The smiles on our faces as we presented our choices dis-

tracted our parents from the fact that, though we were twins, our ideas of what would amount to 'the best of everything' for ourselves would more and more drift away from being identical.

Four years later Emma had resolved to be an aeronautic engineer while I would fantasize about my future radical days in the Nigerian judiciary. Loving us equally, they let us pursue our choice of careers. This, however, was against the advice of our uncles – who insisted that Emma should be a lawyer, while I should settle for something more modest like taking a course in catering. My parents would not accept that and isolated us from our uncles, who would not give up on their stance that girls should not be lawyers or they would intimidate their husbands; and that those who are only sons should not leave their homeland – let alone the continent – as they are custodians of the family tradition.

Shortly before Emma left for Europe to study, we had a picnic – 'we' being the nuclear family – wherein our parents reassured us that they were impressed with our choices and believed that if we both worked hard enough at what we did, we would excel. And when I looked into their eyes I saw happiness, and satisfaction with themselves that they had not stopped keeping their promise: to give us the best of everything, even when that did not mean the same thing to us as to them, to the rest of the family, or even to each other.

Similarly, Nigeria promises to give us the best. The preamble of the Constitution of the Federal Republic of Nigeria provides amongst other things that our state is '**dedicated to the promotion of inter-African solidarity, world peace, international co-operation and understanding**'. I also say that the purpose of our constitution is to promote good government and the welfare of all persons in our country, on the principles of **FREEDOM, EQUALITY and JUSTICE, and for the purpose of CONSOLIDATING THE UNITY OF OUR PEOPLE.**

While I agree that our preamble is a beautiful piece of literature, its implications are heavy, tricky and extremely demanding. This is more so the case if we take it that the preamble should be the standard of regulation for the enforcement of the rest of the constitution. Now, how do we reconcile the various demands of the preamble, varied, confusing and individually difficult and subjective as they are?

In this post, I shall discuss the principles of equality, unity and justice. Shutting my dictionary, I dare to say that equality and unity have identical implications: they imply that the existence of diversity is accepted and highly regarded in the society. Equality indirectly means that diversity is recognized and encouraged: if we were all exactly the same, there would be no need to speak of equality, it would be a given. And unity requires that subjects of diversity are willing to co-exist alongside each other – that is, to accept and respect each other's individuality.

We could say that justice is about bringing the defiant offender to book, but this is only a single story. And the danger of single stories, as explained by Chimamanda Adichie, is that 'they dispossess and they malign... they can break the dignity of a people.' I similarly opine that those who embrace this definition of justice too religiously, strap themselves to the fierce wheel of ignorance, setting themselves up for destruction.

Descriptively, a term such as Justice – derived from the word 'just' – suggests a good, peaceful or a happy ending. A resolution. Ordinarily, this would only happen in fairytales. If it were to translate to a society like Nigeria, we would have to contend with a big question: what would a happy ending mean in the context of a diverse society?

We should recognise that happy endings are not the same thing for our various groups: Christians, Muslims, Igbos, Hausas, Yorubas, students, teachers, employers, employees, dancers, traders, investors, women, men, homosexuals, bisexuals, heterosexuals, transgenders, politicians, activists... even if they all insist on it as our goal.

The question is: Is justice possible, or not?

I believe that my homeland, Nigeria, is as potentially phenomenal as any other place in the world. We only need to trick our hearts to live up to this: the reality is that we can deal with equality and unity even while we embrace justice. We simply have to meet each other halfway. And it is only from that point that we can stretch out to reach the gift of Freedom – the liberty to stay alive in the midst of ourselves and achieve the greatest possibility of living 'in unity and harmony as one indivisible and indissoluble Sovereign Nation under God...' In this light, Nigeria would be keeping her promise to her people, as my parents have kept their promise to me.

I loved Ella's simplicity. To think that she was almost invisible in class. I saw another interesting post, from a fellow student of hers, Isaac Nanigi:

The argument of the Same-Sex Marriage Prohibition Act 2013 is that the Nigerian custom and African tradition is not accepting of same–sex affection and neither has or will ever condone it. But for heaven's sake, there is no such thing as 'the Nigerian custom' – besides the brown-uniformed public servants in charge of exports and imports of goods into Nigeria. Sexuality is neither goods, nor a container, nor a vessel. It cannot genuinely be bought or sold by humans, nor can it be given or taken away.

There is also no such thing as 'the African tradition', because Africa does not have 'the tradition' to say that it is the original, only or objective one. What is to say that African loins or hearts cannot naturally churn same-sex attractions, or non-conforming genitals or gender expressions?

Africa means us, the beautiful diverse realities that

should have a common ground of tolerance, and just tolerance. Beautiful realities like those of the Azande people of Sudan whose ancient male warriors sought the affection of male lovers because the affection of their wives would neutralise their potency for battle; the Pangue tribe of Cameroun, where same-sex affection is an ancient tested and trusted charm for wealth creation; the Zvekumombe practice of teenage Zimbabwean shepherd boys who sought each others' affection in the cold fields beneath the night's stars; the 2000 year old painting of two male lovers sitting in the public glare of the Zimbabwean state.

Africa means me, and the several interesting and diverse possibilities that I may want to explore academically, spiritually, financially, socially, emotionally, and more fiercely, sexually, when, how and with whom I may want to explore them.

Africa also means us, the little strands of hair that can't make it neatly into the kinky bun. The realities and practices that are common and widespread, yet secret and untalked about.

Of course not all my students were progressive, and not all were deep thinkers. It would be unrealistic of me to go on without making mention of a few of the other, more boisterous ones: Camilla Tonye and her like. They too were full of opinions, and intelligent, but their ways of refusing to knuckle under to the ways of the authorities were rather different. They taught me how impatient I could be; indeed at times, how old-fashioned.

One morning I bumped into Camilla on my way to class. I was driving in. It was lecture hours, yet she seemed to be heading out of the campus, and was dressed in indecently tight and too-revealing clothing. I wound down my window and called out to her, but she did not respond. So I pulled up, got out and stalked up to her.

'Why are you dressed like this, and where are you going to?' I asked sternly, disgusted by the loud crackling noise made by the bubble-gum she was chewing.

'I'm not in your lecture hall, so why do you care?' she said rudely.

'Now, you look here, miss,' I said, raising my voice and deliberately creating a scene. 'This is K.U. and I am responsible for my students. And hell, yeah, I am responsible for you whether or not you are in my lecture hall.' The bubble gum froze in her mouth. 'You have absolutely no business skipping lectures, and definitely no businesss being dressed in this despicable outfit.'

'S-sir... sir... I was just go-go-going to the bank,' she stammered.

'Dressed like that?' I snapped. 'I don't even want to know. I am going to your class now, and I want to see you there in seven minutes dressed like a lawyer in training.'

Pushing down tears, she hurried back to her student accommodation and changed, made it to the class only a few minutes late, and hardly ever missed my lectures again.

Despite these sorts of small dramas it is fair to say that at this point these students rocked my world.

I considered it deadening to the mind to dictate my lectures from 'immemorial and priceless academic bibles' brown and stale with age and dust, as was the tradition for a good few of the academic aristocrats at K.U., some of whom still insisted that computers and PowerPoint presentations were the Anti-Christ; while others simply converted the brown notes into unrevised on-screen copy. My methods gave me more time than other lecturers to finish my academic outline and revise thoroughly with my students before the first semester exams kicked off in April. This was crucial: my radical approach had to be seen to yield traditional results, or it would be impossible to defend.

In accordance with the K.U. tradition, at the end of my final lecture of the term, before the beginning of the exam season, I held hands with my students and said a prayer with them.

They then had a week for private revision. Having submitted my exam questions to the Exams and Records Department, and with no more lecturing to be done, I was free to spend more time in my room attending to my rather neglected private life.

After months of both of us being strapped to our very different, but equally consuming, worlds of work, Tega and I were now back on Skype most evenings. Though she was still dedicated to the Afrospark Project, she said it had come to feel more and more like a spy job. By nature a forthright and open person, having to always speak over the phone in code, and be more discreet amongst her friends than she had had to be before, was wearing her down. And from what she was saying it seemed that Lola's commitment was waning fast: she kept dwelling on the recurring arrests of suspected homosexuals, and of staff members of LGBTI rights-focused organisations, and on how humiliating and frightening it would be to be arrested. Wole kept reminding her that Afrospark is a *human* rights-focused organisation, and as such she should not be so worried, but we all knew that provided only a limited insulation. In truth we relied far more on Brother Gbenro's high standing within the State Security Service for protection than on our maintenance of a fine distinction between 'pro-LGBTI' and 'pro-human-rights-including-LGBTI'.

Wole, meanwhile, was going through his own dramas. He sent me an email on the morning of S[t] Valentine's Day that seemed to me painfully confused:

Dear Wale,

I trust that things are going smoothly for you at school. Skipping the formals, I'll just get to it...

Today is S[t.] Valentine's Day, and I will be unreach-able most of the time because Lola insists that I give her my all today. I can neither be in the office nor take any calls. We will be at her place doing a list of things she has already planned out. And hey! We are wearing matching pink T-shirts today. Pink is her favourite colour, and our couple theme for the day.

But Wale, I'm scared.

Lola is my friend, my sister. There is never a dull moment with her. I look forward to seeing her every day because she is open to me. She is not afraid of being a little girl in my arms. I love her so much for that. She is playful, exciting and adventurous. When she is playing lawyer in the office she is, yes, I can say this, sexy. When she is enraged, she is so beautiful. Whenever she smiles, it's like time stops for me. We have our moments, and I truly wish they would last forever.

We are now only a few months away from our wedding and till now you and I have stuck to our decision not to let the girls know about our sexualities. Then again, I am realising how increasingly homophobic Lola is. By the day she makes it clearer to me that both the film and the Save the Colours *project for her is just business. 'I believe that everyone has a right,' she always tells me, 'and so I have the right to what I like and what I don't.' One would have expected that her support for the fight against gender discrimination would endear her to LGBT issues, but it hasn't.*

I don't want to fight her any more on this issue, so I'm willing to hold my peace for now. But we need to have this conversation soon, Lola and I. Whether or not homosexuality is something she can live with for the rest of her life. She is still in the dark about me never having wanted to be with a woman, and I'm very anxious about our wedding night. I can get all up on her with my eyes closed, visualising Tayo or Akon, but I'm never really aroused long enough to unbuckle my belt. It's really shameful. But I keep trying. I can't walk away now.

I am strong, regardless, and getting set to have a lovely Val's day. Too bad you have to make do with cam calls with Tega for now.

I miss you. Tega misses you. She is such a wonderful person. She's always here for me when Lola has one of her crazy sessions. I am glad we are keeping her. I always tell her that someday I would pretend to be you and run away with her, and she laughs.

Please come home soon. It's never the same without you.

I love you sir. Don't ever forget this.

Your Brother,

Wole

Ogbeni, Listen

If bones will rise
So will truth
And life, breath
And your godly fruit
If truth be told
So should you
And this gift of life
And time given you
If you will speak
They will listen
To your time, Ogbeni
Your lesson:
Don't be still
Don't be missing
Release your soul
Be the reason.

Eyimofe/The One I Love

O nce our marriage plans were announced and the invitations were sent out, I received two replies from faraway friends, Ahmed and Kwame.

From: ahmed@sugarbooks.com
To: waledamian@damianbros.com

Dear Wale,

I'm so thrilled that you guys decided to make Save the Colours *part of your joint wedding celebration and vice versa. It will be so colourful an event, especially now that it is being held in Kola University. There is quite a buzz here in the Netherlands about the* Eyimofe *feature-film which shall be premiering at the event also, especially after the many production difficulties you have shared with me. It will be so exciting to finally see some home-grown material that is objective, academic, spiritual and yet realistic on the issues of sexuality and sexual identity.*

Come August, all roads lead to K. U. – for the first time in years I will be in Nigeria. Really, I can't wait to see the Damian twins for the first time, live!

OMG, Wale, I have so much I want to say and ask you in person. Yeah, yeah, cam chats are great, but nothing beats a nice warm teddy-bear hug and firm handshake.

> *Keep it real bro.*
>
> *Excited!*
>
> *Ahmed*

From: kwame@kwame.com
To: waledamian@damianbros.com

Dear Wale,

I almost gave up on ever seeing you or Nigeria again. Often I wanted to reach out to you, but given the circumstances under which we parted ways, I thought it better not to. I was under the impression that you had deliberately kept your distance. I was, I have to say, shocked by your invitation.

I feel honoured that you deem me worthy to speak alongside the remarkable individuals you listed at the Save the Colours *event. This is more so as it borders on issues of sexuality and sexual identity. However, I must confess to you that I have never been so sure of what to say, or not to say, as regards these two delicate topics. But I promise to give my best. I shall also have rounded off my Law degree programme by then. What better way to celebrate it than to be in the company and at the wedding ceremony of the Damian twins? Lola and Tega are the luckiest girls in world for bagging men of your calibre. And I wish you both all the stamina in the world.*

Had I known you were not mad at me, I would have written earlier. I have so much to tell you.

I have come out to my family. I came out to my parents first. My dad has not said much to me since then, asides from when he insisted that I take a HIV test in his friend's hospital the following day. I came out negative. My mum has been moody. She now reads her Bible more and attends church services more. My dad told my siblings after the test results came out, but he maintained that it was a family secret, so we don't talk about it. I proceed to the United States for further studies shortly after I have honoured your invitation in Nigeria. When I told my parents about you and your brother and the weddings, they were happy. They believe that this shall be an equally remarkable experience for me as regards my career and the journey towards maturity. I suspect they also hope your wedding will be an inspiration to me to consider getting married to a girl some day. I don't think so.

Then again, I respect Wole for taking this bold step into matrimony in spite of, well, what can I say?

Anyhoo, I shall get to work immediately on my presentation. It shall not be easy combining this with preparations for my exams. But hey! It's all part of the experience.

When our paths crossed before, I thought God loved me. But our paths crossing again? He can't deny being madly in love with me – neither can I with Him...

God keep you,

Kwame

I knotted a white bow-tie about my brother's neck and hoped that I looked half as handsome as he did. He brushed a speck of lint from my lapel with his fingertip, and nodded his approval.

We rode, together with our best men, Tayo and Kwame, in the first of a convoy of five cars, flanked by two power-bike riders. Wole insisted on driving. Tayo sat beside him. I sat in the back with Kwame. He placed his palm on mine and squeezed gently. I squeezed back, and we held hands while looking away from each other and out at the passing scene. It was the final day of the *Save the Colours* show, and the perfect morning for a wedding – save that a little too much of what had happened in the last couple of days had been unanticipated, and everyone was still a bit startled. And even after all that, Wole preferred to feign oblivion. He was in high spirits, undaunted.

So much had stormed the week.

After hours of at times heated debate we had been permitted to host *Save the Colours* on campus. 'I believe that this will broaden the minds of both the student and staff bodies,' Professor Brown declared during the board of trustees meeting, to which I had been invited in order to shed more light on the concept behind the show.

'I quite agree,' said Professor Ibinabo, head of the Arts Faculty. 'The past few months have really seen hell as regards these gay rights. You know, to address them as though they are a different niche of rights is misleading. Human rights are human rights whether they belong to Christians, Muslims, blacks, whites, lesbians, gays, children, women, boys... they are simply rights, and they should be respected, or else our so-called democracy becomes even more of a façade than it already is.'

Every time the word 'gay' was mentioned, I noticed that one of the trustees pursed her lips and hunched her shoulders in disgust. Several of the others looked embarrassed that the subject was on the table. Yet everyone listened courteously. Professor Brown darted a glance at me every now and then.

'I don't quite agree,' Professor Hussein spoke up. 'Our democracy has almost nothing to do with this. I believe that the better part of Nigeria simply does not know enough to decide wisely. Even the Bible says that the people perish for lack of knowledge.'

'Yet is it not precisely events such as these, that are a bit daring, that help impart the knowledge people lack?' said Professor Ibinabo.

'The main issue here,' Dr. Onoja of the Sociology department chimed in, 'is whether such an event supports our vision as an institution. And that's a bit dicey because our own personal visions are not the things that are, on the balance, necessarily the vision of the school. The school has only recently been privatised, and so much attention is on

K.U. now. A wrong move may put us in a very bad spot. This isn't – let us be honest and face facts here – just about artistic freedoms or freewheeling academic debates. This is really a celebration of homosexuality and bisexuality – intense criticism of which is the only point of confluence for the rest of Nigeria – besides Lokoja and soccer.'

This last remark drew a little laughter.

'We have to be mindful also,' Professor Hussein said, 'of the kind of impression we give to both the sponsors and the parents of our students.'

'And I'm wondering,' Professor Ibinabo said, 'why engaging the students actively in positively productive activities of this class, and boosting their chances of making good contacts nationally and even internationally, should give the parents a bad impression of this institution.'

A sometimes irritable individualist, Ibinabo had been an unexpected ally in my struggle to get this event to happen. However, at this point two trustees opined in unison that the substance of *Save the Colours* was contrary to our traditions and culture as Africans. And that in fact we should actively discourage such indecency amongst students and ourselves.

'What do you mean by "indecency"?' Professor Ibinabo shot back. 'What is indecent about seeing a feature film that is clearly so accomplished that its script won the Kaka Foundation Grant? What is indecent about talking about these things that are clearly already very much part of our lives and this school, and that bother us?'

Another trustee spoke up sharply: 'Perversion is not part of our school.'

'Perversion?' Professor Ibinabo asked.

'This western idea of men sleeping with men, and women sleeping with women. And the worst of it all, making it an issue for discussion!'

'We might as well discuss pornography and masturbation,' her neighbour added in an outraged tone.

'And we should too,' Professor Ibinabo said. 'Look. There is really nothing perverse about having an intellectual or academic conversation. Whether the sexual act itself is wrong or right is for God to judge.'

'Well.' Doctor Kemi, who had been thumbing through the

proposal quietly, spoke up now. 'Looking at the fabulous and high-ranking endorsements it has gained, I'm certain that this project is a big deal. Besides, everyone has been going on and on about in on Facebook and Twitter already. It'd be shame if we can't tap into all that enthusiasm and publicity.'

At the mention of the endorsements everyone went back to their own copies of the proposal. Soon they began nodding amongst themselves.

Doctor Shola, another quiet faculty member, said that the fact was that the school could encourage a conversation about sexual orientation and gender identity without taking sides.

Professor Amarachi, the trustee who could not stand 'gay', whose shoulder-pads jutted out like airplane propellers, and whose head was wrapped in thick, navy-blue velvet which must have been fifty yards long, finally spoke up. 'Look, I don't know what you are all saying about endorsements. Endorsement or no endorsement, I will not be party to this show of shame. Can't we just avoid this wahala? Ehhh... Chineke! Nigeria is hot now o! Why can't they take their human rights programme wahala somewhere else? Does Amara not have a very good cinema and very good halls? Then let them go there with this.' In summary, she argued that her Christian faith did not permit her, nor, she was sure, anyone else, to even talk about the evil of homosexuality, never mind homosexuals being entitled to anything but condemnation. 'Flee all the appearances of evil!' she concluded.

Some of the other trustees murmured amens.

I wanted to argue that the true Christian also embraces everyone, regardless of who they are and what else they believe, as long as they accept Christ as the Messiah and Saviour; that Jesus consorted with sinners; that He told us not to cast the first stone; to judge not lest we be judged.

I wanted to tell her that she had no right to call *Save the Colours* a show of shame – a project that had drained so much energy from my life, and that stood for everything I believed in as a lawyer: human rights, equality, and inclusion under the law. Above all, I kept wanting to tell her that her headwrap was the size of Lagos, and that perhaps it had overheated her brain. I thought of other, more creatively vicious statements as the meeting plodded on. I jotted them down to vent to Wole when I told him about it that night.

Thankfully Professor Ibinabo liked Professor Amarachi no more than I did. He said, 'Our duly-constituted government, in framing, debating and passing the Anti-Gay Marriage law, as it is popularly known, did a lot of discussing of homosexuality, as have our newspapers, and of course it is debated endlessly online. Goodness knows our religious leaders have said a great deal about it. The cat is out of the bag, Professor Amarachi. I think it is better to discuss these things responsibly than leave our students to discuss them, as they are surely doing already, without guidance.'

At the end of the day it was thrown to a vote and *Save the Colours* won by a modest margin.

'I'm glad we can agree that Professor Wale's project is a step in the right direction and should be supported by the institution,' Professor Brown said in conclusion. 'And since it's in August, we could pull the convocation ceremony a little closer so that everything is run and concluded within the same week. In that way we could also make time to attend "Uncle" Professor Wale's wedding.' Professor Amarachi pursed her lips and eyed me coldly. I smiled back graciously: I had won – that round, at least.

Professor Brown invited me to dinner that evening at his place, where he introduced me to James Fela, a blogger and alumnus of K.U. who had been the best graduating law student of his set. He had been commissioned by the school authorities to chronicle the transformation of K.U., and make progress reports on the success of those K.U. alumni who were excelling in diverse fields of work. He had followed the Tani Cross story in detail, spoke intelligently about the intricacies of the case, and offered a shrewd analysis of what the various Nigerian newspapers had written about it. He was excited about *Save the Colours*, and seemed pleased that we were getting married soon after. He was happy, he said in a rare moment of tactlessness, that it meant the rumours of Wole and me being homosexuals would stop, adding perceptively, 'It's important for minority rights that those advocating for them aren't always members of that minority.

Otherwise it can be dismissed as mere self-interest.'

Once the meeting was over, and after I had agreed the dates formally with Professor Brown, I called the team back in Port Harcourt. Wole was excited, and he and I agreed to move the wedding service to the Campus Pentecostal Fellowship.

'What?!' Lola screamed when she first heard of this.

That was wahala. *Save the Colours* might as well take my place as Wole's bride, she must have thought. He had to pacify her all through the flight to Amara, Tega told me when we were alone together: talking, joking, cuddling... and still her frown did not in the least tilt, never mind turn upside-down. Tega herself had hardly jumped at the idea, having already approached the pastor of the church she attended in Port Harcourt, which was where most of her friends and many members of her family lived. She too had lashed out verbally when she was told – or so Wole told me later – but had cooled by the time she and I spoke about it, perhaps because Lola was being so histrionic it left her no room to be dramatic.

The fliers and handbills for *Save the Colours* landed, and with the help of the students from the debate team they were pinned up on every notice-board in every building in the school, and given to students who visited the library as they left.

I collected Wole, Tega and Lola from the airport. Tega hugged me so warmly I felt I had won some lottery. We drove to the hotel in Amara where they would be staying, and Lola, who had by then, it seemed, decided to be both professional and a model supportive wife-to-be, held Wole's hand all through our discussion of everything that was going to happen, soothing him with pep-talk when the pressure of all the endless organising and co-ordination got too unbearable: 'Wole, we can do this. We are all in this together.'

It was a relief. But when Tega and I got some private time together over dinner, I asked how come she and Lola were acting so nicely when I had been given the impression that they were mad at the hastily-changed arrangement.

'Nicely ke? There is nothing nice about this o. The only reason we are calm is because we all worked so hard on this

Colours kini.'
   '*Save the Colours.*'
   'Whatever. We still plan to get back at you guys for this horrible, horrible arrangement.'
   'Plan abi?' I asked.
   'Yes o,' she said, sipping from her straw and smiling to herself.
   'No be Naija we dey. No worry.'
   'I'm not bluffing.'

Mum, who had flown into the country several days before, arrived at Amara, as did our many guests and sponsors from the United Kingdom, United States, and other parts of Africa and Nigeria. These ranged from private individuals to representatives of international corporations and NGOs, movie-stars, authors, undergraduates, doctoral students and academics. They were received excitedly at the airport by student delegates from Kola University – it was, after all, their convocation week, and the publicity had blown up nationally: Ebony Life TV had caught it, and so a substantial swathe of Africa knew something about the upcoming events. Dignitaries from throughout the country would be coming to grace the graduation of their children and relatives, and so would other parents and guardians, many of them persons of wealth and standing. *Save the Colours* was planned in such a way that the fliers and advertisements in the national and pan-African papers, on the television stations and in the media, made it appear to the public as if it was the theme of the convocation. Of course there was no one definition of 'Save the Colours': the promotion spoke mostly of exploring human rights issues. Those students who might well have been uncomfortable with aspects of our event were delighted by the calibre of those who would be associated with their convocation as a consequence of it.
   Nonetheless, security was tight. We had received many unpleasant anonymous calls, along with warning signals from highly-placed and sympathetic government officials, pastors, administrators from other universities, and concerned private individuals who had heard rumours: they all came pouring in, getting more intense as the week of the

event drew closer.

In addition to the regular – and, I was relieved to be able to say, efficient – security system on campus, Brother Gbenro had arranged for some mobile police security to support us. Some were allocated to the hotels where our guests were lodged; the others were positioned strategically around the campus. After a tense meeting with the Vice-Chancellor, at which he suddenly worried it might be better the event not take place, it was agreed that the extra security were to be fully armed.

It was seven p.m. Over in Amara it was dark, but the campus was well-lit. The atmosphere was peaceful. Here and there were parents sharing moments with their children, while others strolled down the main road that curved through the grounds, some holding hands: former students, perhaps, revisiting the years of their early love. Wandering guests took pictures of themselves and had brief chats with the students and staff they ran into; cars gently cruised by; graduating students walked the paths in groups of two, three, four, discussing animatedly whatever session had just gone by.

It was otherwise a typical evening at K.U., save that the lecturers had not retired to their lodges as they usually would. Instead they could still be spotted on the sit-outs, in the foyers of the eateries, and by the roadside, engrossed in conversations with the parents of their students and other guests. They could be seen seated in their vehicles, all four doors flung open to let the fresh air in, enjoying the K.U. space, and the anticipation of the approaching unknown. I too was enjoying the energy building in K.U. A slight breeze embraced me, running its fingers through my hair. It was the eve of the kick-off of *Save the Colours* and I walked the paths of K.U. proud of my brother and myself, and Tega and Lola.

I met Wole and Mum at the Falcon Arena. Mum was still sultry, slender and beautiful, but her hair was kinky and afro now. She wore her contacts less, and her glasses more. Her smile seemed to me more and more like Baba's, and a little less like Genevieve Nnaji's. Baba had passed in our final year on campus, a year after Maami.

Lola and Tega were already there, in the depths of discussions with the technical crew and organisers – there are always a million last-minute problems to sort out, however slick the façade of an event. They were clad, like twin sisters, in blue jeans and white pinstripe blouses, their long Brazilian hair extensions oscillating behind them. Twins for twins...

'Such sweet ladies. You don't get them like this anywhere in the world. Black is beautiful,' Mum said, and seeing them then, gesticulating passionately, furrowing their brows in displeasure then laughing freely, I could not have agreed more.

Though white lights blazed above us, the hall was cool. Posters from our many sponsors were mounted on boards and stood on display around the entrance. Silk rainbow ribbons ran in pairs down the edges of each of the four black-carpeted aisles, tactful international symbols of Gay Pride. The hall dazzled in black, white and rainbow. Beautiful.

I thought to myself how a thing as simple as a rainbow could stand as a symbol for the most complex things. I thought of love, mercy, forgiveness, grace; limitedness and, simultaneously, limitlessness. I thought of the beauty of the world and of God, and how great His mind must be to have willed such a beauty into being. And how the rainbow would go on for centuries and centuries, yielding so much meaning to all those who could identify with it.

('Hot pink,' Wole said after I had made him promise to at least keep the rainbows out of our wedding, under the circumstances, stood for 'sexuality, everything inexplicable but true that pulls us closer to each other and away from everything else. Red: the life that lustres and leaks second by second, each one a chance to embrace, deny, live or die. Orange: our healing, the resilience that God affords us that we may do all we should and can, loving, loving and healing when there is no-one to hold our hand. Yellow: the sunrise and the proof and symbol of God, something, someplace more beautiful and real than the pain and pleasure of the passing time and life's short phase. Green: the large carpet of big questions that spreads over the earth and sustains it, giving, and giving life, in ways more special than one. Turquoise: the sparkles of art, beauty, speed, magic, love, bliss, and the wonders that we can neither help feeling,

control or avoid. Blue: the peace, silence and control that
makes a shell over all that is, was and will be, giving us all
the gifts of our future and right now. Violet: the energy that
runs from side to side, from the top to the bottom and back
to the top again, belonging to no-one completely, but held in
trust by us, for us, from God.' Whatever you say bro, just
keep those ties out of my wedding.)

My phone rang: one of the trustees. I answered and Mum
went over to chat to the girls.

They were engrossed in conversation, and I was wrangling about the special arrangements we had made for the
delegates of other universities, who turned out to have been
booked into a more exorbitant hotel than the one we had
budgeted for, when I caught sight of Wole leaning heavily on
a wall and sucking on his inhaler. I excused myself from the
call and hurried over to him.

'What's up, man?' I asked, guiding him to a seat.

'I don't know o,' he said wheezily. 'I guess it's just the
stress.'

'Stress ke? Which stress be that one? You have been carrying on so well before this morning. Wetin dey happen?'

'Okay... yawa fit gas this week o,' he said.

'How?'

'You know we receive abusive and harassing calls at the
office all the time, the more so since the new law. You even
got some yourself here. Now, as though the ones from the
"top guys" are not bad enough, since morning I have been
receiving anonymous threat calls on my personal mobile. She
started calling a few months ago – '

'She?'

'Yes. She says I have something that belongs to her. She
says she would ruin me before I ruin her marriage.'

'Are you seeing anyone other than Lola?' I asked. Then,
lowering my voice: 'Do I know him? Is he from the Rainbow
Talk? Cos if you are, then you shouldn't – '

'Wale, chill.' He flapped his hand at me. 'Are you going to
listen or not?'

'Oya, sorry, go on.'

'I am very faithful to Lola. I will not hurt her. To start off
with I was finding this all so amusing because even before

Lola I never encouraged any married man. I just cannot stand men who know they are not ready for the commitment of marriage but take the vows anyway.'

When he said that I gave him a look to see if he was somehow joking, but he didn't seem to be.

'This mystery chick is so full of adrenalin sometimes,' he went on. 'I thought it was some sort of prank by one of my friends until she started crying in the course of her ranting. Then I thought, well, she is crazy. After that I felt it was safer to reject her calls. But she began calling from so many other numbers, and with all this organising I can't just ignore a number because it's unfamiliar. Omo I tire o. Anyway, the koko now is that she called to say that she has had it with me and that she is coming after me.'

'What did she mean by that?' I asked.

'It beats me. And I have absolutely no idea who she is.'

'Did she talk of anything save for her marriage?'

'At all, brother mi. I offered to send her an invitation via mail but, no surprise, she would neither give me her residential address nor even her email address.' He cupped his head in his palms. 'For the first time since I began this, I have this feel. I am afraid. My heart jolts as though someone is about to get hurt. I just wish I could place my finger on who it is. I... I...'

He was wheezing again. 'Hey, hey, hush,' I said. 'It's okay. Remember when Harvey Milk was about to give that speech and he was threatened?'

'Yeah,' he mumbled.

'What happened?' I asked, putting my arms around his shoulders.

'He called their bluff.'

'And what happened after the speech?'

'Nothing.'

'Look, nothing good comes easy. Great men always have great stories to tell.'

'So I'm a great man?'

I smiled and shrugged.

Monday began with the opening ceremony and the premiere of *Eyimofe*, our feature film. The red carpet was anchored by the Afrospark Media Department K.U., represented by three incredibly hardworking student volunteers, foremost of whom, to my delight, was Ella, the Chimamanda fan from my I.H.R. class. Paparazzi, magazine feature writers, international news houses, bloggers and publicity officials from Abuja, Lagos, Calabar and Enugu were present. Even Ebony Life TV was rocking the red carpet in that Africana-fab style of theirs – I hoped they would feature us on *EL Now* – and I looked out for Denrele Edun, one of the few media personalities capable of setting an event on fire. To my great relief *Save the Colours* was being seen not as a despicably pro-gay event, but as a test-case for artistic and academic freedoms in the face of a government that was increasingly keen to pander to the most vulgar and oppressive aspects of popular sentiment and religious fundamentalism. K.U. as a private institution was not reliant on direct government patronage, and that gave us a certain freedom. It had already been remarked on that we had invited no government ministers to attend.

Save the Colours would be broadcasting the events for the rest of the week via our YouTube channel.

I had never seen so many people troop into K.U., yet nonetheless that evening all seemed calm, save for the soft hum of speech as they made their way into the amphitheatre. I stood at the entrance with some of our more enthusiastic students to welcome guests and hand out popcorn and soft drinks. Shaking hands, saying hello, welcome to K.U., we are happy to have you here, being warm generally – normally reserved outside a teaching setting, tonight I was someone else, and it felt good. I wished I could stand there forever and that people would never stop coming in. Every handshake differed. Some were impersonal and brusque. Others were soft and embracing. Firm and serious ones came every now and then. And then there were the ones that came with a lingering locking of the eyes and a smile. Some of these were strangers, though I recognised a few men from the Rainbow Talk meetings. Those I pulled into a hug or gave a fist bump.

Danjuma – Iska – came in the company of Tani Cross and his family. He received a brief handshake and nod of acknowledgement. Tani was now looking well, and was smartly turned-out, and managed a smile as he and his parents got hugs from some of our student organisers, who knew the case, and my part in it, well. His father, who I had never met before, stood by him, looking awkward in a sharp suit, his hand on Tani's shoulder. I was pleased that he had come round to supporting his son to the point of attending our public and high-profile event.

Kwame appeared, looking handsome. He gave me a hug, and made sure he shook the hands of all the students who stood with me before he went in. Interestingly I got warm handshakes and smiles from a number of very straight-acting and very beautiful men, who looked deep into my eyes while introducing the organisations/sponsors they were representing – the kind of looks that could give any unyielding target a fever. Wahala.

Lola drew me aside, looking annoyed: she had just got an email from Apple Cards, a smallish printer we were using because they were based in Amara, saying that our souvenir brochures would be arriving late owing to some in-house logistical problems. She had called them angrily on receiving this message, and they were making light of it, she suspected because she was a woman. I had to step outside and speak with them, and threaten that if the brochures did not arrive within the hour we would arrange for Plan B – which included getting the police to shake them a little before sundown. Perhaps more effectively, I said we would not pay for the brochures if they did not arrive in time. They promised to rush them over by express courier. Courier ko, carrot ni.

Tega, meanwhile, was in the control room with Craig and the technical crew, shuttling between updating the Afrospark Facebook community page and monitoring the blogs, Twitter feeds and websites of those whose representatives we had invited. She now buzzed me to report that the delegate of *X-blazzer* online magazine, who should have arrived the day before, had called to say that her editor would not pay her flight. I suggested that we paid, but Tega did not buy the idea.

'Lola and I have been pleading with her to raise awareness on their website for weeks, to no avail. She just wants the free flight, and Afrospark needs all the money it can save now. We are getting super online coverage anyway. I'd rather we lay her off.'

'Do what you have to do, babes.'

'How are things out there?'

'Everything is fab. I think we'll have a packed house for the screening.'

I ended the call and returned to the venue. The last few attendees were straggling in. I followed them. Across a now almost fully occupied Falcon Arena I saw Wole shaking hands with the delegates from the Kaka Foundation, who sat in the front row along with some of the trustees of K.U. Just then Craig announced from the control room that the movie would begin in five minutes, and advised everyone to please be seated and turn their mobile phones to silent. He was extremely nervous, and had asked that we not introduce him to the audience before the film. 'If they like it, you can bring me up afterwards,' he said, grinning sweatily. 'If they hate it, I'll slip out the back way and run!'

Wole and I took up our positions on either side of the stage, and awaited our cue. The lights dimmed, then went out. I removed my glasses and tucked them in my breast pocket. A hush fell over the auditorium. Audible from behind the arena was the sound of two generators chugging mutedly: we were determined not to be sabotaged by a sudden loss of power.

Two spotlights came on.

Dressed alike in blue jeans and white button-up shirts, we stepped into them. Alternating sentence by sentence we introduced ourselves, welcomed the guests and the sponsors, and praised our alma mater for hosting the screening. When Wole introduced the film he said that it was not just another chapter in Nigeria's history book, and I added, 'It's painfully, however, one of the most colourful.'

On cue the spotlights snapped off, and the auditorium was plunged into darkness. As Wole and I slipped into our seats a light but masculine voice announced over the speakers, 'Eyimofe, I'm scared.' Rattling drum beats followed as the screen gradually turned white, displaying 'EYIMOFE' in block letters, subtitled 'An African Gay Story'. Someone who was sitting behind me said, 'Blood of Jesus!' and my heart sank: we had debated this subtitle for hours, eventually committing to boldness. Had that been a fatal mistake? Another person said, 'Chei!' Someone else said, 'Tufiakwa,' snapped her fingers, got up from her seat and made her large-bottomed way clumsily and ostentatiously along the row in the middle of which she had been sitting, up the aisle and out of the hall. I prayed that no-one else would leave; that people would not walk out en masse.

The drum beats got faster and louder – I was pleased with the density of the bass: Tega had told me that sound quality had been another subject of much heated wrangling in post-production – and the title text exploded into tiny CGI fireflies. This was as new to me as to the rest of the audience: though I had been on set at various points during filming, due to my job at K.U. I hadn't been directly involved in 'post' – the shot-by-shot editing of scenes, the adding of music and credits, the picture-grading and so on. Wole had sent me vague assurances over the months that things were going well, but no more than that. Now I was kicking myself for not having watched even a rough cut ahead of time. I had attempted to at one point, but at first could not get the Vimeo account to open, and was then defeated by K.U.'s WiFi's modest download capacity. Now I wondered uneasily how the more intimate moments, which of course I had read in the script, but had forgotten about amidst so many other worries, would be handled, and how the audience would respond.

To my relief, after the initial flurry, no-one else walked out. Most of the invited and international guests were either progressive or actually LGBT themselves; and I think our students were enjoying taking part in something that was provocative and rebellious, but was supported by the institution, and happening on the comparatively safe terrain of the K.U. campus.

I glanced at Wole, who was sitting beside me. He was gazing up at the screen entranced, his face lit up by its reflected brightness. All I could do was imitate him. I settled back in my seat and tried to relax and enjoy the screening.

I wholly failed.

Eyimofe opens with a lengthy single shot of a man walk-

ing on the side of a very busy expressway in slow motion
while other people and vehicles scurry by in the opposite
direction. He is weary and preoccupied, too busy to notice
the people who occasionally bump into him, and the bus that
speeds past, splashing mud over his white jalabi. 'A happy
accident,' I recalled Lola saying of that unscripted moment:
'The bus just happened to pass by and hit a pot-hole on cue!'

The man is Prince Haleem, a slender, dark and strikingly
handsome man who we will discover later is a successful
entrepreneur.

The actor playing Prince Haleem, James Konteh, is Ken-
yan, and looks much thinner in person, as I had seen half an
hour earlier, when he walked in escorting an extremely
pretty young woman who had a minor role in the film. She
too was slight, but on screen appeared pleasingly full-
figured. The camera really does add pounds, as they say.
From Craig's report James had been quite expensive to get
on board, and, though full-bloodedly heterosexual, had been
something of a diva, going on and on on the final day of the
filming, when of course things were overrunning and there
was a general air of panic, about how he had to leave for
South Africa first thing the next morning for another shoot.

In the movie Haleem is white-blooded Nigerian royalty,
born Muslim but turned free-thinker, husband to two wives
and father to three sons and a daughter. He reflects, via a
montage of still images, on his graduation day, and how his
parents and family were there to support him. Through
another montage he reflects on the birth of his children. This
cross-fades into a pan along a row of framed photographs –
stills from the montages – hanging on the terracotta painted
wall of a large modern office. All seems orderly and prosperous, and then the screen goes black and there is the sound of
an intensifying heartbeat.

We flash back to fifteen years earlier, the bath hall of the
boys' dormitory of his secondary school, and Prince Haleem
watching his classmate masturbate in the bath while simultaneously having a weird conversation with him about his
holiday 'sexcapades' with girls, an experience that intrigues
but visibly troubles Haleem.

I was impressed with how Craig managed the masturbation scene. I had been worried when I read that part of the script that his American-influenced outlook would mean his opting for a far greater level of explicitness than an African audience could take. However, while it was still clear what was going on, he was careful to avoid shots that would have been too graphic. And the classmate's talk of his carryings-on with girls was comical, and was entertainingly performed, offering the audience the release of laughter amidst their uneasiness.

We then see Haleem haltingly attempt to discuss the incident with his parents on visiting day, but they instead berate him as a failure because he came second instead of top during the previous term's examinations. While the previous scene had created an uncomfortable stirring in the audience, at this there was appreciative murmuring and nodding: I think all Nigerian children have been there. Usually this would be through statements like, 'Does the person who came first have two heads?' or, (possibly and), 'When I was in school, I always came first!'

'Na so na,' a male student beside me whispered. 'Parents no dey try for that side sha.'

'Preach it,' the female student next to him whispered back.

Through a series of short scenes we see how invisible to and distant the prince felt from everyone around him when he was young, and the boy they found to play Haleem as a child in these early scenes looked remarkably like the adult actor. An only child, the prince blames this in part on his having no siblings to grow up with. Soon he gets beaten up for being so skinny and having such a light voice, and is categorised by his classmates as girly because he neither sags his trousers nor gets into any trouble with the school authorities.

Two years pass and another boy, taller and darker than himself, who constantly smacks other boys in the crotch, crawls into his bed and he doesn't cry out. He is called 'homo' by the same boy publicly a few weeks later – the first time he has ever heard the word – who goes on to allege that the prince tried to rape him the night before. The prince is mobbed in his hostel.

As this harsh scene unfolded onscreen I wondered how Tani Cross and his family were reacting. I glanced round, but didn't know where they were seated, and of course the auditorium was dark.

The next day the prince is called out in the course of the school's morning prayers and flogged in front of the entire student body, enduring several lashes of the cane on his bare back, the welts from which are shown in painful close-up. His angry, mortified father is invited for a meeting with the principal. The stigma and pressure gets to his dad, whose political ambition is, we discover, his top priority. He pays the principal to ensure that his son's misbehaviour remains a tale forbidden to tell even amongst the students. The prince is then removed from the school.

Transferred to another school, one without boarding facilities, the prince meets another boy, Dele, who is a student functionary, and is gentle and attentive. For the first time the prince is listened to, and he finds himself yearning deeply for the constant, uninterrupted company of this functionary.

Dele accepts the prince as his brother. The prince falls in love with the idea of having an actual romantic relationship with Dele, but through a series of awkward, allusive conversations, finds the latter's loyalty appears to be to the school, academics and his future. Dele is evasive about his own sexuality, and nothing happens.

A few years pass. The scandal at the previous school is forgotten. The prince has graduated. He is being groomed to take on the leadership of his father's business empire, and is now living in Lagos. He is also exploring, recklessly and unprotected, all the sexual opportunities that present themselves to him in the big city, though is smart enough to keep his encounters discrete. He is betrothed to his father's choice of bride – a precondition for his assuming the post of CEO of the family firm. He gets married, gets promoted, and lives the life of a successful business leader who knows how to get the best from his staff. Later on he takes another wife, and is blessed with children with both wives.

By now he has abandoned his reckless pursuit of sex, but all this time is carrying on low-key affairs with thoughtful, gentle and attentive men, while taking care to avoid anyone in his work-circle.

Dele resurfaces as an employee in his company. After much pressure from the prince, including the promise of promotion for Dele, they embark on a week-long buying trip to Amsterdam. There they rekindle youthful memories, take tours, and spend nights together in exotic places, including bars and clubs that are gay-friendly, where they see all sorts of intimacies taking place. These sequences, Wole told me, had been filmed 'mute' – that is, without sound – and with hidden cameras in real gay bars, and so had a documentary look and a sense of authenticity to them.

On the eve of their departure for Nigeria, Dele and the prince get drunk and find themselves wrapped in each other's arms. They talk about the strangeness of the week, the successful lives they have built for themselves, and the wisdom in letting things just slide. Nonetheless, in the heat of the moment, vulnerable as they both are emotionally, they explore each other more intimately than they have ever allowed themselves to do before, and, for Prince Haleem, more passionately and deeply than he has ever done in his life. He finds himself falling in love with Dele.

The tension in this lengthy sequence played out in two opposite ways for the audience, I think: those who were LGBT longed for this consummation to finally happen, while those who were heterosexual mostly dreaded it. There was much squirming in seats as the two men kissed.

Craig was, to my relief, a master artist. How he got the actors to do these things in a way that felt so real, that made me believe they had had some real-life experience of what they were doing, was extraordinary. Perhaps really being in Amsterdam – they had spent a week filming there – freed something in them. Craig's placing of the camera hid enough to make it not porn, but showed enough not to make it a cowardly evasion.

The prince and Dele return to Nigeria to face their work and lives, agreeing that no-one need know about their adventure in Amsterdam, and that it's better to return to being 'straight' and put it behind them. And so the situation would have remained, had a sweaty, tearful Dele not burst into the prince's office in the middle of a board-meeting, raging and charging towards the prince, blaming him for his just-discovered HIV status, raining abuses on him in front of the board-members, calling him a 'sick faggot'. And so the word is out: The Boss might be gay. He has to attempt to clear his name by taking a HIV test and –

My phone buzzed, a text message from Wole:

Oga, sorry to cut your fun. I am at the parking lot. Someone from Sugar Books is here to see you, Mr Azeez.

For a moment I was confused: I had become so involved in the film I hadn't noticed Wole leave his seat. I slipped quietly from the hall and made my way to the parking lot.

When I got there I found no-one and was confused all over again. An armed security guard was standing by a limousine belonging to one of our more prestigious guests, a machine-gun slung across his stomach, a blank look on his face. Feeling a growing sense of unease, I tried calling Wole's phone but it was busy with another call. It was only mid-afternoon but dark clouds were rolling in, conniving to spread gloom. I tried to reach Wole again as I wandered between the rows of parked buses, but he was still engaged.

A call came in from Tega: 'Babes, where are you?'

'I'm in the parking lot.'

'Why?'

'To meet Mr Azeez.'

'Mr Azeez is here in the lobby, and he's been waiting for a while.'

'Where is Wole?'

'He had to rush off to the airport just now to receive Tayo. Please speak with your guest so that his mind will be at rest.'

'Hello? Hello?' Ahmed's voice on the other end of the line.

'My brother Ahmed.'

'Wale?'

'I'm coming to you, just stay where you are.'

It began to drizzle, and by the time I got back to the building my shirt and jeans were stained with arrows of wetness. As I made my way to the student competition registration-point I was tingling with anticipation.

Tega wasn't there but Ahmed was, sitting waiting on a

bench. He rose to his feet, reaching for a handshake, but I found myself sliding my hands around him and he engulfed me in return – I felt the warmth of his palm on my nape – holding me firmly as he whispered, 'I'm proud of you. I'm so proud of you.'

He pulled back to study my face. His eyes sparkled with excitement. He was clad in a deep grey suit and black shirt, the first few buttons of which were undone, showing the pleasing curve of his collarbone. Clean-shaven, with perfectly arched eyebrows and perfect-length lashes, his presence seemed to say, 'I'm here to take you away.' I felt him deeply: crazy, but I did. I was here with Ahmed. All of me aware, arrested and here.

'Where is Tega, the girl who called me on the phone?' I asked when our hands were back in their places. At that moment she was no more to me than a work-colleague.

'She dashed off just before you came,' he said. 'Something to do with fifty boxes of gift brochures. Omo e, this is huge. See the vehicles parked outside. See the publicity you guys are getting. And it's all happening in Nigeria!'

'Na God o, my brother. The school has also been of great aid. Look at all these: five hundred student volunteers, all staff hands are on deck. Honestly, after all our work it still feels like a dream.'

'Really, this is amazing. You look amazing,' he added, smiling widely.

'Abeg, Abeg, calm down,' I said, glancing at my watch. 'Walk with me. I need to be sure that the welfare team is ready. The screening is about to conclude; it's almost tea-break.'

'I wish I had been in time to see it.'

'I can have a disc burned for you, or give you our Vimeo password.'

From the auditorium came thunderous applause: our film had been a hit.

The day had been beautiful but the night was magic. At the opening dinner – a buffet – that followed on from the screening, one of the guests walked up to me and introduced herself as Ibingo. She was there representing *Cashmire*, one

of the United States-based magazines we had invited. She
said she had done some research on Craig and the Afrospark
Foundation, knew about the Tani Cross case, and she wanted
to meet with Tani and his family, and do a documentary on
us, our work, and Tani's life in the light of the Same Sex
Marriage (Prohibition) Act. She gave me her card.

Just as I was taking her to meet Craig, who was now the
life and soul of the event and extremely eager to meet his
public, Joseph, an elder brother to one of my students,
embraced me hard and whispered, 'Africa needs to see
Eyimofe.'

It was not all good though: James Konteh told me about
an elderly woman with a large velvet headwrap who told him
in a loud voice that he would burn in hell for being in the
film. I suspected this was Professor Amarachi, though, if so,
it surprised me that she had attended. Tega also told me of
some student volunteers who had been dragged into cars and
zoomed away by their panicky parents for fear of arrest, even
after the policemen on duty had assured them that the school
was safe from any such heavy-handed intervention.

Kwame came over to congratulate me on a successful
screening, and asked that I point out Tega to him. I did so,
and he went over to say hello to her.

After the dinner came the gala. Put together by the Theatre Art Department, it took place just outside the amphitheatre, the moonlight that bathed the grand, grassy space helped
along by several strategically-placed floodlights. We took our
seats on rows of folding chairs. By then it was pleasant not to
be talking.

Knowing the calibre of audience they would be performing in front of, the Theatre Art Department had gone all-out
to impress, and presented dance group after dance group:
first the Igbo atilogwu, then the akombi from the south,
followed by others that were northern, central northern and
Yoruba. After that, the students unwound with karaoke. It
was their convocation week, and they had had all week to
rock it, so everyone was glamorous in one native Nigerian
outfit or another, bright colours splashing everywhere, and
the sequins on the women's – and some of the men's –
outfits bounced light like ray-darts into my eyes.

Our invited guests were in full attendance, and so too was the majority of the cast and crew of *Eyimofe*. After the gala performances concluded, Tega introduced me to them one after the other, and also reintroduced me to Kay, star of *The Broken Wind*, who it turned out had come with Baba-lola, the man who played the character of Dele. Was is it me or did she feign that we were meeting for the first time? Under the circumstances, it was probably for the best. Everyone was extremely happy and wildly praising everyone else's work on the film.

For a while I stood quietly to one side and watched. James Konteh – Prince Haleem – who was Lola's escort for the evening, was chatting away with her and some of the delegates from the Kaka Foundation. After a while I saw them move on to charm the delegates of other sponsors of the event, and felt pleased. Craig and Wole were being scourged under the heat of the high-powered camera lights as they gave one interview after another. I went over to speak with the Kaka Foundation delegates, mainly to discuss the possibility of their sticking around for the rest of the week. One had to return to South Africa the following day, but the other two promised to stay on. All of them seemed pleased with the professionalism of the film, the academic setting in which it was being presented, and the buzz of publicity around its premiere.

Mum was particularly pleased that she had been a part of the process from the beginning. 'I told you that this will be hot-cake,' she said, and when she hugged and kissed us both together several camera flashes baptised us.

I took Tani Cross to meet James Konteh and made sure to get a picture of them together. Tani told me that he was now done with his O-levels and was considering a degree in Mass Communication at K.U. Though I commended the idea, I advised him to try other schools outside the country. He asked me why. I brushed the question aside, and was telling him that his newly-added weight looked great on him when Danjuma approached us. I greeted him courteously and asked after his family.

'Please stop this Wale,' he said.

Stop what? I thought. There was no way I was acting like

we were best friends. Or friends at all, for that matter. I gave Tani a side hug, excused myself on the grounds of having many guests to attend to, and vanished into the crowd. I was pleased to see the students swarming around the cast of *Eyimofe*, snatching as many star-struck selfies as possible.

Tega had been absent for much of the evening: she had had to ensure that all the publicity and Afrospark video coverage was on point – the unglamorous behind-the-scenes stuff – and hadn't been there for me much after a cuddly time-out in my lodge on the night of her arrival.

Okay. The plan was that she would share my lodge so that we could stretch our 'maturity' – that is, trying not to have sex – for a few days before she went to the hotel where Wole, Lola, and all the other Afrospark staff were staying. Of course as a man and her husband-to-be I felt a duty to make a move, but on the night of her arrival she was too exhausted to be tempted. On the second night we were both equally exhausted, after having spent the whole day in Amara town with Wole and Lola, sealing the arrangements for the souvenir brochures, posters, programmes and stationery at the printers' office. We spent most of the third night in my office revising details with Lola.

On the fourth night we were in bed together, watching pale, languid American teenagers whisper to each other in *The Vampire Diaries*, when Tega drifted off in my arms. I put the iPad away, and we would have had another regular night of no sex if I had not run my palm speculatively across her belly. She woke up long enough to give me a long lecture on the virtues of premarital celibacy, then dozed off again. I turned over and faced the wall. I was by now extremely aroused and, frustrated, my thoughts went to Kwame, and how full of desire for me he had been. And there I was again, in the overlap of the two circles in the Venn diagram of my life.

I suppose Tega felt that she had to stay with me until I had made a move on her and she had rebuffed it, though I was doubtful of what that would accomplish for her. Proof that she was a virtuous woman and I was a normal man, perhaps. The next day she had me drive her to her hotel, and since then she had been jolly, fresh, friendly and cute around me. I hated that: it seemed so staged.

So there I was, swimming through the crowd at the after-party, now very tired, forcing a smile and greeting as
many people as I could, even when some of them mistook me
for Wole. How wouldn't they? – Mum had insisted that we
both step in the identical white kaftans Brother Gbenro had
sent us from Ilaro. Wole and I had snuck off to Mum's hotel
room just before the after-party to change into them,
(agreeing between ourselves to ditch the abiti-ajas – native
Yoruba dog-eared hats – that Brother Gbenro had also
thoughtfully included). On our return Wole quickly vanished
amongst the guests. As usual I got shy, and found myself
standing by myself and wishing I could retire to my room.
This would be a long evening for a man who did not like
parties.

I was sipping from my second bottle of water when Ahmed's call came in.

'Hey! You mean you'll walk through this night without
alcohol?' he said.

'Says the good Muslim. Where are you?' I asked, looking
around, hoping to glimpse him in the crowd.

'I'm enjoying watching you from here.'

'C'mon... n,' I said. 'I just want to retire to my bed.'

'You know,' he said, 'we could run away right now.'

'That offer I'll take if it sticks around for twenty minutes,'
I said. 'I have to give a speech near the end of the evening.'

And I did, after Wole and I had mounted the stage to
thank everyone who had kept an open mind and come to see
Eyimofe, on behalf of the Afrospark Foundation and Kola
University. We thanked our funders, the Kaka Foundation,
and apologised to anyone who was shocked by the theme of
the film. We emphasized that the subject of sexuality and
gender was one with many sides, and our contribution to it
was simply to show that it is very much part of the human
and Nigerian story, and as such should be studied, discussed
and thrown out there for analysis and debate like any other
topic.

I specially thanked all the members of the K.U. family
who had not flipped out as we had expected when proposing
the project, searching with my eyes for Professor Ibinabo as I

did so. I found him, and he nodded. And, stating the obvious and ending our talk on a light-hearted note, Wole and I announced that we are identical twins, and encouraged everyone to try to tell us apart as the week progressed. Speeches over, the music began. I prised Mum away from where a group of my students were making a fuss over 'the Prof's mum', kissed her goodnight, and slid away to a cab Ahmed had pre-arranged to take us over to the faculty building so that no one would see us walking away.

He snuck some cans of Smirnoff Ice into my office and talked me into having one.

The obligations of the evening finally over, I was feeling much more relaxed. 'My wedding is only a few days away you know,' I said, hoping to start up a conversation – or rather, to head one off.

'Did you really write *Hot Sundays*?' he asked, his eyes meeting mine across the desk.

'Of course I did.' My mind went to Kwame, standing at the window of my hotel room in Addis, asking much the same question. 'Why?'

'Nothing... it still amazes me. Anyway, don't pay any attention to me.' He sipped from his can. 'The day has been eventful.'

'Yeah, quite,' I said, looking away from him and out at the still-spotlit performance area beyond my office window, where the gala raved away on K.U.'s lawn.

And so here I was, a closeted bisexual man with a looming heterosexual wedding, alone with a man I found extremely attractive, and who, despite his own proclamation of heterosexuality, clearly found me attractive too. I had spent the day with my wife-to-be and with several men who fired me up sexually – some of whom I had been romantically and sexually involved with, others not – and a gay brother whose body, I was convinced, did not believe one inch of the lie we were about to tell the world. The irony: that we had returned to this historical place of ours to tell the story of same-sex affection and assert its legitimacy.

It had been decades before when the likelihood of this first struck our lives. I was fourteen, and in JSS3.

It was an early Saturday morning. In the Junior Boys' Hostel it was still dark. Outside it was drizzling lightly. I lay awake on my bunk in a room I shared with nine other students – mostly classmates, and one boy from the class below mine – contemplating whether to go downstairs to fetch water before the queue at the tap formed. The others slept. Then the door crashed open and three older boys came in fast.

One of the three called out for Tobi, my class- and bunk-mate. These were the most dreaded prefects in our senior class – dreaded because they beat students with canes or leather belts so recklessly that the resultant scars turned septic and did not heal for weeks. They had visited our room the previous day and dropped a message with us to tell Tobi to report to the senior prefect immediately after the evening meal. It seemed he had not done so, for now they were searching him out amongst his jolted-awake and terrified fellow-students with big, scorching-bright torch lights.

The next sound I heard was the loud crack of a belt on bare skin. It must have landed on Tobi but I did not hear him cry out – he was never known to respond to pain. Grabbing his uniform from his closet, Tobi was pushed out of the room wearing only his grey plaid boxers, the belts of the prefects slashing his shoulders and back as they followed him.

The rest of us rushed out onto the balcony to see where they were taking him, but it wasn't just him: there were seven other students who had been called out in this way, and were all now awkwardly pulling their clothes on in the yard. Once they were dressed the prefects led them away from the hostel in a single file.

A few minutes later Senior Tosin, Wole's school father and the prefect in charge of our hostel, banged heavily on the hostel gate, mustering all of us downstairs.

'Look,' he said once we had gathered there, 'this is my hostel. If there is any problem, any problem at all, bring it to me, and if I can't handle it we will find a way around it. "Homo" is a serious offence in this school. These boys are going to face the music now because someone amongst you blabbed to higher authorities. Look, we all came here to be educated and we must focus on that. I don't know who

reported this, but in the future I want you to report yourself
to me before I find you out, because then it will be too late.
We are all brothers in this hostel. I won't be taking this
lightly next time. Is there any complaint?'

'No sir!' we answered.

'Today will be hostel rounds. You know what you are all
supposed to do.'

Immediately after we were dismissed I went to Wole's
room, which was on the ground floor, to get more information from him on this 'homo' issue.

'Nna e, this school sef,' he said, speaking Pidgin as he
usually did when he wanted to sound rugged and disen-
chanted.

'O boy, calm down first. How far this homo thing? What
is it about?' I asked while I tried to make some space to sit on
his bed, which was as usual cluttered with textbooks, pieces
of paper, and a mosquito net that had never been hung.

'I don't know how to go about this,' he said, 'but it sha
has to do with when a boy touches another boy when he is
sleeping and someone catches them.'

'You mean touching... as in ...?'

'Touching now... You sef. Touching as in...' he said, nudging me.

'I don't get,' I said impatiently. 'Abeg nak me yan jor.' –
insisting he tell as plainly as possible.

He leaned close and whispered, 'You know na... touching
a boy the way a boy touches a babe.' Sitting back, he said,
'This is terrible. Tobi is now involved. This is just too bad.'

The hostel rounds were postponed to the following weekend. Tobi was absent all day and did not return to our room
that night.

I was woken at 5:30 the next morning, which was Sunday, by muffled crying. Flashing my torch round the room I
saw Tobi standing there naked, dripping with water, his back
and buttocks striped and swollen with wide and still-open
cuts from caning. He was facing his locker. Nobody else was
awake yet. I greeted him softly. He neither responded nor
turned to look at me. I slipped down from my bunk so as not
to wake the others and got close to him. Then he turned to
look at me. My chest exploded at what I saw. His eyes were

red and swollen from crying and he was still crying, and his cheeks were swollen with palm prints from being smacked one time too many.

During church service in the school dining hall that morning there was a heavy-duty sermon on Sodom and Gomorrah and the heinous sin they committed that got God so angry.

At first the preacher said that the 'spirit of homosexuality and lesbianism' possesses someone who is touched by a homosexual, and that the touched person becomes a homosexual as well. Then she said that the sin of homosexuality is fast spreading in the world, and that those involved will go to hell if they do not change their evil ways. As she spoke she marched from one end of the stage to the other. Once she tried to march into the congregation but the microphone stopped working, so she marched back to the stage. It was a very lively service, with everyone shouting loud amens and 'preach on, pastor!' at intervals. Whenever the preacher sank to hinting at the sexual practices of homosexuals and how unholy they were, I would hear roars of 'tufiakwa!' or 'Kai God forbid bad thing'. It seemed to me that everyone except me knew how dangerous and bad this 'homo' thing could be. It must be so poisonous, I thought. I hoped that Tobi, who was sitting next to me, would not die of it.

I was scared – of the preacher; of what she was saying; and for Tobi.

All the while he sat beside me, clad in a white shirt and trousers and brown sandals. At intervals I would turn to look at him. Once I caught him wiping tears from his cheeks. I had never seen him cry before that day. My heart sank and I felt my own eyes get teary.

The prayer session was exceptionally heated up but I did not pray. I could not pray because watching Tobi on his knees crying and praying, probably asking God to take 'homo' away from him, filled me with uncertainty as to who to pray for and what to pray about. Yet in my heart I was convinced that God saw how all this was playing out and that, understanding how it seemed to me, He forgave my silence.

By the afternoon the news had spread amongst the students. Everyone who had borrowed Tobi's notes – he was a good student, and until then had been popular – returned them to him during prep, hissing at him and leaving without saying a word. I watched him sit by himself all through the two-hour duration of the prep with his head laid on his desk. His seatmate had relocated from their desk in the middle row to another at the end, returning at intervals to clear his desk drawer one item at a time, similarly without saying a word to Tobi.

In the days that followed, students from other classrooms came into our classroom, pretending to borrow one thing or another, really only to get a closer look at Tobi. As though this was not bad enough, senior students came in at intervals to demand that Tobi Johnson jump to his feet, and when he wearily did so, they would look at him with so much disgust in their eyes it was painful. I sat in the back row watching all this, imagining what the other boys who had been called out were facing. Tobi had not spoken to anyone I knew since he was taken out on Saturday morning. I wanted to sit beside him as I had at worship on Sunday; I wanted to hold his hand in solidarity. But it was difficult for me to stand out. It was difficult for me to face all that ridicule and humiliation when I could just stay silent.

Then again, I was baffled: if Wole's description of 'homo' was so accurate, if sex outside marriage was so terrible, why were the SS3 boys who sneaked into the senior girls' hostel at midnight to 'visit' their girlfriends on the eve of their passing-out parade celebrated as heroes and big men on their return? Why was it a custom for some SS3 boys to connive with each other to secure the classroom buildings while one of them was inside having a 'conversation' with his girlfriend on Sundays, just a few minutes after lifting holy hands? If two people touching each other was so bad then why did I catch some of my classmates indulging in it during prep periods? Why were these transgressions hardly ever talked – shouted – about during church service? I wished that Tobi would speak to me. Yet why should he? I had done nothing positive to show myself a friend. At least I had not yet moved from our bunk-room, as several others had done.

After we had had our evening meal and were back in our

classrooms for night prep, Senior Tosin walked in.

'Class...'

The whole class roared, which was the usual way of greeting the senior students, stretching out our arms with fists clenched and pushing our chests out.

'Olawale Damian,' he called out.

'Yes sir,' I said, getting to my feet.

'Come with your mathematics textbook and writing materials. Hey, relax,' he said to the rest of the class, motioning them to put their arms down and return to their studies.

On our way out Senior Tosin ducked back into the classroom and ordered Tobi to come with the same materials. Tobi and I walked behind Senior Tosin in silence till we got to Wole's classroom, where there were fewer students. We were directed to settle down in a corner of the back row with Wole. We said a short prayer, led by Senior Tosin. Then, to our great surprise, he revised geometry with us all though the prep time. We had a math test the next day, and Senior Tosin took it upon himself to ensure that we weren't lagging behind in Math and Introductory Technology.

Senior Tosin was Wole's big brother in school. He was light-skinned, tall and hairy, and ranked amongst the most 'fly' guys in school. Tidy, sophisticated and spiritual, he had been Wole's bunkmate since Wole came in, and often teased Wole for not being able to speak or understand Yoruba well. I was always in and out of his room because of Wole, and we all got along. He watched out for both of us, and consequently Wole and I became untouchable. He was renowned for never using his cane save in extreme cases – in which case he would be fierce and thorough in his thrashing – or during the occasional all-prefect inspection patrol; or when his superior asked him to. Despite his friendliness towards me, asides from when Wole was there I felt quite uneasy being with Senior Tosin. There was always a jolting about in my chest whenever he smiled at me on the assembly ground, especially when it was just after he had thrashed some other student for some minor offence, such as having unkempt fingernails, during the all-prefect inspection patrol.

Tobi responded very well in the course of the session: asking questions, offering Wole his other pen... The calm normality of it amazed me.

Monday came, and we were in the middle of taking the test when a naval recruit came into our classroom to demand that Tobi be excused. As Tobi stood up to leave, the teacher asked loudly whether Tobi was one of the 'homo' boys but the naval recruit did not respond to the question.

At the close of school that day, the eight 'homo' boys were seen pulling their boxes along the tarred path, headed towards the parade ground where their parents' cars were waiting to take them away. I caught sight of Tobi, his white shirt and stockings blazing in the sun, his cape fluttering in the breeze. He had visibly lost weight over the weekend. A few minutes later we watched the car his father had sent heading for the gate, and I never saw or heard from Tobi Johnson again. After the holidays it was rumoured that he had slit his wrists on the eve of his flight to meet up with his parents at their Abuja home. But Senior Tosin later told Wole and me that he had left the country to continue his studies in the United Kingdom.

The prefects who had brutalised the boys were stripped of their posts, disciplined and replaced. The school did not take kindly to bullying or indecency in the hostels of any kind.

Ahmed and I spent till nearly midnight talking over rather too many cans of Smirnoff Ice. My excitement at finally being with him had not in the least waned, but the day – the culmination of so much preparation, so much stress and worry – had taken its toll on me, and my head was beginning to nod.

We headed over to the staff lodge, strolling across lawns and past well-lit verandas, passing the last few students as they returned to their hostels. The more we walked the giddier I felt. I hadn't been this tired in years. By the time we got to my building we had both stopped talking. I led the way to my room.

'I hope there are no mosquitoes here,' Ahmed said lightly.

'Hope is good.' I replied, hoping the window nets had kept them out at least for tonight.

A while later, after taking turns in the shower, we were both lying on the bed. The air-conditioner hummed. We talked a little more and then he stopped responding: he had fallen asleep. I covered his bare, smooth body with my adireh wrapper. This was the first time since Kwame I had shared a bed with a man who had no blood-ties with me, but I was too tired to be turned on; I was too tired to feel.

My thoughts churned on, however, and reflections on the day just past bubbled up in my mind. Though the screening had gone well I did not know how much support issues around sexual minority rights had in Nigeria, not given what had happened since the bill was passed: the lives that had been threatened; the people who had been displaced; the sharply altered balance in familial and societal relationships that were already so complex.

Wole and I had agreed that Afrospark would not publicly take sides on the bill; that we would not be directly campaigning against it. Our stated position was that we were only interested in having, as we put it, 'a great conversation' with Nigeria, with Africa, with the world about what exactly being lesbian, gay or bisexual, transgender, intersex or a concerned ally might mean in the African context. How shocked Nigeria would be to learn who actually were the homosexuals amongst us! There was a joke I heard that if every homosexual or bisexual person's head turned blue, the rest of us would be frozen with shock and fear at finding that homosexuality is far more widespread and integrated than it seems in Africa; and that LGB individuals – especially if we add in those who have once or twice flirted with the idea in practice, or even just in their imaginations – may possibly even be the sexual majority, and not the minority they are often labelled as. What would the straight people do? Perhaps try to develop a mathematical or chemical formula that would set everything 'straight', or prepare some potion, or package some prayer screeds to burn up these divine gifts that come with no clear beginning and no known end. And what of the asexual, the transgender, the intersex and the gender non-conformists, who smash all the rules and records of gender definitions or sexual identities and desires? Or indeed our allies, with all their unknown personal stories and passion for the human rights struggle?

As for sexuality, personally, I think that it is like race and sex: features that can neither be chosen nor, without extreme difficulty, hushed up. And like race and gender it can be defined and expressed subjectively. It can be developed, stretched, ignored or celebrated. It can determine everything, or become too everyday to matter.

Our event was not Gay Pride, but the affirmation of sexual difference was clearly in view, because for now in Nigeria it begins with sexuality. Everything sexually different is assumed homosexual, so we began with that conversation – hopefully to evolve over time to include the complexities of gender identity and other, more unspoken diversities.

It was beautiful to see academic research, film, theatre and advocacy have this much effect.

I had missed the preview of *Eyimofe* because it was held at the office in faraway Port Harcourt while I was here in Amara, and I had had to leave the premiere part-way through to meet Ahmed, but I was determined to be fully present for the rest of the week. Owing to the quality of co-operation our team had received from the student volunteers, the institution and our sponsors, bar a few small problems, by the second day everything was, as far as my own role was concerned, running on auto-pilot.

For the following morning we had slated *the Secrets of the Silhouettes*, a theatrical presentation using light, sound and speech. Masked LGB individuals, or actors performing as if they were LGB, (a possibility we stressed in all the promotional material, for their safety in case their names became known), were to be reading personal statements, or letters sent in by LGB individuals who could not make it to the event, and rendered into silhouettes by colourful back-lighting. At the time, trans, intersex and asexuals were in the main invisible and unready to be heard.

The participants would be talking about their secret sexual and emotional lives, the similarities to and differences from heterosexuality, and the added challenges and excitements that African society afforded them. The masks were made from black and white adireh fabric stitched onto thin denim, and covered participants' faces from the forehead down to the end of the nose just above the nostrils. For theatrical effect, and to heighten our involvement in a symbolic way, we audience members were also issued masks at the entrance to the hall.

'Today anyone could be anyone,' Ahmed said as we put them on.

The Secrets of the Silhouettes, which had been put together by Tega, with no input from me beyond introducing her to the head of the Theatre Art department, turned out to be the highlight of the week so far as I was concerned. All the staff of Afrospark except me were sitting in the back row. Our police escorts were outside, and their presence created a sombre mood, as all present knew that these same police had been making arrests in other parts of the country. The police officer who we call our friend today is the same policeman in whose hands the anti-gay law catches fire, and whose brutality homophobia fuels. Yet the crime that attracts homophobia is not homosexuality but vulnerability: it is poverty, effeminacy, outspokenness. In the face of dangerously hot, homophobic Nigeria, only the protected, wealthy, ruthlessly self-serving and politically connected could ride, win, laugh, and lead normal, if not ideal lives – as people of means have done in the past, do today, and will continue to do in the future – for homophobia is innately cowardly. But expelling it demands audacity, and to be audacious and hope to survive demands at least the façade of being shielded – even if one is not actually so.

In the theatre people played along with the ushers, putting on the masks they were given as they arrived, and there was less talk than one would expect in a crowded auditorium before a performance. Everyone was seated by ten a.m., and the hall was full. Along with the board of trustees and other academic staff I sat in the front row, next to a masked Professor Brown. I almost did not know it was him until he reached out, took my hand and said, 'Some gay students will be a part of the presentation today.'

'How do you know they are gay?' I asked.

'I'm the father and best friend of Kola University. I'm open to my children, and they are open to me too.'

'Wow,' I whispered. 'Okay.'

'But not to worry, they will be wearing their masks. Nigeria is not ready for their faces yet.'

There was a loud drum roll and the lights dimmed. M.I.'s 'Imperfect Me' played in the background as the performers, shadowy figures in the darkness, processed from the hall's entrance to the stage, applause escorting them down the aisle. One of them, I knew, was a student of mine. I wondered which he was.

Earlier in the week Lola had called to get my confirmation for someone who claimed to be a student of International Human Rights at K.U., and who wanted to fill in for an absentee speaker, but had not sent a letter proving he was registered here. His name was unfamiliar to me, and I emailed him rather suspiciously: just one undercover policeman, or even a journalist gathering names and personal disclosures, could be real trouble for us. He gave me the name of his blog and I checked it out. Yep, he was my student, Emenike Thompson. His academic writing did not particularly stand out; and his blog, though personal, wasn't particularly revealing. I thought he was one of those quiet students who managed to dodge being heard. He was taking a bold step, but I would not get in his way.

On taking their seats – a row of chairs lined up at the back of the stage – I could tell that the performers were all men, and young. One seemed to have braid-like ridges on his head under a fabric covering. Looking beautiful but rather nervous, Tega came up to the spot-lit lectern to introduce them, naming them with random letters of the alphabet, which I initially thought were the first letters of their first names – until she finished without mentioning 'E'. She emphasized that these were performances: that we should not assume the sexuality of the performers because of the words they spoke, which might not be their own. Then she stepped down from the lectern. The spotlight dimmed and a row of lights that had been set at floor level behind the performers' chairs began to brighten. They had been filtered to create a muted, translucent glow that, while silhouetting the actors, would not dazzle the audience.

The men took their turns to step forward and deliver

their speeches. The first four speakers all followed a certain pattern. First, they began with how they had always known that they were different and how everyone taunted them for being so. They were all slight in stature and effeminate in their speech and mannerisms generally: those who could not hide who they were, and so were forced to be brave. They talked about how hard it was for them to truly be themselves around their families, and how it was hard for them to find or keep friends, when to be friends with them was seen as a shameful, even a dangerous thing. One seemed to be an American returnee, for he talked so much about the divergence in attitudes towards sexuality that existed between Nigerians and Americans. I thought of Kwame and his plans to go to the U.S. It was primarily a question of waking up, the returnee said, and refusing to be tied to no-longer-relevant traditions.

'Individuals are born gay,' another said. 'Being gay is simply a sexual definition, a description, a programme written and embedded in your hormones. You can't just wake up and decide to rewrite your sexual programme because the world doesn't like it.'

Many interesting views and perspectives were thrown up as the men talked. 'There was nothing I didn't do as a teenager to cure myself of homosexuality,' a third young man said. 'I prayed. I attended fasting and deliverance sessions. I was taken for therapy. I was given herbal portions to drink. I even heard of shock therapy being conducted outside the country, in the course of which a homosexual only needs to be electrocuted for a while to be "normal". But I am gay.'

They actually did say a lot. And when each man finished, the audience applauded, whistled and cheered. One of the first four burst into tears when he talked about how his father told his brothers to hold him tightly by his hands and feet as he was whipped thoroughly. I thought of Tobi.

Most of what I heard was familiar: they were places I had been to; they were voices I had heard. These boys were people I had known, victims of the same fate that dealt with us all, and to what end? What was the point of all this suffering, this misery?

I cried.

Professor Brown sat in the darkness beside me, tears trickling from beneath his mask, his lips quivering, but he was very still.

My muscles felt painfully cramped. I wanted to shout out. I wanted to leave the hall. The air-conditioners were all on and working perfectly but the space had somehow become unbearably warm.

I was half on my feet when the fifth speaker came forward. He was of average height, but big build. His hair was long and locked. I was confused: I had never noticed such hair in class. There was something electrifyingly eerie about him. He was calm, each step a feathery leap off the ground. He requested that the lights be brightened slightly, and the backlights turned down. His voice was deep, and the words seemed to roll softly off his tongue slightly spiced with an Igbo accent. I was excited and a little worried. A wave of murmuring swept across the hall – not all those in the audience necessarily wished their presence at this event to be known. I looked round to see Tega having a hushed conversation with a technician off to one side. The masked man insisted that the lights be brightened. I saw Wole's silhouette as he made for the lectern.

'I don't think he should be doing that,' Professor Brown said, 'for his own safety.'

'I'm sure he knows what he is doing,' I said, though I really wasn't sure.

'This is purely art, man,' the Professor said. 'It's not worth putting yourself in danger for. Besides you can never tell who is amongst us. The next thing you know he'll take off his mask.'

Wole was there at the lectern for a while, whispering with the masked man, before I decided I should make for the stage too. Halfway there I met him on his way back to his seat. He said it was okay: 'The situation is under control. We'll give him his lights.' He turned and gestured to Tega, who nodded. The lights brightened just a little, and the backlights dimmed slightly.

'There are so many Nigerian stories,' the speaker began, moving to the lectern. 'Unfortunately, I only know so much.'

The spotlight slowly came up. The hands that held the

top of the lectern were illuminated ghostly white. The face
behind the adireh mask he wore was ghostly white too, and
his lips were pink and smiling. His dense blond hair flowed
down his back in thick locks bunched together by a flowery
pink ruffle. The pink ankara shirt and trousers he wore
contrasted sharply with his skin. He was spectacular; he was
albino.

'I'm a Nigerian Christian. I am a son. I am my dream, yet
above all these things I am just another human reality. I have
an adorable mum, whose dream is to see that I am called to
the Nigerian Bar and afterwards lead the rest of my life as a
practising lawyer, with all the opportunities and possibilities
that any of my colleagues would ordinarily have. I have a
body that is so delicate that every day of my surviving the
sun is victory. I have hair that does not look or feel like that
of my friends here in Kola University' – this was him, then;
this was Emenike – 'I have so many other things that make
me outstanding – too outstanding – and many things that
are usual and common to others are great aspirations for me.
Sometimes I can't help wishing I could say fímí sílẹ̀ forever
to these differences, this skin.

'I discovered another difference in my life at age fifteen,
when the death of my best friend Segun almost took my life
too. He was soft-spoken, bossy, selfless and kind. He was
also anaemic, and at a crucial moment he needed a blood
transfusion. Our blood types matched, but no matter how
much I pleaded, the doctors refused to take mine because of
my fragile state of health until there was no other alternative.
Yet after all done, he died. At his funeral it dawned on me
that I had left so much unsaid and undone in my relationship
with him. There were so many times that I craved for Segun's
touch, so many times I wished to tell him how much I loved
him. There was so much pain and fear that melted away in
his presence. Segun was gospel to me.

'Even today, seven years later, I live my life with the regret that I let my first love slip away without even kissing
him, for shame of how dirty or scandalous it might be seen
as; for fear that I might become the person I had always
really been anyway. I was gay; I'm still gay. And in the midst
of all these differences that set me apart from most of my

friends, I am a boy – a man, still outstanding, proud of every
lock of my hair, the brightness of my skin and the difference
of my heart. Only I can define it, because God has given me
the spirit of strength, love and good judgement. He has given
me a mind that is always growing and learning better things.
I am not ashamed of my sexuality. I am not ashamed of my
life. I am proud of everything that is here, expectant of
everything that should be here, and appreciative of everything that is not and will never be here, because I have God,
and I'm certain that He is above all the madness that labels
and definitions may try to throw at me, and above all the
sadness there is in this world.'

He finished. Instantly, the hall split into clatters, slamming applause... a roaring standing ovation. Emenike was
different. Sexuality is strength, he said. As I stood in that
near-darkness, clapping hard with tears in my eyes, I
wondered at the courage of this boy, this man. And was glad
that, even though he fell into the category of students who
never made it to lectures – I could hardly have failed to
notice him if he had done so – he was still actively involved
with our online work. He had always been part of that circle,
it transpired, and now he was a visible part of our world.

Emenike's was the last speech. The other performers
stood and came forward to join him for a group bow. Then
they were led off the stage and through to the back, where
they could unmask and change from their costumes unseen
– we were still in Nigeria, after all, and anyone could be
amongst us. We took off our masks too. It had been a
gathering of spirits, speaking, sharing, listening and feeding
each other's souls and cores. Masks are an important part of
our lives, as a people. Chinua Achebe in his *Things Fall
Apart* described masks as spirits of the ancestors, and, as
such, superior to mere human beings who led human lives –
and that the men who wore them were possessed by the
ancestors' spirits or even the ancestors themselves – or so
the spectators believed. But masks in the context of homosexuality are not claiming superiority: they are a shield, a
shell, a façade. Masks in the context of homosexuality in
Nigeria are not just worn against the glare and beliefs of
hostile spectators, but also for the bearer to shield his heart,

and to help the survival of his plastic peace and the world that he is building for himself – a place that does not yet, and perhaps will never exist. This is necessary. But there is a danger that in wearing such a mask he teaches himself to take on falsehood perfectly, and becomes comfortable enough with it to detest everything that is natural and genuine, in both others and himself.

We all wore masks, and in a few days those worn by Wole and me would, we believed, permanently become us.

The rest of that day I was in a lighter mood. Ahmed seemed rather blown away by the show: all through lunch and afterwards, on our returning to the lodge, he kept talking about Emenike's speech. When we were in bed later that evening Ahmed went all FBI on it (he had demanded a transcript from our gratifyingly efficient student journalists), scrutinizing it to the very last detail, and highlighting many interesting issues.

'Do you know that Emy would have been killed more than once if he was born into the wrong home?' he said.

'Haba! Ahmed, that's rather extreme,' I said. 'And you can't be killed more than once.'

'Dey there now. Take a look at this,' he said, waving the transcript at me and handing me my spectacles. 'Wear your bottles o!'

'I dey look jor,' I said as the frames of my glasses embraced my face.

He pinpointed every issue in the speech, beginning with the possibility of the chap being an illegitimate child who could have been abandoned in the gutter, as are a good number of unwanted newborns. 'Terrible.' He went on about how some African beliefs include the use of albino skin and internal organs for black magic and fortune-creation rituals. 'So barbaric. It is terrible, so terrible that so many amazing guys like Emy should be subject to so much. Even his dreadlocks – '

'But this is 2014,' I protested. 'Things are not as bad as you make them seem.'

'Really?'

'Look, I've got locks too. And it's not like people go

around calling me possessed. There are also very remarkable Nigerians who are locked: Daddy Showkey; Jide Macaulay...'

'Abegi...You of all people should know Daddy Showkey's being locked isn't an issue because he is a brand. He is "Daddy Showkey"! So he is automatically forgiven for wearing long hair that unrepentantly rebels against anything with the semblance of a comb. And Jide... he is equally a brand. Anyway, he is not in the country, and there are so many other things that shout out for him, his locks are the least.'

'So many other things ke?'

'The fact that he is a gay pastor and all.'

'So you are saying that if you are neither Daddy Showkey nor Reverend Jide – or a law professor in a prestigious private university – you will be stoned for being locked?'

'No, no. Don't jump like that. I'm saying that you are excused from public scrutiny or condemnation for a certain thing if you have something else that is more eye-catching and distractingly good – or bad – enough to take their eyes off the earlier shebang.'

'So you saying that shame is shameful but can be haloed up by another shame more shameful than the first?'

'I'm saying that our flames and fumes can be overlooked and even ignored if our light puts the sun to shame.'

Funny the way he said it. It was less a truth than a hope, but I understood exactly what he meant.

'Look bros... e, finally, talk is cheap o,' he said, jumping to his feet. His bare chest caught my eyes. 'What do you say we make this thing more practical?' He arched a brow, handling the bulge in his shorts and curtsying slightly to ease his crotch.

My heart raced. 'What do you mean?'

'Look, Afrospark can go beyond just this one-week programme.' He slid back into bed alongside me, placing his palm on my thigh and looking deeply into my eyes.

'I don't quite follow,' I said, as I contemplated breaking through the wall I was now pressed up against in order to withdraw from the many alarming – intriguing – possibilities the night was threatening to offer me.

'Tomorrow is the competition element of the festival. Am

I correct?'

'Yes.'

'Good. Now, the best of these stories, paintings, poems, essays, whatever – the best of them should be published in a compilation that shall back up your new novel.'

'What new novel?'

'The sequel to *Hot Sundays,* where you respond to the child you were. Your journey since then – '

'I don't think it's a good idea,' I said, lying back and looking up at the ceiling, unwilling to continue with the conversation. Even if I had the time and space to write an entire new novel, which I did not, I wasn't ready to serve my guts up again. My life was public enough as it was.

'What part of it?' he asked.

'The part about a sequel to *Hot Sundays*. And I'd rather we don't talk about it any further.' I turned to face the wall.

'Aaa... na vex be this?' he said, a comic lilt in his voice.

'Ahmed, please leave me alone. I've had a rather long day,' I said, a feigned sternness in my voice, avoiding turning back to look at him because then he would know I was putting up a front.

'Wo! That one na grammar o! Oya seat up jor,' he said, nudging me.

I stayed put even after subsequent nudges. The next I knew was Ahmed rummaging every part of my body with tickles. 'You no want sit up ba?' he said as his tickles got speedier and more intense. I tried in vain to quit laughing loudly and unculturedly as his fingers touch-typed along my sides and round to my belly. I laughed and laughed, trying so hard to stop him, to push him away – just get him away from me, but he went on and on, and I laughed on and on until I felt my thighs between his and our moist bodies touching. I found myself in the arms of a man, arrested even as I warred against the larger world that was telling me it was wiser, so much wiser to push him away. His eyes locked onto mine as I felt his palm in the small of my back, gently pressing me to him, his breath bathing my face.

The Paper and Performance Arts competition took place on the third day. The prizes were three brand-new SUVs – given

by our sponsors – so there were many entrants. The technical sophistication of the art was not as important to us as the
clarity and originality of the intended message. It was to be
held in a large tent on the school's playing-field. Inside, it
was white and spacious, contrasting sharply and beautifully
with the sea of grass that surrounded it. From outside it
looked as if it was carved of icing-sugar.

The two categories – paper and performance arts – were
open to any undergraduate participants who had registered
on the first day of the *Save the Colours* festival, whether or
not they studied at K.U., and the central theme for both
categories was 'The Millennial Spectrum: Celebrating
Diversity'. The Paper Art segment comprised two elements:
essays, poetry and short stories, to be penned in three hours;
and drawings and paintings, to be executed in four. On
entering the tent the students had spectrum-coloured tapes
fastened around their wrists.

We had a great turnout, with almost two hundred students taking their seats for the paper art segment – all clad
as stipulated in white tee-shirts and blue jeans; an even mix
of boys and girls. Save for the rustling of the leaves in the
morning breeze there was pin-drop silence within and
around the tent. The contestants who were writing were
issued with the requisite stationery while the artists set out
their pencils, pens, paints and brushes, jars of water and
cloths, and supervisors were strategically positioned to see
that the rules were being followed.

While this went on, auditions for the Performance Arts
contest were being conducted in the school's auditorium at
the other end of the campus. The judging panel comprised
five performance artists, three movie producers, our director
Craig, one of the delegates from Kaka Foundation, and two
recent alumni of K.U. named Tolu and Bisi, who had both
graduated from the Mass Communication department the
previous year.

Kwame and Lola, alongside some other staff from the
Afrospark Foundation, and teachers from the K.U. art and
literature departments, oversaw the paper art competition,
while Wole, Tega and I oversaw the performance art auditions. Wole had had an asthmatic attack that morning and

had passed out again an hour after being resuscitated, but insisted he could see everything through till the end of the day. This was the last major event of the Afrospark week before the grand finale: the award presentations at the graduation after-party on the Friday. Today was Wednesday; Thursday was to be a lower-key and more academically-focused day of panel discussions and guest speakers, most of whom had been invited by the university, which would give us enough time to assess the competition entries without feeling unduly pressured.

During a break in proceedings the three of us went and sat outside the auditorium to get some air, Wole holding tightly onto his bottle of water. Tega and I were still not talking much. Wole had noticed that the air had been tense between us at the gala, and that she had sat by him instead of with me during the *Silhouettes* show. Earlier that morning he had asked me what the matter was. I told him that Tega was just overstressed by the *Silhouettes* segment, and that at times she had gotten so bad-tempered I had had to remind her we were on the same team, and that if she was feeling overwhelmed I was there to help. He said that when he spoke with Tega about it she snapped that some stranger from the Netherlands was doing a better job of keeping her husband-to-be occupied than she was.

'You both had better stop acting up,' he said now, taking a sip of water. 'Your wedding is only a few days away.'

'Everything is fine,' Tega said, avoiding my eyes.

'Well, I wouldn't quite agree with that,' I said.

'Why?' Wole's brow furrowed.

'She's been avoiding me since she got here.'

'That's not true,' Tega said. 'I was at his room the other day and I fell asleep and he tried to... Never mind. It's stupid.'

'He tried to what?' Wole asked, beginning to sound mischievous.

'Well, he was getting all out of control,' she said.

'Are you calling my love for you out of control?' I asked, feeling relief that the 'stranger from the Netherlands' was not the main issue.

'True love knows self-control,' she insisted.

'Really?'

'You both stop it,' Wole said. 'Just sort yourselves out. Wale, Mummy is beginning to ask why you don't come to the hotel. Tega, wedding jitters or no wedding jitters, Mummy has noticed that you are suddenly not as fond of your husband-to-be as much. Your people are arriving on Friday; is this what you want them to see?'

'Wole, you know we've all been giving this project our best,' Tega said defensively.

'This project is about real lives, Tega. There is no way you will truly appreciate it if you don't have one yourself.'

At this point I should have kept quiet, but instead I tried defending myself with my having to host Ahmed properly.

'The last time I checked Ahmed represents Sugar Books, which is one of our sponsors, and as such he is Afrospark's guest, not just yours. Afrospark made arrangements for him. Stop this.' Wole was now beginning to sound oddly upset but he caught himself and gulped down the last of his water. 'Tegs. Please could you get me a refill.'

As Tega disappeared into the auditorium, she glanced back at me uneasily.

'You are getting married in a few days,' Wole whispered behind clenched teeth.

'And so are you.'

'Yes.' His breath sounded constricted.

'Is everything alright?' I reached out to feel his neck.

'Stop it, Wale. Don't play naïve,' he said, gently stopping my hand and holding it between his two palms. 'We made a pact to settle down peacefully. Baba would not have approved of this nonsense.'

'What nonsense?'

'Ahmed!' he said. 'Who is this Ahmed guy? What does he want? Is he that good that you want to throw away all that God has given you?'

'Nothing is happening between Ahmed and me. He is a good friend and that's all.'

'I have eyes, Olawale. All week I have been watching. Silent but watching, hoping it is nothing, as you say.'

'I promise, it's nothing,' I said. 'It's just this idea that we want to – '

'Please don't lie to me,' he interrupted.

Fed up with his sanctimonious talk, I lashed back: 'What about your several guest popping in and out of your office?'

'What guest?'

'Now don't you play naïve.'

'What?'

'Don't "what" me. What is going to happen to all those hard-armed shellehs after Lola has slipped the ring on?'

'Wale, this is not about me. I'm not the one who's squabbling with his fiancée a few days before his wedding.'

'At least that's better than having a penis that has never truly responded to his fiancée, not now and perhaps never.'

Heat spread to my face. He looked away across the lawns.

'That was out of line. I'm sorry.'

'We are both under pressure,' he said.

'I'm sorry.'

'I'm not mad at you,' he said. 'But I'm tired. I'm really tired.'

'Of what?'

'Of this dick and where it wants to lead me.' He sighed. 'I believe you'll do the right thing.'

'I just wish – '

'Shhh, your babe dey show.'

'I'm sorry I took so long,' Tega said as she approached. 'Here is the water.'

By the time the Afrospark curtain was due to come down publicity about the event had spread to every corner of Nigeria. Headline succeeded headline, each telling a different version of the Afrospark story. According to some we were trying to sneak 'gayism' into Nigeria. Others wrote that Afrospark was a western initiative targeted at corrupting the young, impressionable leaders of Nigeria's tomorrow. I did not get this conspiracy-minded approach: does nobody train these journalists to do their background research properly? Well, as somebody said, 'Never let the truth get in the way of a good story.'

There were also more pleasant pieces that described the Afrospark initiative as expanding the scope of activism and debate, some even praising it for 'breaking all the rules'. Internationally Afrospark also made waves, owing especially to the screening of *Eyimofe* and the performance by the Masked Albino. *Eyimofe* would later make it to nearly a dozen international film festivals that focused on black and/or gay subject matters and film-makers, and won several minor awards.

And then it was done.

By Thursday morning all the Afrospark props, posters, banners and flyers, all the rainbow tape and bunting had been cleared out from the main hall as the students prepared for the traditional convocation pre-party.

Most of the police support was withdrawn.

Ahmed and I moved from the campus to the hotel, which was where the other guests were staying. He was lodged on the tenth floor, while I moved in with Wole on the eleventh.

I let myself in when I arrived and found Wole in bed asleep. He still had his jeans and undervest on from the previous day. He looked so adorable that day, with his lashes stretched out in subtle curves and his silky beard slightly bushy. His breathing, which had been so troubled of late, was regular, reassuring.

I unpacked my things quietly so I wouldn't wake him. There I was with my twin, heart of my heart, yet the room felt somehow empty, as if something that should have been there was missing.

Ahmed's scent.

Wahala. That was stupid.

More stupid were my imaginings. I saw myself dash from the room into the arms of an Ahmed who, conveniently, would be waiting just outside the door. I saw myself pull him into the shower and give him my all. I saw myself giving into his domination while trapped firmly in his grip.

'Stop it!' I lashed out at myself. Slightly too loudly: Ahmed – no, Wole turned round in his sleep. I held my breath. He didn't waken.

The idea of being with Ahmed had stirred up my libido and raised my blood pressure. When I was with him thoughts of building a life with a man filled my mind, thoughts that obviously threatened my impending marriage.

More threatening than my domestic fantasising, however, was that I was now fighting the urge to tell Tega that, while loving her no less, I had also fallen in love with a man. But then, hadn't she guessed already? If not, and if she knew me as well and as deeply as she was supposed to do, then why hadn't she? I sighed, and went and had a shower.

That evening a few lecturers, the competition judges – which included Ahmed as publisher for Sugar Books – and the Afrospark team converged on the hotel's conference room to jointly consider the entries, agree on the final results for the paper art, and arrive at the three finalists for the performance arts. Wole lectured us on the primacy of substance over form, and reminded us that for the purposes of this competition the skilful execution of the art, or the accomplished use of poetic or literary form was not as important as the vividness and originality of the intended message. The aesthete in me was tempted to disagree with that rather didactic position, but I decided to keep my counsel. Either that, or I was distracted by Ahmed's occasional glances at me across the table.

My mobile buzzed. I excused myself and stepped outside to receive Craig's call. He had left in the late afternoon to escort the Kaka Foundation delegates to the airport, and was in good spirits. They had been more than pleased with the screening of the film, and with the event overall, he said. 'I pitched them a follow-up feature as we drove along and they sounded very excited,' he went on. 'And we can engage lots of NGOs around issues of HIV prevention and stigma and access to treatment and those kinds of things.'

Eventually I managed to conclude the call and returned to the conference-room. We began by weighing up the performance arts competitors, tweeting the names of the three finalists, who would each be given ten minutes to storm the stage at the graduation after-party, the ultimate winner to be decided by audience applause. It was slightly past midnight when we arrived at the ten finalists for the paper arts: five for pictorial, and five for written work. Though there had been a lot of lively debate, in the end there hadn't been too many disagreements about who deserved to be chosen; nor about the eventual winners.

The judges dispersed, yawning. Wole and I were gathering up the last of the students' work when Ahmed returned: he had forgotten his ID card. He stayed till we were done, and the three of us went to the elevator together bearing armfuls of files. Only Wole could fit in the first elevator that arrived, as a crowd of other guests had just come in, tipsy, from a night out, and crammed in ahead of us.

While Ahmed and I were waiting for the next one with our awkwardly-held stacks of papers he enthused about a manuscript a student had pressed on him during the week. 'Provocative and a possible bestseller,' he said. 'She could be the next Chimamanda!' I wondered if it was Ella. I hoped so.

The second elevator chimed open. We went in, followed by a smartly-dressed waitress who was carrying a bottle of white wine and two glasses on a metallic tray that reflected glints of light on the side of Ahmed's neck. Balancing his files in the crook of one arm, he reached out to push the button for 10.

'Please push for five,' the waitress said, and he did so.

'Oga, punch eleven there abeg,' I said.

'We are going to my room first: I'd like you to see the manuscript,' Ahmed said. 'It's unbelievable, I tell you.'

The waitress got off on the fifth floor, and as the elevator doors shut Ahmed asked me why I refused to leave his mind. I smiled tiredly. *If only you knew.*

In his room I spun him round and pinned him savagely to the wall, my chest pressing against his back, my fingers in his front pockets clawing on his thighs, my hips against his firm derrière. *The fabric hides so much.* We were both panting, fully clothed. My mouth was dry. I refused our kissing or undressing.

'I want you,' he said.

'I belong to another,' I said, pressing my hips against his butt harder, my boner throbbing.

'Then why are you here?'

The intercom rang. Ahmed reached for the button.

'Mr. Azeez here,' he said breathlessly. 'Yes, he is here. There was something I wanted him to look at. We'll be up right away. Thanks.'

'My brother?'

'Let's go up to him before someone gets in trouble.'

That's how I predicted it in my head. Here is what actually happened: Wole was on the tenth floor, waiting for us at Ahmed's door. So Wole and I went in with him together. Ahmed gave me a new hardback copy of Paulo Coelho's *The Alchemist* – there was no manuscript. He thanked us for the chance to be a witness to the week and offered us drinks from the mini-bar, which we declined. Wole and I were ascending the stairs two minutes later, Wole saying, 'I don dey talk am now, E go be like say Wole like to dey talk.'

On the morning of the graduation ceremony Mummy and our other guests were taken from the hotel to the campus by taxi, while Wole and I went to the airport to pick up Brother Gbenro. His flight was due in from Abuja at ten but had been delayed by an hour, cutting things rather fine for us to make the ceremony, which, as a faculty member, I both wanted, and was obligated, to attend. But I also very much wanted to be there when Brother Gbenro arrived: he had told us that he was flying in with a surprise for us, and had insisted that we both come to the airport to receive him. Clad in well-starched oxblood-and-royal-pink kaftans and oversize sunglasses we waited in Arrivals sitting opposite each other, our locks neatly braided in four rows and bound back in a bunch, looking more identical than ever. While we waited we followed the build-up to the convocation ceremony on Twitter, Facebook and BlackBerry Messenger. At some point we noticed that we had become quite a spectacle, with people looking us over every now and then. Yep! Two identical dada boys identically dressed pinging away!

Brother Gbenro's plane eventually landed at noon. After a tedious further wait he finally emerged through the crowd of disgruntled passengers, holding the hand of a man who was a taller version of ourselves: Toluwani Damian, Daddy.

He had cut off his locks and his now low-cut hair was entirely silver. He was neatly bearded and pierced in the earlobes, sleek and prosperous-looking and as handsome as ever, wearing a navy-blue kaftan that matched the one Brother Gbenro had on. As he came closer, I saw that his eyes seemed a bit tired and teary. He looked at Wole, then looked at me, searching our – my – eyes for an embrace, for pardon. I would give him more, and so would Wole, who ran into his arms. Both of them were trembling, sweating, crying, laughing. I followed suit. I couldn't help myself. A feeling of wholeness overcame me, a feeling I had missed so much, like a drought swept away by the endless gush of fresh water. I had always wondered what my first reaction would be when, if ever, I beheld my father again, but suddenly I did not have time to think... this man was my being, my life.

The convocation would have to get by without me.

We were chauffeured to the hotel by Tobi, my driver. In the car Daddy and Brother Gbenro plied us with questions about the week just gone, deflecting us from asking them about themselves. We lodged them in the same room, which they insisted on paying for. We were still there making sure they had settled in when everyone else returned from the convocation for lunch and to get ready for the triple party-night ahead – the graduation after-party, our bachelors' eve, and the bridal shower for the girls.

We came down to have lunch with our guests and announce that our dad had arrived. Though it didn't seem to have entered Wole's head that this might be a problem, I was rather worried about telling Mum. Her reaction was almost shocking: she embraced Dad warmly and teased him about his never-waning good looks, and how no-one would believe that he was born four years earlier than Brother Gbenro. Brother Gbenro too was all smiles and laughter. Though this was a relief, once again I had that feeling of secret stories, narratives to which neither I nor Wole were privy.

Lola and Tega, looking gratifyingly stylish and elegant, came and joined us. They appeared thrilled to meet our father, both of them teasing us that they all of a sudden preferred the low-cut look to the locks they been crazy about until that day. We took our places around a large table, Tega beside me, dusting cake-crumbs from my beard; Lola beside Wole, splitting his chicken, both of them performing the part of model wives-to-be. It was endearing, and I was thankful, and yet my mind went back to masks and their meanings. Mummy, stylishly turned out herself, was seated between

Brother Gbenro and Daddy, and seemed relaxed, laughing at their jokes, often pointing out to both girls how adorable her sons were.

I looked at Brother Gbenro laughing, and wondered what he really made of Dad's return. I also wondered why Dad had resurfaced after so long. And Wole and Lola: if only she knew the storm approaching. Wole taking the leap anyway, worried sick all the way. Mum, looking solid and comported amidst all this. Yet did she really not know about his sexuality, or my own? When we had been planning *Eyimofe* she had spoken up for gay rights in a way that implied they mattered personally to us. Despite that, did she see our upcoming marriages as some sort of victory over our father and the potential chaos of same-sex desires? Was that why she was being so pleasant to him? The graciousness of the victor?

I wondered about myself, and how, upcoming marriage or no upcoming marriage, part of me still wanted to meet up with Ahmed to round off the previous night's unfinished business. He was sitting at a nearby table with a woman I recognised as Bukky, one of the K.U. administrators. I wondered how much more luck I could have if I kept on being discreet. Then again, I do not think I was being particularly discreet: people only saw what they chose to see, and I had been counting on that. But beneath the laughter, and Tega's now-annoying submissive wifeliness, I could sense tension in this circle. A circle that to an outsider would look so simple, but was in fact many circles overlapping in the most complex ways.

Our group sat chatting on for a long time after everyone else had left the dining room except Ahmed – and Bukky, who was stocky, dark and beautiful, with low-cut hair, rimless spectacles and a smile that seemed eternal, and who he had presumably met that morning somewhere. Suddenly she laughed, and quite unreasonably this unnerved me. *What the blazes was he saying to her?*

Ahmed looked over then and caught my eye. Mum noticed, and Ahmed noticed her noticing, so he brought Bukky over to our table and I introduced them. Dad was thrilled to meet my publisher. 'You are a very lucky woman, ma,'

Ahmed told Mummy.

'Thanks, dear,' she said, smiling. 'God is always surprisingly faithful.' She then gave him an intent look, holding his eyes until he blushed and looked down. A moment later he excused himself, nodding at me and guiding Bukky by the waist. Turning back to wink when he knew only I would still be watching.

We had the evening all planned out. We would first converge at the Atlantic nightclub, an upmarket venue on Omore Street where the graduation after-party/award night celebration would be storming away, to round off Afrospark; then part ways to attend our respective bachelor and bridal parties.

While everyone else took buses or went by car, Dad and Brother Gbenro insisted that we ride with them on rented power bikes – both of them taking the handlebars while Wole and I, all suited up, clasped them tightly from behind. We rode between the professional riders and the rest of the convoy, our dreadlocks flying from under our helmets. I rode with Dad, holding onto him like paint to a wall, the world thinning out around us as our speed increased. I found myself healing from everything that had come before, and insulated against everything that lay ahead, as we darted along the expressway, riding into a future that was most uncertain yet somehow, we knew, surmountable; winning like the men who came before us, and the men who would come after.

For men of their age, Dad and Brother Gbenro had quite a hold on their 'beasts'.

It was nine p.m. when we arrived at the Atlantic. The Afrospark finale commenced half an hour later, beginning with the presentations of the performance art finalists.

The Master of Ceremonies was my 'special' student Camilla, looking fly in a fitted cream-coloured jumpsuit that was cinched at the waist and sequined at the neckline and ankles, her hair in a waist-length ponytail, a narrow stone-studded white leather belt and white peep-toe killer heels showing off her glistening, ebony-coated toenails – stunning, decently stunning, looking so grown up, and speaking with maturity and assurance that made me proud of her.

The lights went down. Darkness and hubbub fading, then a bright spotlight and silence. The first presentation, of a poem titled 'Beni Perhaps', was made by a boy who stepped quietly into the spotlight wearing nothing but a white cloth draped around his waist. Half his chest and the left side of his face were coated in opaque white make-up, and a flowing red scarf was tied on his head. He began by rattling on a dun-dun drum with its stick then stopped. He recited his poem, drumming at well-judged intervals, the rise and fall of his voice by turns seductive, sensual, at one point mischievous, at another stern. I was most thrilled when he said, 'Let's forget all the nonsense we're told that we should know,' shutting his eyes and turning his head away as though feeling deeply, slowly running one of his palms horizontally across from the white part of his chest to the part not coated, smearing the white make-up, and running the palm of his other hand from the uncoated part to the coated part, smearing and distorting its plenitude. This signalled to me a sensual caress, a call to liberalism... a sign that nothing is really either white or black; a call, perhaps, to unity.

He earned lively applause, whoops and cheers. The second speech was delivered by a plain, bespectacled girl in a plain black skirt-suit and white camisole, with low-cut hair. She talked a lot about dictionary definitions of diversity. Then she delved into the meanings of diversity according to several well-respected authors; the theories and perspectives of notable national and international heroes and thinkers from history. Her choice of words was rather too academic and high-flown for the audience, who began to stir restlessly and clear their throats. I sat there hoping I would hear the simple sounds of her soul's message in place of over-flogged echoes from dictionaries, research and history. I waited until she said 'Thank you' and stepped back from the lectern, and polite applause clattered through the room.

It was frustrating because I knew she was a bright student with a strong sense of fairness and natural justice, and even, in private, a lively sense of humour. I had hoped she would say something that would sing to me, but she had not.

As soon as she left the stage the speakers blared with the

instrumentals of a song that struck a chord in my heart. Then I heard *his* voice. He walked out, his presentation a cover of DJinee's 'I No Dey Shame', a song about a lover who constantly reminds his beloved that his love is shameless and to be flaunted. The masked albino sensation – his locks and lips instantly gave him away. He was clad all in black now, a black adireh shirt and trousers, his hair neatly tied in a black bandana. He wore rimless spectacles and, on his left wrist, two red-beaded bracelets.

Two red-beaded bracelets.

I stood still, perhaps a little stuck, frozen – okay, very stuck and frozen – listening to every word, every line, each with its several meanings. His voice sounded nasal, almost extraterrestrial, yet it was charming.

I felt hot memories slash me through. Baba, saying, 'This will remind you to be true to yourself. This will remind you to be true to God. Never compromise your peace.'

I said I love you many times, yet I walked away.

Once I had a similar pair of bracelets but now I have just one. The other is at Ilaro. With Seun.

I found myself crying.

Someone touched my arm. It was Tega. 'Are you alright?' she asked. I nodded, unable to speak.

The song finished. Just before the lights came back up I slipped away from her, on the pretext of having to make a call. I could feel her eyes on me as I went. My mood fell southward and would stay that way. Once more, it occurred to me – this time in an ominous way – that I was only a night away from wedding her, in spite of every promise I had once made; every secret thing I had once believed in.

Seun.

The awards made and the certificates given, Wole and I left the club and, taking one of the cars, returned to the hotel for our bachelors' party.

All the while I could not shake off the weight lying on my chest. Wole noticed my altered mood but didn't say anything. I wondered what thoughts were in his head. Why were we doing this to ourselves, to Lola and Tega? It seemed to me then as if we were being controlled by some power outside ourselves. I wondered if it was God, or tradition, or fear; or a mixture of the three. It was like we were actors in a play, saying lines that had somehow somewhere been written for us. I had felt that at the dinner earlier, and I felt it more strongly now. If the Devil is the Prince of Lies, what were we doing?

But this was the right thing, I thought. This would expel the rumours of our homosexuality. This would make everything okay. The mask would become the truth, all divisions collapsed together.

The party had heated up, and everyone was drowning in loud music and the mixed spicy aroma of suya and alcohol beneath colourful flashing lights. I sat by Wole on a stool at the bar as the party stretched on past midnight and into the early hours of the morning, my face aching from forcing smiles as he introduced me to his seemingly innumerable friends and associates as they passed by or clustered round us. Most of them had flown in earlier that day especially for the party, while a few had been around all week – friends from our schooldays and Port Harcourt. Almost everyone I knew or cared to know was now in the hall. But a few had not appeared, and it still bothered me that Seun had threatened not to come when I last spoke to him.

This was a few months ago. I had called him to tell him that I had fallen in love with a girl, and that I would be happy. I did this out of anything but good will. Seun and I were once fiercely in love, and once upon a time I could not think of life without him, and out of the love that we had shared I wanted him at my wedding. But I also fiercely wanted to spite him. I wanted him to feel the way I had felt when he betrayed me; like the heavens had snatched my soul away.

It was a sort of unfinished business. I had this with Ahmed too: we had not spoken since our last night together.

We were in the function-room on the tenth floor. The girls were having their bridal shower two floors beneath us.

We – Wole, Tega, Lola and I – had all had our phones confiscated by our over-enthusiastic wedding planner Annabel, a college friend of Tega's. As she gave us our final orientation in the elevator she made us promise not to 'accidentally' run into each other till the wedding ceremony. She, Tega and Lola got off on the eighth floor, and we continued up to the tenth.

Wole was pulled up to dance at some point. I held tightly to the bar's marble counter when someone pulled at me, then saw it was Kwame. Though I was not exactly afraid to dance with him, I resisted. I so badly wanted to disappear from that entire scene, from the reality of being a groom the next day or any other day, and from the temptation that was being so freely offered. I wanted to flee from the possibility that I would be thrown into a new life I might not be able to live but would have to somehow bear, like a scar I could not erase but only conceal.

Kwame danced away smiling. I felt a hand on my shoulder. It was Ahmed. 'Mind if I sit?' he asked, sliding onto a stool beside me.

'Sure.'

'This is a great party.'

'I understand you are leaving tomorrow,' I said.

'First flight.' Taking a cocktail the bartender offered. 'Mee... n the energy here is superb.'

'Are we going to talk about this?' I shouted over the music, my lips brushing his ear.

'Nope.' He was moving his head to the rhythm of the song that was now streaming from the speakers.

'I'm sorry,' I said.

'Sorry? Nonsense! C'mon, this is your bachelor's eve. Your last night of freedom.' He was on his feet now, swaying his hips playfully in front of me in a way that would be seen by others as a joke.

'So you are just going to pretend that nothing happened?' I asked, convinced that he was feigning his excitement on my behalf. He was equally not at peace: I knew it. But here he was, smiling and seemingly thrilled for me, gesturing for me to join him.

'Yep. Hey, ten minutes k, then we'll talk. I want to teach you some lessons on the dancefloor.'

'No, don't do that,' I protested. 'Let's talk. Please.'

'Ten minutes. Just ten minutes.' Now he was immersed

in the vortex of coloured lights. 'Please, now.' I did not move. He tugged at my arm. 'Okay? You want to play hard to get?' He put his hands on my sides, pulling me swiftly off the chair and to himself, our bodies meeting at the pelvis. 'Dance now. Talk later.'

The next I knew I was on the dancefloor, rocking real. Dancing dangerously in a circle of clapping people that quickly formed around Ahmed and me. It was a dance-off – a naughty dance-off – Ahmed sacrificing his age and integrity on the altar of flexibility and style. But I would not let him win. The room grew wilder as we got caught up in the thrill of it all. We danced and danced. I found myself caring less and less what happened, what people might guess, what they might know. The future seemed to be flying away from me and it was a relief.

Suddenly the lights went off and the music cut out – it was a power failure. And in that brief moment, someone pulled me to him. I felt lips meeting mine, a tongue thrusting into my mouth, hands squeezing my derrière and holding me firmly, touching places only 'he' would touch.

Seun?

I could not move. I could not think. I could not fight. Just stood there in the crowded darkness, drowning in the chatter but hearing nothing, giving myself over to this moment. I felt his breath circling my neck, then he whispered from behind me, 'You still can't say fimí sílẹ̀ to me.'

'Seun?'

At that the lights came back on, and then the music, followed by a roar of applause – everyone was still in high spirits. But I was frozen with shock. *This is impossible.* I looked round and I did not see him. I just saw Ahmed, who with a grin resumed his dancing.

'Did you just kiss me?' I asked him.

'What? I can't hear you!' he shouted, trying to out-scream the music.

I took his hand and pulled him away from the dancing crowd over to the bar. 'When the power went out someone kissed me.'

'Don't be silly. There is no way I'm getting physical with you. You are getting married tomorrow.'

'But someone kissed me in the darkness,' I insisted, my heart pounding.

'Well, it wasn't me.'

While Ahmed was still under the heat of my anxious interrogation the music got turned down. Wole called for quiet and gave a brief vote of thanks. I was expecting him to wave me over to say something to our guests before the dancing resumed, but just then an announcement came from the hotel management, through a member of staff, that for security reasons all the parties would have to be suspended. A confused hubbub broke out.

'Our guests are all here, for Christ's sake!' Wole protested to the manager when we both stormed his office a minute later. 'That's over a hundred people!'

The power went out again and we stood in the dark, our chests heaving, as he fumbled for the rechargeable lamp on his desk and switched it on.

'This is for the best reasons, sir,' he said coolly. 'We understand that someone believes we are hosting a gay party in our facility and as such reported it to the State Police.'

'What?' Wole shouted.

'It's our bachelor's eve, for God's sake,' I insisted.

'I'm quite aware of that sir. And your safety is of utmost import to us. There have been thirteen locations blacklisted for raid and thorough search tonight. And regrettably this hotel is on that list.'

My heart dropped. What was happening? Had the manager known in advance? Something was closing in around us.

Wole turned to me. His expression was blank. 'The best we can do now is ask that the hotel staff shall guide us all to our individual floors and rooms with torches and we shall remain there till morning,' he said. 'We shall have a nice wedding and we shall leave Amara tomorrow for our honeymoons.'

An hour later I was back in our room on my knees beside Wole. Together we were declaring God's authority and invoking His protection for the hotel, our guests and our wedding. We were declaring in faith that everything was perfect, even at a time like this; and we prayed especially for the safety of the many LGB people we had summoned to

Amara, some of whom might have been targets. I felt sick
thinking of the recklessness with which we had invited them
here; at our assumption of immunity when the entire nation
was being turned against us. Amara had seemed so safe in
the glow of K.U.'s protective aura. I said a silent prayer in my
heart that God would preserve the balance of things according to His will, and that my wedding to Tega be sealed before
His Throne of Grace.

'I know You are in this, Lord. If Tega is mine to marry,
then no force seen or unseen can contest that. But I wish that
above all things Your will be done. Everything is beautiful
even now. In Jesus' name. Amen.'

In the morning I had a sudden craving for my phone. I
needed to call Seun and confirm whether or not he was in
Amara, and both Wole and I needed news about the raids.
He had dreamt that we were both arrested by the police just
before taking our vows at the altar. We had not heard
anything from the hotel management about the raids.
Thirteen locations, the manager had said. How had he
known this? We wanted to ask him if there were any specific
spots where gay men would ordinarily hang out, and if these
had been targeted. We wanted – needed – to know what had
happened in Amara the previous night. However our two
best men – Kwame (for me) and Tayo (for Wole) – would not
have it: we were trapped in the room till they got the cue
from Annabel to take us straight to the cars.

I caught multiple reflections of us in the elevator mirrors
as we descended. 'It's happening,' I thought. 'There is no
going back now.'

And so we stepped out into the lobby, all of us men who
had enjoyed intimacy with and loved other men, pretending
to be four heterosexual guys totally disconnected from the
whole gay business. It all felt so unreal. But still we made
strikingly handsome fits, all of us in dark grey-blue suits,
white shirts, and with silver silk ascots tucked into our black
velvet waistcoats. Starred with red rosebuds pinned to our
lapels, black glacé shoes on our feet, dark shades, balmed
lips and oiled beards bouncing off the sun.

As though the morning was not tense enough already,

Tayo had to tease Wole about his having a sweaty wedding night to look forward to. I shot him a look, but Wole laughed. He seemed a bit less tense now, but the gut feeling that I had to get hold of my phone grew in me. I had dreamt of some of my male students, who were in my dream wearing lipstick, being beaten, dragged through the streets, and lynched.

Annabel was waiting for us in the lobby. 'You're both looking smashing!' she enthused, singing it like a Beethoven sonata. 'Oh, your publisher Mr Azeez said to give you this,' she added. 'He had to rush off this morning.' – handing me a thin white envelope.

'Annie, please... I really need to make a call,' I pleaded.

'We had an agreement, remember,' she said, adjusting my pocket square and lapel. 'No communication.' She wagged a playful finger.

'Until we get to church, I know. But this is an emergency.'

'There is no emergency, don't mind him,' Wole interrupted. 'He just can't wait till we get to church to hear his angel Tega's voice.'

'It's not that,' I said, irritated, and confused as to why last night's events weren't worrying Wole more. 'It's – '

'Gentlemen, we are running late,' Brother Gbenro called from the hotel entrance. He too was looking smart, in a flowing white agbada, with white shoes and a blindingly shimmering silver wristwatch. His voice was tense, but perhaps that was just to do with escorting a tardy wedding party.

I gave Annabel a pained, pleading look. 'Okay, okay,' she said. 'I'll give the phones to your best men on the absolute condition that they give them to you only once you get to wedding venue. Okay?'

She did so. We piled into our waiting car, and our convoy headed for the campus. Lola and Tega's party were to follow on shortly after; their and our parents, Brother Gbenro said, were already at the church, along with most of our other guests. I looked at the envelope but decided that I had had enough of Ahmed just before my wedding. The previous night's stunt was taking it too far. Part of me thought it couldn't have been him who had embraced me, but there was no other logical explanation.

Kwame passed me my phone as we arrived at the church. It had been on all night on silent mode, and the battery had almost run out. I had eighty-seven missed calls and twenty new messages, with the implication that many more were waiting to flood into my inbox. They were almost all from my students. I looked back along the road and saw Lola and Tega's convoy, following along in the distance. My heart skipped. This was real: I too shall be a husband. Several cars bearing guests pulled up behind ours, blocking us in. Chauffeurs emerged and opened doors for their immaculately turned-out passengers. We got out. Wole hurried into the hall to speak to the officiating minister. I stood on the red-carpeted steps of the church, looking around blankly. So many people were here. So many seemingly friendly faces. Again I felt my reality split open. I was drowning.

Wole came out of the fellowship hall and hurried up to me. He was panting heavily. 'There is a problem, man,' he said. 'Don't freak out.' After looking about to make sure no-one could see it, he handed me his phone. A picture was on display – a picture that would change my life. I felt goosebumps attack my body like a wild splash of frosty wind, and sweat trickled down my back like ants.

A car horn sounded, then another. We looked round and saw some way down the road a convoy of five cars, Lola and Tega's party, were pulling up and making an awkward U-turn, obstructing the flow of traffic. I turned to Wole.

'Ah! Ejo! This is not happening today o,' he exclaimed. Simultaneously we tried to call their iPhones, but they weren't taking their calls. 'They must have the photos now.'

The photos.

A photo of Danjuma and me hugging at the Rainbow Talk meeting while he leaned in to kiss me; an old photo of me and Seun stripped to our boxers kissing in his hostel room; a photo of Wole being fucked by a man whose face was outside its frame, taken in the smeary mirror of some anonymous hotel room.

We jumped into the front seats of the frontmost SUV in our convoy, Wole getting behind the wheel, but it was boxed into the jam-packed arena by all the other cars. Everyone was asking questions. It was taking too much time for them to make way for us, and they were not smart about it at all, however aggressively we blared our horn, and there were just too many drivers to look for anyway.

Daddy, Brother Gbenro, Mummy, and Lola and Tega's parents came out of the church then, wondering what all the racket was. Wole and I rushed up to them and pulled Daddy and Brother Gbenro aside. After quickly flashing them the photos, and them giving us an 'Aaah! At this time?' look, they went and negotiated with the professional riders to release a bike to us. Wads of notes changed hands, we jammed helmets on our heads, and a minute later I was clinging to Wole's back as he sped us through the campus gate towards Amara.

The roads felt bumpier than they had the night before. Trucks, tankers and trailers carrying petrol, water and Fanta seemed to be conspiring to make it impossible for us to catch up with the girls' convoy. Wole was overtaking dangerously, swerving into oncoming traffic, weaving between trucks scarily close to their huge, whirring wheels and earning us lengthy soundings of oncoming car horns. Our wheels thudded into one pothole after another, jarring my spine.

We had thought that they would return to the hotel but they were going in a completely different direction. Who was driving? Which of the cars were the girls in? Were they together or apart? I could not make out my thoughts any more, and the thick black smoke and white dust that lashed at my eyes made it impossible not to cry.

We hit a traffic jam where the vehicles were packed in too tight for even our power bike to squeeze through, and a petrol tanker beside us belched soot in our faces. Coughing would only make us inhale more pollution than we had already, and we tried to hold our breaths.

I watched from outside myself as Wole stood up on the bike's pedals to look ahead.

The girls' party was held at a police checkpoint, he informed me. 'They're stuck there. We'll catch them now.' He sat back down and I slid my arms round his waist again. His body vibrated less now, his heart throbbing slower but heavier. I realised we had not planned an explanation for the photographs, or certainly I had not. Perhaps he had some clever lines in his mind that would make it all okay, but I didn't think so. In that instant I wished the girls away. And just then they were let to move on. The traffic ahead of us moved slowly forward, by chance opening a gap our bike could fit through. Wole put his foot down and sped us past the checkpoint, leaving police officers shouting at our backs, but for me all excitement was gone. I prayed we would never catch up. I did not have anything to say to Tega.

Our speed increased, and I wondered in an abstract way if Wole too wanted not to succeed, if he was in fact trying to kill us. His cheerfulness about his wedding had, it struck me now, the quality of someone who has decided to commit suicide: no more worries, no more cares. One time we narrowly escaped colliding with a vehicle head-on, and another some kids flew off the road to avoid being mown down by us, and nearby pedestrians shouted curses.

We were now on the outskirts of Amara and in a part of the town I had never gotten to know. The broad, four-lane road was not as clogged here. We could see the girls' convoy only a little way ahead. Nothing rode between us save for two big trucks that drove in parallel and moved at top speed. A narrow space was left between them. Part of me wished that the space would close up and the girls vanish into the distance. Another part wondered what Tega thought of me.

Wole rushed us into the space between the two trucks. I could feel the heat and vibration radiate from them, and hear the clanging of metal and the roaring of the trucks' engines as they seemed to be closing in on us. I heard Wole shout 'Jesus, Jesus, *Jesus*!'

Images flashed into my dust-stung eyes: the ones of trucks colliding on Nigerian expressways; the ones of skulls cracking like popcorn beneath heavy tyres to expose oceans of blood and islands of brain, and blood-bathed bodies lying unidentified and unidentifiable on the glass shard-sprayed tarmac. Time stopped when a metal flap from the truck on our left flicked up and ripped through my sleeve. I froze and could not feel a thing, not knowing if I had been cut or not. I knew our skulls were crushed when the truck on our right puffed dark smoke at us and wavered inwards. 'Stop! Stop!' I screamed at Wole as I held him so tight I must have made him want to vomit. I was certain I no longer wanted to get married today: I just wanted to stay alive.

Wole darted us through the smoke and we burst out ahead of the trucks with him still shouting 'Jesus! Jesus!' Then he led out a loud scream, then mad laughter.

The girls' convoy was close. We were moving at as fierce a speed as they were. Nothing rode between, or beside, us now.

A T-junction appeared up ahead. At it the first two cars went left, while the other three went right. The traffic lights turned red before we could make a decision about our brides' destinations, and what to do; and to my relief Wole pulled up sharply rather than ploughing into the thickly criss-crossing traffic that now streamed before us. He put his foot down to balance the bike.

My phone shivered in my pocket. It was Professor Brown. I answered. He told me that some policemen from outside Amara had visited the Atlantic shortly after we left the previous night on a 'special assignment', and had rounded up everyone in attendance on charges of homosexuality. We could only guess that Brother Gbenro's influence had shielded me and Wole, as our names must have been mentioned to them, and our involvement in campaigning around LGBT rights was well-known.

'Return to the school immediately, please. The parents and guardians of these students are on campus with some of our staff. Reassure them that everything is under control. I will call Abuja for help from my contacts in the government. Please, nobody leaves the campus until I confirm that it is safe to.' Then he sighed, 'So much for peace and unity.'

Just then, an SMS came in from Tega: *I hate faggots. I hate you.*

Be ni Perhaps

Let's forget Valentine colours and Christmas bows
Let's forget all the nonsense that we 'should' know
And let's drift some maggi into milk
Let's use some sugar for egusi
And nibble some okra with ketchup
Hmm... Perhaps *Be ni*?
Perhaps not.
Let's start a new parade
Of Christian girls and Muslim boys
Playing okwe and drinking kunu with nkwobi
Be ni Perhaps?
Perhaps? Perhaps.
Let us make KJV Arabic
And roast masara in the open
Let's celebrate those *Be ni* moments
And let's forget the difference between Daudu and David
And understand that Hussein isn't worse but only slight-
ly different
Let our lips sincerely say *Be ni*
And let our hearts agree
With rib-cracking laughter when Yusuf and Ikenna mis-
quote Shakespeare
Let's help Zainab with her hijab
And help Funke sustain her gele
Let's teach Nma the bridal dance
And let us let Edikan marry for beauty and for love
Let's have one festival of our several songs
Unveil the brides, say they belong
Perhaps *Be ni?*
Be ni Perhaps

Oremi True

Oremi,

Often, I think, life is not as black and white as we like to make it seem. If you were not so stuck up with your high regard for public endorsement, you would be open to this fact too.

No, really, let's think of it: How can a father say he loves his son and still can stand to watch him cry? How can water be so good yet it drowns people? How can a child who has been raised to be courteous and poised turn out to be a bully? How can a life which should be so perfect – or is seen to be perfect – turn out to be a whirlwind?

I am struggling with these questions of black and white. I'm struggling with these questions of you. Of us. Five months into matrimony and I can no longer recognise my reflection. It's like each time I hold Kikelomo in my arms I'm acting out a script. It's like everything I see in her is drawn from the songs you sang to me. I love Kike. I'm sure I do. I respect that she is hardworking, directed, fierce and passionate. Yes, and she smiles. She smiles like you.

Olawale mi, it's difficult. My dreams are now filled with pictures, so many pictures of us. The other day I was kissing her, and really I was kissing you. Whenever I feel her hands around me I have to believe first that it is you so that I don't freak out.

But I'm strong Wale. I'm strong but I miss you. I really miss you. And though we can't be together, I'll always have you. I'll always want you.

I love you man. I really love you. Come home soon.

Wild Silence,

Prince Seun

SCRIPTURE LIGHT

MINISTRIES

Port Harcourt, NIG

www.scph.com, 08011111111

Dear Olawale,

How are you today? How have you been? I trust that you are ready to move on to the next phase of your life. How are your mum and brother?

I am writing this to share a few thoughts with you on what has been on my mind for a while.

When your mother first invited me to your place to meet with you and your brother, I was a bit nervous. I often do not know what to expect when it comes to young people. They are so alive and different from the older ones, because they are too young to be afraid. They are too young to pretend.

But our meeting and several conversations have come to inspire me in several ways. It reminds of the first reason I opted to become a pastor – that I saw how much pain and confusion young people go through, and I wanted to help direct them, God helping me. It has not been easy. Each young person is different and often has an interestingly unique reality to his or her life. But they all require the love of God to be sorted out.

The last time we met, you confided in me. I love that you deemed me worthy to be a friend to an amazing you. I call you amazing because everything about you radiates the Glory and the Presence of God. I call you amazing because you are the perfec-

tion of God. Before now I have read of great men in the Bible, and in our recent history, men who were and are still being celebrated for their successes. I found one thing common amongst them all: They wrestled victories from their battles. Victory isn't a one-man sport. It is you continuously dominating yourself and the rest of the world. They learned to subdue themselves and the forces blowing their lives this way and that. They took over, and insisted in spite of everything else on living up to the God within them, their Purpose. You have never been just another child. Seventeen means that you have come a long way. I need you to rest assured that nothing and no-one can stop you as long as God is on your side. Just do not get in the way of your victory – nor let anyone or anything else – and everything will be fine. God says you are perfect so you are. He is holding onto you in everything and in every way. Let nothing steal your peace, my brother. Let nothing blind you to the presence of your Father. I celebrate you every day because I see the victor you've been made to be. You'll always be in our prayers. Godspeed.

Hopefully, we could have lunch together when I visit. I also hope that you and Wole will let me drive you to church – not ours, but another one that I think might interest you.

Much love,

Pastor Makinde

Whenn I told Seun that I was leaving for Port Harcourt with Mummy, he was sullen. He kept staring into the distance, and it seemed to me that the whole of Ilaro Grammar School thinned away until it was just the two of us sitting side by side at our desk. For the rest of the day he refused to discuss anything with me, and I came home disgruntled.

That night, after dinner, Baba and I were out on the balcony. It was dark but the light from the moon bounced white off his shiny head. He began to tell me a long folk story about why the sea washes ashore and recedes almost immediately. I looked up at him from where I was sitting on the floor and watched his hands move in silhouette as he talked. Stories for him, for us, were more than just a pastime. Whenever he told a story, there was something he wanted me to learn.

The earth, he said, was a prince amongst his brothers, the other elements of creation, and they all lived happily under their father, the sun. One day water decided that he should be next in command to the sun. Everyone else disagreed, not just because they did not think that water was good enough to be next in command, but because he was such a proud fellow and, if promoted, would lord it over the rest of them. Water, regardless, went on and on in his bid to assert his superiority over the other elements. Still, they rejected him. Sun stood aloof, insisting they decide the matter among themselves. Then one day, while they were asleep, water flooded over his brothers in a deluge, subjecting them to his density. They were trapped. When the sun discovered this, he was enraged with his son, and blazed forth and dried most of him up in retribution. The other elements were furious with water, and, after agreeing amongst themselves that leadership was needed, they decided to make their youngest brother earth the second in command in his place. They charged earth with the authority to make sure that water never leaves his place again. But since then water has not stopped trying to reclaim what was never rightfully his. So when he tries to wash ashore the earth drives him back, teaching the world that everything has its place in creation for the balance of things.

'You have your place too, Olawale,' Baba said.

'Yes Baba,' I said.

'Have you told your friends that you will be leaving for Port Harcourt?'

'I don't have any friends, Baba.'

'Seun nko? What about him?' he asked. 'You always talk about him.'

'He said he doesn't want to be friends any more because

I'm going away.'

'Is that so?'

'Yes Baba.'

'Come and take these.' He placed two beaded bangles on my upturned palms and closed my fingers around them. 'Always be true to yourself and to your God.'

'I don't understand, Baba.' I sat back on the floor, smoothing out the bangles between my palms.

'Just don't ever forget. Be a man.'

That night I dreamt of Seun and our first meeting. It was my second day at Ilaro Grammar School, and the English class was on, when Miss Nike paused in her disquisition on the role of the sheep in George Orwell's *Animal Farm*: 'When they chant "four legs good"...' – she seemed to have caught sight of something – or someone – at the door. She stepped out briefly and returned with a boy as small as I was. His skin was deep chocolate and his eyes were bright and large, but the hair on his head seemed to have been sprinkled with ash. Miss Nike introduced him to us as Oluwaseun Alabi and directed him to share a desk with me. His eyelashes were long and looked soft. Somehow we were friends at once. As the days passed, I discovered that I craved school more and more. And it was not that the school's skies had started raining candies. But perhaps they had, for me. My spirit accepted Seun. And soon I found that my core submitted to him. His lively intelligence quickly made him most sought out by the other students, but he insisted on being with me and shied away from everyone else. We shared everything from pencils to the fruits we gathered during the break period, to the sandwiches and juice his mum packed for his lunch. From the first he attracted special treatment from the school staff and management, and with time I learned that this was because he was royalty.

A life without Seun's friendship would be different, I knew. Emptier. And yet at the same time my shallow young spirit was growing excited about the move to Port Harcourt.

Ah, Port Harcourt: the long stretch of Aba Road, bisecting the city in a gash bejewelled with vehicles. Port Harcourt with her predictable traffic jams: seven to nine a.m. and five to nine p.m. The too-young salespeople hawking their wares on trays or from their hands. The light-skinned immigrant children already skilled in our three major languages – Igbo, Hausa and Yoruba – who would cling tightly to you till you parted with twenty naira – just before five others rushed over from only-God-knows-where, singing, 'Uncle marama. Aunty marama,' demanding their share too. Port Harcourt and her multifarious routes and junctions: Artillery, Mile One, Slaughter... each offering a poor alternative to the other: it's clogged in one, it's clogged at all. All this making us thankful for the great radio stations we have: Ray Power, Rhythm 93.7... connecting everyone across the airwaves.

P.H. is pretty too, when the sweet sun rises above her and overwhelms the blaring flare of gas at Eleme, which casts a gold shadow over Akpajo, Aleto and Alesa all night, itself perversely beautiful... An interesting place to live in, socialise in and just be in, she bears a sizeable chunk of Nigeria's oil and gas and political history. She was the playground, place and pride of Ken Saro-Wiwa, Ogoni's voice and valour, his story and work almost unknown to today's indigenes, who should be retelling and reliving his struggles.

P. H. is also Nigeria's garden city, and World Book Capital for 2014. However for me she is special for other reasons. She gave me a chance to learn of the other side of me. The me I am when I am in the company of my brother, and sharing the amazing experiences and dreams that bound and keep us together.

Up until our last year in secondary school I idolised Wole as an ideal version of myself. Everyone liked him – the teachers, the junior students, the girls in our class; the boys in our class... I felt that they only put up with me because more often than not Wole was with me, and while he was with me they couldn't help coming over to him. So there I was, silent most of the time in our group conversations, but present. Then again, he knew how to retreat and take me with him when our termly examinations were approaching.

The third Saturday of the month was visiting day. Mum would come to us with home-cooked rice, or egusi soup and garri, or vegetable soup, and she never showed up without fried goat-meat. Eating was Wole's favourite part of visiting day. I had come to love it too, and its 'juicenessness'. Mum

would sit with us by the school's parade ground and listen to
Wole tease me about this or that girl who said she liked me,
and to whose flirtatious tactics I had been oblivious. She
would talk about Wole's asthma medication, or my sadly
unimproved grade in mathematics: simple, everyday matters. Sometimes she talked of things at work, but always
lightly. She told us once how her car had packed up in the
middle of the road one afternoon and she had simply left it
there and gone home.

'Wo. I can't shout o,' she said, laughing. 'The poor thing
insisted on observing siesta, and I was in no mood to car-sit
that pile of metal!' She had had to take an okadah home
under the blazing sun.

At the end of the evening she would take our hands and
pray with us. Afterwards we would watch her drive out of the
school compound, and feel melancholy.

She never missed a third Saturday except once, and then
she sent word to us ahead of time that she would be out of
town, and Brother Gbenro came instead. He did not bring
any food: we had to make do with gala – sausage rolls – and
Pepsi – but he did bring us letters. He gave one to Wole,
from Baba, and two to me – one from Baba, the other from
Seun.

In Baba's letter he said he had been having negative
dreams about me. He did not describe their contents, but
advised that I be wary of the boys in school, and that I should
look out for my brother more.

Seun's letter was an apology for the way he had told me
off the last time we met. He said he wished we had talked
more, but the line that stayed with me was, *Wale, it's never
the same without you.* I kept the letter folded in my bible,
between Malachi and Matthew. Somewhere along the line I
got another bible and stopped using my old one. I did not
reread the letter as often after that, but thoughts of Seun
flashed into my mind whenever the boys in my class talked
about homos and how disgusting they were, and my face
grew hot.

In all that I felt totally alone. It wasn't until a few weeks
before our last Christmas holiday as students at Nigerian
Navy that I got wind of Wole's fondness for Peter, a boy in

the junior class. Initially I thought little of it because Wole was now a school prefect, and his interactions with Peter seemed related to his duties – duties that had drawn him so far from me that I now only got to see him during classes and late at night, after he had made sure that the other students were quiet and in their beds. We were speaking very little by then. I had not been invited to become a prefect, and was – belatedly – beginning to see him as an entity separate and different from myself. This made me bottle up my feelings, and I became someone else too. Needing to find a niche, I put up a façade of toughness.

Peter visited our room too often, I thought – even after I warned him to never mistake me for Wole. He was slight in build, somewhat effeminate, and spoke delicately. For this reason he never really got on with his classmates. Wole knew I did not like him, but never stopped trying to make him 'our little brother'. Wole would go to study with him in his classroom, and sometimes they wouldn't return until thirty minutes after prep time was over. Wole often ironed Peter's clothes on Saturdays along with his own, when usually it was the junior student who ironed for the senior student.

I had let all this slide until one particular Saturday. Wole and Peter were doing their laundry together near the tap and I came to get our locker key. I teased Wole about his hanging out with his 'boyfriend' and he gave me the most shocking response: 'Not all of us are like Seun o.'

He could not possibly have known of Seun unless he had read one of my letters. I angrily demanded an explanation.

'Wale, somebody loves you.'

He grinned mischievously at me and Peter chuckled shyly. This enraged me. I imagined Wole waiting till I left the room to comb through my locker. I imagined him reading Seun's letter with Peter and their eyes widening in excitement. I was mad at him. I was mad at Peter. I did not see my hand darting across Wole's face, though I felt the stinging impact on my palm. He was shocked. I was shocked. Everyone watching stood amazed. For the first time in my life I had hit someone, and that someone was my brother.

Wole felt his face and shot a glance at me. I had hit him harder than I thought: blood trickled down from his nose. He made to walk past me towards our room, but returned, took another look at me – this time fiercely into my eyes – then kicked at a plastic bucket filled with water that sat on the floor beside me. Water splashed on both us, and blood ran down his foot – the bucket had split and cut him; I had cut him. Both his fists were clenched at his sides. He turned to walk away again, and this time he didn't turn back. Peter looked at me, then followed him out.

We didn't speak for weeks.

A fortnight later Peter fell ill. Wole nursed him and was hardly ever in our room. He only returned to jump into bed without saying a word to me. He sometimes tucked Peter in at lights out and spent the night on the floor next to him. In class we did speak, but he was extremely formal with me. I wished so badly that he would hit me back. Get it out of his system. But he didn't.

Peter's condition worsened and he had to leave school for an operation.

A few days later, after school hours, Wole unexpectedly slipped his hands into mine and, looking into my eyes intently, asked, 'Who is Prince Seun to you?'

'He is my friend from Ilaro,' I responded.

'Will he come between us?' he asked.

'I don't understand.'

'I can't bear the thought of anyone coming between us.'

'But you place Peter above me.'

'I don't place Peter above you, Wale. '

'That's not true, and we both know it.'

'Peter is my school son.'

'And I am your brother, Wole. Your twin! Besides, Peter you will leave here in Navy. Me you will go home with and live with.'

'I won't leave Peter here.'

'What are you saying? Will you ask Mummy to adopt him?'

'No, it's – I don't know.'

There was a long pause and he looked away, worry spreading across his face. His eyes got teary.

'Wale, you are my brother, and I love you. But Peter, he is very special to me.'

'More special than I am?'

'It's not the same thing, Wale.'

'Really?' What the hell did he mean? How could Peter be more special to him than I was?

'Wale, I feel for Peter what Seun feels for you.'

My heart dropped to my stomach for a second. *Wole is ti bii.*

From that moment on I saw my brother in a new light. I connected with Wole on a whole new frequency, and saw I no longer needed to feel in competition with Peter. After that I let myself be vulnerable around and to him. I think I fell in love with my brother then.

After Dad had eloped with Uncle Ola, and we had returned from school to Port Harcourt, Wole was depressed for about a month, and neither Mum nor I could reach him. He came to the dining table only to say good morning and have breakfast, and in the evenings would eat his dinner in silence. I knew this was because Peter was still in hospital.

In the meantime we awaited our O-level results and hoped-for admission to university.

At some point I noticed that Mum had beefed up her commitment to the church. We were used to attending Sunday services together, but now she went on Wednesdays and Fridays too. She read her bible more, and one of the pastors from the church, Pastor Makinde, started visiting regularly. Sometimes when he came around he would ask to see Wole and me together.

We would talk – or, truthfully, he would mostly talk and we would mostly listen – until late in the evening, and then he would leave. He talked about the Bible, about the Ten Commandments and how beautiful they are. But he was always quick to remind us that they demonstrated that independently we as humans are weak and fallible. He said they were more aspirations than commandments, because we would never be able to perfectly keep them; that to err is human and forgive divine, but that nevertheless we had a duty to try all through our lives to get better at keeping them. He added that some of them, such as the commandment to honour our parents, though singular, translated to a whole range of other commitments, while others, such as the prohibition against stealing, were less ambiguous and more precise – though even these had their complications: is it wrong to steal to prevent your children starving? Would the fundamental command to love justify the commandment broken? Were some commandments more important than others, we asked him. Did the commandments of the New Testament supersede those of the Old? Pastor Makinde said that our lives were built around the beauty of the commandments, and perhaps the complexities they gave rise to too, as the norms surrounding them varied in different times and places.

Our conversations grew in intensity. He talked about love, and mistakes and imperfections. He also got around to sex, adolescence, and what he called 'human expectations'. Once he asked us about our girlfriends. We said that we did not have any, and further asked whether it was not unchristian to be in a relationship this early. He said that it depended on how we decided to express our romantic yearnings. He further told us that generally our human cravings are not as evil or inappropriate as we often label them to be, providing that we direct more energy to expressing them appropriately than we do to seeking out the right label.

After he had gone, that evening over dinner Mum talked to us about the use of condoms. When Wole told her that he did not need to know as he was not having sex, she said he could teach his friends who were. 'No knowledge is a waste. And you, Wale,' turning to me, 'you haven't introduced me to your girlfriend.'

'Mum, I'm not having sex either,' I said.

'That does not mean you can't have girlfriends,' she said. 'That goes for you too, Wole.'

'I guess girls don't like boys with dreadlocks,' Wole said.

'That's not true,' Mum said. 'That's so not true. Anyway, as far as condoms, it's best to know beforehand. You should know road signs before you ignite the car.'

The next day Wole asked Pastor Makinde if he had a girlfriend. 'I'm very married,' the pastor responded, flashing his ill-fitting wedding band, though he wouldn't tell us anything about what his wife was like.

On the whole I enjoyed these sessions, as they got Wole out of his room and saying more syllables to us, and there was an undercurrent in what the pastor said that suggested tolerance of different ways of expressing love

However one time, looking around himself shiftily, the pastor announced that we would be talking about the Sodom story, and why God destroyed the inhabitants of that city. Wordlessly Wole got up and left the room, locked himself into his bedroom, and came out only for dinner.

This meant I had to sit through that session all by myself. Usually Pastor Makinde was light and jovial, but that day he trashed the topic of homosexuality and was very dramatic, shaking and sweating profusely. He talked about 'dirty' behaviour, and said there was an evil spirit that subdued everyone who practised it, and also showed me parts of the Bible that said no homosexual shall be allowed into heaven. He said the only way out was to confess our sins and undergo thorough spiritual deliverance from the spirit of sodomy.

After that he gripped my hands and said a very energetic prayer casting and binding the spirit of sodomy, spraying my face with saliva and soaking my palms with his sweat, making my whole body vibrate. In the middle of all this, one of those thunderous Port Harcourt rains began to fall. Lightning flashed and thunder cracked. It was very windy outside and the wind blew into the living room, clattering the blinds and scattering papers. The power went out, and in the half-dark I was terrified. I feared that Rapture was beginning. I did not want to go to hell, so I called out to the pastor, who was rocking back and forth with his eyes closed tight, praying loudly. At that he opened his eyes, his lashes dripping with sweat. In a choked voice I told him I was possessed by the spirit of sodomy and needed deliverance. He smiled and said, 'The Lord has revealed it to me a long time ago. It is an ancestral curse we must break. Or else you and your brother will never know peace. Get on your knees. Let's commence the deliverance immediately.'

More terrified than I had ever been in my life, I did as he said. He clamped his hands around my temples. My heart was racing. My head was threatening to pull itself from his grip, his large, sweaty palms pressing against it on both sides, drowning me in sweat, olive oil, tears and saliva. He went on and on praying.

Following that night I struggled with nightmares and a severe headache. I could not discuss what had happened with Wole. Even now I cannot articulate the experience enough to discuss it clearly. I believe in the existence of angels, God, divinity and evil. But I was – and remain – stricken with questions. If homosexuality is genuinely an evil spirit, how come no-one has been able to cast it out? How come it still occurs and is reborn effortlessly in the human race? And above all: how come it is a nest and inspiration for so much warmth, art, kindness, community, sisterhood and brotherhood? How has it spun so many intellectuals, role models, philanthropists, spiritual and political leaders, experts, artists, stars and lovers? How come God occasions so much good with, through and in spite of it? And if it's a distraction from the proper business of life, how come it genuinely and independently causes, interferes with or stops nothing – even the having and raising of children?

A week later Peter visited Port Harcourt with his family for a medical check-up. We learned that he had been admitted to the University of Port Harcourt Teaching Hospital. Mum would not let Wole go by himself – she did not think he was emotionally stable enough – so I accompanied him in a taxi Mum hired for us. We said little to each other on the journey, and Wole grew increasingly tense. On getting there we learned that Peter had been moved to the intensive care unit, and they would not let us see him – only family members were allowed in, on the doctor's orders. His mum came out and told us distractedly that he was all strung up on drips and life-support tubes and wires.

'Everything was okay after the surgery until two days ago,' she said. 'We were at the market, shopping for school. He started complaining that he was feeling dizzy and that he could not feel his right leg. On our reaching home, he lay down on the couch, closed his eyes and right in front of me he stopped breathing.'

Having knowledge of first aid, she had managed to resuscitate him. They had come from Lagos to Port Harcourt because his medical files had been transferred there in the course of his first surgery, and they trusted the doctor who had operated on him.

We sat with her until Peter's father returned a short while later – he had been making calls outside. We were allowed to see Peter briefly. He was unconscious, plugged with tubes, and a plastic mask covered his face, a tube running from it to an oxygen cylinder by the bed.

After that we waited in the reception area with his parents, in the hope that he might wake up.

By seven p.m. Mum's calls were coming every five minutes, and we had to go. Peter's parents thanked us for making the journey.

On the drive home, Wole slipped into his solitary mood again. I reached out and took his hand and we shared a short prayer in the back of the cab.

A few days later Peter's father called to tell us that he had passed on.

At first Wole acted like nothing had happened. Superficially he seemed brighter, but his eyes showed his pain. Everyone knew that he was putting up a façade. Everyone knew that he so badly wanted to grieve. But how manly would that be? He went out on his own more often, to see former classmates of ours who lived in the neighbourhood. I became aware he was drinking beer, and sometimes he smelt of dope. Soon I noticed that he laughed more than was reasonable at things that before would not have been in the least amusing to him.

He still mostly kept up his church attendance though, as did I. One day we were coming home from one of our midweek church functions when we sighted Obinna, one of our former classmates, in the midst of a group of boys wielding canes and belts. They looked like they were about to lynch him. Wole and Obinna had at some point had a confrontation in school over something Obinna refused to tell me about when I asked him. I never raised it with Wole, so I never quite understood their relationship. Wole and I ran over just as one of the boys, who was holding Obinna by the shirt, shoved him off-balance. Obinna landed heavily on the ground on his backside and the boy caught hold of him and pulled him to his feet again.

'Oga, wetin dey happen here?' Wole demanded as we pushed our way through the growing ring of angry boys. 'Abeg calm down, leave the boy shirt first' – trying to pacify the most provoked of the group, who kept a fierce grip on Obinna's shirt.

Ranting and yelling 'Tufiakwa!' they loudly accused Obinna of being homosexual.

When Wole asked them how they knew, or if they were sure he was homosexual, they said that Obinna's story had gone round the neighbourhood, that everybody knew about it.

'Aaa... you serious?' Wole asked sarcastically. 'But eh... him done do you before?'

'Choi! God forbid!' the boy holding Obinna's shirt shouted, stepping back and letting go of him.

'Abi him done do you?' Wole asked the next boy, and the next, until they all agreed that they had no proof.

'Even if him na homo, na by to dey beat am you go beat the homo commot for him body?' Wole continued. 'Oya you now. You be Timi no be so?' he said, pointing to the leader.

'Na my name,' the boy confirmed sulkily.

'You dey smoke "Igbo" you know say if I tell police now, na sanko you dey go straight!?' The crowd grew a little sobre. 'Even you sef,' I said, pointing at another boy, Tonye, whose lips were black from marijuana smoke. Meanwhile Obinna had slumped to his knees, watching and blinking, lips torn and bloody from a blow which had earlier been dealt his face.

Wole and I successfully convinced Timi that the mob was not justified. He was reluctant at first, but he connected with Wole as if he had known and already begun to respect him before that time.

'Oya everybody, dey go una house,' Timi shouted, dispersing the others. Reluctantly they went, tossing sticks aside, feeding belts back through loops around their waists. He stayed back to shake hands with Wole and me. He apologised to Obinna, who was still terrified and shaking.

Wole helped Obinna to his feet. As Wole embraced him, five or six small granite rocks seemed to fly from nowhere, missing me and Obinna but hitting Wole and, ironically, Timi on the back and thighs. It was Tamuno, another boy, who threw them – we could see him taking to his heels some distance away. Timi pursued him shouting, 'Thief! Thief!'

Later we learned that Tamuno got caught and seriously beaten.

Some months after this incident, Wole, Mum and I moved from Port Harcourt: Wole and I had been admitted to Kola University to study law, while Mum had been transferred to a new branch of the hospital she worked for that had opened in Abuja.

Seun, meanwhile, wrote to tell me that he had gained admission to the University of Port Harcourt. I wanted to reply, to at least say I was pleased for him, but felt I couldn't: following my session with Pastor Makinde I kept so much bottled in. I had pulled back from Mum, because it must have been her who told him she was worried about my and Wole's sexuality. But as I began to count down my weeks in Port Harcourt I needed to tell someone how all my life it had been there, peeking out at me in odd places and at odd times: the reminder there was something about me that was not quite conventional. And it wasn't merely that my mind was at war with my body: it had been a string of wars. The whole of myself against the whole of myself. I had always sought a name for it and, ironically, through the intervention of Pastor Makinde, I had now found one.

It was our last Sunday in Port Harcourt, and the church was full. Makinde preached a sermon on 'Openness to Our Purpose'. After the service I excused myself from Mum and Wole, went to his office, and told him that his deliverance had been ineffective. He blamed it on my lack of faith.

I slapped his face twice, in my head, and left.

Fimí sílẹ̀ Forever

Guide me in my today
And kindle my seemingly distant tomorrow
Sing to the halo around my heart
That she may realise her inherent fire
Sing to the bird inside me
That she may instinctively whistle back
So I may learn from your wings how to fly
And from my lips to sing
And command my body to dance
In subtleness, in speed and in love
Sing to my distant tomorrow
But teach me to dance heartily today
And when the sun sets
Teach me to stop for discipline
Teach me to say Fimí sílẹ̀ to the arms of passion
And return home to the ones who truly love me
That I may sing to their hearts too
Tomorrow I promise to return
Because I have been sung to
But if I say Fimí sílẹ̀ forever,
It will be pure and true

Iwonikan/just you

Dear Wale,

Look, you have every reason to think that your place in the world is one big mistake. But for God's sake why should God put you against God? I have no desire to complicate what seems like the perfect life that you have built for yourself. I would love so much to see you happy.

But only you can let yourself listen to the truth. God is always speaking. He is always there.

If you decide to get married today I need you to know that I love you and I'll always be a phone call away.

Hugs,

Ahmed

After the girls had left us, we were told later, the extra police security at Kola University had been abruptly withdrawn: even Brother Gbenro could only do so much.

Professor Brown and a team of lecturers rushed down to the police station to see our graduates. So many people had been arrested in the raids that night; some had even been killed.

According to the police report there had been 'many people who did not look like graduates' at the Atlantic, and the officers had been given an anonymous tip that there was to be a gay party held at that same club. They were given, they said, descriptions of the location and of certain individuals who would be present, and the range of people they would find there, so when they got to the club they were convinced that they had received a very good tip. And so they raided the 'den of homosexuals and its patrons', in the process gunning down several the police claimed tried to overpower them. The dead men, we later heard, were only trying to flee the scene, and all the bullet entry wounds, it was noted when the autopsies were performed, were in their backs. Their blood spattered the walls of the lobby and stained its pale marble flooring.

Among those killed were James Fela, the 27-year-old alumnus of K.U. turned freelance blogger who had been commissioned by the university to chronicle the *Save the Colours* week for the school's archive; and three other past alumni of K.U., all of whom had been guests at *Save the Colours*. The surviving suspects were rounded up violently by the police, and were even briefly attacked by the inhabitants of the neighbourhood before they, and the bodies of James Fela and the others, were taken away by the police. The gateman of the club was forcibly evicted, and the Atlantic was burned to the ground by the righteous local community.

Professor Brown was reliably informed that most of those arrested who were not alumni had been rapidly bailed by their lawyers, their names struck from the records as though they had never even been in police custody. The celebrities caught up in the affair – Nollywood actor Amobi Dike, celebrity blogger Ken Fubara, and celebrity model and philanthropist Fola X – all of whom had been guests of *Save the Colours*, and who had been photographed in handcuffs at the impromptu press conference the police gave at the scene of the arrests – received official apologies for the 'mistake'. Our alumni, however, were all refused bail. No reason for this was given, just a terse, 'It is at the court's discretion.'

It was a criminal matter, a felony having been committed: flagrantly violating the provisions of the Same Sex Prohibition Act of 2013.

The police shootings, by contrast, were not criminal.

As one of the organisers of the controversial *Save the Colours* event, I was instructed by the vice-chancellor not to say or do anything. He would handle the matter personally, he said. He had had confrontations with the Amaran police in the past, and had won; and he wanted to wield all the influence of Kola University and her recent affiliates to get the students in his charge released without the case coming to court.

It terrified me that these students – the same students who I had shared classes and lectures with; who I had encouraged to be bold and assertive in expressing themselves and claiming their human rights – stood the chance of becoming convicts, and I could do nothing about it.

The administration split into factions: those who felt that the students deserved whatever was coming to them if it was true that they had really 'indulged in homosexuality' and it was a gay party; those who were keen on making as many phone calls as possible to get the students out of police custody as there was, thus far, no provision for bail; those who did not want to talk about it at all; and those who were already applying for transcripts to leave the university because its good name was on the chopping-block.

Nigeria was hot, and we had chosen to dive into the cooking pot, so to speak: this was our comeuppance. In a perversion of democracy we were to be shown that the new law indeed applied to all: to students from a prestigious private university as much as to male prostitutes privately shipped in the dead of night from one upmarket hotel room to another, and afterwards thrown back onto the streets like trash. What I did not understand was why the K.U. students were being held back so intently. As time went by most of the other suspects who had not been bailed straight away were released, 'thorough investigations having been conducted.' But not our students: they had been charged, and were to be taken to court.

Their increasingly frantic and frustrated parents, and some of our more engaged lecturers, had meeting after meeting to try and find a way forward. The school chapel had more prayer sessions than usual, and the Muslim students, parents and teachers tabled the issue before God too. We had a candlelight vigil for the men who were shot dead. It was well-attended: even those most vocally against 'homo business' were troubled by the police shooting young partygoers dead at a graduation ceremony party in an upmarket nightclub. Professor Brown spoke at the vigil, and asked the students who attended to be calm. He also asked, without being in any way specific about what, that everyone be careful.

The semester ended, but our worries did not. Over the weeks of the summer break I watched my boss's morale drop. Meeting after meeting, he was not the same person. Each time the case was mentioned he seemed to age a year or more.

The trustees had agreed that Wole would defend our students. I badly wanted to, but Professor Brown would not let me. I pleaded and pleaded, but I was asked to stay away from the case, and instead prepare to take some of our other students to England for an international debate competition. I did not understand this. My brothers, sisters, friends were involved, I had the right to be heard in any court in Nigeria as a legal practitioner, yet here I was being instructed to stay away from the case by the very people who had previously told me that I came highly recommended as a practising lawyer. I would not have it.

'I know what I am doing, Wale,' Professor Brown said. 'Trust my decision. We can't put all our eggs in one basket. I know that you are as good as your brother. But because you are a lecturer here, you may be seen as part of the problem.' I was about to interrupt when he cut me off with a gesture. 'Then again, we are praying that it doesn't get to court. I am making some progress. Our kids should be released soon enough.'

As I left his office the thought flashed into my mind that perhaps he was trying to get me out of the country so I might claim asylum abroad. Whether that was the case or not, I commenced preparations with the students who had been selected to represent K.U. in the debate competition, though with little of my usual zest: Amaka, a sweet girl of nineteen, who had swift steps and a power and energy in her voice unusual for one so young, and Zainab, (nineteen and veiled, as demanded by her faith), who was more diffident, but had an unexpected gift for comic timing. We worked hard together and I thought they would do well, but the dark clouds still hung close and heavy above us, and every member of the K.U. family.

Of course I met regularly with Wole, and I met with the trustees. I visited the police station in my capacity as pastoral mentor, attempting to see our students, though in this I failed. It was an ugly situation: we had learned earlier in 2014 that 'investigations' as regards men suspected to be homosexuals involved some sort of forcible examination of their rectums with medical instruments. There was no telling whether or not they were subjecting our boys to these same degrading 'medical' examinations: it tore my heart to think so, and not being allowed to see or talk to them to confirm one way or the other worsened my fears.

By this time Mum and Brother Gbenro had returned to Abuja. Setting aside the disaster of our wedding day and its causes and consequences, Mum did not want to leave Nigeria until she was sure of the fate of the arrested boys. Dad too was extremely unsettled, and wanted to stay in Amara with us to watch things unfold. Behind the scenes Brother Gbenro pulled as many strings as possible. He kept calling us to ask if we had received any call from the Inspector General of Police. We had not. He sent us the personal phone numbers of highly-placed politicians to call. Sometimes our calls were well-received and we were offered positive assurances. Other times their personal assistants would tell us that they were in one meeting or another, perpetually unavailable.

The Naija blogosphere had already begun to spread the rumour that Wole and I were homosexuals; that that was why our brides had left us practically at the altar. Some of them even had video footage of the brief drama outside the church and us hurrying away. A national magazine we had struggled to get to notice Afrospark's work in the past was now calling us repeatedly, eager to secure an exclusive interview. When we declined they went ahead and did a piece anyway: 'Gay lawyers jilted on wedding day!' *T-mag* published random pictures of us standing about with some of the male attendees of *Save the Colours* above taglines filled with innuendo. The silliest version of the story I read claimed the girls were undercover policewomen, who had discovered enough to nail us under the Same Sex Marriage Prohibition

Act.

The girls, however angry they might have been, were sensible enough not to grant any interviews either, thank goodness. They were also avoiding any contact whatsoever with us. But still the rumours were getting stronger, and all that was needed to see us arrested, and in all likelihood convicted, was the pictures they had been sent.

These had not gone into circulation yet. Whoever started this had other plans for us, it seemed, than public humiliation, and we tensely awaited the first blackmail demand.

We were now being followed whenever we left the campus. Wherever we went we felt the stares of people who recognised us from our faces being on the covers of magazines. Dad, Brother Gbenro and Mum were once more urging us to leave the country. Their reasons were unarguable: the danger was real. But we could not abandon the kids.

Earlier in the year there had been reports from some of the residents of Omore Street, saying that they strongly suspected the Atlantic was a gay club. The recent raid that had trapped our alumni seemed to confirm those reports. But were they true?

Hotel Castro was on the same street, and in an attempt to establish a narrative other than the official one, I went there to ask a few questions of its staff and, with luck, some of its regular guests. Unlikely as it seemed, I hoped to dig up some information that might help our case. Either that or I wanted to be by myself for a while.

Set in its own grounds, Hotel Castro was a huge white structure of fifteen floors or more, with, as I saw when I went inside, whitewashed floors. Its environs were professionally landscaped, the bushes spherically topiarised, the lawns clipped short. Everything there seemed to have been properly planned except, oddly, the parking lot, which was far too small to accommodate all the customers' cars.

Men – the effeminate ones who I suspected had attracted the attention of the police to Omore Street in the first place – catwalked their way in and out of the hotel's front entrance.

By chance I had been there earlier in the year, to pick up Professor Brown when his car broke down in front of it, and had witnessed this unexpected parade. Now I was here again, and they were here again. Presumably whoever owned the hotel had powerful friends, and so this blatant display of what was surely barely-concealed male prostitution apparently drew no hostile official attention.

I took a seat at the poolside, sipping a drink and staring into space, hoping to speak with one or two of these men on the subject of the raid. I was rehearsing my opening lines and strategy for winning their confidence when suddenly, as if projected out of the depths of my mind, Seun emerged from the pool.

I wanted to jump up – to go to him; to leave – but I couldn't move: my prince had frozen me.

He had seen me, and now he was approaching me. He was wearing only form-fitting swimming trunks. He was unchanged from the last time I saw him: tall, skinny but firm-bodied, hair spread across his chest, tapering down in a narrow track to his navel. The hair on his head was still snow-studded, but his goatee and chest hair were dark, velvety and trickling with water. His hands that once meant, and did, so much to me; his shoulders firmly-framed, slight biceps and, in his forearms, lacy veins... all that magic was drawing nearer. Hide me. Kai! He still had those eyes – and I remembered with searing longing the things he did to me with that look in his eyes.

'Adewale,' he said, squinting in the glare. 'It is you, Wale?'

'It's me,' I said.

An hour later I drove back to the campus to pack my things and run away from Amara. I needed to flee everything that I had once feared and now so urgently desired.

Seun was everything to fear. He was a fierce lover, a devoted friend. He was never caught between worlds. He was someone who knew what he wanted, and who he wanted to be with. He was blunt, witty and sometimes obnoxious. And he caught me. He caught me every time.

While an undergraduate at K.U. I was over at the University of Port Harcourt almost every weekend, visiting Seun. He

playfully insisted that because I did not know where any of
the clubs were I was a bore, and that I did not know enough
of Port Harcourt's nightlife and secret places to prove my
claim that my family was once based there. I usually spent
Friday lunch periods with Wole at K.U., then zapped out of
Amara on the last flight to Port Harcourt to see Seun,
returning to Amara on the last flight on Sunday. His family
was wealthy, so most of the time he paid for the flights.

With Seun, Port Harcourt, a city I had thought I knew so
well, became a tourist trail with an expert guide, a vista
scattered with unexpected monuments and delights. He had
learned the history and politics of the city as thoroughly as
though he had lived there all his life, and though I was not
particularly interested in all that, I was impressed that he
had been able to garner so much information about the place
that had been my home. Thankfully, he also knew how to
chill and make the most of his free time: Port Harcourt was
his playground, and when I was with him it became mine
too. I would often steal glances at him while we cruised
around the city in the red Golf his dad had bought him, and
my heart would skip one beat too many as I looked over at
him navigating the manic streets as relaxedly as if they were
wholly free of traffic. I felt captured and complete. I was all
the more thrilled because it seemed that I had no more than
blinked and he had grown up on me from child to youth to
man.

The Seun I knew at Ilaro was coy, reserved, solitary. He
spoke very little but let his actions speak for him. His deep
glances at me, and his simple, direct questions when he did
speak, affected me powerfully.

His parents were elated that finally he had made a friend
– one whom he felt comfortable enough with to bring home.
I once spent a weekend at their place. A large, dark chocolate
edifice in the midsts of a ring of hibiscus bushes, it was
guarded by a dwarf wall into which was set a white, tiara-
shaped gate.

Seun and his family are royalty, and their home was
drenched in affluence. At school the principal personally
checked on him daily, which always embarrassed him; and
no matter how angry the teachers were they never flogged

him, even when it was supposed to be a mass punishment. Initially this immunity did not extend to me. Seun did not like this, and he would cry and sulk when they segregated him from me and the rest of his classmates. Soon enough our entire class became untouchable, and his popularity among his classmates rose hugely. Despite this, if he was not with me, somehow he was usually alone.

I had been reluctant to meet his parents, given they were royalty and mine were – as I believed at the time – a petty trader and a farmer, but they were friendly and unexpectedly informal. They looked like siblings and nothing like other couples in Ilaro. His mum, tall for a woman, and dark, kept a modest afro topped by an Ankara Bow. Her lips shone with crimson lipstick and her eyelids dazzled with either blue or gold eye-shadow – or both together – even when she was just staying at home. Her skin was flawless save that she had more than one shade of brown on, making her face lighter than the rest of her body. She kept her legs crossed and to one side most of the time, and leant against her husband on the sofa. She was an exotic brand of Yoruba, the type that did not have to fry akara, mix moi-moi or dice the hell out of ewedu leaves herself – as her well-polished nails declared. She also seemed the sort who insisted that amala was not as classy as semo-vita because of its smell; or that English was too good to be mixed with Yoruba – but that Yoruba always sounded better with a splish-splash of English, '...a leetool hee and leetool dee'.

His dad was of average height, and he was dark too. His hair was dense, and his Elijah beard made him look as though he wore a helmet made of hair. The thick lenses of his spectacles were like the bases of Coca-Cola bottles, and his eyes appeared swollen and amphibian when he looked at me, each blink like the slamming of a pair of heavy doors. When he laughed, which was often, his tummy shook. He was not one to be caught without his brightly-coloured tee-shirt, thick-volume book and large, blaring radio-set – anything but the regular Ilaro man. His voice was lighter than his wife's, and neither of them had the Yoruba spice to their speech. Their English seemed to be singing while their Yoruba sounded like French. They had lived for a time in

Britain. Their talk – of books and films, politics and current
affairs and fashion – was, I suppose, bohemian, and, though
lively, tended to make me feel ignorant and uncultured.

On the second night of my visit, after sitting out on the
veranda with his dad for a while talking of education and
career plans, Seun and I retired to his room and lay side by
side on his bed in the darkness, laughing over the grammati-
cal blunders and comic gesticulations that our less impressive teachers regularly made at school. Suddenly, the mood
changed.

'Olawale,' he said, 'do you want to run away sometimes?'

'I don't know. Maybe sometimes. Do you?'

'Yes, but not lately,' he said.

'No?'

'No.'

'Why did you want to run away?'

'My parents said that I was gifted and bound to Ilaro. It
frightened me.'

'Bound ke?' I asked. 'What do you mean?'

'While we were in London I got so sick my blood was
always running dry. The doctors tried so many things but
they all failed. My parents contacted home, and they were
told that because Dad was next in line to the throne my
destiny lay here in Nigeria, that my blood was tied to Ilaro.
They also said that I would die if I did not return home
immediately. The next thing we were on a plane headed for
Nigeria. My parents seem modern, but they're not.'

'Do you regret coming home?' I asked.

'I used to,' he said. 'I'm scared. I'm so scared.' He began
to sob.

Though I could not have put it into words at that age, I
thought I understood: that he was afraid of being claimed by
a life he had not chosen and did not want, and that he feared
he could not live.

'It's okay,' I said, but he just sobbed harder. He tried to
speak but his words were lost. I held his hands for a while
but he would not stop, so I tried doing what Maami always
did whenever I cried. I embraced him. I patted his back and I
sang him a lullaby:

'Thank you sir o, baba mi o masheh

O dami l okunri ti o damil obinri,
Thank you sir o, baba mi o masheh'

As I threw an armful of books onto my bed in my lodge room at K.U. I caught sight of my reflection in the mirror.

Seun had held me once in front of a mirror.

It was the second semester of my first year, and he wanted to show me his new apartment off-campus in Port Harcourt. He came to Amara by bus to get me. He spent two nights with Wole and me, and afterwards he and I left on the bus to Port Harcourt together. Seun insisted that we sat at the back of the bus. He held my hand for the better part of the nine hours' ride. It was Saturday. The following week had just one lecture slated, and that was on a Friday: I had almost the whole week to myself.

We got in quite late, but he had arranged for a cab to pick us up from the bus park. The following night he had three of his friends over for a chicken suya and beer dinner. There had been no formal introduction – I hadn't met any of them before – but as the night advanced and he got drunk, Seun started to refer to me as his cousin. The other friends followed suit.

I quizzed him about this in the late morning of the following day, when his breath reeked of alcohol, just before he threw up for the seventh time, then passed out again.

On my third night he apologised with a tin of chocolate cookies and sprawled out on the bed beside me, wriggling like a salted worm and torturing me with his mutilated version of 'Soledad' – screamed at the top of his lungs – threatening not to stop singing until I accepted his apology.

His antics tickled me eternally. Once he came into the room after his bath with just a short white towel wrapped around his waist. I acted asleep. He called me, and I chuckled, with eyelids tightly closed. 'Oh. You are sleeping abi?' he said, just before pouncing on me, lavender-scented limbs and skin dripping gloriously. I felt a sharp rush, a shock. My eyes opened and met his, a few inches away, staring down at me.

'Get off,' I whispered.

'Sleeping men don't talk,' he said, his eyebrows neatly

aligned, smelling of freshness, his toned thighs binding mine between them. I'd rather die than move. I didn't want to...

'You are breathing hard,' he said.

'Please get off me.'

'You're hard,' he said, getting off and walking over to the wardrobe, his 'ifetinye' jutting gloriously before him, making the towel hug his butt more.

I could not pack fast enough. A vein had struck like lightning from my widow's peak to my left eyebrow, my face was dripping with sweat and tears, my shirt had been savagely creased and several buttons were missing.

I hated him.

I hated that he was audacious, stupid and extreme.

It had been dark and we were half-asleep when my hand ran gently down his torso. 'Baby...' he moaned as he moved closer to me, breathing my air, his wet tongue gently sliding in between my lips. I felt a thousand drum-beats run through me. I didn't know what my hands were doing or where they went, but it was like I knew things I had not known before. We gently took off each other's underwear, and he slid on top of me, ticklishly tonguing my ear lobes and the sides of my neck. I heard myself moan. My core was awakening. Then suddenly he got off, lay down beside me and did not say a word.

The following day, the eve of my return to Amara, he took me out for dinner at a restaurant. He carried on like nothing had happened, and for some reason I felt I had violated him, made him break his moral code.

'I'm sorry for last night,' I said finally.

He waved it off, smiled, and changed the subject.

Later, while I was asleep, I felt warmth shielding me. His arms were around me. And we talked. We talked about my telling stories about Ilaro and my dad in *Hot Sundays*. We talked about his trips back to England for holidays. He had learned so many things. He said that things were simpler there. People were open to learning and talking about 'stuff'. He explained that he had stopped the previous night because he did not want to walk into something we had not prepared for. 'If we must do it, we must do it right' he said. Sex was not just pleasure to him. It was also about candour, stamina – and responsibility. He spoke about safety and consciousness. 'I need you to know enough to want to, or not want to. We are different; we have to take extra precaution.'

'I know about condoms,' I argued.

'Do you know how to use them?'

'No.'

'Do you know about lubricants?' he asked.

'What are those?'

That night he showed me his bottle of water-based lubricant, and he showed me how to use it. He asked that we continue from where we stopped the night before. He taught me how to safely wear a condom so that there were no bubbles – 'air bubbles are bad for condoms.' He let me in, oscillating gently. Moaning. Gripping me tightly. Sprawled across me, his heartbeats louder than drums. It was our first time since Ilaro. Our first taking of this road. I could not think. He was melting around me, pelvis to pelvis. Sweat sleek all over our bodies. We had stopped being men, being like trees in the wind. Here there was no need to be firm or to control anyone. There was no need to be anything. As the seconds expanded, time stopping every now and then, my thrusts gained momentum, his grip became firmer around my nape. All I could feel was complete and out of my body. Being man, woman, tree and wind, being everything there was to be. Seun laughed. My core had woken.

A few hours later, while I lotioned myself in front of the mirror, his warmth shielded me again from behind, and he locked me in his arms.

'You should write about this,' he said.

'About what?'

'Everything'

'Last night, Ilaro, everything.'

'I don't think so,' I said.

Hot Sundays was birthed a few days later, in one of the reading cubicles at the law library in Kola University. It was my attempt to resolve the complexities that came with the men in my life, using the slightly distancing form of the *roman à clef*. The man who flashed in and out, my dad, at that point too timid to stay still; the ones who were to stay forever, the one who had unleashed a whirling inside me and who defied the labels of lover and friend, Seun.

Two years of writing, editing back and forth, and circling around themes and meanings followed for me, Seun, Wole, and my English teacher back at Navy, who was excited that a student of his was bold enough to seriously attempt a novel, if rather a traditionalist when it came to matters of style and punctuation.

When I was in my third year, with Seun and Wole's encouragement, and through links Kola U. had with literary networks in the U.K., U.S. and Europe, *Hot Sundays* was accepted at Sugar Books, an English language press in the Netherlands.

Before then all I had written were letters to Seun, and the secret ones to myself that no-one ever got to read. 'At the touch of love everyone becomes a poet,' Plato said. Plato is right!

I loved Seun, madly. I could never be objective around him. The way he looked at me. How he touched me. I could never say fimí sílè, and he knew it. With him there was neither wind nor tree: we were both and yet neither of them. With him I did not have to be a man, be firm, or tearless. And he knew it.

He once joked that all our lives our hearts are sculpted by the *Romeo and Juliet*s and Nollywoods of the world. We all know how a boy is supposed to court a girl. But no-one ever talks about how a boy is supposed to court a boy, or a girl a girl. Is one of the boys supposed to become a girl, or are the rules the same? 'The point is I want you, like this, exactly what and how you are, not a girl!' He was wrong. It is our lovers, not Romeo and Juliet and Nollywood, that sculpt our hearts. They fortify us or crush us forever.

It was beautiful and vulnerable with him. And I was bare. But being visibly vulnerable makes you an easy target for the cowards who know where and how to hit. Cowards like Seun. I should have masked it: indifference, distance, anger, silence, anything!

Two months after I had been called to the Nigerian Bar, Seun wrote to inform me that he would be getting married to a girl to whom he had been betrothed. Custom demanded that before he assumed his position as the Oba's priest he had to be married to a bride who had been chosen for him by his family. Her name was Kikelomo. Seun took me to see her once. She was attractive, courteous and made us a delicious meal. She was studying architecture at Obafemi Awolowo University.

'I love you,' he often said to me. 'Sometimes I pray that we fall asleep and you wake up a woman, just like Eve.'

Such statements disturbed me. 'Or you,' I would say.

He repeatedly told me that we did not have all the time in the world to say I love you, but we would have opportunities. He said some of us go through life knowing that destiny is somewhere close but never finding it. As the days and weeks advanced, he started speaking more and more in parables. Whenever we were together he made love to me like it was the last time. More passionately, speaking less and less, keeping his eyes open, crossing all the lines he had never crossed before. Our sessions also grew remarkably in duration, and it felt us though we would literally diffuse into each other and either become one or vanish entirely.

Initially it felt dangerous to let myself be handled the way he handled me: to become used to it. I had resolved not to be devastated by the forthcoming transition: Seun and I had weathered the distance, the times and our initial speechlessness. We would weather this marriage too.

In spite of this enduring confidence in my partner, part of me was terribly frightened and counting the moments. He was mine, and when we were together I knew that nothing could contest that. But he also belonged to his family, and to Ilaro, and to the priesthood. All these forces had for a while somehow been in balance, but in time everything competes for control, dominance and focus. The only thing that did not stand a chance in this competition was me and our transient forever. Marriage was coming. I had seen this happen to others: I never expected it to happen to me.

Wanting to be closer to Seun was the reason I let Wole pull me into taking a job with him in Port Harcourt when Abuja offered juicier professional opportunities. Like Wole,

Seun made me believe in the strength and the reality of me. He told me that I was perfect, and would always be, and that everything which was had already been. He talked about the possibility of our having met and loved each other in a previous life, and said that our love would continue in the next.

I was startled from these fierce thoughts by Dad taking a seat on the bed beside me.

'Going somewhere?' he asked, indicating my part-packed bags, which were now piled on the bed.

'I have an official assignment to attend to,' I said, getting to my feet and turning away from him to conceal my tears.

He stood up too, turned me to him, and placed his hands on my shoulders. 'We both know that is a lie. I may not be the most fantastic person alive but I am your dad. Come.' He embraced me. It was as if the walls collapsed around us. I felt a rush in my chest. I was home. He would listen. My tears poured out.

Afterwards we sat down again, and I told him how confused I felt. How Tega's leaving without giving me any chance to explain things hurt me. How I wished that I knew the words to use if she ever decided to listen. How the men who were gunned down could have been any of us, because we also had been there that night, but had had the good fortune to leave before the raid began. I wanted to tell him how Seun and all these crazy men with whom I had no possibility of a future kept walking into my life, and how I couldn't shut the door on them no matter how hard I tried. How the men never wanted to leave. But I couldn't. I cried and he gently stroked my locks. He listened to what I did manage to say without speaking, and when I broke into tears again he whispered, 'It's okay. It's okay.' And years of tears and repressed confusion flowed, and my chest ached but felt lighter. I never knew I hurt this much.

We left my cases unpacked and drove into the centre of Amara. In an attempt to get away from the tensions of the looming court case we wandered the shops. Then we visited a cinema and caught an action-packed sci-fi blockbuster. It was a relief to just look and not think. Afterwards Dad caught sight of a boutique and led me in. He took a coffee-brown fedora from a mannequin and placed it on my head.

'Almost perfect,' he said, tugging on the brim. 'Just needs a little something. Sit down.' I sat on a chair for customers waiting for those they were with to try on outfits. Dad loosened the single braid I had tied my locks into and ran his fingers through them severally. The attendant hovering nearby watched this; everyone in the shop eventually noticed and stopped to stare. But my dad did not care, and after a while they resumed their browsing.

While I felt his fingers go here and there in my hair, he talked about how beautiful dreadlocks are.

'It just stands you out like the gift you are,' he said. 'When I was growing up eh, kai! If you had dreads people thought you were either demon-possessed or that something was fundamentally wrong with you.'

'Baba and Maami always likened locks to having the gift of Samson,' I said.

'Did they? I always thought they disapproved. Funny how time puts everything in perspective.'

'Why did you cut yours off?' I asked. He smiled and didn't answer.

As we talked I looked at my reflection in the large mirror wall, and I saw generations passing and time closing in: a past wide as a nation, a future narrowing to a point. Everything seemed to drift out of focus except the memory of a few minutes earlier, when we were sitting next to each other in the dark and largely deserted auditorium:

'I'll never leave you again,' he whispered as he held my hand and squeezed it gently. 'I'll always be here to listen when you are ready to talk.'

'What about Uncle Ola?' I asked.

'Ola is fine. He is doing well.'

'I mean, what is the stand between the both of you?'

'We are standing up,' he said, chuckling.

'Okay,' I said, and turned away, irritated that he had deflected a serious question with a joke. We were mute for a while as on the silver screen UFOs hovered and CGI cities exploded into rubble.

'Walemi,' he said, 'if you want the black answers you need to ask black questions.'

'What happened after you eloped with Uncle Ola? Your life together, how was it?'

I needed to know. Did he understand how important his answer to this question was to me? He smiled.

'When Ola and I left Ilaro we headed straight for Lagos to start afresh. His belief in me was a dream and I never wanted to wake up. Every day with him was like we were sixteen again. Every morning had a sweet flavour to it, and everything was like we had just met for the first time at the Ifa Festival.

'A few months later, he flew me to England for an MBA, sponsoring everything and somehow, I don't know how, getting round the problem of my criminal record. He stayed behind in Lagos, calling Brother Gbenro every week to ask after you and Wole, and he visited me in England every three months, bringing pictures and updates from Gbenro on your welfare.

'After my studies I returned to Nigeria. We were together for a year in Lagos before I got a job in South Africa. I left and he relocated with his family to Abeokuta. We still keep close contact. He works here in Amara.'

'His family?'

'He is a married man.'

'You mean, you...?' I asked.

'No. He was already taken.'

'How so?'

'He got married to Ezinne while I was in prison. And when we got to Lagos he introduced me to her. We simply struck sex off our relationship and remained loyal friends to each other.'

'Simply?'

He shrugged.

'You mean, in all your years with him you never – '

'He decided that he wanted a woman in his life and I had to respect that. Ola is a very spiritual and decisive man. And being with him taught me so many things. Every morning I woke up to the fact that he in fact lived the charmed life. Ola, so sensual, so deep, suddenly became Ola contained and sexually distant. While I was in Nigeria he taught me that the greatest pleasure that a man can have is true satisfaction.

Not the momentary one that comes with orgasm; nor the "freedom" that comes with indiscipline. But the peace that comes with knowing that your life is complete because it is fed by one and it feeds another. We, as gay men, could also decide to direct our vigour, beauty and diversity into work, investments, art, families and friends.'

'I don't understand, Dad. Are you saying that gay people should pretend not to be gay?'

'I will be the last person to ask you to pretend, son. Hey!'

'Then what are you doing, if not that?' I asked. At this point he had my hands all wrapped in his and I enjoyed the feeling.

'I'm so Bruno Mars right now,' he said, 'loving you just the way you are.'

'So what are you saying?' I asked, irritated.

'I am saying that my sexuality isn't a function of if or when I spread my legs or dive between another's. But the countless "no"s and "yes"s I have to say and believe in to survive and, more importantly, to succeed, are not just for me, but for those whose happiness and victory I have become.'

'Become?'

'It's really up to me to define and live out. Are you Christian now?'

'What does that have to do with anything?'

'Well, are you?'

'Yes, Dad, I'm Christian,' I said. 'Why shouldn't I be?'

'A little bird told me that someone was flirting with both Islam and Christianity at one time.'

'Well, yes, I was,' I said. 'While I was at university. I had so many questions on my mind and I needed answers.'

'I was at that point too. But I flirted with a lot more than two religions. I stretched to drugs, depression, self-hurt, so many things.' I remembered him lying face-down on the bed in Ilaro, the traces of cocaine on the book-cover, and nodded. 'What I am saying is that questioning yourself or your circumstances is a weak man's work. And my bible tells me that I have been given a spirit of strength, love and good judgement. And so have you, son.'

'Dad, I'm bisexual,' I said.

'Says who?'

'I have a history. They think I'm gay. Mum, Wole, Brother Gbenro: everyone knows.'

'How?'

'Seun told them,' I said.

'What Seun?'

'Prince Oluwaseun, my classmate at Ilaro,' I said. 'And later, during and after university, we were lovers. A few years ago he was due to get married, as his parents had arranged. I wasn't happy with this. But I knew our love was not enough: the world he belonged to needed him to be "normal" and stay that way. He didn't love her, but we had to accept that time eventually catches up with us all. And I did accept it: I understood why he had to do it.

'Seun asked me to be his best man. I said fine. At the time Wole and I had just been admitted at the University of Western Cape to pursue further studies in South Africa. Then he dramatically announced that the wedding date would be adjusted to coincide with the day of our departure for South Africa.'

'Why?'

'He said it was because he had to be distracted from the pain of my leaving. I said okay, whatever he wanted. But then a week before the wedding he turned up at our place in a rage and told Mum, Wole and Brother Gbenro that I was making unwelcome passes at him, and he warned me and my dirty requests to stay away from him and his family.'

'And so on your own wedding day he ruins your and your brother's marriage even before it happens? But why?'

'I don't know. His wedding to Kikelomo went ahead without me. I didn't even try to see him after that. But then he sent our fiancées a photo he and I took in Port Harcourt on one of my visits,' I said. 'It was – well, you know, you saw it.'

'But Seun was incriminating himself too. That's crazy.'

'Very crazy,' I said. 'But it was taken on his phone, so it had to be him. And then some other person sent other incriminating photos too, of both Wole and me.'

'Who?'

'I've no idea. Some woman with a grudge against Wole,

we think. And as if it was not bad enough that his marriage crashed – '

'His marriage?'

'Yes, and now Seun is here in Amara, begging for my forgiveness, saying he never sent the photo, saying that he wants me back in his life just after crashing my marriage before it began. It's why I was packing up. I just have to – '

'He is in trouble, son,' Dad said.

'No, Dad, he is a demon, and I'm in trouble.'

'No, he is here because he is confused. He is here because he could not stand living without you, and it's this ugly because you both are yet to decide what you want.'

'How do you mean?'

'Look, when you are ready to say fimí sílè to these battles, God is here to make it happen,' he said.

'Are you saying that God can zap my bisexuality?'

'I am saying that heaven gave it to us, and only heaven can take it away,' Dad said. 'Your life is delicate, son; so is Seun's, and when it's up, it's up. Only you get to live it. Just you.'

'So?'

'So decide for yourself,' he said. 'Look, when you type in the word "gay" or "homosexual" on Google, you see photos of men in the nude, kissing or getting all amorous and reckless indiscriminately. If that's all of who you choose to become in the brightest day, or the darkest night, if that's all you see when you look in the mirror, then that is totally up to you, and nobody else.'

'Dad, I can't decide who my mind and body choose to love,' I said. 'Or who to desire.'

'Yes, true. I believe that one scatter. Trust me I know. But you can decide *how* your mind and body chooses to love a person. You can decide how your life should or should not touch them. You can decide what memories they will have of you years after time and distance have separated you. You can decide whether or not they will feel blessed or cursed by having met you.'

He took handfuls of my locks. Hairpins and rubber bands went here and there. Like magic my hair was bound and flowing down my chest in two elegant braids.

He replaced the fedora on my head. 'Perfect. My prince,' he said. I felt beautiful.

'I think I'm ready,' I said.

'For what?'

'To say fimí sílẹ̀.'

Olalekan/Wealth, here and increasing

Light struck me
And everything else came to a halt
Light kissed me
And all these sours became salt
You touched me
And my dreams felt breath
Ola, wealth that is here
Ola, wealth that is true
He touched and I was full
I came alive
Ola wisdom, Ola true
Ola, the one they all called fool
He held me
And everything returned
He felt me
And everything took form
Olalekan, God's beauty holding my hand
Olalekan, God's beauty in all that I am.

Amutorunwa (Heaven Gave It To me)

Olawale mi,

*Ilaro holds so much memory for me. The most diffi-
cult of its memories is the night you and your brother were conceived.*

    *Gbenro and I had shared an eventful day with
both our families. Soon it was late and just three of
us were left in the room – including Tolu. Tolu, your
father, was very witty and charming – as you know
he still is. Tolu had stayed back because Baba wanted him to. Baba was very fond of him.*

    *As I served him dinner, he asked that I ate with
him, so I did. Gbenro went home; Baba went to bed.
Tolu and I talked about my approaching marriage
to Gbenro, how well-suited we were, and how we
would grow old together. I was happy, and caught
up in thoughts of marriage and the happy future
ahead of me. By then he was drunk, but not aggressively so.*

    *After dinner we went to our separate rooms to
sleep. A few minutes later, he was in my room, in
my bed. I was surprised by this, and as you can imagine, alarmed. He told me that he had never felt
women, and was numb no matter which one he was
with, then apologised for talking to me about such
things. I did not know what to say, but tried to
speak kindly and lightly. He told me about Ola and
how much he wanted to be with him. He also told
me what Gbenro did to them. He cried. Because I
loved Gbenro, I felt guilty, as if I was somehow responsible for his actions. I panicked, and in my panic, my emotions got the better of me, and I let myself
conceive. He was truly numb all through. Afterwards he cried again.*

    That was one mistake. My second was in telling

Gbenro. He was very angry with your father, and took many years to forgive him, and nearly as many to forgive me, though I believe in all that time he never stopped loving me. And he always loved you and your brother, because you came from me.

I have not told anyone of this but you.

I have not addressed the issue of the rubbish that Seun said on that ugly day, because I know better. I know how pain and fear can make people act contemptibly. But I see the spark of your father in your eyes. You must understand that God does not give you more than you can handle. You are up to whatever challenge your mind, body, spirit or soul poses you, because you are impeccable. You are phenomenal.

I have nothing against you leaving Nigeria the way you did or needing some time to yourself.

Grieve, but don't grieve forever.

The world awaits you. Heal quickly, and be strong again.

We miss you,

Hugs,

Mummy

Speaking with Ahmed was like rewatching *Letters To A Stranger*. The first time we saw it was online. We were in separate locations, his internet speed was faster than mine, and so we shared it out of sync: I would hear dialogue revelations over the phone a few seconds before my characters reached them. Despite this, we were both equally drawn to Jemimah's need for a peculiar blend of adventure and reality that would last forever; and to Sadiq's simplicity, and the way he struggled with few resources to get things to fall into place. Perhaps it was a similar storyline that Ahmed and I shared.

He flew in from Abuja in the morning, and came with me to the Amaran High Court for the first day of the trial. Our students were charged jointly with offences contrary to Sections 4(2), 5(1) and (2) of the Same Sex Marriage (Prohibition) Act, 2014. The paparazzi were waiting outside the courthouse when we arrived, their cameras flashing. This was a lost battle, I feared. The peaceful protest march the parents' union of the students of Kola University had led the previous week in the state capital – five hundred of them, all clad in white shirts and holding up placard-sized photographs of their imprisoned children and wards – had not swayed the authorities in our favour.

The day of the protest had been warm. Professor Brown had been unable to keep me from joining the procession, providing I attended only in a personal capacity. We assembled on campus, marched to the state government house, then made our sweaty way to the Ministry of Justice, where we made our stand at the front gates.

'Even if they were gay,' Pastor Bola, an old alumnus of K.U. whose ward was now in her first year, screamed at the top of his lungs, 'they are Nigeria's present, her future.'

A law that does not see all her people, one of the placards read, *is no law at all*.

Although I was scared of the unpredictable outcome of the demonstration, I knew there was a reasonable chance that nobody would officially stand in its way. Several members of the now resurrected Rainbow Talk had connected with me at midnight the Friday before. They were younger men, and there were five of them, two undergraduates and three entrepreneurs. Bayo, the most assertive, spoke only in pidgin and Yoruba. They were all calling from Abuja, and they all seemed to be in the same place. They were furious about the arrests, but had no clear plan of action. However, a few of these new members were also connected, and it was they who turned out to have the key to how the situation might be turned around.

'I no go lie you, oga,' Bayo said, 'this thing na big fuck up.'

'Since they want to play rough,' Onome said, 'we are up to it.'

'Fola get strong connect for government,' Bayo said.

'What connect?' I asked.

'I'm dating a member of the House of Representatives,' Fola said.

'Which one?' I asked.

'I'll send you photos,' he said.

'Eddy na strong guy too,' Bayo said.

'I'm laying one of the Commissioners at Amara,' Eddy said.

'Wow!' I exclaimed.

'Tari na expert.'

'One of the female government ministers has been toasting a roommate of mine,' Tari said, 'and this roommate is on our side.'

'I'm dating Captain Caeasar,' Onome said. 'He is a naval officer and the Vice-President's cousin.'

'Kayode is my partner,' Uche said, 'the governor's son.'

'Which governor?' I asked.

'The governor of Amara.'

'All we need is proof,' Bayo said, speaking English for the first time. 'Proof of these secret affairs. And we are very close to having it. Look, if every ti bii in Nigeria has to to be out for us to save these children then it has to happen. We are all in this. Every one of us. Uche and Kayode will be flying down to Amara to march with you. When they see them there, they will have to keep it all quieted down.'

'And it's not just about self-interest and covering up,' Onome said. 'Kayode has already threatened to come out if there is any criminal conviction.'

'And he has some serious dirt on his dad,' Uche said. 'Remember the elections are around the corner. And so many of them are eyeing a second tenure.'

'This is more than double impact on the governor,' I said.

'We just got started,' Tari said. 'It has come to that point. We need to do what we need to do.'

By three a.m. on the morning of the march I had received emails Bayo had bcc'd me into and sent to the target lovers. He attached links to password-protected websites containing explicit pictures and videos of the guys and the lovers they mentioned. He made no threats, simply stated he hoped that nothing 'stupid' would happen in the course of the march.

By 7 a.m. Kayode and Uche had arrived at the campus in

government vehicles with tinted windows, along with seven other men who discreetly identified themselves to me as part of the LGBTI community. They had with them ten white envelopes, a red 'X' neatly and boldly marked on each. We wanted to give the impression that these contained DVDs and copies of the compromising material, though since that same material would have condemned our own members, in fact they were empty. The possibility would be enough, we hoped. We said a prayer and accepted God's Grace.

We made our way through the marchers, ten of us, bearing the envelopes conspicuously, eventually reaching the front. Photographs were taken of us apparently leading the march and immediately circulated to our targets, and of course appeared a short time later on various current affairs blogs and websites. 'What's with the Xs?' read one of the titles I later saw. The next day pictures of Kayode's face – and he was seen as one of the jewels of Amara – as he seemingly led the march, were plastered all over the news. Could he be gay, the blogosphere wondered feverishly.

We arrived at the Ministry of Justice with our envelopes and placards. We were out there from mid-morning until late in the afternoon. Groups of police officers watched but did nothing: apart from the effectiveness of the Rainbow Talk's behind-the-scenes activities, many of the protesters were well-off, and might have influence. The sun burned down on our heads. Eventually one of the commissioners came out to address us in front of Government House. He mustered a smile.

'My good people,' he said, 'good afternoon.'

'Good afternoon,' we replied.

'We appreciate that you have come this far to have your voice heard. But you must understand that the state, the country operates on the rule of law. The law is very precise on what is allowed and that which will not be condoned. I can't say much to you. I am only an officer. But the government assures us that the accused will be given all the rights due to them in the course of their trial.'

It was not much. We had not expected much. But we kept trying. The K.U. students were all over the internet, blogging and uploading protest videos. The fact that Nigeria deemed their colleagues – educated young people from good homes – too dirty to be free had compelled their response. It had ruptured so much in them. In addition, both the regular news and dozens of independent blogs were constantly broadcasting updates.

As usual there was a series of interviews on television. Everyone was getting a spotlight; everyone was having his or her voice heard. Most, of course, agreed that Nigeria would not condone the thought of homosexuality. The cliché lines were: 'This is against the order of nature'; 'Our culture and religious values are very precise that homosexuality or anything that hints it is obscene, immoral and abominable'; 'It is a product of the western world from which we differ on so many levels.'

In spite of all the madness, God was there. Every night I would return to my room and Dad and I would pray together. He had the gift of speaking in tongues. And whenever we prayed together I felt confident in the next day's work. He said that no matter what we do or say on Earth, God always gets to have the last say. He also said that everything we were experiencing was part of God's story, and that each of us was to pick a lesson from it. He was always confident and smiled for a long time after prayers. In amongst the boiling confusion of behind-the-scenes game-playing, wars of influence, and legal strategising, his faith was my bedrock.

Wole visited the lodge most days, often early in the morning, before going on to the school's administrative block. He was confident, or at least he seemed so: he always seemed strongest when there was a clear battle to fight.

In the midst of all this we missed Tega and Lola so much. We had not had time to grieve about what had happened with them, and they were still not taking our calls. Initially we tried hard to reach them: they were so tangled up in our business and campaigning lives, as well as our romantic ones. But as the pressure intensified, and so many other practical matters pressed in around us, we stopped trying. And what, truly, was there to be said? They vanished from the Afrospark office: all they had been doing, we had to do. Soon it stopped coming up in our conversations: it was less painful that way.

When we heard that despite everyone's best efforts our students were being charged, the heavens could no longer hold water. The walls around us fell apart. The world laughed at us. Once more the 'fags' would come to their Biblically-destined end. In the face of all that our marital concerns seemed small and petty.

We knew that the best of our youths were soon going to be unveiled for the world to gawp at. It was going to be a full-blown criminal proceeding. And even though the majority of them were not gay, everyone knew that in cases of suspected sexual deviance the conviction began the moment you stepped into the court, or were sighted by the public. How could you prove you had not desired what it was forbidden to desire?

At times I cried for them. But Dad would not have it.

'Do you think it is enough for you to just sit here and cry?' he said angrily. 'Who will be strong for those boys in there? They are the ones who are getting the real heat. Whether or not they get out of this, their resumé, their history is forever scarred in the Nigerian community. And perhaps in the eyes of the "cultural and spiritual" half of the world who are too dang sanctimonious to see beyond – ' He cut himself off, concluding abruptly, 'You just can't be doing this now.'

It was a fierce and massively unbalanced battle, the entire weight of the government, supported by the massed opinion of the Nigerian people, against the progressive part of Kola University, Wole and myself, but my dad was right: tears were worse than useless.

On the evening before the first court sitting I got an august and unexpected visitor: Professor Afolabi, knocking at my door at a most ungodly hour. If it were not ajar already I would have simply ignored him. Eleven p.m. for Christ sake!

'I know I should not be here now,' he said as he came in, closing the door gently behind him. 'I only returned from my leave yesterday. I was shocked to hear what happened.'

With all that had been going on I had not noticed his absence. But as he spoke, I realised the last time I saw him was the day before convocation. We had run into each other at the campus entrance and he had told me quite unexpectedly, 'I think you are all doing a fascinating job here. You and all these pro-gay people...'

'But then, I might as well say that I did warn you earlier about your methods,' he said now.

'With all due respect, Prof,' I interrupted, 'this is not the best of times.'

'Of course, man,' he said. 'This is perfect timing. Everything is crumbling in your face. You and your blogs, stories, Facebook. All that nonsense. And for God sake the bloody dada. You came here to mock academia and the very sanctity that it stands for.' Mischief was glinting in his eyes.

'I'm sorry Prof,' I said, disgusted by his presence, 'I can only take so much. Please leave my room.'

'This room is K.U.'s property,' he said. 'And the sooner you and your kind leave K.U., the better for all and sundry.'

'Me and my kind? '

'The first week you came here I could tell that you are a flamboyant homosexual. You are no better than the sluts flaunting themselves on Omore Street.'

I was speechless.

'You think we wouldn't know? Oluwaseun is my son-in-law.'

'You are Kikeh's dad?'

'I'm her uncle, her dad is late. And no pervert is going to wreck my niece's marriage on my watch.'

'What are you talking about? I haven't seen Kikeh for years. Besides Seun and I are not even in contact,' I said.

'If that was true then you would have thought twice before returning to Nigeria after your doctoral degree.'

'What do you mean?'

'The moment you stepped back into Nigeria, Oluwaseun turned on Kikeh. She became the very picture of the devil to him. He avoided speaking to her or even touching her. He began frustrating Kikeh even in her pregnancy. He tortured her.'

'How does that relate to me? I can't tell a man how to treat his wife. His family life is exclusively his business. It's cruel that you think that I'd want to even relate with a man who slew me on the altar of his matrimony simply because he thinks that demonizing me would make him the saint.'

'Exactly,' he said, his eyes now bright and eager. Kikelomo, it struck me, had his eyes. 'Kikeh found the so-many emails he sent to you, the pictures he kept. Newspaper clippings and your travel itinerary, filling up a file in his office desk.'

'What?' I was dumbfounded.

'What? What? You hypocrite! Even after she called you and begged you stay off her husband, the father of her son, you were still seen with him.'

'She never called me!'

'He kept late nights for you. He ignored his son for you. He is sacrificing his marriage for you. You devil incarnate!' He drew nearer.

'You have absolutely no right to – '

He slapped me across my face. I took it.

'By the time I am through with you,' he railed, 'and these, your useless Harvard returnees, you would know that flames are not toys.'

He stormed out of my room, banging the door shut behind him, leaving me both shocked and extremely confused.

'Court...!' The court clerk announced the entrance of the judge.

We all rose to our feet. The trial was finally about to begin. The best or worst would occur. We – me and a few of K.U.'s lecturers, who sat in the gallery along with the students' parents – murmured a prayer amongst ourselves and softly said our amens. Ahmed, who sat beside me, said amen too.

Wole, in his wig and gown, was seated in the third row of the bar, the seats reserved for lawyers. Two other smaller matters were to be entertained before our case was announced. They dragged on. Our levels of anxiety rose. The line of defence Wole and I had discussed until our heads were spinning with exhaustion was now a jumble in my mind, and worse, it seemed horribly flimsy. Could we really challenge and disprove every single piece of so-called evidence the prosecution produced? Even if we could get the anal inspections excluded, for instance, on the grounds that they violated individual human rights, our protests would in and of themselves imply that we thought they had harmful evidentiary value. In or out, they would contaminate our case. We could certainly not hope for a sympathetic judge.

It was one p.m. The complainant, the State Counsel, had just finished opening his briefcase and setting out his papers when the court door clicked open and two men were let in, Dad and, to my great surprise, Uncle Ola. They both wore crisp black suits. Dad gave Wole a small nod, which Wole returned. While Dad searched about for me with his eyes, Uncle Ola headed straight to the complainant's table and handed him a white envelope.

Dad slid into the row beside me, taking an unoccupied seat on the other side from Ahmed. 'Two syllables,' he whispered. 'No-leh'.

Time stopped and everything stood still.

He meant *Nolle Prosequi*.

I did not believe it until Uncle Ola winked at Wole with his right palm to his chest. As he was empowered to do by sections 174 and 211 of the Constitution, the Attorney General had stepped in to discontinue the proceedings.

A few minutes later, after some hasty whispered exchanges between court officials and a grumpy announcement by the judge, the dock was opened and the handcuffs were taken off the confused-looking young prisoners.

Through eyes hazed by sudden tears I saw my boys running to me and to their parents. Looking thin, bruised and violated. Part of them had been stolen. But they were free. Free to embrace me; to cry, laugh, scream 'Thank God!' They were free to be the Nigerian dream that they were. The court burst out with hallelujahs and 'Praise God!' as our graduates hugged their parents and friends. I palmed tears from my eyes. I had doubted this was even possible and I did not know how it had been done.

Dad, Uncle Ola, Wole, Brother Gbenro, Ahmed and I assembled that night for dinner in an eatery on campus – daddy's treat. There was a television set on in the corner of the room, and we were raising a toast to the freedom of our students when our gist came up on the news.

The crowd that had gathered outside the courtroom had

been fierce with the Attorney General's entering of *nolle prosequi*: 'Look o, this was a very serious matter and it should have left for the court to handle normally o,' one almost toothless old man said.

'This is pure corruption I tell you,' said another. 'This is not justice at all. This is a crime. These are criminals involved. Why else would they go scot-free if money had not exchanged hands?'

They said so much about the Attorney General of Amara on the news, these people, these ordinary citizens: they wanted the blood of those Nigerians who had failed to safeguard the nation's morality; they so badly wanted to make their point. The Attorney General's job was on the line for helping our graduates, but we were just relieved that the drama was behind them – behind us – and our mood remained festive. Ahmed was happy to be there with me to celebrate this victory, and I was happy too.

But we all knew the hard truths that had tarnished our victory.

After I had informed Brown about what happened between us, Professor Afolabi was stripped of his official duties on campus. In retaliation Kikeh went to Brown's office and delivered copies of the accursed pictures to him personally, threatening to release them to the press if he did not instantly restore her uncle's appointment and terminate mine. She called my phone to confirm that she had made the threat, and tell me that she and her uncle were going to ruin me. Curiously she did not ring off at once, but allowed me to draw her out. Perhaps because there was no-one else she could discuss it with, she was eager to tell me the story:

After they had discovered photographs of me on Seun's desk where one would ordinarily expect to find images of a wife or sweetheart, she and her uncle hired a private investigator to follow him around. This investigator took pictures of Seun with various other men on several occasions – some of them in compromising positions.

I realised as Kikeh talked that he had also taken pictures of Seun and Wole when they ran into each other at a gym, and subsequently one time when they were coincidentally scheduled to travel to Abuja on the same flight. I knew about that because Wole had told me about these chance meetings over Skype, when he had also told me that Seun was trying to reach me to apologize for outing me, since I was not replying to his emails. Kikeh, I now saw, had assumed Wole was me, and had concluded that Seun and I were clandestinely continuing a relationship that, in fact, we had broken off after the scene he had made with my family. The photo she had sent of Wole having sex with some anonymous guy had been intended to wreck *my* marriage, not Wole's, as Kikeh had assumed the man in the photograph was me. She had, it turned out, only ever sent these photos to Tega, not Lola – but Lola, unlike Kikeh, *had* known the difference between Wole and myself when Tega showed them to her: she had known it was her fiancé being penetrated by another man. Meanwhile Tega picked me out in two other photos of me kissing a coloured man outside a gay bar in Capetown.

According to Kikeh, what broke the camel's back for her was an email Seun sent me to which he had attached photographs of intimate moments we had shared in Port Harcourt – she had guessed his password from his usual line, 'You can't say fimí sílẹ̀ to me.' She shared the email with her uncle, Professor Afolabi, and after our encounter in class on my first day back at K.U. he had informed her that he had found the enemy. I was to be crushed.

They decided to start with my wedding. Wole and Lola were just collateral damage.

She was cold and sounded deadly on the phone. But I was done being scared of being outed. I knew Brown did not intend to reinstate her treacherous uncle, threats or no threats: if she went through with them, he could accuse her and her uncle of blackmail. So I called her bluff: the students were out of jail, and, though I knew Wole and I could soon be going in, I resolved to enjoy the rest of my open days before the arrest, if it eventually came, and not live in fear. I knew that Wole would likely refuse to flee Nigeria, and I was going nowhere without him.

She eventually rang off, dissatisfied with my explanations, and repeating her threats of exposure. Days passed and nothing happened. In spite of pressure from all sides, the Attorney General insisted on throwing the students another party to replace the one that was disrupted by the police. It was held in the conference hall of the Spectrum Palace and was themed 'Heaven Gave It To Me'. Colour-coded white and silver, it was packed with dignitaries, commissioners of state, students from other schools who had been specially invited, the parents and guardians of the students, the graduating students of Kola University them-selves, and the incumbent finalists of the performance arts competition, who now had a second chance to shine. The Attorney General was there himself and the security was top notch – double that for *Save the Colours*. And as usual the paparazzi were out in force.

As I looked out across the crowded, joyous room I asked Brother Gbenro, 'How did you do it? He must have known it was an extremely unpopular decision.' I knew that the influence exerted by our Rainbow Talk members could not have achieved this.

'Well,' he said, avoiding a direct reply, 'we need to pray that it does not come up again. We need to pray that there isn't a backlash. This is only temporary. But we have started and there is no going back.'

The party was pumping and Wole was nowhere in sight. He was flying back from Port Harcourt, having briefly returned there to sort out a few issues at the office – and to see Lola. It was the only fair thing to do: the air was too thick for silence, and regardless of what had happened he still wanted her to be part of Afrospark. His return flight to Amara had taken off late.

I had flown back to Port Harcourt myself a fortnight ear-lier, shortly after the release of our students. I had gone on a weekend, to reduce the chances of running into anyone I knew. On Sunday I had dressed up intending to go to church, but on pulling up at the church's gate in my rented car and seeing the people walking in, I reversed and drove straight to the office instead. I couldn't face being quizzed: I still was not set to give answers – or not to anyone but Tega.

I was at the office, where I had intended to plough through a mass of neglected admin, but was in fact sprawled out on one of the chairs in the conference room and lost in

thought, when Tega barged in. She saw me and instantly
turned on her heel. I jumped up and dashed after her.
Ignoring me, she stumped into her office and picked up a box
packed with her things: she was leaving.

'Aaaaa! Ifemi! No!' I said, falling to my knees dramatically, making sure to block her way. The office was bare: her
pictures, her books, her posters: everything was gone. She
wouldn't look at me.

'Wale. Please leave the way.'

'Aaaaaa, ejor, I can't o. We need to talk.'

'Mr. Damian, please leave the way or I'll scream,' she
said, sobs trickling into her voice.

'Nooo. We will shout together o,' I said.

'Wale, please go. Go!' she screamed, bursting into tears,
throwing the box to the ground and falling down as well. 'Oh
my God, Wale. I was going to spend the rest of my life with
you.'

'I still want to spend my life with you Tega,' I said, crawl-
ing closer to hold her.

'Don't touch me!' she said, pushing me away as I slid my
arms around her, but I held on tight.

'I won't let you go. I can't let you go.' Holding her firmly
as she pounded softly on my chest, jerking while she cried,
tears trickling from my eyes. How did I let this happen? I had
hurt this woman so badly. I had snapped in this wind.

Taking pity on me, and perhaps confused herself, Tega
invited me to stay with her. I jumped at the chance, not
realising she had moved in with her aunt. Besides being policed by the aunt, whom I had only just
met, sleeping on the sofa for the first time, watching her
sit up late searching for jobs online, I thought there was
some possibility that she could be my Tega again. But my
hope misled me, and somehow we failed to talk about
anything that mattered.

She dropped me off a few days later at the airport.

'I don't think I could ever stop loving you,' she said after I
had checked in.

'Come with me,' I urged. 'I really, genuinely want to
spend the rest of my life with you. You are my soulmate, Tee.'

Looking in her eyes, holding both her hands as delicately as if they were made of warm glass.

'You are bisexual,' she said.

'So?'

'What do you mean, "so"?'

'I mean I don't see why I can't make a good husband for you and a father to our kids when they come.'

'I don't want a good husband. I want *my* husband, whose love I don't have to compete for.'

'What do you mean, compete?'

'I don't just want to be the only *woman* in your life. I want to be the only *one* in your life. And you can't guarantee that.'

'I swear I'll try.'

'Forever is too long to be a gamble.' she said. She reached up to touch my face and tears rolled from her tired eyes: she had been crying for days.

'I love you,' I said. 'Oh Tee, I love you.'

She smiled and kissed me so deeply as she slipped an envelope into my back pocket, her warmth and her tears caressing my face.

'Goodbye Wale,' she whispered, avoiding my eyes, and I watched her as she walked off briskly, her long, flowing bridal hairdo bouncing, and vanished into the crowd of other passengers.

Once on board I opened the envelope: it contained her resignation letter and engagement ring.

Wole's flight back to Amara had finally touched down, and he had gone to my room on campus to freshen up before coming to the party. I stepped out to call him again.

I was trying to get as far away from the music as possible when someone called my name. I turned. It was Seun. He looked futuristic in silver and white, and yet still a bright slice of the past's cake, the young Seun who conquered me.

'You know you shouldn't be here,' I said.

'I came to say goodbye.'

I thought I was done saying goodbye to him, but seeing him again sent an ice trail down my spine. Memories flashed. Feelings erupted. But this was not like before: it wasn't the time or the place to be 'Walemi', or contend with whether to say fimí sílẹ̀ or not.

'I have nothing to say,' I said.

'Let's walk,' he said. 'Please.'

I took a breath. 'Okay,' I said. 'Okay.'

We walked, and we talked, and before me he transformed. Again he was twenty-four, a student at the University of Port Harcourt. Again he was fiercely beautiful, silver-tongued in silver. He talked about how much he had tried to be straight after he said, 'I do'. He talked about his wedding night, how he had ingested stimulants but still had to masturbate himself in the dark to be with Kikeh. He said that Kikeh was an amazing woman, phenomenal in almost every way. With her, he said, he came home to a trophy. She made every day a festival for him. And he tried not to hurt her. He talked of the many books he had read about how to please a woman, and how often he went for counselling and prayer sessions.

'For her sake, I wish I could give this sexuality back, or take another one,' he said sadly. 'Perhaps one that would let me feel her hands when they touch me, and let me feel her when I touch her... Sometimes it's like I'm losing my mind. And I need to talk to someone who shares the same wound with me. Matrimony is great for society, but often it's overrated. Look at how many married couples have affairs, get divorced, or beat each other. And that's without the gay thing in there. We focus on making it seem like the solution to everything. Like a flawless doll, if it seems like nothing is wrong on the outside, the world sees nothing.'

'What do you see?' I asked.

'It's difficult to say. Often I see a friendship that is yet to be. A life that is yet to be lived. Or perfect lips that are too perfect to say anything at all. A thing that is being slowly poisoned.'

'So what is it going to be?' I asked, thinking of my father and the decision he had made, a decision I thought unliveable. 'Are you going to hang on? She might be going to prison.'

'What do you advise?'

'It depends on what you intend to achieve.'

'How?'

'You are a gay man, married to a woman who has had a son for you. Now she knows that you are gay, she has become the devil to protect you from yourself. But still she is the mother of your kid. Whether you admit it or not, your kid needs her. You need her.'

'How does a gay man need a woman?'

'This is not just any woman,' I said. 'This is a woman who sees you. Who knows you, and who is – perhaps – willing to stay with you regardless of your sexuality.'

'Exactly! How do I continue as a gay man married to a woman? I'm no stone.'

'Half of you would be paradise for many.'

He snorted a laugh and shook his head. 'That's no answer,' he said.

'And yet we can't have it all,' I said. 'First you are a man, then you are gay. And now you are daddy. Yes, it is important to embrace your sexuality. But it is also important to be a good father and mentor to your kid. You have the option of letting this young boy have the best childhood you both can offer him, or let him grow up in a broken home, denying him the full knowledge of either his mum or his dad.'

'Full knowledge,' he echoed. 'Does that mean lies?'

'There are so many important things, but some things are just more important than others. You choose.'

'Do I choose for Kikeh too? She isn't a stone either.'

'You can only choose for you,' I said.

'I wonder if you are trying to convince me,' he said, 'or yourself.'

'Another friend of mine, Kwame, is going to go to the United States,' I said. 'To be himself. That's the right choice for him, and I support it.'

We wandered back to the conference hall. I did not know we had been outside for so long until Ahmed emerged from the building, looking magnificent in a sparkling, silver-threaded white agbada that contrasted sharply with his complexion, like a Yoruba groom at his engagement party.

'I have never known you to be a fan of parties,' he said to me, stretching out to shake hands with Seun. 'I'm Ahmed.'

'Oluwaseun,' Seun responded, shaking Ahmed's hand.

'*The* Oluwaseun?' Ahmed asked, prolonging the contact.

'I guess,' Seun replied uncertainly. 'The Oluwaseun.'

My phone buzzed. It was Professor Brown. 'Good evening, sir,' I said.

'Where are you?'

'I'm at the A.G.'s party.'

'Okay, right.'

There was something in his voice that troubled me at once. 'What is it?' I asked.

He didn't reply at once. I could hear his breathing. A girl in impractical white and silver high heels staggered past us, leaning on her escort, who wore a white tuxedo and silver bow-tie, and giggling tipsily.

'There has been an incident on campus.'

'An incident?'

'It's Wole.'

'What?'

'He was found outside your room.'

'What do you mean, found?'

'In a pool of blood.'

'Is he – ?'

'He was shot.'

Mind Scent... the world, the same

We walked this earth
They never knew
To hurt, heal, make anew
Dreams sent from Throne to home
To give us reasons in lieu of alone
Minds of pure and silky truth
Minds that didn't know their own fruit
We hunted ourselves
We thought we were at war
We cursed ourselves
Now in place of rising we fall
Great was great till we came
Though we couldn't break those walls
We didn't leave the world the same.

Bawoni?

Dear Ola,

How are you today? How is the family? How is work? I am sorry I have not got around to responding to your last two emails. I have been swarmed with work.

Today is another anniversary of my arrival here in Pretoria, South Africa, and I sit back in my study to reflect on how things have played out so far. I think of the so many possibilities of how wrong things could have gone and I am thankful.

I remember our arriving here together, and your promising me that South Africa would offer me a brand new life. I had been scared and worried for so long I could not imagine being free of those feelings, especially as half of me still did not forgive you for getting married. However, I confess that I had dreams of meeting someone who will genuinely turn my heart from unforgiveness, someone who is not afraid of shining on me as father, brother, friend and a partner. Someone who could be as fierce a lover as you were to me. But this time without the sneaking around and pretending.

After you left and I was granted asylum, I was quite determined to have a life. My heart craved another.

I prayed desperately every night. And foolishly I saw 'Mr. Right' in every man who made himself available to me. So I became somewhat of a 'Don Juan', cashing in on the myth that Nigerian gay men are savagely intriguing sexual beasts. In a few weeks, my lips ached from kissing and my body cringed from the so many bodies and flavours it had

*to adjust to. I lost my sanity trying to get someone
to fall in love with me. I failed. So I stopped, withdrew into my shell and became worried again.*

*I joined the LGBTI support group at my church and
slowly began to heal. I broke out of my all-male circle and made friends who were lesbians. I also met
real life transpeople for the first time. I questioned
God and myself for the first three nights – neither
answered. So life continued, each of us learning and
being.*

*South Africa is a great place to be. Sometimes I find
that I have the energy and stamina to socialise,
laugh, be naughty or flirty like the old days, and
that I have the charisma to walk into a room and
engage everyone.*

*However, there are times that socialising feels like
World War 3. Like I am drowning in an ocean of
sounds and souls that are out to get me. Like every
laugh mocks me, and every stare, handshake or
compliment has some lethal flavour to it.*

*There was this instance: we had an event at the
church and I had to be in a group photograph. While
the photographer was arranging us, I stood in a
'safe place' where I could stand quietly and not be
spoken to. Suddenly at the last second she moved me
to a spot beside a refreshingly stunning-looking tall
white man, probably in his late fifties, whose blue
eyes prior to that moment almost drowned me. In
the course of the shots, he complimented what I was
wearing and I froze. I should have simply said
thank you but I couldn't. I had to avoid him and his
eyes the rest of the evening.*

*I became more committed to the support group and
I have had the opportunity to travel both around
South Africa and Africa more widely. Did you know*

that love really is everywhere, not just in the loins of a prospective partner? Love of landscape, of nature, of a well-prepared meal or a comfortable bed.

However, I find it unsettling that I have cultivated a habit through the years. The habit of insulating myself from hurt and therefore from wonderful possibilities. Wherever I travel in the world, when I run into a Nigerian – and I always do – the first thing that occurs to me is the longing to trust and connect. But at the same time, I ponder on the issue of whether he or she has brought homophobia from home and will reject me, perhaps viciously. When I feel strong enough to take whatever comes, I throw all the caution to the wind and connect. However, in my vulnerable moments I feign a plastic accent or simply become unapproachable – it works.

My expectations of an intense monogamous love returned, though I had evolved considerably. Unfortunately, as soon as I left the LGBT circle I encountered attacks. Subtle attacks on my colour and on my sexuality. I thought that South Africa with her progressive law would be a bed of inclusion. I was foolish. The laws of inclusion are locked away in books while in the streets blood pours, and homophobia, transphobia, misogyny and madness flourish. LGBTI individuals suffer immensely here also. The law in all its beauty cannot instil love and patriotism on the subject. It cannot change hearts.

When I read about the Tani Cross case and what Wole and Wale are doing, I was worried because LGBTI visibility had not started achieving much yet in Nigeria. They are clearly into a revolution. And we all know that the revolution often consumes those in the revolutionary vanguard first. I wish I could tell them that homophobia cannot be cured by court cases and revision of legislation. I still do not think it's the right time – though no doubt they would say, what is the right time?

As you know, Fabian, my half-South African and half-Caribbean partner, and I have been together for six months. I suppose I should not be telling you this but I cannot help myself. He is sweet, but he does not feel like a Nigerian. Nigerian gay men may not be savage sexual beasts, but there is an intensity in our gay subculture that I have not found here. Perhaps the pressure, depth, secrecy and secret beauty of who we are, where we are and how we are makes us a distinct breed. I hope freedom, when it finally comes, (and I do believe it will), does not take this away. The intensity I think is spread across the weeks and months of proper dates and court-ship. He proposed marriage last week. I have not said yes yet, but I think I will.

However, I am dying to return to Nigeria, or at least make contact with my sons. I wish I could see you again.

Warmly,

Tolu.

When the issue of relocating to South Africa came up, I did not jump at it. This despite the fact that the police had not been challenged for what they did in Omore Street; indeed now the case had been dismissed no-one was saying anything about the arrests, or the deaths. The unknown assassin who attacked Wole was still out there, threats were pouring in, we were all frightened, and it was hard to separate paranoia from danger that was real. Relocation would mean starting over, and I was in no mood for that, at least not at a time when I was finally getting to do something that really engaged me, teaching. But leaving was a necessity.

Ultimately it was not my decision to make: our elders had decided, and we were all on board and air-bound before I could say adieu to Naija properly. Brother Gbenro thought I was being unreasonable, but squeezed my hand softly at the departure gate just before he bade us farewell, and wished me love and luck.

I had read Nelson Mandela's *Long Walk to Freedom*, and that was as much as I knew about Amandla and the politics of race. I understood that South Africa was a place where the liberation struggle was neither about the sugar from the ground nor notes from the bank, but about inter-sections of humanity – of race, gender, sexuality, language – liberty, equality, rights, living standards, and the joint expectations of a people who were well aware of, and embraced their need for, each other. South Africa, I thought, was a story of a people who had resolved to cross the line.

Dad has crossed the line too. He is happy and the sky did not fall after all. We have one more parent, Mr. Fabian. Slender and light-skinned. Their wedding photos are sprawled all over the wall. He insists that we call him by his first name, and has gone into therapy. He is more on the quiet side, and quite adventurous with food and wine. However, he is yet to adapt to the Nigerian taste for spicy food, for all his talking so fondly about suya and pepper soup!

We have not been here long. Some nights it rains and it gets so cold I can't sleep. And when I go into the living room I see Wole – who has now resorted to spectacles – watching the Nigerian news on his laptop.

Other nights I have nightmares of being arrested. Other times I am shot dead, or Wole actually dies. But I wake up and am consoled by my distance from the heat, the wahala. But then what about the heat that has come with me, the consciousness that I will never stop being both Nigerian and part of a group 'democratically' scripted for the gallows by my fellow citizens? I also think of South Africa, this new place and how different it is, for better and worse.

Wole, whose shoulder is, under thick padding and ban-dages, now a crisscross of stitches and scars, seems unstop-pable. Having narrowly escaped death he has finally abandoned delusions of heterosexual marriage, and has bounced back, delving into his roots, finding himself and coming out, working on ways to rebuild our lives and preparing the Nigeria we left behind for our eventual return.

We have commenced arrangements to apply for refugee status. When Dad's friends, who are also refugees, visit, they say that we are lucky to have our dad and Fabian to fall back on: 'Things are not as rosy for others o!' We should be flying out to Capetown soon, once Wole has recuperated sufficiently to join the queue for asylum seekers. Dad is coming with us. It feels as if he is over-compensating for his many absences from our lives. I wish he knew that it is difficult to bear a grudge in the heat of desperation and the quest for survival.

When Wole is not on his laptop, he is with his men. And his men, they never stop coming. It is like someone forgot to turn off the fawcett – or better, smashed the pipes open. I can't blame or judge him. In fact I applaud him for his strength. Challenging everything a man should be.

For myself I cannot think of love or companionship right now. This is not the time: we cannot build a house when the floor keeps moving and there is constant risk of subsidence. Ahmed is still in my life, and has been patient with me so far. He did not mind the Grindr app on my phone when he visited, or that girls chat me up on Whatsapp.

'Don't you ever think of forever?' I asked him once. 'Settling down?'

'I do. I live it in my every day, and in my "right-nows".' He won't give up on me. Bisexual or not.

I do not know what happens next. Everything as it is now seems so freighted by uncertainty. I fear that I may not find a Yoruba word for 'amandla', and that this hurricane may rage too long. Regardless, I am preparing for the sun. Alhamdudillah, it is coming.

Ajatala

I see approaching silhouettes sashaying in the distance
I see skies and stars behind them
I see stubborn resistance
And the blinded love attacking them
I see wild oats fall on lovers' backs
And betrayals, upsets
I see broken hearts and dreams
And ocean-rivers that were once streams
From all these I see Ajatala
Rise like lightning from the rubble
I see the sun melt his mask and salute him
I see the rains streaking rays
And the blinded love growing dim
I see a new love
A love that threatens everything we were taught to be-
lieve
A love that makes us drop our stones
And dart at the waves with faith of our own
I see Ajatala, a reflection of our birth heat
A stubborn replica of our grounds that meet
But before all these I see fear
And silhouettes sashaying in the distance
Hurricanes falling from the sun
And nothing will grant victory a gold platter
He lets them make the flames hotter
He wants to show us that we don't burn.

Epilogue

They said our sunset was a savage little flame on the horizon, taking back all our unused energy at the day's end; that she took back our unsaid words and our unlived dreams, all the things we ignored, forgot and had belittled since the sunrise. So the world indeed falls asleep, not because she is weak from work, but because the heat of this flame has exhausted her: a little savage flame that takes away all that would have made the day better, all that we would still have to account for.

Then again, the sunset is Oluwole, fierce in everything that touches him. She is Seun, warm in everything that left him; she is Lola and Tega, distant in everything that should have been close. The sunset is Nigeria, beautiful in all that is hoped for, and all that is reality. But the sunset is not me. She has refused to take my regrets and my pain. She has left me aware and still here. She has ignored my wishes, and left my past with me. She has given me this past, and now my home calls me a criminal, my nature a crime. Not because I have done or forgotten to do anything, but because I am. In this light Wole shares. Even those who should understand have failed to.

Oluwole and I are now far away. Somewhere people can love and dream freely. Somewhere heroes before us fled to, planning a return in due time. Afrospark is still alive, criminalised, but now beyond Nigeria; perhaps beyond us too. Wole still does one thing every day to embrace Naija: speak, write or pray. And me? I hope. And I'm nervous. Even while hoping.

And yes, we are still waiting for a second sun to rise. One that might have pity on us, and perhaps permit me to say fimí sílẹ̀ forever to those things that challenge my dreams of a simple life. I am finally working on the long-awaited sequel to *Hot Sundays*

I will always be in love, madly in love with all the things that are, these things that I can't change. Until God decides otherwise I'll let you contend with yourself, but leave me out of it. Hate, love, fight, live, regret, laugh, cry, run, whatever!

It's your life. Live it now that it is here. But don't forget the days and the sunset, the turning tables and the day when we will get to say when and why.

I still love you, Nigeria, no matter what you have chosen to say, do or become. I have given you the power to heal or hurt me. And with you I'll always walk, in my thoughts, dreams and prayers. I'll walk this road. I'll never say fimí sílẹ̀. Perhaps because you are my dream, Heaven's gift to me. I'll never say fimí sílẹ̀, because just as no-one is a slave, no-one is ever truly free.

The End

TELL THE WORLD THIS BOOK WAS		
GOOD	BAD	SO-SO

About the author

Nnanna is a Nigerian lawyer and story teller with a Master of Laws degree in Human Rights and Democratisation in Africa from the Centre for Human Rights, University of Pretoria, South Africa. He runs his personal blog, 'Letters to My Africa', (nnannaikpo.blogspot.com), and is presently with the Sexual Orientation and Gender Identity (SOGI) Unit, Centre for Human Rights, at the University of Pretoria, South Africa, where he is also a doctoral candidate. He is also an avid lover of 'Ofe Ezinwanne', a soup invented by his mum, Doris Ikpo, and only properly prepared in their family kitchen.

Also available from Team Angelica Publishing

'Reasons to Live' by Rikki Beadle-Blair
'What I Learned Today' by Rikki Beadle-Blair

'Faggamuffin' by John R Gordon
'Colour Scheme' by John R Gordon
'Souljah' by John R Gordon

'Fairytales for Lost Children' by Diriye Osman

'Black & Gay in the UK – an anthology' edited by John R
Gordon & Rikki Beadle-Blair

'Tiny Pieces of Skull' by Roz Kaveney

'Slap' by Alexis Gregory

'More Than: the Person Behind the Label' edited by
Gemma Van Praagh, John R Gordon & Rikki Beadle-
Blair

CPSIA information can be obtained
at www.ICGtesting.com
Printed in the USA
FSHW022032311018
53454FS